SALESMAN MATEO

THE LONELY HEROES SERIES, BOOK SIX

SAM E. KRAEMER

This book is an original work of fiction. Names, characters, places, incidents, and events are either the product of the author's imagination or used fictitiously. Any resemblance to actual persons, living or dead, business establishments, events, or locales is entirely coincidental.

Copyright © 2018 by Sam E. Kraemer
Rerelease Copyright ©2021 by Sam E. Kraemer
Cover Design and Formatting: Arden O'Keefe, KSL Designs
Editor: Beau LeFebvre, Alphabitz Editing
Proofreader: Mildred Jordan
Published by Kaye Klub Publishing 2021

These characters are the author's original creations, and the events herein are the author's sole property. All rights reserved. No part of this book may be reproduced, scanned, or distributed in any form, printed or electronic, without the express permission of the author. Please do not participate in or encourage piracy of copyrighted materials in violation of the author's rights. Purchase only authorized editions.

All products/brand names mentioned in this work of fiction are registered trademarks owned by their respective holders/corporations/owners. No trademark infringement intended.

THEIR STORY

A strong sense of loyalty courses through the lifeblood of the Torrente family, and as a member, Mateo is duty-bound to move to America to assist his favorite cousin, Gabriele, when threats are made against the family. Mateo possesses a skillset that is required to protect Gabriele's children and to assist in identifying a traitor in their midst.

The job seems easy… until Mateo meets the one man who reminds him that, in his profession, it's wise to remain without encumbrances—emotional or otherwise. No one with a conscience will accept Mateo's profession, so he fights his own desires for the kind of happiness he sees around him in New York, resigned to be forever without love… though a little fling never hurt anyone.

Shay Barr is a talented hair stylist and barber. His reputation is golden, and his prestigious client list is a who's who of New York society. His future is bright as long as his secrets stay buried in the past. When Shay receives unsettling news from home, he's reminded why he ran at eighteen, and now, it seems history is set to repeat itself. The pack of religious zealots Shay barely escaped as a teen have found another lamb—to convert or to slaughter—and Shay is determined to save him, but how?

When Mateo Torrente walks into DyeV Barr with a teary-eyed little girl Shay thinks of as part of his found family, the chemistry is explosive. Unbeknownst to either man, the other is exactly who he needs. With one "Torrente" smile, Shay is enraptured by Mateo, but there is danger lurking in the shadows.

Will the Salesman and the Barber be able to escape the perils at their heels or will they become love's martyrs to save each other?

New To The Lonely Heroes Series?

Start at the beginning!

Ranger Hank (Book One)

You may also grab the boxset –
The Lonely Heroes Series – Books 1-3

Other books by Sam:

The Men of Memphis Blues Series

May/December Hearts Collection

On The Rocks Series

Weighting… Complete Series

My Jingle Bell Heart

Georgie's Eggcellent Adventure

The Secrets We Whisper To The Bees

Unbreak Him

FREE Books by Sam:

Kim & Skip (The Men of Memphis Blues #0.5)

The Holiday Gamble

The World was Perfect

Seth – Mi Guapo Amor

STALK SAM E. KRAEMER'S EVERY MOVE

Join Kraemer's Klubhouse

Get Sam's New Release Alerts

Follow Sam on Bookbub

Follow Sam on Amazon

Follow Sam on Instagram

A FEW WORDS OF THANKS

I'd like to take a moment to thank my team—Arden, Beau, and Mildred. Without them, I would never be able to tell my stories and put them out for your entertainment. I appreciate all of the work that goes into these books, and I'm sure I don't tell you enough, but thank you so much.
I'd like to thank my patrons on Patreon for their interest in what I publish and "how the sausage gets made!" I offer future book ideas, exclusive excerpts, and first-look cover reveals. If you'd like to become a patron, go to Sam's Patreon and choose your level!
Finally, I'd like to thank Special K and Sweet A for their support and listening ears. I can't tell you how much it means to me that I have both of you in my corner.
I truly hope you enjoy "Salesman Mateo!"

PROLOGUE
MATEO TORRENTE

I could hear my father yelling at someone the moment I opened the front door of our home. I'd been summoned to the villa in Siena for a discussion, and the explosive, clipped words bouncing off the walls of the foyer didn't give me a good feeling.

Giuseppe Torrente's brash voice and thick accent always made me laugh because it was all for show, as was Rafael's, my brother. Papa used the accent to intimidate those with whom he came into contact who weren't in his inner circle, and I supposed it worked.

My brother claimed it gave him street cred as a chef. Rafe swore his employees and the food critics who came into his restaurants took him more seriously if he spoke in the thick accent of our grandparents. I doubted it, but I let him think what he wanted. Accent or no, his food was fucking great, and he had a James Beard Award, so no one could take that away from him. The guy had talent.

My family had moved back to Rome after Rafe, Allegra, and I finished grade school because Nonno Lorenzo fell ill. He was a lovable old curmudgeon to everyone but family, but even he couldn't bully the grim reaper. Of course, we all missed him because he and Nonna Bianca held the family together, but she made each of her sons promise they would remain a family before she passed about a year after Lorenzo.

My grandparents left the family property to their sons, who all shared the large villa in Siena when everyone was in Italy for family functions. Aunt Graciela and Uncle Tomas spent time with us in Italy when they could, so the families had remained close over the years, just as our grandparents had commanded.

When they were younger, Lorenzo and Bianca Torrente had a marriage everyone longed to emulate, fueled with a passion that sometimes spilled over into zealous shouting matches, according to my mother when we reminisced about the old days when Papa and Zio Tomas came to America to live after they graduated university in Italy.

Uncle Tomas went to work in law enforcement in New York, while Papa took a job working for the Teamsters' Union as a business manager before he met Mama. She was the reason my father stayed in New York as long as he did, going against Lorenzo's wishes for my father to return to Italy to take his place to work with Uncle Luigi at the vineyard. Papa's participation in the vineyard never happened in any real way because Giuseppe started his security company when he walked away from the Teamsters, claiming they were too fucking corrupt for him, but everything turned out for the better in the family.

My parents, Giuseppe and Teresa, had allegedly married for love, which eventually grew into a marriage of convenience. It seemed my father had developed a roaming eye over the years, which wasn't to my mother's liking. I was guessing over time, Mama decided to look the other way regarding his philandering because she didn't want to upset her seemingly perfect life, but I chose to still believe they had their own particular version of love.

I never had any confidence that I'd find love for myself, but I knew the idea of a happily-ever-after gave my little brother, Rafael, hope. While Rafael and I were busy becoming the sons Giuseppe Torrente expected to carry forward his legacy, neither of us gave our little sister, Allegra, any attention. That was until we got word she'd gotten into trouble with drugs and had overdosed. Allegra survived, but she had suffered brain damage due to one mistake in judgment.

Mama and Papa had done everything they could to protect my sister, or so they believed. Unfortunately, it was someone my father had known since childhood who'd had a hand in my sister's situation. The man who had fed her addiction, having supplied the drugs in the first place, was the son of a man my father had known his whole life. Mama told me who was responsible, but Papa would never confirm her allegations, nor had he ever requested we make a move to deal with the man. Of course, my brother and I had other ideas about it, though we never expressed them to anyone.

Allegra lived her life in our home in Siena, next door to Uncle Luigi's vineyard. Her compromised state of mind took up most of our mother's time, which was why Mama stayed in Siena more than she was in Rome.

I was guessing Mama's absence from my father's life in Rome could have contributed to his dalliances over the years, though I didn't give him a pass for his actions. Rafe and I used to joke in private how we'd never be surprised if a brother or sister showed up we didn't know about because our father was quite careless with his dick, or so we'd heard in roundabout ways from conversations we weren't supposed to witness with Zio Tomas and Zio Luigi.

Papa's cursing in Italian as he disconnected the call brought me from my reverie. "Stupid bastard! Mateo, son, thank you for coming out on such short notice. It seems we have an issue, and I want you to look into it. Your brother has always been careful with his activities, but this latest stunt with Giancarlo Mangello is bringing a bit too much attention from those we'd rather not engage, what with the newspapers writing articles on body parts turning up all over the world like those children's books where you had to find the odd fellow with the spectacles in the crowd," Papa ranted, his hands flying about in the air as if he was juggling knives.

I nodded, having reminded my brother of that very thing when I heard it being discussed over coffee at Gabriele's place of business. Even though we were in a secure location, it wasn't safe to discuss such issues where a stranger might fall privy to them and decide to make a little money off of someone else's misfortune.

Papa stopped and rested his hands clenching and unclenching on the back of his burgundy leather chair, his eyes solidly fixed on me. "We need to shut it down because the attention hinders us from effectively doing *our* jobs. I've also learned Francesco Mangello has come to Italy again. He's in Venice at his brother's home, and he's brought his wife along, but he didn't bring his son. The only son he has left alive. Now why would he do this?" my father asked. His guessing games were annoying as fuck.

"Papa let's cut to the chase. What do you want me to do, and when do you need it done?" I asked in Italian. My father's chuckle made me smile. It reminded me of cranky Lorenzo, who I missed. When my father was busy with work, Nonno Enzo would bring Rafe and me out to Siena to work at the vineyard and spend time with Uncle Luigi and Tomas, our cousin, during the summers. Those were golden years I missed very much.

"I need you in America with Gabriele because I believe Francesco has left the U.S. because he's ordered a move against the family and doesn't want to make himself a suspect. I think he knows we had some hand in the deaths of his sons, and he will seek revenge. I'm worried he may have a hint about the true parentage of Searcy and Dylan, and if he does, he'll come for his grandchildren," Papa finally cut to the chase. I nodded, mentally compiling a list of things I needed to do before I made the trip.

Papa continued. "I believe Salvatore Mangello is digging into who killed his brothers, and we know where the trail will lead him. In the event he's somehow using the American authorities for his search, I want him gone before he leads them to our door. I want you to help Gabriele keep his sweet children from harm. They mean a lot to this family, and I want them safe."

"Okay, Papa. Anything else?" I asked. He didn't look like he was done complaining at all.

"I also want you to get your brother to stop his foolish antics and get rid of any evidence in his possession. I realize he has been set on seeking the truth regarding your sister's attack, but his ridiculous game of cat-and-mouse is making him conspicuous, and the rest of the family by extension. I'll track Francesco's movements here. You need to be on the lookout for Salvatore and protect the family when he comes.

"We know the devil, son. Let's not allow him into our house again. Two of my operatives were ambushed in Berlin yesterday, and all of the evidence points to Frankie's personal guards. I'll handle things here if necessary, but I need you to deal with the situations in America. Tell Gabriele as little as possible for the time being because I haven't explained some things to him yet. I don't want Dexter and him to worry if we can contain the problem without their knowledge," Papa ordered. That wasn't a surprise to me.

Papa always kept everything close to the vest, even with Rafe and me. It was aggravating at times, but I always had to assume it was because he was trying to keep us safe from something. It did, though, make it difficult to plan at times without knowing from which direction catastrophe was going to strike.

Papa poured the two of us glasses of Torrente Grappa, handing one to me as he took a seat behind the huge, hand-carved mahogany desk. He slid forward and glanced at me to see if I was listening. I knew better than not to be. "Gabriele doesn't know many of the things we do in Italy, even though Nemo and Smokey are familiar with our methods. I'd like to keep it that way. Please, stay safe and protect the family at all costs," my father beseeched.

I was many things—a former law enforcement officer with the *Carabinieri*, a salesman for the vineyard, a contract killer when necessary—but I wasn't someone who would be a disappointment to my father, to my family. I walked around the desk and hugged my father, offering him a kiss on the cheek, before I went in search of my mother and sister before I returned to Rome to pack up the things from my small flat to take with me to America.

I didn't know what I'd encounter there, but I knew I would protect my family until my death. I was a Torrente, after all.

1

MATEO TORRENTE

I stepped off the elevator, juggling my suitcase and garment bag as I tried to find my keys. Exhaustion had settled into the soles of my loafers a long time ago, and all I wanted was a bed.

I had finally arrived at the apartment where I would be staying in my cousin's building, and I was fucking dead on my feet from the whirlwind that brought me there. My father, Giuseppe Torrente, had directed me to go to the States to help out my cousin, Gabriele, the head of Golden Elite Associates-America.

Papa had assured me he had things in hand at the Italian headquarters, but he said my cousin, Gabe, had some issues at his office in need of investigation, and he needed someone to look out for *his* family…namely, *me*. My father didn't have to ask twice because Gabriele meant the world to me.

My brother and I assisted Gabe with cases when we were in the States, but one of my father's former *frenemies* in Italy, who had moved to the U.S. years prior, was pulling some bullshit, which my father didn't approve of.

Those actions had my father on high alert because the people involved were heartless and wouldn't hesitate to do harm to anyone they believed stood in the way of their activities' success. According to Papa, it became essential for me to be available to my cousin for an undetermined amount of time to neutralize the threat if it became necessary. I had a feeling it would become *very* necessary in too short a time, but I was ready.

I looked around my new apartment, seeing all of my personal effects had arrived ahead of me, thankfully. All I needed to do was unpack, but I was too fucking exhausted to care at the moment. Dexter's mother had lived in the same apartment before her untimely demise, and then Dexter took it over after. The aftermath was a very long story involving some dark and scary moments for the family, but at the end of the day, no one outside Golden Elite Associates knew where Dexter's sister and her lover had ended up, nor were they aware Dylan and Searcy were actually Francesco Mangello's long-lost grandchildren. It was my job to ensure that truth remained buried, and I took that job very seriously.

Just as I was about to go back to my bedroom and pass out until the next morning, there was a quick knock on the front door. I went to the box marked as "kitchen" and found my Tanfoglio Witness Stock II 9mm in a slow cooker I'd been learning to use when I was still in Italy. I quickly retrieved the mag and slid it into place, loading a cartridge into the chamber.

I held it behind my back before I went to the peephole and looked out, relaxing when I saw it was Dexter with his children, Dylan and Searcy. They were carrying bags, and even through my bone-deep fatigue, I was thrilled to see them. I shoved the gun into the back waistband of my pants and quickly untucked my shirt to cover it before opening the door to see three happy smiles aimed in my direction.

"Come in, come in. It's good to see all of you. I thought we were meeting at the Victorian tomorrow morning," I stated as I relieved Searcy of the bag she carried and then picked her up for a hug. Dex and Dylan followed us to the kitchen where we put the bags on the small island.

I watched as Dylan looked around the place before he walked over to me and extended his hand to shake. "Ciao, *Cugino* Mateo," he greeted with a nervous smile. I laughed and ruffled his hair.

"*Molto bene, giovanotto!* How've you been? How's the summer?" I asked. I remembered Gabriele mentioning that Zia Grace and Zio Tomas had been teaching the kids some Italian so they didn't feel left out when all the cousins were around. I thought it was very sweet, but I was the big softie in the family. My brother, Rafe, would have laughed at me.

"Summer's fun. Well, mostly. Mr. Chambers isn't very fun, though. We brought some food from Cousin…I mean, Cugino Rafe's restaurant near our house. We used to live here, you know?" Dylan explained to me.

I kissed Searcy on the cheek before I set her on the floor. "Well, what have you brought me from my brother's restaurant?" I asked as I began pulling things out of the bags.

Dex stepped forward and handed Dylan a tablet, officially changing the subject because it was a gruesome tale regarding their time spent in the apartment. Dex's mother had been watching Dylan and Searcy the day she died, and what happened in the aftermath was horrific. "Why don't you guys go watch a movie in the living room. We'll go in a few minutes. I want to speak with Mateo."

I felt a tug and looked down to see Searcy, the little beauty, tugging on my dress slacks. I knelt down to speak with her. "Yes, *bella regazza*? What can I do for you?"

"Can I call you *Zio* Cugino Mateo? Papa said we should call you cousin, but I wanna call you *uncle*," the sweet little girl asked with a cute tilt of her head that could melt the coldest heart. I glanced at Dexter to see his soft smile, and the love in his eyes for those children overwhelmed me. I'd easily give my life for them without question.

It wouldn't surprise me if the Mangello family came after Dexter to get those kids if they ever learned the truth of their parentage… that Dino Mangello was their father. I was sure the Mangello family suspected we were responsible for the deaths of the two *princes* based solely on the revenge my brother sought because we believed our mother when she told us the drugs Allegra took were supplied by Giancarlo Mangello.

"How about you call me *Zio Teo*? Allegra calls me *Teo*. Since I don't have any nieces or nephews yet, I'd be honored if you'd consider me your *Zio*," I explained. She gave me a big kiss on the cheek before she scurried off to the living room with her brother.

Dexter was busy folding the bags he brought with the food before turning on the oven and setting an aluminum container inside to keep warm. After he was finished, he turned to me and took a seat at the island. "I can't thank you enough for coming to help Gabe out with work right now, Mateo. It's a lot to ask for you to put your life and job in Italy on hold to move here. Gabriele won't discuss things of this nature with me, but I have a feeling this has to do with the kids' father and his family. I realize if they figure out…" Dex whispered before the tears started to fall and his voice broke into silent sobs. I couldn't help but walk around the island to give him a hug.

I could see the man was extremely upset about the possibility the children were in danger, though I tried not to give him any indication that was the reason I was in New York. I felt for him because I could see the love he had for Dylan and Searcy. Dex was such a gentle soul, and he wasn't used to the violence that was ever-present in our family. I prayed he never found out the darkness the family was capable of.

"Hey, Cugino, no need to worry. Uncle Luigi is sending me some sample bottles from the vineyard for me to shop around while I'm here, so there's no suspicion of my true mission. Hell, maybe I can expand the family business while I'm in the States. Anyway, where's the new operative? Uh, Duke?" I asked.

That was the latest information Gabe had given me when we spoke before I'd left Italy. He had a new Operative, Duke Chambers, and the man was in charge of looking after Dexter, Dylan, and Searcy. I'd met him in Italy about six months prior when he came to work at GEA-I, my father's leg of the business, for a short stint before Papa sent him to the States to work for Gabe. I didn't know him well except to say he didn't seem to like Rafe or me when he'd met us. Of course, we didn't give a shit what he thought about us, but his disdain for our mere presence was nearly instantaneous as I recalled.

I had no idea where the man came from before he went to work for the organization, and Rafe and I didn't like not knowing the background of the operatives in both Italy and America. Word was Duke had been a Marine—that much Papa confirmed—but how he came to work for us in Italy in the first place was something my father wouldn't discuss. I wasn't really surprised because it was Giuseppe's way.

There were a lot of things Papa kept to himself. I was forty-two years old, and I'd grown used to the silence a long time ago. My brother? Well, Rafe had his own way of handling things, which usually involved him in the kitchen in the middle of the night at his best or something far more sinister at his worst.

I looked at Dex to see he wasn't very happy about his new companion. "He's outside in the Escalade. He refused to come inside. Do you know him at all, Mateo? Gabe said he came from Italy."

I sighed. "*Non tanto*...not much. I worked one case with him toward the end of his time in Rome. We were escorting a Russian woman who was defecting to England because her life had been threatened in Moscow. We kept her safe until we could deliver her to MI6 so they could put her into protection. After Duke dropped her off, Papa sent him here," I answered, leaving out a shitload of details.

"Anyway, when does Gabriele expect me to check in with him? I'd like to unpack a little, but I can be available tomorrow if he needs me," I offered.

Dexter smiled. "How about you come to the house for breakfast in the morning. I have a full day at the studio, and Gabe is busy working on several cases, but we make time to have breakfast as a family, and you, *Cugino,* are most definitely family.

"Duke refuses to join us, but I hope you will. The kids love you, but they're scared of Duke. I'll feel better having you with him, so they feel safe. Sorry, but you'll have to deal with Duke on your own," Dex determined, offering a smirk. Clearly, he knew I had about as much patience as Gabriele, which was next to none.

"Why are they afraid of him, have they said?" I asked. Those kids were so easy going, I couldn't imagine them not getting along with someone, even a cold son of a bitch like Duke.

Dex seemed to hem and haw a bit before he rested his hands flat on the table. "They, uh, well, Dylan said he doesn't talk to them. He just barks out orders… *'Get out.' 'Get in.'* He isn't friendly, at all, and Searcy says she's tried to be his friend, but he just doesn't like her. I understand someone not enjoying kid duty, but they're not much trouble, really. Just ask Mathis or Cyril. Hell, call Abra. She still talks to them on Facetime about once a month, even with her pregnancy."

"He has growly eyes." We both turned to see Searcy standing in the doorway of the kitchen for just a moment before she scampered off to the living room. How long she'd been listening was a good question.

So, for whatever reason, Duke Chambers didn't seem to like our family. Why my father sent him to work for Gabriele was a mystery. I'd give Chambers another shot before I took shit up with Papa because I wanted more information on the man and why the fuck we had to tolerate his rude behavior. It made no sense.

Duke might have been a Marine, but I would *not* allow him to continue to intimidate those two, sweet kids. "I'll deal with him. So, what time is breakfast, *Yogi?*" I teased, offering Dexter a patented Torrente grin.

He slapped my shoulder and laughed. "You're just like Gabe, Mateo. We'll see you in the morning at seven." With that, Dexter gathered his kids and headed out after hugs for me from all three of them. After they left, I locked the door and went into the kitchen to retrieve what smelled like my brother's lasagna.

Of course, Rafe hadn't made it, but Parker Howzer was the next best thing. The kid was a hell of a chef, and Rafe was lucky to snag him when he did. I was looking forward to the meal, but I was eagerly anticipating the sleep I'd get once my belly was full. I needed to be up early, and I knew jet lag would fuck with my system, but I was actually excited about the change in my work environment.

A clear head would be essential in the morning because I had two very important assets to guard… the most important assets I'd ever had under my watch. I would keep them harm-free at all costs because they were irreplaceable, and their protection was the most important thing in *our* world.

The alarm was on its third snooze, so I sat up and stretched. Working in different time zones all the time kept my system in a constant state of chaos, so I'd learned years ago to set the alarm earlier than necessary so I had time to get my senses about me. It took time for it to sink in that I needed to get up, and my method of beating jet lag had yet to fail me.

I checked my phone for messages, seeing nothing. As far as I knew, nobody except Gabe and Dex…and now the kids… knew I was in town. Well, probably Chambers if Dex had told him why they stopped by the apartment building last night. I was sure Papa told Gabe to keep my arrival on the downlow so as not to alert the wrong people that I was in New York again. We were sure Francesco had people watching us just as we had people watching him.

I was honestly looking forward to seeing Nemo and Smokey. We'd worked together in Italy years ago and developed a strong bond. They were men of honor, and I counted them as more than friends. We shared loyalty and respect, and the fact I would be working with them gave me a level of comfort I didn't feel a lot of the time when I was on assignment.

I worked alone most of the time. My specialty wasn't exactly a group skill, and Papa only called me in when things were dire. I'd worked other assignments, but when things went in a direction that was detrimental to our undertaking, I was tasked with setting things to rights.

We'd kept Smokey and Nemo from the wet work, but Nemo had asked for certain responsibilities from time to time because he had his own ghosts, and Papa had obliged. It wasn't discussed with anyone, which was why what my brother was up to was of particular concern. I needed to get to him as quickly as possible.

I quickly showered, shaved, and dressed for work. I heard my phone buzzing on the box next to my bed, which reminded me I needed more than just a bed frame, mattress, and box springs. I was fucking grateful I'd thought to order the bed in the first place, and I was happy Nana Irene, Dyl and Searcy's nanny, was able to let in the delivery men for me, so it was already set up when I arrived the previous night. I owed the woman a thank you and maybe a cookie bouquet when I had the time.

I hurried out of the bathroom and grabbed the buzzing annoyance—my phone, smiling when I read the message. Apparently, Gabe had told someone else about my arrival.

Outside. Hurry the fuck up, Dickhead

I laughed as I grabbed my briefcase where my Tan was secured along with extra mags. New York was a real bitch when it came to registering a handgun, so I probably wouldn't bother because I didn't have my detective's license either. I'd borrowed a gun from Gabriele when I'd visited before to help out, but that wasn't exactly legal, either. Luckily, I was good at my job and kept things under control. All the state and local officials knew about me was that I was a wine salesman for Torrente Exports, International, and I had a distributorship license, all nice and legal. That was all anyone in the five boroughs needed to know.

I took the stairs instead of waiting for the elevator, happy to see Smokey in his big ass truck with a sarcastic smile. I just laughed as he pointed to his watch. "You're late," he snapped as he stepped out of the vehicle and offered his hand to shake before pulling me forward into an uncharacteristic hug.

When he worked with us in Italy, he wasn't the hugging type, but it seemed as if he'd mellowed since he fell in love with the handsome Parker Howzer. It actually looked good on him.

After we pulled apart, I walked around the truck and hopped in on the passenger side. "I'm not late yet, Smokey. By the way, I heard you got engaged, so when's the wedding? If you decide that chef is too much for you, I'd be happy to take him off your hands," I teased, knowing I was older than Smokey, so the big guy probably had a lot more game than me. His fiancé, after all, was a hot, young guy. Shep Colson was a lucky son of a bitch.

Smokey chuckled in the confident way men did when they knew they'd met the right person who would never leave them when another idiot came along and made a play. "You're welcome to try your hand, Mateo, but you won't get too dang far. My man's in love with *me*, and we're getting married next spring. Since your surly ass is in town, I might have to keep a better eye on ya, just so you don't make a fool of yourself."

We both laughed at his comment before he drove us from my place to Gabe's fancy house. After he let me out at the curb, Smokey waved before he headed to the Victorian. When I knocked on their front door, I heard running feet headed my way. There was an answering knock from the inside, which made me laugh. "It's *Zio* Mateo," I informed, hearing Searcy giggle through the door.

"I need Daddy to open the lock. Stay there," she instructed, which had me laughing hard. She was going to be just like Gabby with that "giving orders" bullshit. I understood why my father was so adamant those kids remained safe. They were incredible, and since I was pretty sure I would never have any of my own, they would have a very special place in my heart, no doubt.

The door opened, and there stood my cousin Gabriele. He'd put on a little weight since the wedding, and I would take *every* opportunity to point it out. "Wow, when's *it* due? Dex didn't mention he'd… hello there, my pretty girl," I greeted Searcy when I saw her step from behind Gabe with her infectious smile, not finishing my burn on my cousin, though I did pat his little overhang.

Gabe laughed and flipped me off after I picked up Searcy, kissed her cheek, and headed toward their kitchen behind him. "Mateo says I'm getting fat. Am I?" Gabe whined as he stepped into the room ahead of us and to the right. It was then I saw he was talking to

Dexter, who was cooking scrambled eggs. Gabe walked up behind his husband and kissed his cheek and neck, covertly squeezing the man's ass.

It was blatant territory claiming, and it made me laugh. "You feed your husband too well," I teased as Dylan came into the kitchen.

"Hi, Cugino," Dylan greeted with a fist, which I bumped. He handed his glasses to Gabe. "Dirty, Papa." The little guy rubbed his eyes as Gabe went to a drawer and pulled out a pump bottle of eyeglass cleaner and a special cloth.

He sprayed the liquid and looked at me with a smile. "There are two bottles and two cloths in the console of the Escalade. He doesn't like his glasses to get dirty, so if you wouldn't mind helping him clean them, I'd appreciate it," Gabe explained as he held them up to the light to examine the lenses as he continued to wipe them with the rag.

"He's picky," Searcy told me as she played with the back of my hair, making me laugh again. She was priceless.

"What's on the agenda for today?" I asked as Dexter filled plates with eggs and pulled out a platter loaded with bacon and biscuits, setting it on the table.

Searcy scrambled from my arms to shoot around the table to a booster seat in one of the kitchen chairs, and I removed my suit jacket and flipped my tie over my shoulder to keep it from getting dirty when I dove headfirst into the tempting food in front of me. It smelled incredible.

"Nana Irene called me this morning. She has to go to the doctor because she has a pain in her leg. We're eventually going to need to find a new nanny for the kids. Nana Irene is going to be seventy-two," Dex explained to me with a worried look.

"Ah, okay, uh… what would you guys like to do today?" I asked the kids. Hell, I had no idea what to do with two kids aged six and nine. I glanced up to see Dexter shaking his head while Gabriele laughed quietly as he buttered and jellied a biscuit for Searcy.

"We wanna go make pottery," Searcy stated.

Dylan quickly spoke up. "That's sissy stuff. I wanna go to the beach at Nonna's house and skim board," Dyl demanded.

Gabriele, my asshole cousin, laughed, but thankfully Dexter came to my rescue. "We're going out to Long Island for the weekend, so you're not dragging Mateo and Duke out there today. Why do you think pottery is sissy stuff?" Dex asked Dylan as he took a seat on Gabe's left thigh and began eating off his plate.

Dylan ducked his head. "Girls make dishes and shit," he stated. I almost laughed before Gabe reached up and popped him on the back of his head, just as I remembered our fathers doing to us when we were about Dylan's age.

"You wanna taste the soap again? I told you about that mouth," Gabe scolded, sounding far too much like Uncle Tomas. I was trying very hard to hold the laugh to keep from getting Dylan in more trouble. Of course, I knew where the boy heard the language… it was just like all of us growing up all over again.

Searcy giggled, the little minx. "Told ya," she stated to her brother before she dug into her biscuit.

I could tell things were getting a bit tense, and I already had a battle on my hands when Duke Chambers showed up that morning. I didn't need another. "Okay, uh, how about we go to Central Park and ride those paddle boat things before we get lunch? We can also go to the zoo. That oughta take up most of the day.

"After that, we can stop by the Victorian to check in with Nemo, Smokey, Casper, Sherlock, and Mathis, and by then, your dads should be about done for the day," I suggested, knowing it would take them at least an hour to get cleaned up after breakfast, which would make it after eight-thirty. The boat ride would at least burn an hour, and then lunch another. The zoo? I was guessing a person could kill a lot of time at the zoo. Sounded like a good day to me.

Gabe laughed. "Good luck with that shit, man," he said before he patted Dex on the ass. The yoga instructor hopped up to allow Gabe to stand. He kissed each of his children on the head before he rushed upstairs to pull on his shirt, tie, and jacket and finished dressing. I glanced at his plate to see it was mostly still full, which made me laugh.

"Yes, you got to him, Mateo. He'll probably eat salads for the rest of the week, and I expect him to be running more than usual. Now, let's go over the rules," Dexter told me as he dug into the eggs left on Gabe's plate. I couldn't help but laugh as I dug back into my breakfast, as well. Being with family was good.

2

SHAY BARR

"Marcella, you know better than to use a cheap, over-the-counter kit. Why didn't you call to tell me you'd had your eyes done? I'd have come to you, sweetheart," I chastised one of my regulars who took it upon herself to allow someone other than me to touch up her roots. The woman had a brow lift earlier in the week and was still suffering from residual bruising and swelling which wasn't subsiding as quickly as she'd hoped.

Marcella didn't want to come into the salon to undergo the scrutiny of my other clients... or maybe by me... but when she saw her hair after she washed it, Marcella knew there was no choice but to beg me to help her. I assumed it was something horrific when she came into the salon with a scarf and large sunglasses covering most of her head.

I couldn't imagine the damage done to her hair until I relieved her of her disguise. Once I saw it, I held the evil laugh. *Some women never learn.*

Throughout my examination of the carnage, Marcella confessed she'd instructed one of her maids to go to the local discount pharmacy to pick up a touch-up kit for her roots, which was something Marcella had seen on television as she was recovering from her plastic surgery. Knowing the woman as I did, no doubt the request was more like a command.

I'd have bet the maid picked up a kit for red hair instead of brown, likely substituting the contents of the red kit into a brown kit box so Marcella wouldn't catch on to what was about to happen until it was too late. I was pretty sure the maid was only too happy to pay her boss back for the shitty treatment she'd endured during her employment, much as I assumed all of Marcella's employees had suffered over the years.

Marcella's hair looked like some sort of wild creature had taken up residence on her head. There was a good chance I'd seen something very similar on *Animal Planet* one Sunday night. It was a bat with red fur and dark wings, which looked like Marcella's red roots and chocolate ends. Let's just say the woman was a hot fucking mess.

Of course, Marcella fired the maid, but that was probably inevitable because Marcella was a bitch, and I was pretty sure all her maids meted out retribution on her one way or another before they were dismissed. The line for revenge was likely a long one.

Many of my clients were bitchy snobs, unfortunately, but that was what happened when one had a great reputation as a stylist. The rich, rude women only wanted the best, and it seemed I was the best in Brooklyn at the time. I wasn't about to make any apologies for it, either.

I was certain I could have been the best in Manhattan had I decided to remain, but there were too many snotty socialites fighting for too many celebrity stylists in the city for my tastes. I moved to Brooklyn when Maxim Partee decided he was moving over the bridge to start his own business. He sparked my desire to be my own boss, so I went for it… and I took another friend with me. The woman who would become my salon manager was only too happy to help me relocate our business to Brooklyn.

Sonya Torres was my girl-Friday, and I'd never trade her for anyone. She'd been the shampoo girl at the fancy salon where we'd both worked in Manhattan years ago, but I saw potential in the woman and believed she could be so much more.

When I finally walked out of Upper Cut, the pretentious salon where I worked at the time, I talked Sonya into going with me because that Latina had flair. She was a stunning beauty, and she had a certain rapport with customers which Ingrid Acton, the owner of that uppity salon, didn't appreciate. I, however, *did*.

"I know, but I was embarrassed because I hadn't told anyone I was getting them done. I had no idea I'd have so much bruising, and Morton has an award thing tonight that I have to attend. I thought I could wing it, Shay, but obviously, Venita had it out for me, that little wall climber. I'm glad I fired her," Marcella complained.

Venita, who came into the shop on occasion to pick up Marcella's shampoo and hairspray, was from Pelham Bay in the Bronx. She lived with her two sisters and her grandmother. Her parents still lived in El Segundo where the Santos girls were born, and her father was retired Air Force, for hell's sake. She hadn't climbed any walls to get to Brooklyn.

I glanced up to see Sonya's face was bright red with anger at the woman's derogatory remark about Venita. I saw her stomp her foot and shake her head with the evilest look I'd ever seen. *"Ese chinga polvoriento tuvo suerte de que todo lo que Venita hiciera fue follar con su cabello. ¡Hubiera afeitado la cabeza de la puta!"* Sonya taunted as she walked by with a fake smile plastered on her pretty face. I couldn't hold the laugh because I actually knew enough Spanish to understand the gist of Sonya's comment.

Marcella picked up on the word, "Venita" and frowned. "What did she say? Is she saying rude things about me, Shay?" the woman snarled. I could hear Sonya cackling in the back room at the comment, but I was pretty sure Marcella hadn't, and relief slid down my spine.

"She said Venita messed with the wrong woman," I offered as a pathetic explanation.

Of course, it was a lie because Sonya said Marcella was lucky all Venita did was to fuck up her hair because my sweet Latina would have shaved her head, and then she called her a 'puta'...bitch. I certainly didn't translate it for the woman because Marcella was a steady, *wealthy,* customer, even though she was probably a dusty pussy as Sonya had mentioned in her rant, but I really didn't want to lose her business. I had to deal with all kinds of personalities in my chair, so I tried to remain diplomatic as often as possible.

I was sympathetic when possible and a sniping shrew when necessary. In my profession, word of mouth was the best form of advertising at my disposal, so my fake concerns for my customers' ridiculous problems paid off in the long run. I didn't offer an opinion one way or another when a conflict was presented. I was supportive of whoever's ass was parked in my chair, and it worked for me.

I glanced in the mirror as I brushed the corrective die on Marcella's roots and offered the woman a fake smile. "She's not rude, Marcella. Sonya's just a straight shooter, much like yourself," I patronized.

Once I was finished applying the color, I placed a plastic cap on Marcella's hair and put her under a dryer on low to help the color develop faster… and keep her from talking to me anymore. I walked to the back with the bowl and began cleaning up the mess I'd made.

"I don't know why you put up with her bullshit," Sonya complained.

Maybe I put Marcella under the dryer to keep her from hearing this particular exchange?

Marcella Kastle believed she was one of the entitled who lived in Brooklyn, simply because her husband, Morton, was a big-shot realtor who worked in the Spires Tower in Manhattan for old Randolph Spires himself.

The woman had bullied Sonya into approaching me for the appointment, and I'd been the weak idiot to cave and tell Sonya to move the four other clients thirty minutes incrementally so I had time to color and style Marcella's hair between appointments.

I hated the fact that I had to kiss ass, but it was the way business was conducted in my profession. I wasn't thrilled about it, trust me. I knew my other clients would be upset at me for pushing off their appointments by thirty minutes, but I'd make sure they were smiling when they left so they would give my salon a good review for their other pretentious friends who would call for the much sought-after appointments.

Marcella wasn't the first client I'd shifted things around for, and she wouldn't be the last. Besides, I had no reason to rush home in the first place… well, except for a pissed-off rescue cat, Sir-Mix-A-Lot… or Mixer, as I called him.

The black and white cat had wandered into my Red Hook neighborhood in Brooklyn, and the fucker set up shop under my first-floor, bedroom window, yowling every damn night for a week before I fed him. It sounded like someone was being murdered at night, and I didn't need the bags under my eyes from the lack of sleep after listening to his non-stop complaining. Besides, I was a soft touch, and I felt bad for the homeless animal.

I took Mixer to the vet to get him checked out, and after he was dewormed, neutered, and caught up on his shots, I took him home. He was an independent bastard and not appreciative that I'd had his balls cut off, but he had two meals a day and a nice place to live. He could adjust, just as I had when I came to New York from Hot Springs, Arkansas. We all learn to adjust to better surroundings unless we're on a suicide mission. *Mixer and me? We're meant to be.*

"Sonya, *mi amiga*, you know how much I abhor comments like the one Marcella made, but instead of tossing her out of my salon on her saggy ass and having her bad-mouth us to all of her friends, I'm planning to charge her seven-hundred-and-fifty dollars for the color correction and the disruption to my schedule. I'll be giving away products to my customers for the rest of the day, so Marcella owes me that much to be sure.

"Take deep breaths and try to find Venita Santos if you can. Ask her if she's found a job yet, and if she hasn't, tell her to come by when she can talk with me. I'm sure Maxi might have a spot for her on his crew. If not, we'll give her a job here, but I'll have to make sure she doesn't work on the same days Marcella comes in for her appointments. It'll all work out. Trust me, chica," I instructed, trying not to piss off the Latina because the woman ran my life, and I loved her for it.

Sonya was muttering until she heard the bell indicating the front door was opened. She was mid-snack, so after I dried my hands, I turned to her and grinned. "I'll get it. Finish your food while it's hot, doll."

With that, I poured myself a fresh cup of coffee and hurried to the front desk to see a handsome man standing there with a teary-eyed Searcy Torrente in his arms. A huge chunk of the girl's hair was gone, and I turned to see Dylan staring at the gorgeous man with a healthy dose of fear in his eyes.

I walked around the desk and looked at Searcy, one of my favorite people in the world. "Sweetie, what happened?" I asked. She began wailing like someone had cut off her arm, so I scooped her into my arms before turning to look into the eyes of the most gorgeous man I'd ever seen… well, seen *again*. I'd never been introduced to him, formally, but I'd seen him at Dex and Gabe's wedding. He was only there for a hot minute, but a blind man could see he was related to the handsome Gabriele Torrente.

"Can you tell me what happened?" I asked him as I tried to sooth Searcy by snuggling her into my neck where I felt the tears streaming into my shirt.

The man appeared to be at his wit's end, and the other guy with him, a big blond beast, was laughing and not even trying to hide it. "I, uh, Dylan said you cut their hair, so we came here. It seems someone put gum in her hair and then proceeded to cut it out with a pocketknife *he wasn't supposed to have*," the gorgeous brunet stated as he eyed Dylan, who was starting to look quite squeamish.

I tutted at Dylan. "You know better than that, young man. What did I tell your father? Peanut butter—not scissors, or in your case, *a pocketknife*," I scolded, but not too harshly.

Searcy had the most gorgeous dark, wavy hair in the world, and there was about a two-inch by six-inch chunk of it missing from the left side, right near her ear. "Come on, all of you… oh, except you, *shoulders*. You can stay right here and wait," I addressed the large blond man who didn't appear to have a sympathetic bone in his body.

I turned to the other man and smiled. "What's your name?" I asked the Gabe Torrente look-alike.

"I'm Mateo, Gabriele's cousin. Their sitter couldn't watch them today, so I volunteered to take them to Central Park for the day. We were eating lunch at one of the restaurants around the park, when one of us put his *gum* in his sister's hair instead of in a napkin. When Searcy found it and started to cry, he hacked it. He has a pocketknife I'm sure his Nonno Tomas gave to him, just like he does all of the grandsons in his family," the tall man explained.

I looked at Dylan to see the guilt on his face, and it was so adorable that I almost hugged him. Unfortunately, I still had the little brunette in my arms who was crying... *hard*... and wiping her snotty nose on my shirt.

"I hope you got rid of the evidence before your dad sees her hair," I alerted the kid. The large man, Mateo, reached into the pocket of his very sexy slacks and pulled out the pocketknife, showing me the small weapon. There were a few strands of dark hair hooked into it that appeared as if it still had the roots attached. The poor little beauty had suffered, for sure.

I gently placed Searcy in my chair and turned her to look at me, taking a few tissues to wipe her gorgeous green eyes. Dyl's were a beautiful brown, just like Mateo's appeared to be as I glanced up to see him studying me.

"It's not the end of the world, and your hair will grow back, I swear, Searcy," I told her, pointing to my short hair which I'd hacked off a month earlier after a horrific weekend.

Of course, it was the wrong thing for me to say to the little brunette because she only cried harder, which wasn't my intention at all. "You're not very good at this, are you, *roba caldo*?" I heard the handsome man criticize behind me.

I wheeled around and studied him for a moment before I stood to all of my five-six. "Maybe not, but I wasn't the one who allowed the nine-year-old to carry a pocketknife, now was I? My name is Shay, by the way, and if you want me to do you a favor, I'd suggest a change in attitude, Cousin Matthew," I snapped back as I cocked a perfectly manicured eyebrow at the man, purposely not using his correct name. *Bitch, don't fuck with me. Dex will have my ass for this, but I ain't going down alone.*

I looked at Searcy and smiled. "Okay, it's still summer, so how about we try a new style while we let this chunk grow out? I can call your daddy and have him come over for approval."

Dylan groaned as he stood next to the chair. "Daddy has classes until six tonight, and he'll be upset if he has to cancel them. Why don't you just cut it even and let's go? We were going to the zoo, I thought," the boy whined at Mateo-the-Manly.

"I'm not laying a scissor blade to her hair without one of your parents giving permission," I responded to Dylan. I wasn't one to be bullied for damn sure, even by one of my favorite people.

Mateo-the-Manly threw up his hands. "Fine, *bello*, let me get Gabby on FaceTime so you can get permission," he responded, pissing me off like there was no tomorrow by using words I didn't understand. It was Italian, I was sure, but I had no idea if he was calling me an angel or an asshole.

Just then, a timer on my station clanged. For a moment, I forgot what it was for until I turned to see Sonya pointing toward the hairdryer under which sat Marcella. I hadn't meant to leave her under the whole time, but I lost track of everything when the handsome man came in with a crisis.

I folded my hands in prayer, issuing a subtle request across the shop, and saw Sonya roll her eyes. She quickly nodded before she walked over to the dryer and released Marcella, taking her to the shampoo room before returning to me with a snarl. I made a motion with my right hand as if I was eating soup, which meant I'd take her out to dinner, and she smiled. *One crisis down, one to go.*

I felt a tap on my shoulder and turned to see the beautiful Mateo holding a phone out for me. On it, I saw a very annoyed Gabe Torrente. "Hey, before you get peeved at me, let me show you the damage, *Mr. Carrington*," I stated, reminding him of his husband, who was going to throw a fit.

I guided the phone to show him the chunk of missing hair before I handed the phone to Searcy, who started crying again. "He cut it, Papa," she whispered in the most pitiful voice I'd ever heard in my life.

"Oh, sweetheart, it's not that bad. Let Shay make it pretty, and it'll be fine. How about if Shay asks that nice lady to put some pretty make-up on you after your haircut? My treat? Tell your brother he's in trouble when he gets home," Gabe told her before he instructed her to hand me the phone.

I looked at the screen and cocked an eyebrow. "Whatever it costs, Shay, okay? Put that smile on my little girl's face. *Please?* I'll handle Dexter, no worries. I forgot Dad gave him the pocketknife, so I'm in deep shit over it as it is. Charge my account," Gabe requested.

I glanced at Dylan to see he was teary-eyed, too. "I'm going to trim Dyl's hair, as well. Maybe we don't have to have a full-blown meltdown over this? I'm sure Dylan remembered the last time gum was in Searcy's hair and how Dex cut off a bunch of it instead of calling me. Take gum away from your children, Gabe. And maybe make sure the nine-year-old isn't armed next time," I joked, seeing the handsome man smile.

"Thanks, Shay. Hey, do I look like I've gained weight to you?" Gabe asked, which caused the tall, handsome man next to me to totally lose his shit with howling laughter.

Mateo grabbed the phone from me and looked at the screen with a big smile before he disconnected the call and turned to me. "Can you work us in, or should we come back later?" he asked with, dare I say, an eager look.

"I'll get Ari to trim Dyl's hair, and I'll get Searcy shampooed with some very special shampoo. I'll dry Mrs. Kastle's hair before I cut Searcy's. It's fine. I have time before my next appointment," I explained before I motioned for Paige Morten, the makeup artist who worked for me.

She hurried over and smiled. "Yes, Shay? What can I do for you?"

"After Searcy gets her hair washed, can you give her some subtle shimmer to make her feel a little happier? Also, can you fix up Marcella Kastle? She has a thing tonight, I think, and she had her eyes done, so there's bruising. I'll pay for Marcella," I told her since she was an independent contractor in my salon.

Paige rented the space from me and had her own clients, but she brought in business to my salon which was profitable for me, just like my nail technician, Ahn Lee. I also had a masseuse and an esthetician who worked at my salon so I could offer full-service to my clients. That day, the only service Searcy cared about was her shimmer.

I had Maxi Partee to thank for that one because we'd done the hair and makeup for Dex and Gabe's wedding. Searcy fell in love with the subtle makeup Paige had applied, and when Gabe offered it as a way to make his daughter happy, I wasn't about to decline his request.

I took Dylan to the back and gave him his choice of what he wanted to drink while I grabbed sparkling water for myself. I sat Dylan down and combed my fingers through his hair to give Ari instructions regarding the cut for the sweet boy who was in big trouble. "Tell me why you put gum in Searcy's hair, and why on earth did you cut it out?" I asked.

Dylan stared at me for a few seconds before he sighed, seeming to have decided to trust me. "Everybody likes her better than me. She has pretty hair, and she smiles and laughs a lot, stealing everybody's heart. Both our dads say it all the time. I'm sick of hearin' it," he told me, reaching under his glasses to wipe his eyes with the tips of his fingers. He was such an incredible kid, but I could see he had a bit of a rebellious streak in him, as well.

I sighed. "I wish I had a little sister. I used to be jealous of my friends who had little brothers or sisters because they had someone who would look up to them and depend on them. I didn't have that growing up," I lied to him.

I had older brothers who hated my fucking guts, but when my ass left Arkansas, I became an only child to anyone who would meet me in the future. I didn't go on to tell young Dylan about my father who had been so damn cruel to me I couldn't wait until I could get away from him, and I still prayed he died an agonizing death. The jury was still out on my mother.

My family still lived in Hot Springs, Arkansas, from what I knew after calling the only cousin I spoke with, Dani Barr. Her father was my dad's brother and a preacher at a Pentecostal church back home. That didn't make him a good guy.

Uncle Brett hated me with a hellfire-like passion because I was the queer of the family, but somehow, Danielle didn't share the family's distaste for the rainbow community. We exchanged emails and phone calls on occasion. She was how I found out my grandfather, Joseph, had died a few years prior.

I wished I could say I missed the old man, but he was the one who raised my father Bob and my Uncle Brett to be the mean sons-a-bitches I grew up to hate, just like I hated my three older brothers. I didn't shed a tear when I learned Joe had died, and I caught myself before I prayed my father, mother, aunt, and uncle didn't live much longer because those were negative thoughts I didn't want to harbor. I took Dex's yoga and meditation classes, and I knew karma was an unforgiving bitch. I wasn't ready to tangle with her anytime soon. I wanted to be as Nama-gay as Dexter, but I had a long way to go.

I looked at Dylan, seeing a little boy of nine trying to get some attention for himself, and I could relate to him. Yes, Searcy was the one who drew everyone in like a moth to the flame, but I remembered Dex telling us about Dyl getting bullied by one of Gabe's nephews, and I wondered if there was more to it than Dylan just being an ornery little shit like most boys his age.

"I know it's hard for you at this age because you're not sure what to think about most things. You need to be around boys your own age who aren't assholes, but there aren't any in your neighborhood. Are you going to any camps or anything? I know your fathers are worried about you being out of their sight for a minute, but do you want me to talk to Dex? I think I get where you're coming from," I told Dyl, seeing his face light up for a second before he totally deflated in front of me.

"I already asked, and they said no," Dyl reported with a hopeless voice, covertly reaching up to dry a few more tears.

I grabbed a towel from the basket on the table. "It's okay, Dyl. I'll tell you what. I'll talk to Dex about me coming over to teach you my soccer moves. I played when I was in junior high and high school. Do you know how to play?" I asked him.

"A little, but I know baseball better. Smokey and Nemo taught me how to pitch," he explained with a proud smile. *At least the tears stopped.*

I felt the hair on the back of my neck stand up before I heard the chuckle. "Okay, *Sling Blade*, tomorrow night, how about we all go to a Liberty's game? Nobody likes the Spires," the tall man stated with a sexy voice that made my insides melt.

I let an embarrassing giggle slip out before I turned to look at him. "Don't say that too loud, please? My customer's husband works for Randolph Spires," I whispered.

Sexy Mateo smiled at me and winked. "Understood. You're coming with us, right? I mean, I'm trying to get a head count. My treat," the man offered with a big grin that had my panties on fire.

"I, uh, I'll have to check my schedule and get back to you later, if that's okay?" I mumbled, sounding like Karl Childers from the movie that Mateo had referred to earlier. I was only seven when it came out, but I'd seen it at some point in time. It was creepy as fuck.

Mateo took my hand and reached for a pen from the table next to where I was standing by Dylan. I'd been working on the New York Times Sunday crossword before I opened the shop that morning. The damn thing usually took me all week because I wasn't diligent at it, but based on the fact I was actually a dumb hick, I gained a huge sense of accomplishment when I finished the fucking puzzle.

The studly Italian man flipped over my hand and leaned forward to smell my arm before he wrote a number on the underside of my forearm, offering a soft kiss to my wrist before he released me. He tossed the pen on the table and winked at me before he left me with Dyl.

I sighed like a lovesick girl as I watched the sexy man step out of the kitchenette, but I was brought back to the moment when Dylan laughed. "Are you gonna shave my head like yours?" the kid asked as he pointed to my very short hair which was finally growing out, thankfully.

I grabbed him gently by the ear and pretended to drag him behind me, hearing him laughing the whole way before I put him in Ari's chair. I was too stunned at Mateo's gesture to do more than make scissor gestures over Dylan's head to Ari, who laughed at me as if I'd lost my mind before I walked away.

Speechless wasn't a look I could pull off easily.

I sat with Sonya at our favorite Mexican restaurant, *Fiesta en mi Boca*, which literally meant *'Party in my Mouth.'* I loved their food, and the drinks were to die for. Maxi and I used to go there for lunch or dinner all the time before he stopped drinking. The margs were delicious, but his boyfriend, Lawry Schatz, had liquor issues, so Maxi decided not to drink in solidarity when they got together.

It was yet another example of the things we do for love, as an old song stated. Maxi and I were still good friends, but he had a man in his life, and I didn't. I understood it—the need to be there for your man. Friends were fantastic when you were single, but when a significant other came into your life, everyone forgot about their friends who had been supportive through thick and thin. Yeah, I knew the drill, but it didn't make me happy that we didn't hang out as much as we used to do.

"*Jefe*, what's wrong? A tall, sexy, Italian man got your tongue?" Sonya teased as she stirred her drink and offered me a smirk. I couldn't hold the chuckle at bay. I was unable to hide anything from Sonya, really. We were truly simpatico.

I considered her comment before I decided to change the subject because I was still reeling about the encounter in the kitchenette. I still had Mateo's number written on my arm, and I couldn't exactly say when I'd try to wash it off. "How's that guy…uh, what's his name?" I joked, knowing his name was Alonso Flores, and Sonya had been playing hard to get with the handsome man since he was assigned to our route. He was the UPS man who came into the shop at least three times a week for deliveries, and the guy was stunningly handsome in all his Latin glory.

Alonso hit on Sonya every time he came in, usually bringing her a flower of some kind and a poem to go with it. I thought it was sweet, but my dear girl thought him annoying. Alonso was a few years younger than her, but he seemed to be a good guy. My thoughts on the age thing? The younger the meat, the sweeter the taste. Except for me, of course.

I loved older men who I believed to be so much more refined and steadier than men my age. They knew how to treat a lady... or a gay boy. It reminded me of Mateo Torrente's sexy gesture before he left the salon with Dylan and Searcy, both happy with their spa day.

"Thank you for making an awful situation much better. Searcy loves her hair, nails, and makeup, and Dyl feels very cool with his new fauxhawk. Could I make an appointment to get my hair trimmed?" Mateo asked as he ran a long, elegant hand over his long locks. He reminded me so much of Gabe Torrente, I was about to drop to my knees and worship his cock as I stood there.

I swallowed my tongue before I smiled up at him. "Check with Sonya for my next opening that works with your schedule. I'll, uh, let you know about the game tomorrow night," I told the man as I held up my arm where he'd written his phone number. Once again, he kissed the inside of my wrist before he winked and herded the kids out. I... not surprisingly... was left breathless.

Sonya's laughter brought me back from some *very* lascivious thoughts. "Oh, he's got you, doesn't he? Don't talk to me about Alonso Flores. He's cute, but I would chew him up and spit him out, and you know it, Shay. How about you and Mateo Torrente? He's *muy bueno, sí?*" she teased me.

I chuckled. "Yes, he is, but Mr. Torrente's not interested in me at all. *Oh, my! What's a girl to do?*" I joked as I picked up my menu and fanned myself in Southern-belle style. It made Sonya laugh, and it changed the subject, thankfully.

I sipped my margarita and worried about what I would do the next day because it would be rude not to respond to the man regarding the ball game. I didn't know who he was inviting, but he'd made a point to invite me.

Was I setting myself up for heartache? Could it be any worse than what I'd suffered the last time I'd... well, it wasn't dating by any stretch of the imagination. His name was Mr. Franzl, or so he told me, and he was a mean bastard. After the Frenchman abandoned me, I needed the physical reminder I was worthless and nobody would ever love me because I was the abomination in the family due to my orientation. It was something shameful, making me unworthy of seeking love and happiness.

Mr. Franzl was only too excited to punish me for my actions, just as I'd asked him to do. He didn't ask my name, choosing to call me *'slut'* the entire time we were together. If he somehow found me, would I go back to that club and allow that man to beat me again? *Probably.* That answer made me sick to my stomach.

3

MATEO

"All you fucking Torrente's believe you're special, don't you?" Duke Chambers taunted as he aimed a front kick to my chest on Monday morning, which I dodged and returned with a roundhouse to his head, taking the mother fucker to the mat. His animosity wasn't warranted as far as I knew, but from what I'd learned on Saturday night by talking with the other operatives at GEA-A, Chambers treated everyone with the same shitty attitude. It appeared the Marine hated all of us with equal measure, and I wondered what the fuck my father thought when he sent the prick to work for Gabe.

I'd taken many of my new colleagues and their significant others, along with Searcy, Dylan, and the beautiful Shay Barr, to the Liberty's game on Saturday evening. After Searcy's haircut meltdown Friday, Shay had impressed me with being able to calm her and Dylan, along with diffusing the situation of my cousin and his husband getting pissed at me about the 'gum incident' in the first place, and I was grateful for his help. It became the excuse I used to organize a baseball outing with most of the crew, but I had more selfish reasons for asking Shay to join us.

I'd asked the handsome man to dinner before the game, but he told me he had appointments scheduled until six that night. The game started at 7:05, so he'd barely have time to get a shower in and rush to the stadium. I accepted that without argument because I was a patient man, but the strawberry-blond pushed all of my buttons without question... much like the fucking asshole I was about to stomp into the blue mat beneath us because he was pissing me off something fierce.

"What the fuck's your problem, Chambers?" I snapped at him as he sucker punched me in the nose. I stepped back and reached up to feel the blood flowing from my nostril, yet a-fucking-gain. Rafe had broken it not long ago while Casper had been in Italy, and now I'd just taken another shot to it that I didn't feel I deserved.

The man started to come at me again when Smokey stepped between us. "Back off. What the fuck is going on? This is a workout, not a goddamn cage match, Chambers. We're all on the same team, not adversaries," Smokey told him as he reached into his pocket and pulled out a handkerchief before examining my nose. He wiggled it and set it back in place, which was exactly what any fucking doctor would do.

I stepped away from him and held the cloth under my nose as I kept my head tilted forward to keep the blood from draining down my throat. It wasn't a new practice for me, unfortunately. "I'm fine, but I'm gonna have black eyes," I bitched, hearing light footsteps on the stairs.

"What the hell?" I heard Dexter complain. We were in the basement of the Victorian where Gabe's people worked out, but I knew for a fact we were more aggressive in Italy than Gabe's operatives, so a bloody nose wasn't really a disaster considering some of the other injuries I'd received at the hands of a co-worker.

Clearly, Chambers had a fucking grudge or a score to settle with me, but I had no idea why. It wasn't that I couldn't take the beating because I was used to it with my crazy brother, but Chambers' level of aggression had me worried, especially since he was my partner on kid duty.

The summer was nearly over, and as far as I knew, there had been no news regarding the Mangello family and their movements. Rafe had been in North Carolina with Nemo and his primary before Papa called him back home for a job. St. Michael went down to help Nemo, and I was in New York to ensure nothing happened to those sweet kids we all loved. I wasn't sure if Chambers had read the memo, but we were to protect Dyl and Searcy at any cost, not try to kill each other while sparring.

Dexter stepped forward and turned me so he could examine my face. "Jesus, guys. Come with me, Mateo. Let me ice this," Dex demanded.

"Yeah, go with your little pussy friend and…" The sound of a body hitting the mat behind me caught my attention. I turned to see a very pissed-off Smokey, who I thought was a peace-loving mother fucker since he'd gotten engaged to Parker Howzer. He had Chambers flat on his back with his hand around the man's throat, and it didn't look like the cowboy wanted to let go.

I pulled away from Dexter and went over to Smokey, fighting to break his hold on Chambers, who was turning blue. "Let him go, Shep," I gritted out as I frogged his bicep until he pulled back. I'd seen blood in men's eyes, but not more than when I looked at Smokey Colson at that moment.

"Get your shit and get the fuck out," Smokey demanded of Duke Chambers once he backed away.

I glanced around to see everyone was there at once… or almost everyone until Gabe came galloping down the stairs, looking ready to kill someone. I stepped in front of him as Dexter tried to grab his arm. "Stop now," I commanded as I pushed against my cousin because he was closer to killing Chambers than Smokey, and I couldn't imagine how that was possible.

Dexter got between us and gently put his hands over Gabe's cheeks, drawing the big man's gaze downward. "I'm fine, Gabriele. He didn't touch me. He hurt Mateo, but I think he's okay. Just fire Duke," Dex suggested.

Gabe pulled Dex into his arms and whispered something to him before he kissed him and led him upstairs. I walked over to Chambers and extended my hand which he refused. "Man, I don't know what you got against me, but I'll fight it out with you if it makes you feel better. I'd urge you to refrain from making comments about my cousin, though, because I think Gabriele might have a shorter fuse than me. We'd have to dig a huge fucking hole for you, big boy," I told him before I walked away and went to the locker room to shower. If that joker thought Gabe would kill him before I got to him, he was misjudging me completely. I hoped I didn't have to show him the error of his ways.

I showered and dressed before going upstairs to see Casper. I needed some intel on Salvatore Mangello, and Papa had told me to use Casper if possible because Lotta Renaldo, our IT guru, had her hands full with a new case in Berlin. Papa didn't know if it was a Mangello hit or someone else, but the world was a fucked-up place to be sure.

As I was leaving the locker room, my phone buzzed in my pocket, and when I unlocked it, I saw a text from the hot barber.

Can I change your appointment this afternoon to six instead of five? I have a hair emergency to handle. Don't laugh. You know it can happen. SB

I snickered and replied to the hot man's request.

Sure thing, Sweeney. See you at six. M

My teasing reference to *Sweeney Todd* had happened on Saturday night while we were watching the *Liberty's* kick the asses of the *Milwaukee Dells* something awful. It was a delightful conversation if I did say so myself.

"So, what got you interested in being a barber...err...stylist?" I asked as I offered Shay some of my popcorn. I shook red pepper flakes and parmesan cheese on it at the pizza stand, and Shay commented he'd never thought about doing it before as we all walked to our seats, which I'd ensured were next to each other when I handed out the tickets.

"The chance to use a straight razor without anyone questioning me.

Anyone pisses me off, and it's this," he joked as he dragged his thumb across his neck, making me swallow a kernel down the wrong pipe so I nearly choked to death. Shay pounded on my back on one side while Sherlock pounded (much harder) on the other. I elbowed that prick in the ribs, praying I broke one. My little brother, Rafe, loved to tell me I was still a fucking child. I was kind of starting to believe him.

"So, Sweeney Todd, how many men have you killed in your chair?" I asked before taking a sip of my beer.

"Who says I killed them? Maybe I just used my demonic magic to make them do dirty things to me?" he teased, which caused me to spew beer all over the back of Smokey's head.

Everyone but Shepard Colson had laughed like we'd been watching a sitcom. His comment to me? *"I'll get you, you mother fucker."* I was certainly going to keep an eye out for the man because I knew those Delta bastards were ruthless and stealth.

That reminded me, I owed Smokey something for stepping between Chambers and me the previous day because I was about to kill the mother fucker. Smokey wasn't quick to temper from what I remembered when he worked with us in Italy, but he'd stepped up pretty quick when Chambers brought Dexter into the discussion. I was grateful for it and also grateful that he got Gabe out of the mix because I knew my cousin was an overbearing asshole when it came to his husband. I actually envied him for it.

I walked down the hall to knock on Casper's door. We didn't know each other very well, but everyone else gave him a thumb's up, so I was looking forward to working with the Spook. *"Avanti!"* I heard, recognizing the tongue of my ancestors.

"Sono io, Mateo. É bello vederti!" I greeted as I stood in the open door.

The guy stood up and smiled. "Mateo, I only know how to say a few things in Italian. Hell, English is barely my native tongue. Good to see you again. What the fuck happened to your face?"

Casper walked over to me and offered his hand to shake which I took, pulling him closer for a hug. We'd seen each other in Rome when he was there looking for an old lover before I was sent to

Greece with St. Michael to look for Sally Man. When we found he'd left Athens before we got there, we returned to Rome, where I stayed for a bit before I was sent to New York. It was good to see Casper again.

"I said it's nice to see you, man. I could use a little snooping if you're free. Lotta's busy with another case. You got a minute?" I asked the man.

"Sure. I'm not too crunched for time. Shoot, what can I do for you?" Casper asked while pulling out a pad and pencil to take notes, just as Lotta Renaldo did every time I went into her lady lair. I seriously respected the woman because she was excellent at her trade. There was a time when Papa hoped one of us would marry the genius, but the gay and bisexual genes ran deep in our family.

I was as gay as a prancing pony. Rafe was the equal-opportunity lover in our family, just as Gabriele had been before he met the gorgeous Dexter Carrington. Uncle Tomas used to say the Torrente blood burned hot and could not be contained by limiting our options between choosing one sex over the other. My Uncle Luigi laughed the loudest at that one.

"We have a former friend of the family I'd like to see if you can find. His name is Salvatore Mangello. He's the youngest son of…"

Casper nodded. "Frankie Man. I'm familiar with the family. You want to know where he is right now or what he's been up to lately?"

For my purposes? "Both."

"Okay. How much history you want on him?" the guy asked, just like a good Spook would do.

"Give me, uh, give me his activities since the death of Giancarlo, his older brother. Check out what he was doing in Athens about two months ago, for sure. Maybe go back six months or so if you can?" I asked.

Casper looked at me and smiled. "Are you in the pool? Some of the guys have a pool about where the next pieces of Carlo will turn up. There was a report that his hand was found stuck on top of a stick outside his father's house, which was why Frankie took off for Venice. It was giving the house the finger," Casper told me, making me laugh.

"You don't say? Someone has a very sick sense of humor," I stated...*and several walk-in freezers, the stupid fucker. I need to cut that shit off before it leads people in directions none of us want, namely, my idiot brother.*

"Yeah, I'd say. I'll get right on this, Mateo. Let me know if you need anything else, okay?" Casper stated with sincerity before he gave me an odd look as if something had just clicked into place for him. I waved to him as I hightailed it out of there before anything stuck with the guy, unsure of where his thoughts might be leading him. *Curiosity killed the cat...and the sloppy operative.*

I went to the men's room and looked at my two, blooming black eyes in the mirror. They were becoming darker by the minute, and I didn't want to scare Shay when I went to get my haircut, so I made my way downstairs to see Dex in the studio with a class. He held up his hand to show me five as he pointed to the clock while in some pose that had his body contorted in a way that had me jealous of my cousin's fucking luck. I glanced up to see it was five of four, so I was guessing his class ended at four. I nodded and walked over to the reception desk where Sierra and my cousin, Dom, were stuffing envelopes.

"Hello, troops. How's it going?" I asked, seeing a scoff from the woman who had worked for Gabe for a few years. I didn't feel I deserved her nasty look because I hadn't asked her for anything. She hopped up from her chair and left the scene without a word for me.

I turned to look at my young cousin, seeing him unfazed. "What's up her butt?" I asked Dominic, who didn't stop working. Apparently, her cranky behavior wasn't a new thing?

Dom chuckled as he licked the last envelope, placing it into a box lid where two rows of envelopes were lined up like soldiers in the ranks. Dom smiled at me before he picked up the box lid and placed it on the counter for the mailman. "What do you want me to say? I've come to believe she's just a bitter woman. Hell, isn't it obvious? She said her boyfriend took off on her some time ago, and I think she's having a hard time meeting someone new. From what I've learned in the few years I've worked here, the last guy was a lazy fucker and left her with an assload of bills, so I'd bet she's feeling the heat of trying to pay that shit off. It's only a guess, though," Dom speculated.

Dom glanced around the place, so I did as well. Finally, he continued in a much softer voice. "Based on some of the shit I've overheard her say when she's talking to friends on the phone, it sounds like the stupid asshole was hurting himself to get drugs because he was an addict. I keep these things to myself, you see. I'm fucking afraid of her, and I'd suggest you be wary as well, Mateo."

I wasn't about to be afraid of anyone, but I wouldn't hold Dom's concerns against him. I was much older than him, and he had a lot to learn—or unlearn. Fear wasn't an emotion I indulged in.

"How's your mom?" I asked after Lucia, one of Uncle Tomas' daughters. She wasn't the friendliest cousin in the world, but we were never exactly close growing up. Aunt Grace kept a tight leash on the girls, so I hadn't really bonded with any of them as I had with Gabriele. I had high hopes with Dom, though.

"God, Mom's started dating someone, but don't mention it around here. I'm afraid if Uncle Gabe or Nonno find out, they'll lose their shit. I talked to the guy on the phone a few weeks ago when Mom had him over for dinner with my sisters, and he seemed pretty nice. He's Italian, so that should make Nonno happy if they ever go public," Dom informed.

"Ah, what's his name?" I asked. I wasn't foolish enough to believe I knew the guy, but maybe I could get Casper to do a little digging on the family's behalf...in his spare time.

"Marco Rialto. Ma says his family is from the boot. I just warned her to be careful. You know how guys can be," Dom stated with a big grin.

I chuckled as I looked at the handsome kid. "I do—do you, *piccolo cugino?*" I teased. Dom was anything but little, to be sure. He was like a beanpole, but he was a handsome young man of about twenty-four if I remembered correctly. The Torrente blood was definitely present in Dominic.

The flush of his cheeks was all I needed to see. "I see the gene pool is strong in you. Welcome to *la famiglia all'interno della famiglia,*" I told him before I took his hand and pulled him from behind the desk, kissing him on both cheeks, which made his face glow.

"The family within the family? Is it that obvious?" he asked as he patted me on the shoulder before he stepped away.

Before I could answer, I saw Chambers ambling down the stairs like the fucker hadn't a care in the world. When he looked at me, he smirked. "Wow, fucking your cousin is cool in the Torrente family? That's goddamn perverse," he sniped at me before he went out the front door.

I turned to Dom, who had a worried look on his face, and I laughed it off. "He's an asshole. Don't let guys like him get under your skin. He's jealous, I guess."

I glanced at my watch to see it was just after four, so I walked over to the yoga studio, holding the door for Dex's students, some of whom looked to be high as a fucking kite, or maybe they were just that mellowed out? Once they were gone, I went inside to see Dex drying his shoulders and arms. For such a small guy, he was fucking cut. *There must be something to that yoga shit? Maybe I should give it a try?*

"How come I don't have kid duty today? You're not still mad about the hair thing, are you?" I asked. Dex hadn't really spoken to me at the ball game, but I was pretty sure that had more to do with me talking to Shay Barr than him being mad about Searcy's hair.

"Today is Parker's day off, and he and Maxi wanted to take them to Coney Island, so Mathis tagged along. I think Parker wanted to go the most of all of them because he's never been, so the kids gave him a good excuse. They should be home by seven. You're back on kid duty tomorrow.

"Gabe told me your father said he couldn't fire Duke. Do you know why?" Dex asked. I shook my head because I honestly had no idea.

Dexter began rolling up a few mats in the studio, leaving me unsure of what to say. Finally, he nodded to himself and looked at me as he placed two mats into a large basket with handles. "Whatever the beef is between you and Duke Chambers, please don't act on it in front of my kids. Gabe said he talked to Duke, and the guy gave his word he wouldn't do anything aggressive toward anyone here again.

"I don't know if I believe him, but I'd like you to let me know if he starts shit with you, Mateo. I don't care what your father says. I'm still not convinced I want that man around my children," Dex stated. Based on the look on his face, I could see he was dead serious.

"Gotcha, Yogi. So, can I give you the third degree about your friend, Shay Barr?" I asked with a grin and a wink. Dexter giggled. *If he weren't my cousin's husband, I'd be all over that man.*

"Sure. Let's go get an iced coffee," Dex suggested. I opened the door for him while he slipped on some flip-flops and wrapped the towel around his neck, heading out to the lobby where Sierra and Dom were sitting at the desk not speaking. The box top of letters was still resting on the raised ledge. I'd noticed it was a mailing about a special yoga class for couples, and it looked very intriguing.

"Guys, thanks so much for doing this for me. Can I bring you something to drink?" Dexter asked them with a bright smile as he touched the letters, thumbing through them to see they were ready to go.

"We're fine, Uncle Dex. Anything else you need us to do?" Dom asked. I glanced at Sierra to see her nose turned up like someone had farted in the lobby. It made me laugh, which earned me a direct scowl from her highness.

"No, but thank you, both. I'll be back for my five o'clock class," Dexter told them as we traversed the stairs, him leading the way. I followed Dex into the kitchen where Sherlock was sitting with his tablet, a big smile on his face.

"What has you so smiley?" Dex asked the Brit before going to make each of us an iced coffee.

"My mum sent me pictures of my new nephew, Nigel. That little boy is going to get his arse kicked every day in the schoolyard with that handle. Do you think Gabby would give me some time off to go home for a visit?" Sherlock asked Dexter.

I turned to see the yoga teacher smile brightly. "Of course, he will. I can talk to him for you if you'd rather. You should know, having been on kid duty before, Gabriele values family very much. He'll happily let you go, Cyril," Dex seemed to remind the guy.

"Thanks for the offer, Dexter, but I'll talk to Gabby myself before I firm up my plans. Where are the ankle biters? I heard there was drama on Friday regarding chewing gum and a pocketknife. Sounds like Master Dylan has a bit of the scoundrel in him. I remember doing something of the sort when I was a lad, but I didn't think to hack off my sister's hair to hide the evidence," Sherlock joked, making me laugh.

We both looked to see Dexter with a cocked eyebrow, so we tried to sober up. He suddenly chuckled, looking at us. "All of you are too easy. So, Mateo, you're interested in Shay Barr?" Dex asked.

"I'm out when the dating game begins. If you find a beautiful young maiden looking for a father figure, send her my way. Mateo, we need to have a bucks' night, you bleedin' bastard. I remember dragging your fat arse back to your papa's house too many times after we got blasted at a pub. I actually miss the fun," Sherlock told me before he left the room.

I turned to look at Dex, who was smiling at me. "You guys never talk about working for Uncle Giuseppe in Italy. Do you do a lot of work like Gabe and the guys do here, or is it mostly something else?"

I knew better than to give him a straight answer. If my cousin wanted him to know the truth, he'd have already told him, so I just smiled. "We mostly work for diplomats. We provide security for some of the lesser state officials, and we help look for people who've gone missing, which isn't an uncommon occurrence in Italy, as you've likely heard from Gabe. It's mostly boring shit, but it's something to do in addition to selling wine. So, your friend Shay?" I pushed onto another, much more interesting topic.

Dex laughed. "Well, if you're really interested in him, I'll give you some insider tips. He's a great guy, but he becomes very defensive if he feels someone he cares about is being mistreated. He's totally a closeted romantic. He's the type of guy who would love to be swept off his feet, but not at the expense of his male ego."

That was all I needed to hear. For the next forty-five minutes, Dex told me some things about the little temptation-on-two-sexy-legs while he put some stuff on my face to try to hide my black eyes. I was grateful for his assistance, and I thanked him before I was off for my hair appointment, new weapons of seduction in tow. I was actually pretty excited to see the barber because I was definitely interested in the man for more than just a quick fuck… likely for the first time in my pathetic life.

4

SHAY

"You want me to stick around, *jefe*?" Sonya asked as she began sweeping the floor around my station. It was Monday, and Mondays always brought disaster-repair duty. The day had been busy, such that I barely had time to grab a salad from Watercress for lunch. It took me three stabs at eating half of it because it seemed as if all the crazy came out on this last Monday of August. All the teachers had apparently tried to cut, color, and perm their own hair over the summer, and I was booked to try and fix their mistakes before classes began the next Tuesday.

There was an overprocessed perm that had turned her already bleached hair vomit-emoji green. The only possible fix was for me to cut her hair into a cute pixie cut, while she sat crying in my chair. I then dyed it a sexy platinum blonde, making her beautiful, petite features and her gorgeous, blue eyes stand out. She looked like a human fairy… even more than me. That thought made me laugh.

My second surprise of the day was from a school principal, Janet Owens, who was pregnant with her fourth child. Her son, little Joey Demon Seed, decided he couldn't see Momma's eyes while she was napping on the couch, so he took his safety scissors, which easily cut paper, and cut the front of Momma's hair, right at the scalp. I cut

Janet's hair into a bob and styled the top of it such that it hid her missing bangs, and then I showed her how to style it herself. She left that day in tears, but thankfully, they were tears of gratitude.

"No, Sonya, go home, love. I'm off tomorrow, remember? I'll be available by phone if you need me," I told her as I handed her the deposit to drop off at the bank on her way. By six when Mateo Torrente was due for his haircut, I was tired and hungry.

I was cleaning the combs in the back room of the salon when I heard the bell over the door, so I washed my hands and walked from the back with a towel to keep from dripping on the floor. "Hello, Mr..." I began until I saw who was standing in front of me. It wasn't Mateo Torrente.

"Danielle? Honey, what the hell are you doing in New York?" I asked as I rushed to my cousin, seeing she looked wrecked. I led the young woman into the back room and sat her down at the table, offering her a bottle of water. After a sip, she turned to look at me, and the tears began to flow.

"I'm here about my little brother because I didn't know what the hell to do, or where else to go. Danielle told me as she held her head in her hands.

Just then, the bell sang out, signaling the door was opened again since I forgot to lock the damn thing after Dani came into the shop. I walked out of the kitchen to see the last person I wanted... my rebound fuck. I pulled the kitchen door closed and advanced into the front of the salon. "Mr. Franzl, what are you doing here?" I asked, addressing the large, bald man I'd met after Frenchie ducked on me. I'd been feeling extremely stupid and vulnerable—a recipe for a bad decision if I'd ever heard of one.

The private club I visited that horrible night after Frenchie ducked out on me was called Master Kinx. It was a BDSM dungeon I'd heard about at a gay bar in Brooklyn, so after wallowing in self-pity for an hour, I left Dirty Daddies and went there. I paid the cover charge, praising myself for venturing out of my comfort zone... without telling any of my friends—Maxi, Dex, Parker—or even my dear Sonya, which was foolish of me.

Most of the available Doms at the club were otherwise occupied, so when I was approached by a man who wanted to buy me a drink, I took him up on it. It was Mr. Franzl, a pure sadist, and after he got done with me, I had a bruised coccyx since the asshole chose to spank me with a piece of wood rather than a paddle. He laughed at me when I couldn't sit down after he got done fucking me through my protestations, claiming he'd had a bad day at his job which was why he showed no mercy to my stupid ass. He even gave me a card with his cell number on it, the stupid freak.

I went to an Urgent Care and told them I'd fallen down the stairs at my home, and my tailbone hurt so badly it was impossible to sit. They did x-rays and found no fractures, so the doctor pronounced it a bruise, gave me a donut pillow plus a prescription for Tylenol III, and sent me on my merry way.

The long and the short of it was that I'd stupidly allowed a stranger to beat me just as I'd been beaten many times when I was younger, and it felt fucking normal, which was the saddest thing in the world. That wasn't normal, but I sure as fuck didn't know what was normal. I was guessing that would be the hardest thing to figure out. I did learn a valuable lesson, however. Make sure you know what you're asking for because you might not like it when you get it.

"You haven't come back to Master Kinx, and I've been waiting to hear from you. You have my number. I got the Dungeon Master to look up your guest information after I tipped him." The man stood in the middle of my reception lounge, taking in the salon. "This is a nice place. What is it you do here?"

In the soft light of the setting sun, he still scared the fuck out of me, and I could tell he wasn't in my shop for a haircut or a shave because he was bald and still had that ugly, bushy beard. The man was large, just as I remembered, and he didn't look happy that I hadn't gone back to the club or checked in with him. I didn't owe him any clarification because I paid my own way in the world, but the look on his face led me to believe he felt differently about the matter.

"I own this shop. It's a hair salon. Why are you here, Mr. Franzl?" I bit out, wanting to be rid of him as quickly as possible.

Mr. Franzl, if that was really his name, appeared to think he had some hold over me that I wasn't about to acknowledge. I had the feeling that if I showed fear, I'd play into his hands, which wasn't something I was about to do. I hoped my cousin didn't come out because the man looked as if he were in the mood for something I was sure would shock poor Danielle. It wasn't going to make me happy, either, based on the fact he pulled out a pair of what I thought were police handcuffs, flipping them around his right hand as if they were a prop.

"You didn't call me as I instructed, *cum slut*. I made you an offer, and I waited for you to accept. I told you I'd take care of you. You could move in with me, and I'd give you a good life. You can sell this… there's no need for this bullshit," he offered as he waved his hand in the air toward my salon. That shit pissed me off. The salon was mine. I'd built it from nothing, and nobody was going to diminish that or take it away from me.

I laughed. "I didn't call you because I'm nobody's *cum slut*, Mr. Franzl. I own my business…" I began before the man approached me and pushed me against the mirrored wall that led to the shampoo room, his large hand quickly wrapping around my throat.

"That's not an option, *cum slut*. I told you I'd make a life for you, and you don't think it's good enough? You're *mine*. You have no say in this matter, and I thought I'd already taught you that lesson," the man stated as he tightened his grip, cutting off my ability to breathe just as the bell over the door sounded again, signaling another visitor. *Lock That Fucking Door, You Idiot!*

I heard a recognizable deep laugh and the engagement of a cartridge into the chamber of a gun, a sound I still remembered from my fucked-up childhood. "Wow, Sweeney, did you give the man that haircut? I'll admit, it's pretty bad."

Before I could respond, Mr. Franzl was on the floor with a gun to his temple. I was on my ass against the wall where the asshole had dropped me because Mateo Torrente wasted no time taking the man down, and when we both noticed the growing wet spot on Mr. Franzl's slacks, I held in the laugh. Mateo did *not*.

"So, tell me, what has that handsome man done that caused you to put your hands on him? To attempt to do him harm? Did you come back because you didn't like your manicure, or did you come here for something else? Whatever possessed you to believe it was okay to come into Mr. Barr's place of business and threaten him? I'm just curious," Mateo quizzed as he grabbed Mr. Franzl by his throat and helped the man to his feet... roughly... not moving the gun from the man's temple.

"He... he's mine. We met at a club, and he's now my submissive. You have no right getting between us," Mr. Franzl snapped as he tried to reclaim his dominant posture.

Not surprisingly, Mateo chuckled at him before he shook his head at the man. "Wait, you're a member of a club where you told them you were a Dominant, and they hooked you up with this firecracker who... Oh, no, this is priceless. Is part of your training as an alleged Dominant to actually piss your pants when a true alpha male comes along?"

I almost felt sorry for Mr. Franzl as I witnessed Mateo's assertion of supremacy over the man... until I remembered the medical bills I'd had to pay. And the pain I'd suffered, which wasn't pleasant.

"Mr. Torrente maybe let him go before he does something worse in his pants?" I requested after I finally caught my breath.

Mateo looked at me with a serious look. "Did he *hurt* you?"

I considered my answer carefully because the truth was that the man *had* hurt me, but I went to that club of my own free will, and it could be said I asked for whatever I received. No, I didn't want to have the man beat me the way he had, but I'd put myself in that position by not doing any research before I just showed up, hadn't I?

"He did, but I failed to define limits before our encounter. I put myself in that position, and it wasn't Mr. Franzl's fault his level of punishment was much higher than I expected. I didn't realize he was a sadist before our encounter, but I was the one who accepted his invitation to join him in a private room that night, so I suppose he took it as me inferring consent. I should have asked more questions before I went into that room, but I didn't. Let him go," I requested again as I stepped aside.

I'd never met a cold-blooded killer with a heart until I looked at Mateo Torrente addressing Mr. Franzl. Mateo removed the gun from

Mr. Franzl's temple and placed it into the back waistband of his pants before he returned the man to the floor. Mateo actually brushed off Mr. Franzl's shirt and adjusted the man's suit jacket.

Mateo stepped back and actually held up his hands as if he was framing a photo shoot before he stepped forward to the man and leaned in close to Mr. Franzl. Mateo didn't whisper as he spoke directly into Mr. Franzl's ear, so I couldn't help but hear what he had to say.

"Mr. Franzl, is it? I'm Mateo, a wine salesman and a very good friend of Mr. Barr's. Do you like wine?" he asked the man, who quickly shook his head that he didn't.

Mateo chuckled. "Well, that's a shame because I have a lovely case of Bordeaux for sale. Nevertheless, I think we have something in common. You see, I do *not* like pussy, and based on what I heard tonight, you don't either, even though you do resemble the last one I saw. You see, I like dick, and I'm not ashamed to pursue it, but I don't push myself on anyone because that's bad form, or so I was taught growing up. Pushing yourself on anyone without their express consent is rude, and I won't tolerate rudeness to my friends." Mateo spoke calmly to the man, and I could see Mr. Franzl was definitely shaking in his boots.

"What I witnessed when I came in tonight was you trying to force my barber, Mr. Barr, into becoming your full-time bitch, but I get the feeling he wasn't receptive to your demands, was he? Of course, when someone tells you he's not into your idea of a party after going one round with you, maybe you'd better learn to back off? I'd appreciate it if you'd leave Mr. Barr alone," the large Italian man stated with a scary smile.

"Mateo," I started, seeing him turn to look at me.

"Just give me a second to show the man out. I'll be back for that haircut, and can I have a shave? You can use that straight razor you've bragged about being proficient with. I trust you," he told me before he looked at Mr. Franzl. "He's very fucking proficient with a straight razor. I'd remember that if I were you. Say thank you," he ordered.

Mr. Franzl looked at me with disbelief. "For what?" he snapped as Mateo moved to stand close behind him.

Mateo Torrente leaned forward and actually licked the man's neck, smiling at me. Mr. Franzl was shaking even harder at Mateo's proximity. "Thank him for the fact I'm not going to extract your fucking brains with a dull spoon because I have no problem doing it. I remember once in Florence when I used an ice pick to scramble an asshole's brains. He didn't die, but he wasn't really alive after our encounter. It's an odd position to be in, don't you think? Caught between life and death?"

I saw Mr. Franzl's eyes squint into slits as he reached into his jacket pocket for something before he grinned, evil seeping from his every pore. "Thank you for not… what he said, and I'm sorry I laughed at you that night when you told me I'd really hurt you. I should have beaten you to death instead," Mr. Franzl gritted out, fire flashing in his eyes at me. His hand lifted, and I saw the overhead lights flash against the knife blade of the weapon he was holding.

I quickly pointed and shouted, "*Knife!*"

Mateo didn't look at me as he stood behind the man, but I saw his body stiffen. He quickly lifted his hands and jerked Mr. Franzl's neck in a strange angle that took the man to the floor without another word, the knife skittering across the tiled lobby floor.

Before I could catch my breath, the handsome Italian man had me by the hand, pulling me back to the kitchen. When he saw my cousin sitting at the table, he pulled his gun from behind his back as he pushed me behind him. "Are you with that fucking cunt?" he asked Dani as he pointed the gun at her.

Not surprisingly, Dani giggled. "Jesus, fuck no. I was ready to grab somethin' and go out there after that jackoff myself, but what was I gonna hit him with? A comb?" she asked as she pointed to a jar of combs soaking in sterilizing liquid.

Surprisingly, Mateo laughed. "I apologize, ma'am. I'm Mateo Torrente. You are?" he asked, ignoring the fact that I had a dead man in my lounge.

"I'm his cousin, Danielle. Aren't you just a white knight, Mr.

Torrente," Dani teased a bit, either not knowing about the dead man in the lobby or not giving a shit!

Mateo chuckled. "Please, call me Mateo, Danielle. I can see the family resemblance. I hope you're not offended, but I find Shay more appealing. That doesn't mean you're not a beautiful woman, though. Now, if you'll excuse me, ma'am, I need to make a call to take care of the mess I made in the waiting area floor. I'll be back in a few minutes. Could you talk to Shay before he passes out or has a seizure?" I stood between them, nearly unable to breathe. It was my first dead body, after all, and I wasn't familiar with the protocol surrounding such an event.

As if he could ready my mind, Mateo touched my cheek. "Stop that line of thinking, Sweeney. Nobody ever asks for anyone to intentionally hurt them, and regardless of the playpen where you found yourself, that shit usually goes against policy everywhere. I'll be right back."

He left the room for a minute as I stared at Danielle, who had a big smile on her face. "Wow, now that's an interestin' prospect. Tall, dark, and deadly. Be still my swoonin' heart," she teased as she stood from the chair and walked over to me, gently patting my face to bring me back to the present.

After a few minutes of me with my head between my knees as I breathed into a bag, the handsome killer returned to the kitchen and dusted off his hands as if he'd done something to get them dirty. "All done. Let's clear out. We can head to your place or mine, Sweeney. Bring your stuff so you can cut my hair," Mateo suggested.

My eyes fixed on him, and there was nothing else in the room aside from the two of us. There was no dead man on the white marble floor, only a beautiful man looking at me with a lustful expression I didn't think I'd witnessed in my life. We both heard a throat clearing next to where we were standing in the doorway of the kitchen, and I turned to see Danielle with that sly grin of hers, one I was far too familiar with seeing over our lifetime.

"I've got a motel room not far. Call me tomorrow," she told me as she began to leave.

"My place it is. Cousin Dani, come back. You're going home with us where we can talk, right Sweeney?" Mateo insisted.

I laughed, still feeling the shock of what happened ricochet through my body. "Can you call me Shay?" I asked the handsome man.

"Oh, I can, but where's the fun in that, *Sweeney*?" he teased.

Of course, he was right, and I decided to just follow his lead. The man had me over a barrel with my ass hanging out, and I hoped to hell he fucked me so I could calm down. Where was the fun in anything else?

5

MATEO

I gave Shay a glass of wine to help soothe his nerves because his hands were shaking badly after my lack of self-control at his salon. Yes, I'd behaved in a rash manner, and in front of an audience, no less, but it was well known in my family that impulse control wasn't my strong suit.

Make no mistake, I already knew I was going to kill the man for beginning to think he had any claim on Shay Barr when I heard his comments through the salon door, but I had planned to do it quietly, not in the flippant fashion in which it had occurred. I hadn't meant to do it in front of the sexy-as-fuck barber, likely scaring the shit out of the guy and dashing any hopes I had of perhaps courting the man, as my mama used to call dating. Unfortunately, the news about Franzl doing harm to my barber and then laughing about it was more than I'd been prepared to hear. When he brought out the knife, he sealed his fate, and I'd acted accordingly.

"Let's forget about this for tonight," I told Shay as I looked at him standing by the table holding the scissors in his shaking hand. No way was I letting him at me with a razor, either. Of course, his cousin, Danielle, laughed at us as she sipped her cup of tea.

"Yeah, good idea," Shay stated as he dropped the scissors on the leather case he'd extracted them from earlier. I refilled his glass from one of the bottles of pinot noir I had in the kitchen pantry. Three cases of wine had been delivered that morning, leading me to believe I wasn't going back to Italy for quite a while. In one of the cases were bottles of the vineyards best Reserves, which I assumed were a bribe for me to stay in New York to help my cousin. I'd need to call and thank my uncle for his kindness and ask him to tell Papa to back off. I wasn't going anywhere anytime soon, but they damn well didn't need to know why.

My phone chimed on the island countertop, so I picked it up to see a message from Rafe.

Bad news, big brother. That was one of Frankie Man's triggers you 86d at the beauty parlor. Name was Herman Geist. What the hell happened? I'm headed to the river, and you're going to owe me an explanation. Come to Mangia soon. I'm in town. R

I put my phone in my shirt pocket and took off my tie, wondering what fresh hell I'd brought on the family. *And how the fuck does Rafael know that guy is a hitter? Does he have a deck of fucking cards with their goddamn pictures?*

"You okay?" Shay asked me, pulling me from my thoughts.

"Yes, I'm fine. Are you two hungry? I have food from my brother's restaurant I can reheat," I offered, remembering all the stuff Dexter brought over on Thursday night. I'd shoved a lot of it into the freezer because if I ate all of it, I'd be as fat as Gabriele.

"I, uh, I think Danielle and I better go to my place to talk. It's family business, and we don't need to bother you with this," Shay offered as he began wrapping up the leather roll where his scissors and razors were contained.

"What family business?" I asked as if I had a right to know.

I turned to Shay's cousin, who was probably twenty-five or six. She had bright red hair and cute freckles. I immediately liked her sassy attitude. "What can you tell me, Cousin Dani?"

"Danielle let's keep the dirty laundry in the family," Shay hissed at her. She stuck her tongue out at him and turned to me, a serious look shadowing her face.

"My daddy's a preacher back in Arkansas where Shane and I were both born and grew up. Our church... well, the church where my father rules with an iron fist... is more like a Klan meetin' than a house of worship on Sunday mornin'. It's just a hotbed of crazy on a good day, but last weekend, I went over to my parents' place to pick up Chase so we could make our annual trek to Little Rock for some shoppin' and lunch, just the two of us, but only my Grandma Betty was there watchin' the dogs. She told me my mother and father were on a weekend retreat with church friends, and Chase went campin'," Cousin Dani shared.

"That's a crock of horseshit," Shay mumbled under his breath.

Dani giggled. "Yep. I happen to know that was a lie for two reasons. One, my brother is petrified of the woods. Hates woodland creatures and would never be caught dead away from electricity because, like Shane, Chase has a way with hair and loves his blow dryer and stylin' tools. He wants to follow in Shane's footsteps and go to cosmetology school as soon as he turns eighteen and graduates high school. Our parents don't know this because they'd have a fit if they knew he had those plans, so he'll have to run away like Shane did when he turned eighteen.

"Two," she held up two fingers for emphasis, "my brother's friends consist of one guy from church who my parents know, Zack Schiller, and a girl in Chase's art class, Drea Weaver. Right now, Zack's in Austin, Texas, with his grandparents because his parents are having marital problems. My own mother told me that just last week when I spoke to her last. She didn't mention a word to me about a retreat this weekend."

Dani was a fast talker, and it took every bit of my attention to keep up, but I liked her instantly. She so reminded me of Shay.

"When I called Drea to ask about Chase, she told me she hasn't seen or talked to my brother since the pair had an argument over Chase's crush on one of the guys who works at the body shop in town with Shane's brother, Corbin. Seems Chase got the crazy idea in his head to ask out Derek Hines, and Drea told him if he did, he'd get his ass kicked for sure. Chase pitched a hissy fit, much like Shane was known to do back in the day, and she and Chase haven't spoken since.

"School just started, and I can't imagine my parents would allow him to be gone right now. They usually make him participate in community service projects along with a bunch of the kids from church, but letting him go camping with friends instead of cleaning up at the church and nearby cemetery? I can't imagine that's the truth," Dani explained to us.

I saw the blood drain from Shay's handsome face. "What?" I asked as he and Dani stared at each other without speaking. It was like when Rafe and I were together; we didn't need to speak to make our thoughts known between us.

It seemed as if all of our lives, Rafe and I had been able to communicate without words. We weren't twins, but we thought alike, and based on the way Shay and Dani appeared to be upset, the *'why'* of the situation couldn't be good.

"It's nothing. Chase probably ran away like I did, not able to take it until his birthday in November. I'll go to Hot Springs with you to look for him," Shay told Dani as he began gathering his things and returning them to his messenger bag. I knew a lie when I saw one.

"I… I can't leave right now Shay. Give me a couple of days to get someone to come to help Gabby and Dex with the kids, and I'll go with you," I offered, feeling a stone in the pit of my gut.

Dani looked at me and swallowed. "Thing is, Shay, nobody's seen Buck, Elvin, or Corbin around lately, either," she stated. Shay grabbed the counter and held onto it, surprising me.

I rushed to my feet and grabbed him by the shoulders, looking into his eyes that were wide and filled with terror. "Tell me what that means, Shay," I demanded.

He closed his eyes a moment before he opened them, recovering his composure a bit. "My brothers are assholes, is all. I need to get home to get my stuff together. Come on, Dani, let's go," he commanded his cousin.

"Wait to leave until tomorrow. I'll get my father to send someone over from Italy, and I'll go with you. Stay here with me, both of you, and I'll go with you tomorrow to look for him," I all but begged.

I saw Shay look at his cousin and nod. "Go ahead to the hotel. We'll pick you up there tomorrow and head out. I'll text you when I'm... we're on our way to get you," Shay told her, bringing a big grin to her face. I looked to see Shay's face was a little pink, which was so damn attractive on him I couldn't help but want to get him naked.

After his cousin left, giving me a nice hug before making her exit, I turned to the sexy barber and pulled him into my arms. I'd wanted so badly to kiss him the night of the baseball game, but when everyone was settling rides back to Brooklyn, it was mass confusion.

Shay ended up getting a ride with Gabe, Dex, and the kids. Smokey and Parker gave me a lift, and my poor dick and I commiserated about the fun we'd missed due to our cockblocking friends, who currently were nowhere in sight. I gently brushed my lips over Shay's, feeling the softness I'd been imagining.

I pulled away from Shay and looked into his beautiful, amber-colored eyes that were lined with teal-colored eyeliner. I could see the hint of freckles on his nose and cheeks that he'd tried to hide with makeup, and I longed to see him fresh-faced. "I think you're one of the most handsome men I've met in a long time. I can see the slightest specks from the freckles on your nose and cheeks. Would you mind washing away the makeup so I can see them better?" I asked, feeling him bristle in my arms.

Shay pulled away, looking defiant. "Oh, you don't want to be seen with the gay guy who likes to wear makeup and paints his nails, huh?" he snapped at me, which surprised me.

"*Wh-wh-what?*" I stuttered, shocked at the look on his face.

"You're just like all the other guys who like to fuck a guy but don't want anyone to know they're gay. You're one of those guys who won't be seen in public with someone like me unless people think he's a bro, right? Well, I'm nobody's dirty secret. If I'm going to be with a man, he's going to know it's a privilege for him to be seen with me because I don't go out with just anyone. A man has to be worth the trouble for me to spend my time, and I refuse to..." he went off.

Hey, speak up, stupid. You're not a shrinking violet, you know? "Oh, *really*? Like that guy I just killed because he hurt you and would have stabbed one of us if I didn't? What did he want to change about you? What's the deal with that shit anyway? I'll spank your ass if you want me to, but I refuse to hurt you like that, Shay. Maybe I have a less-than-conventional job, but I don't cause pain to people who don't deserve it. I... I'm not ashamed to be seen in public with you, and I don't fucking care if you dress up like *Lady Gaga* and strut around Central Park with a bunch of dancing, pink poodles wearing tiaras. I'd be honored to escort you anywhere you wanted to go in whatever you wanted to wear if you'd just go out with me," I defended.

I caught my breath and continued. "I happen to have a thing for those adorable freckles it seems you're trying to hide. I like the way your eyes pop with that teal liner, and the nail polish you wear reminds me how delicate your hands are compared to my big, calloused hands.

"I don't care how much fucking make-up you want to wear if you'll ever go out with me on a date. I just want to see your beautiful face in all its natural glory when it's just the two of us alone. Hell, Dexter put make-up on me today to hide two black eyes I got in a sparring match. *I don't give a shit about you wearing make-up!*" I was shouting by the end, surprised I got it all out without my dick crawling up into my body in protest of my yelling at him, considering how much I was already into him.

Shay seemed a little shocked at what I said, but I got it. I was pretty fucking shocked myself. I certainly didn't expect my impassioned rant to score Shay Barr climbing me like a coconut palm, but when my hands met his delectable ass and his lips settled on mine, I knew what people meant when they said the connection jolted them like a bolt of lightning. It was likely the closest to heaven I'd ever be allowed.

Having Shay wrapped around me was like nothing I'd ever felt before, and I had a feeling I might be kissing my independence goodbye if he would give me the time of day. I felt as if I'd been hit in the head with a brick. The man would be leading me around by the nose...or something impressive much further south, and it would be effortless for me to do it as long as he'd have me.

I carried him back to my bedroom and placed him on the mattress like he was made of the most delicate porcelain. I gently moved us up to the top of the bed and looked into his gorgeous, golden eyes with a soft brown ring around the pupil. "Will you tell me why you went to that club to be spanked? I'm going to guess that guy wasn't the first person you met there. What do you get out of it? Don't answer me now, but when I earn your trust, I'd like to understand what it means to you. I'd like to know what happened to you that causes you to believe it's what you deserve, and I'd like to know how it makes you feel. When you trust me, will you tell me?" I whispered to him.

Shay nodded as he wrapped his arms around my neck and pulled me down to him, kissing me so passionately, I believed I was about to shoot off in my Armani boxer-briefs. We made quick work of our clothes and were under the sheets in record time. Of course, then I remembered I hadn't unpacked my bathroom yet. "Shit! I have condoms, but they're in a box somewhere. I really need to unpack my shit," I whispered to him, loving the idea it was just the two of us in a cocoon of lust.

Shay's smile lit up the room. "I've got a couple in my messenger bag."

His face turned bright red, and I laughed. "Yeah, I get it. You're a sexy man in the city. Well, maybe I can..." I started before my common sense caught up with my stupid mouth. Shay wasn't a guy to be pinned down, and I wasn't the guy who asked for exclusivity on the first date. Hell, we were hooking up. It wasn't even a proper date, many of which I'd actually had in my life, so I knew the difference. I liked wine and romance, unlike Rafe who just liked a good fuck and duck, man or woman.

Shay left the room and came back a moment later, his hard cock bobbing in the breeze. His body was slender and tight, and not surprisingly, he was bare of any hair. I worried about my stamina because he had all my engines racing as my eyes followed his dick like a bouncing ball. "How do I want you?" he asked as he looked into my eyes with a cute grin lighting up his handsome face.

"By all means, Sweeney, how do *you* want me?" I asked.

He smirked. "Anyway I can have you, *Killer*," he teased in return, making me laugh. It was rare for me to find anyone as fucking twisted as me.

I rolled onto my back and motioned for him to climb aboard, eager to get inside that tight body. After he was settled on my groin, he leaned forward and teased my lips with his tongue where I noticed a flat, black thing on it. "What's that?" I asked as I nipped at what I believed to be a small, black star.

Shay laughed, lifting his tongue to show me it was a piercing. "I don't wear the barbell at the shop because it makes me hiss a little, and I think it's unprofessional, but I suffered to get the fucking piercing in the first place, so I'm keeping it. Ever had head from a guy with a piercing?"

"No sir, no I haven't. I've seen a lot of shit in my forty-two years, but I've never been with a guy with a piercing of any kind. I just haven't been that lucky," I replied, seeing Shay's smile.

"Well, maybe next time I'll put in the barbell when we plan a real date… unless this is all you want. If it is, that's fine," he told me, but the look in his eyes said it was anything but fine.

I sat up and pulled him closer to me so my cock was teasing his crease, the tip aware it was very close to that velvet channel. "No, this isn't all I want… well, right now, I think you can tell I want something in particular. If you're not sure I'm really interested, let me show you. You tell me when you want to stop," I suggested as I reached for the tube of lube Shay had tossed onto the bed along with the condom, which I handed to him.

I opened the lube behind his back and squeezed some of it onto the fingertips of my left hand. I slowly slid my fingers down his crease, applying a little pressure with my index finger until I found his hole, leaning forward to lick his neck as I swirled the lube over the sensitive nerves at his rim. I loved having my ass played with when I was getting blown, so I was hoping he was of the same mind. I should have asked, but the way he was thrusting against my finger, I must have been doing something right.

Shay gently placed his hands against my shoulders, pushing me onto the bed as he quickly scooted up my body, holding his hard cock down for me. I didn't hesitate to lick the head, catching a drop of precome and tasted the salty goodness as it exploded on my tongue. I moved my hands to his ass and pulled him closer so I could get as much of him into my mouth as possible while I continued to finger fuck him. I'd learned how to suck cock a long time ago, and I believed I brought some skills to the game.

I swirled my tongue around the mushroom head, nipping a little at the crown because I loved hearing the moans coming from deep inside him. I couldn't get enough, and when Shay tried to pull back, I wasn't ready to stop. "Please, Mateo, I want to come when you're buried inside me," he gasped as I slowly eased off, seeing his cock was dark pink from my work.

Shay looked at my cock behind him and then at the foil package in his fingers. "This will be a close fit," he stated as he ripped it open and rolled it down my hard shaft. I double checked it to make sure it wasn't going to break since I wasn't due for testing for a couple more weeks.

"I think it's fine. I tested negative last spring, but I need to find a doctor to get my next round. Maybe you can give me a referral?" I requested, trying to back myself off a little before I exploded all over both of us since the fun was just getting started.

"Me too. Mine were negative as well. I always play safe. You okay?" he asked as the tip of my cock breached him before he slid down my pole all the way. He was so tight around my cock; I lost my breath for a moment.

After a few seconds to regain my control, I smiled at the sexy man looking down at me with a perfectly manicured, arched eyebrow, waiting to see when I was ready. "Ride on, Sweeney," I encouragingly joked, enjoying the glide inside his slick tunnel as he smoothly rode me. The giggle he offered at my nickname for him did exciting things to my dick inside him.

The man was as beautiful inside as he was out, and he knew precisely how to drive me insane. I flipped us so I could control the thrusts after a while, and then he pulled away and got onto his belly. I slid back inside him with my legs on either side of his hips, and I pounded him into the mattress. I honestly growled when I released into the condom after I made sure he got there with me. He'd hosed down the sheets, but I didn't give a shit. I'd buy more damn sheets. I just wanted the man in my bed and in my life.

6

SHAY

I woke with a start, looking around the room to find I didn't recognize it at first, but then I remembered I was at Dex and Gabe's old apartment. I'd been to the place when the couple was remodeling it, having offered to help them paint the kitchen, but I'd never seen the bedroom. Now, I'd been fucked in the bedroom, and I could attest the place was nice and had a lot of potential, much like the man who had me nearly gagging with pleasure the previous night.

I slid out of bed and went to the bathroom, cleaning up enough to be able to take an Uber home without the driver wrinkling their nose. I needed to pack a bag, get Dani, and head to the airport. I wasn't looking forward to going back to *Dog Patch, USA*, but if what I believed was happening to my little cousin was actually *what* was happening? I was about to take down some hillbillies.

I dressed quietly, seeing it was four-thirty in the morning, an ungodly hour to be up. Thankfully, Dani was getting us airline reservations on my credit card, so I didn't have to worry about it. She'd left her car at the Little Rock Airport after she drove from her home in Memphis to pick up her brother for a weekend away so we would have a vehicle when we arrived in Arkansas.

The worst part would be the trip back to the family compound on the banks of Lake Ouachita, northwest of Hot Springs. It was back in the woods and not easily found unless one knew where it was located. I was sure my brothers would have parked near the front gate and taken four-wheelers back to the cabins, so Dani and I would have to go on foot in order not to be detected.

I wasn't looking forward to the reunion with my closed-minded family at all. Much like my little cousin, Chase, I wasn't a fan of the woods, nor the awful memories that would come with being there. The fact my family believed they could torture the queer out of me had been more than I could begin to contemplate, but I'd be damned if I was going to allow it to happen to my cousin.

I scribbled off a quick note to Mateo so I didn't just leave him hanging because I wasn't rude like that. I'd had a man duck out on me a time or two, and it wasn't fun to wake to the humiliation that maybe you weren't good enough for someone to spend the whole night with.

> Mateo —
> You sure know how to show a fella a good time! Thank you for last night, Killer. It was muy caliente! (I know more Spanish than Italian, but I can learn!)
> Knowing how attached you are to your family, I'm sure you can appreciate the fact I have to do this search/rescue for my cousin. Don't worry. I know how to use a gun, and I know where to get one. I grew up down in the 'holler,' and unfortunately, I know the enemy and what they're capable of doing. I've got your number and you have mine, so I'd like to stay in touch. No ghosting me. I'll text you later!
> Sweeney xoxo

I liked the nickname because it made me laugh. Mateo had been so much fun when we were at the game, it was hard not to throw myself at him, but I had managed to maintain my cool that night. Watching him interact with Searcy and Dylan made my heart palpitate. That man was cut out to be a father, for damn sure, regardless of what I believed to be his profession.

I'd studied Mateo and Gabe at the game, noticing the cousins had a lot of similarities… hair color, facial structure, height. They also had similar personalities, but I noticed Gabe's head kept swiveling around as we sat in the box Mateo had secured for us.

Mateo was a little more discreet in his observations of the area, but all of the men who worked for Gabe were vigilant, and I had no idea why because I didn't detect any danger. But then again, I wasn't a security professional like those men. Dex and Parker had confessed to me they weren't a group of hot photographers, which any fool could see if they looked at those guys.

Of course, the similarities I saw in Mateo and Gabriele had me wondering about other things. Dexter was a very happy man… a man who appeared to be very well satisfied in the bedroom. Naturally, I was curious how Mateo measured up, but I wasn't so much of a slut I was going on a fact-finding mission the night of the ballgame.

When I *did* find out a few nights later? OMG! I wasn't disappointed at all. I also had a newfound respect for Dexter if he could take Gabe's cock… supposing it was anything like Mateo's. I was much more of a whore than Dexter, I was certain, and I felt Mateo's rod deep inside my body as I rode it. If he could take it? Well, I'd definitely be looking at Dexter with a new eye.

My cell buzzed to alert me that my ride was waiting, so I let myself out of Mateo's apartment as quietly as possible to meet my Uber downstairs. After I arrived at my apartment, I packed up enough clothes for a few days, knowing that if I couldn't get Chase out of that camp within a few days, it might be too late for him to escape the shit I'd endured.

Hell, I was sure they'd only perfected their techniques over time. I should have gone back to do something before it ever got to the point where they were now targeting Chase, who was such a great kid when we were younger. I wasn't about to allow the same shit to happen to him that they'd fucking pulled on me. Chase didn't deserve to be fucked up the way I turned out.

Back when I was being held at that compound, I had no one who tried to get to me while I was enduring the same type of bullshit I envisioned my cousin was going through, but Chase had something I didn't have back then because my cousins were too young to stop it, and my brothers were too fucking stupid… or brainwashed… to see it was wrong.

Chase had Dani and me, and we'd do everything in our powers to rescue him from the hell those people were capable of inflicting, all of it couched in the name of saving us from burning for eternity. Their skewed interpretation of the teachings of their religion was more perverse than anything I've ever done.

I sent a text to Dani, letting her know I was on my way to pick her up after I found a cab. I walked out of the lobby to the street, surprised to see one of the handsome guys who worked for Gabe Torrente standing next to a large vehicle, seemingly waiting for me with a bright smile.

"Uh, you're Mathis, *right*? How've you been? I didn't know you lived in my neighborhood," I greeted, unsure of what the hell brought the man to my apartment building in the middle of the night. I'd met Mathis at various gatherings, and I believed he was a nice guy. He wasn't as tall as most of the men who worked for Gabe, but he was still intimidating as hell.

Mathis was leaning against a large SUV just like the one Dex was chauffeured around in all the time. "I'm here to go with you and your cousin to Arkansas, Shay. A buddy of mine from my days on the force is going with us. His name is Jonah Wright, and he lives near the hotel where your cousin is staying. I bet we'll be as welcome in your neck of the woods as a fart in church," Mathis teased before offering a chuckle, referencing the fact he was African-American. I noticed he didn't ask my permission to go along, but I wasn't offended, nor was I about to question it.

Everyone who worked for Gabe Torrente seemed to be strong-willed, overly protective alpha males. I'd been around that group of handsome men before I became interested in one of them, and thankfully, they'd seemed to accept me into their lives enough to let down their guard around me.

I knew for sure they had each other's backs, along with the backs of any who were involved with someone in their circle, which explained why Mathis Sinclair was driving me to pick up my cousin. Someone had asked him to look after us, and I was pretty sure it was Mateo Torrente.

The sexy assassin (which really sounded cooler in my head but horrible when I gave it a second thought) had anticipated I'd sneak out of his place without waking him so I could go home and get my things to go to Arkansas. Apparently, sometime after I fell asleep, he'd enlisted one of his coworkers to sleep outside my apartment building so as not to let me creep off without a minder because he was looking out for me.

I wasn't sure if I was okay with the idea of it or not, but hell, Mathis might come in handy if we were dealing with my crazy, fucked-up family. They were the shoot-first type, and it would be good to have someone with us who knew how to expertly shoot back.

"So, what time did Mateo call you?" I asked as I hopped into the passenger seat next to him.

Mathis was a really hot guy. He was the type of man gay boys dreamed about, what with his beautiful crescent-shaped eyes and the confidence that he could take care of things. He'd mentioned he was a cop in a past life, which I supposed fit the stereotype of people who protected others for a living, it was all new to me.

Mathis laughed. "I got a fucking call at two-thirty after he spoke to Gabe. His plans couldn't be changed, so Gabe suggested he talk to me. I just got back from visiting a friend in southern Virginia, so I wasn't scheduled for anything for the next few days, anyway. Can you fill me in on what's coming at us?" he asked. The guy was super polite, and I liked him a lot.

I gave Mathis the rundown, supplying a lot more details to him than I offered Mateo, really. We stopped to pick up Jonah Wright, who could have been a linebacker for the *Empires*, the New York NFL team. The man hopped in the back seat of the SUV and smiled without really saying much.

The next stop was to pick up my cousin at her hotel. I asked them if they minded waiting outside for a few minutes while I went into the hotel to help with her luggage. I took the elevator to the second floor where she'd told me her room was located, and when she opened the door, I pushed my way inside. We needed to talk for a minute.

"Listen to me because we don't have a lot of time. We have help going in to find Chase. One of the guys who works with Mateo is going with us, and he's bringing a friend. I know you're not like our families, but these guys are African American… well, Mathis… I don't know for sure what his ethnicity is. Goddamn, I sound like a paranoid hillbilly. I just didn't want you to…"

Dani smiled as she pulled her phone from the pocket of her jeans, flipping through a few pics until she turned it to face me. "This was my last boyfriend. I'm pregnant, not far along, but Dante didn't want children, so I broke it off when I found out about the baby. He's a jazz musician, and we went out for a couple of months. We weren't really serious, and he's getting ready to go on tour," she explained as she showed me the picture of a gorgeous African-American man with a big grin. He had his arms around her shoulders, and they both looked happy.

"It's my fault I got pregnant because I forgot to take my pills for a couple of days. I fucked up, not the guy, so I decided it was best to end it and let him live his life. I didn't tell him about the baby, but I'll be fine." I studied her expression to see she really did seem okay, so I nodded and squeezed her forearm.

Something inside me said the man deserved to know he had a child on the way, but the other part of me said he wasn't looking to have a family if he was going on tour with his group, and maybe she was doing him a favor by not telling him? What the fuck did I know?

"Don't look so constipated, Shane. I've got a good job in Memphis working as a dispatcher for a delivery service, and I'm keeping the baby. I'm not pushing Dante for a commitment, but I will let him know about the baby eventually, and I won't stop him if he wants to see his child. I'm not like the family, Shane. I'm normal," she teased as she grabbed her small suitcase from the bed and lowered it to the floor.

"Let me get that, Dani. Gosh, you're pregnant? You're too young!" I gasped, not able to fathom my younger cousin having a baby when I'd barely just adopted a cat. Thankfully, Maxi had agreed to check on Mixer for me while I was gone.

"I'm not sixteen like my mother, Shay. I'm twenty-six," she reminded me, which made me laugh.

"Let's go. I need you to stay as far away from this as possible, Danielle, especially since you're pregnant. We'll stash you somewhere when we get our shit together. Jonah Wright's a cop, or so Mathis told me. I think they used to work together, but anyway, the man looks like he can hold his own.

"Between Mathis and him, I think we'll be able to get Chase out without too many problems before the family figures out what happened. You're okay with all of this, right?" I asked again.

I didn't think my cousin would be as racist or bigoted as our family, but I had to ask. People we didn't know very well were putting their safety in jeopardy to help us find Chase. They were owed respect and appreciation, and I was going to make damn sure Dani was the person I believed her to be, which was very much unlike our family.

Thankfully, she'd grown into a wonderful woman as I'd always wished, and I was relieved and thrilled. She was definitely not *normal*, as far as our family defined itself. Dani was extraordinary, and when she got into the SUV in the back seat with Jonah Wright, I could see the man thought so as well.

Later that morning, we landed at Clinton National Airport in Little Rock, and Mathis went to the rental car counter even though Dani had her Toyota in long-term parking. "He's a little dictatorial, isn't he?" Dani pointed out with a big smile after Mathis told her to leave her car where it was parked, proclaiming he'd pay the parking fees.

Jonah stepped up behind us and placed his large hands on each of our shoulders. "I guess you don't know Mathis very well, but he was a hell of a cop. He got dealt a raw fu…damn hand because he's gay, and I was ready to leave the force right with him, but he talked me out of it.

"He went to work for the District Attorney's office as an investigator, and finally decided he'd rather help people than hurt them, so he started his own P.I. business. When he went to work for GEA-A, I was happy for him because he seemed to be doing what he was best at, helping those in need. It didn't hurt that most of his coworkers are gay as well. He finally has the acceptance and respect he's always deserved.

"Anyway, Mathis isn't one for a lot of explanations, but the reason he wants you to leave your car is that we need to be in an unfamiliar vehicle when we approach your family. If Shay's brothers know you, they likely know your car, and that puts you in danger.

"If they see it parked at a motel, we've lost the element of surprise, and we're screwed. An unknown vehicle won't register with them if they drive to town for supplies, and we have the advantage of not tipping our hand until we're ready," Jonah explained to both of us.

I listened to him, finally laughing when I thought of those idiots… my brothers. I honestly wondered where Corbin was in the mix because I'd always thought him to be smarter than Buck and Elvin, though that bar was set pretty low… *pun intended*.

"A shiny object will take my brothers by surprise, along with her father and mine, but I get where you're heading with this one. You guys are keeping track of these expenses, right?" I asked.

I wasn't a charity case. I paid my way, and I could pay for Dani and Chase as well. I was grateful for my success, and I would share it with those I loved, without question.

Jonah laughed. "I'm here for some fun, and I got to meet a pretty girl, too. You can fight with Mathis over who pays the tab. I'm just hoping to get to see some wild animals outside of a zoo. I grew up in Queens, and I've never been in the country before, so I'll be on the lookout for coyotes and bears and, uh, what are those big cat things?"

"Mountain lions or cougars?" I asked, seeing him nod. Well, I had a couple of wildcat brothers who liked to cook meth as a hobby back in high school without my sanctimonious father's knowledge. Would that be wild enough for him?

We took rooms at a small motel near Hot Springs Village. Dani and I were sharing, as were Jonah and Mathis. We stopped at a barbecue place off the highway and picked up food, sitting at a picnic table in a grassy area behind the motel. Mathis had a map spread out on the table, and Dani and I were attempting to show him the proximity of the cabin to the lake and the best way to get there.

"We're going to have to hike in. The people at the camp will hear ATVs, and if the terrain is still as dense as I remember, we can't get an SUV back there," I explained to our companions.

"Have either of you been to the cabin lately? Could they have made changes neither of you knows about?" Jonah asked as he looked at us. Dani touched my arm in support as I swallowed down the bitter, copper taste of remembered blood in my mouth.

I finally pulled myself together. "I haven't been there lately, but I doubt they've changed it much since I was last there. It was two weeks of pure torture in an attempt to drive the queer demon out of me. As I'm sure you can guess, it didn't work," I teased as I flipped my wrist, adding a giggle to alleviate the tension that seemed to be growing as we sat at the table. I lost my appetite and pushed away my sandwich.

I looked up to see Jonah and Mathis had both stopped eating and were staring at me. Dani had tears on her cheeks, so I took my normal place in the dance. "Come on, guys, I'm fine. I survived," I stated as I wiped my fingers of the sauce from my pulled pork sandwich.

Jonah and Dani stood to clear the uneaten food from the table, leaving Mathis and me alone. "Talk to me, Shay. Tell me what to expect when we get to that cabin because my mission is to extract the Asset, your cousin, without killing members of your family. Tell me what Jonah and I might find when we arrive at the site. It's better if we're not surprised. Surprises bring chaos, and then mistakes happen. We want no mistakes."

I nodded, wishing to fuck I had a shot or seven of vodka. It would make it a lot easier to tell a nice guy like Mathis what took place if I was a bit intoxicated. Only four people knew the truth about what happened to me at that campsite. The rest of the people in my family knew what was likely going to happen, but those four sadists? They took fucking delight in torturing me, which always made me wonder who was the bigger abomination to God… *if there was one?* Me, the queer, or the men who tried to beat and electrocute it out of me.

An hour later, Mathis Sinclair was staring at me as if I had three heads. I hated that I'd told him the whole, ugly story, but I'd gotten through it without crying for the first time in a long time. Well, I didn't tell many people the ugliness of those events, but I used to stand in front of a mirror and tell the story as a way of training my mind to let it go. Unfortunately, I always cried when I used to recite it. When I finally got through without breaking down, I was kind of proud of myself. It was a breakthrough. Unfortunately, poor Mathis didn't seem to see things the same way.

"No disrespect, but that's the most fucked up thing I believe I've ever heard, Shay. What did you do when you got to Little Rock? You had to be terrified they'd come looking for you, right?" he asked, his voice very measured, though I could sense he was upset. I honestly appreciated his compassion.

I wasn't going to lie to him because he was risking his neck for a member of my family, and I felt as if I owed him the truth. "I, uh, I tricked for about a month, which I'm not proud of, to make some cash, and then I made the decision I was going to do something more with my life. I got a job working at a nail salon as a receptionist and emptied the trash at the end of the day. Mrs. Tsoi let me sleep in a back room of the shop to keep me off the streets." I remembered that little back room where I slept on a bedroll. The walls were beige and it was all scuffed up from where supplies had carelessly been stored on the shelves, the boxes leaving behind marks. I had itched to paint it, but I worried that if I did, I'd make it my home, and I didn't want that for my future.

"She also helped me find another part-time job at a beauty salon not far from her place. I worked as a shampoo boy and cleaned the place after it closed, and I scoped out beauty schools. Mrs. Tsoi and Miss Laverne were kind enough to help me find one and kept me employed so I could pay for school and a place to live. When I finally finished beauty school, Miss Lavern gave me a job at her salon where I was able to learn a lot more from her and the other stylists than I'd learned in cosmetology school," I explained. I missed those two women with my whole heart. I'd never called to talk to them because I was afraid my family would find them and do something dire to get information about me. The less they knew—the safer it was for them.

"I owe those two women a lot, but they refused to allow me to do anything for them. Miss Laverne and Mrs. Tsoi both encouraged me to go to New York for a hair and nail show at their expense because they were friends, and Miss Laverne swore I had talent when it came to hair. That trip? It changed my life. I came back to Little Rock for my clothes and to thank them, and I got a bus back to the big city. *And, that's the end of the free show. Good night, folks,*" I joked as I looked at Mathis to see a smile on his face.

"Well, that's quite a tale. I understand a stubborn, Korean woman getting her way because that's my mother. She's a hardass, but she can figure out when people are in need, and she does anything she can to help them. My father's a pastor at Our Shepherd's House church in Jamaica, Queens. They are an odd couple to be sure, but they make it work, and I'm grateful for them every day," Mathis informed. He hadn't struck me as a preacher's son, but I'd bet nobody thought I was one either!

"I'm also beyond thankful that my parents know I'm gay, and that they're not trying to pray it away or anything. All my dad ever says is he hopes I can find the right man to appreciate me. Not everyone who believes in a higher power is like your family, Shay…and, I'm done preaching for the night."

We shared a laugh before Mathis' face turned serious. "Look, man,

I'm sure you haven't told Mateo half of this shit, so my lips are sealed, but I want things to be crystal clear before we ever head to that camp. If I see anyone doing anything hurtful to your cousin? I will take a *Torrente* stance on that shit, and I know you're aware of what that means. I won't hesitate to handle it so it might be better if Jonah and I go in alone," Mathis suggested.

I wasn't completely sure I knew what a *Torrente stance* meant, but based on Monday night's events in my salon, I had a good idea. "Does it happen a lot?" I asked.

Mathis smiled and winked. "I'm not sure what you mean." I couldn't hold the laugh. I could just picture Mateo saying something of the sort.

"Well, handsome, you're not going to find it without me, but I agree we should leave Dani here. I don't want anyone in our family knowing she's involved or even in town because she's pregnant, and she's not going to marry the father. Hell, they don't even have a relationship, and that will piss off her parents to no end. Hillbilly justice isn't pretty," I offered, trying not to elaborate any further so as not to insult the two men who were kind enough to accompany us into hell.

Mathis pointed toward the path where Dani and Jonah were returning to the motel, hand-in-hand. "I'm going to guess *that* won't make her family happy?" he joked before he laughed.

I swallowed the lump at seeing my cousin's big smile. I turned to Mathis and chuckled. "No, it won't, but all she needs is the people who really love her to support her. She's a remarkable person," I offered.

Mathis smiled. "He is, too. Maybe it's destiny?"

I nodded in support. "I certainly hope so."

I walked into the room I was sharing with Dani to hear my phone buzzing, so I rushed over to the cheap night table and unlocked it, seeing a bunch of texts from Mateo. I decided to cut to the chase and call him instead of responding to all of them.

It rang once before I heard his voice in my ear, worry clear in his tone. "Are you okay? You fucking left without waking me, Sweeney."

I chuckled. "You just couldn't help yourself, could you?"

"Help myself with what?" Mateo asked, attempting to sound like a pouting little boy. I wasn't fooled for a minute. He was looking out for me whether I liked it or not.

"You sent Mathis Sinclair to hold my hand through this bullshit," I responded, trying not to sound ungrateful.

"Hold your hand? He damn well better not be holding your hand, Shay," Mateo responded, his harsh tone making me smile—plus the fact he used my given name instead of the nickname he'd given me.

"No worries, *Killer*. He's not interested in me at all. I'm sorry I ducked out on you without waking you to say goodbye, but then again, you knew I would, didn't you?" I teased, hearing his sexy laugh.

"I'm so sorry I couldn't come with you, but I sent a man I trusted, Shay. Please, don't ditch Mathis. Let him and his friend help you, okay? I care too much about you to be objective like Mathis will be in this instance. I'd massacre anyone who tried to hurt you and considering it's your family, that's not the best idea. Mathis will be judicious and look out for you and Dani if you let him. Please let him?" Mateo implored, his worry coming through loud and clear.

"I will, I swear. My brothers are crazy, Mateo, and I don't want them shooting your friends. I want this to be handled as safely as possible," I explained.

There was silence for a minute, and it had me worried. "Don't approach the place until tomorrow night. Can you get there in the dark? Can you get to the place where they're holding your cousin in the dark?" he asked me.

"Yeah, but Dani didn't bring her gun, and as far as I know, Mathis and his friend aren't armed. We can't go into that camp without protection," I told him.

"You won't. I'll talk to Mathis. How are you, *tesoro*? I wish you wouldn't have left without a kiss goodbye," he told me, which was very sweet.

"I gave you a kiss. You were happily sleeping and didn't feel it, but I didn't leave without giving you a kiss, Mateo. I'll be back in a few days, and I'd like to give you that haircut and shave I promised. That dead man isn't still in the salon, is he?" I whispered, remembering I needed to send a text to Sonya that I'd be out of town for a few days.

Mateo laughed, his deep voice lighting me on fire. "I don't know what you're talking about, but you be safe, Sweeney. I'll talk to you tomorrow, okay? I miss you." The line went dead, but it sounded like he was happy to talk to me because I knew I was happy to talk to him. Unfortunately, I wondered if he'd still feel that way when I told him the stuff I'd only told Mathis earlier. I prayed it wouldn't make a difference because I wasn't ready for us to end.

7

MATEO

After I got off the phone with Shay, I called Gabe. "It's date night. What can I do for you that will be very quick so I can get back to what I was doing before you called?" my cousin snapped, not very friendly at all.

"I appreciate you sending Sinclair for this, but they have no firepower with them to go into a bad situation. They flew commercial," I reminded him. Gabe told me he'd send someone to watch out for Shay and his cousin because he didn't want me to leave. I got it. Family before bullshit, but I was on the verge of wanting Shay Barr to be part of my family.

The other issue that warranted Gabe sending someone else to help Shay was a simple fact that in our business… I would lose all objectivity when it came to Shay's situation because I was falling for the guy, and that was when a smart operative sent in a neutral party to take over the protection detail. I'd trusted it to Gabriele, but I felt like he'd failed me, which pissed me off.

"Firepower? Why do they need firepower?" Gabe asked, the fucking asshole.

I felt my temper flare, but I wasn't about to explain it to him over the phone. "I'm coming over," I warned before I hung up. I pulled on shoes and a jacket to walk to their house which was in the neighborhood where I lived, trying to take calming breaths the whole way to keep from beating my cousin to a bloody pulp.

I walked up to the porch and banged on the door until Gabe opened it, not happy to see me at all. "I told you it was date night. Searcy had a tummy ache, so we stayed in. What about that implied an open invitation to come to my house and bother me?"

I pulled him out the front door by his arm so his family wasn't disturbed. "I know my fucking job, Gabriele. I know why Papa sent me here, and I'm doing what's fucking necessary, but that doesn't mean my fucking world begins and ends with you, okay?

"Have you ever heard of that fucking conversion therapy where the religious among us decide they can convert gay men or lesbian women to straight because they believe it's a goddamn *choice*? You ever heard of that shit, Mr. *Carrington*?" I snapped at my cousin.

Yes, Gabriele had a family, and they might be in danger through no fault of their own, but there were other people in the world with their own problems. Gabe was short-sighted when it came to shit that involved him and his.

I had my own situation to worry about at the moment, and Gabe didn't seem to give a shit about anything that didn't revolve around his world. It took everything inside me to fight off the urge to deck the bastard, but he was family, so I didn't.

I heard steps approaching the hallway and saw Dexter's standing at the door staring at the two of us. When he saw me, he flapped his hand at Gabe and moved in front of him. "Mateo, what's wrong? Come inside," he invited.

I heard Gabe sigh heavily before he led Dex inside and left the door open, so I walked into the house and closed the front door, hearing soft music playing in the background. I hated to bust up their date night, but the man I was coming to care about very much was in danger. While I wouldn't leave my family unprotected, I needed something from Gabe. I'd get it or take out my frustration on him and smile when he had black eyes, just as he'd done to me after Duke

Chambers broke my nose. He always enjoyed seeing one of his cousins get their asses kicked the *stronzo*.

"What's going on? Do you want a glass of wine?" Dex asked as he herded us into the living room where the two of them had been watching a movie.

"No, thanks. I'm not going to be here very long." I turned to my cousin and looked at him with certainty. "I need someone in Arkansas. I'll find the secondary, but there's no intel regarding where the fuck he went, so tracking a cold trail is a waste of time. Hell, if we get a hit on the primary, I'll go fucking find him and deal with the whole goddamn mess at once, but I want someone in Arkansas with ordnances," I ordered. I glanced at Dex to see he looked concerned, and since I had no idea how much he knew about our operation, I wasn't specific when I was referring to Salvatore Sally Man as the secondary and his degenerate father, Francesco Frankie Man as the primary. Gabriele knew exactly what the fuck I was talking about.

"Shay's cousin is gay, and if I'm reading that shit right, his family is having an intervention to try to rid the kid of the gay *diavolo*. Shay called me and said they needed help. It's not going to be a simple extraction, Gabriele. Those mother fuckers torture people. I need more." I stated it plainly, and I could see Dexter turn to look at his husband, giving him a perturbed nod.

Gabe looked at me, and I saw the surprise in his eyes before it morphed into regret. "I'm sorry, Mateo. I thought it was just a stupid drug thing, and I was sure Mathis could slip in and handle it while his friend stood watch. I had no idea it was anything this serious."

"Someone will be there tomorrow with enough firepower to blow that fucking place sky high, I swear. I apologize for not really listening when you called me. Please, find the secondary and let's get this shit done," Gabby requested.

I nodded and turned to leave. I stopped at the door and looked back at my cousin. "I'll keep your kids safe, but you look out for Shay Barr. Call to see if Tommy's in the country so he can help Chambers with the kids in my absence and threaten the marine that I'll castrate him if he doesn't play nice in front of Dyl and Searcy. I might be gone for a while if we get a hit, but I'm not coming home without results.

"Tell Shay Barr to wait for me, will you? I'm beginning to believe we have a future." I didn't wait for an answer. I left and headed back to my place. I needed to make some plans because I finally had skin in the game. Who'd have thought I'd ever give a shit about anyone enough to make a bargain? *Not me.*

I sat at the kitchen island scrolling through my phone to see a text I'd forgotten all about because I had a sexy little barber dancing through my mind, all the time. It had come the night of the unfortunate incident at Shay's salon, and after we got naked, I forgot about everything else that happened.

Bad news, big brother. That was one of Frankie Man's triggers you 86d at the beauty parlor. Name was Herman Geist. What the hell happened? I'm headed to the river, and you're going to owe me an explanation. Come to Mangia soon. I'm in town. R

I called Rafe, but it went to voicemail. Since I had no idea where he was or what he was doing, I left him a message to call me. I walked back to my bedroom, which I'd finally unpacked that afternoon because I was waiting to hear from Casper about Sally Man's whereabouts and recent activities. It seemed to me with all of the fucking advances in technology, it would be easy to trace a mother fucker's electronic footprint, but clearly, I'd seen too many episodes of one CSI. Finally, my phone began singing.

"Torrente Wines, Mateo speaking," I responded, not recognizing the number.

"Hey, Mateo, it's me, Casper. I'm sorry it took me so long, but Sally Man has two cell phones registered in his name, and they've both crisscrossed the country twice in the last month. It's taken me some time to sort out which one is actually his, and which one's registered to him but being used by someone…"

"Casper, cut to the chase, my friend. Where is the fucker?" I asked.

"One of his phones last pinged a tower near the Golden Gate Bridge before it went dark last weekend. The other one pinged a tower here in New York last Thursday night, Mateo. The phone in Frisco is a dead end, and the phone here hasn't had a hit since Thursday, so I fear he's changed to burners, which I can't trace. I've tagged all of his credit cards, which he's not using, nor is he using his name to travel, register in hotels, or rent cars anywhere in the world," Casper shared. Fuck! That wasn't good news.

"I've left alerts on everything I can find registered to him so if he touches any of his holdings, I'll know, but it seems as if he's trying to go off the grid. I last had him a month ago in Vegas, but after that, I lost him until I got his signal in San Francisco last weekend. I'm monitoring all of his accounts and last known acquaintances, including his father." *Now fucking what?*

"Frankie Man has a suite reserved at the St. Regis downtown if you want to check it out. I'm not giving up, okay? I'm trying to hack the cameras at Frankie's home here in town, but they've beefed up their security recently, and I'm having no luck. I'll keep on it, Mateo, and call you if anything breaks. Can I do anything else to help you?" Casper asked. I admired the guy's efforts for sure.

"No, but thanks, Casper. How's your man?" I asked, feeling guilty for forgetting the party planner's first name.

"Maxi's busy, but we're fine. Let me know if you want to go to dinner some time, Mateo. I'm sure he'd like to officially meet you. I'll be in touch when I get more," Casper told me before the line went dead.

I actually appreciated the invitation because I knew Shay was good friends with Maxim Partee, and maybe we could hang out as couples? *Yeah, and why don't you head down to the malt shop and meet Betty and Veronica, Jughead.* I was becoming a sentimental sap, and I was close to not caring about it at all. If it would make Shay happy, I'd be on board.

I made myself a sandwich and turned on the tube for an hour before I gave up waiting to hear from my brother. I went to bed, setting the alarm to get up an hour early so I could go for a run. I wanted to have another discussion with Duke Chambers because I knew he was a concern of Dexter's, and I wanted to know what the fuck his problem was with me and mine before I went on the prowl for Sally Man. Contemplating popping a cap in that asshole's head was becoming my happy place. Chambers was turning into a huge pain.

As I thought about things, I had to be honest that Duke was a concern of mine, as well. I wanted to know what the fuck the guy had against us, and why in the world my father had told Gabe not to fire him. I should have called Papa and asked him directly, but getting a straight answer from Giuseppe Torrente was like finding a goddamn needle in a haystack. It rarely ever happened.

I walked into the Victorian at six that morning and headed directly downstairs to find Duke and Smokey going at it in the gym Gabe had built in the basement. I wondered what Parker Howzer would think when his boyfriend came home with bruises because Duke was showing no fucking mercy on the man as he had Smokey on the mat before Smokey kicked him off. What I didn't expect to see was London St. Michael standing to the side appearing to be ready to go next.

"Gents," I greeted, seeing Smokey turn to me just as Duke threw a punch that took the big cowboy down to the floor. I rushed over to Smokey to see the man was out... cold.

I grabbed Duke Chambers by the throat and held him up as I closed my hand, cutting off his windpipe which was becoming my signature move if that fucker Franzl was any indication. "What the fuck is your goddamn problem? What did he ever do to you?" I snapped at Duke. His foot came up and connected with my ribs, taking me down to the mat next to Smokey.

I heard a rustling on the mat and saw St. Michael had Duke on the mat with his arm behind his back. "Dude, seriously? What the fuck is your damage?" London hissed at Chambers. I could second that shit.

Chambers wiggled away, wiping the blood from his mouth before he spoke. "I was hired to get you jackoffs into shape, not coddle your candy asses. I'm just doing my fucking job," he snapped as he hopped up and left the area.

Those of us in the basement looked at each other, not sure what the fuck was up Duke's ass. When Smokey came around and was helped up by my cousin, Tommy, who had just appeared out of nowhere, the cowboy laughed as he rubbed the bruise forming on his cheek.

"Fuck, maybe we are going soft? I know I could use more time in the gym, but maybe not such that I look like I get mugged in an alley every day."

I chuckled. "Have you forgotten how we all looked when we were working out in Italy? For some fucking reason, this is what we do, torturing each other at the whim of crazy men. Anyway, I'm headed out to Queens to see who's staying in Frankie Man's place if he's staying at the St. Regis in Manhattan. Any takers?" I asked.

St. Michael walked over and smiled. "I would, man, but I'm headed to North Carolina to relieve your brother because he's been summoned back to Italy. He was helping Nemo with the Senator. The election is coming up in just a couple of weeks, and then I should be free if you still need me," he offered.

I didn't know what any of that meant, but I nodded in appreciation. Smokey waved me off as he left the area because he was headed off for a romantic weekend with his man, as I'd heard through the grapevine.

Of course, Chambers wasn't going to be any help, the cocky fucker. It was going to be me, but then again, it was the way life progressed. It was, however, the first time I worried about *my* safety. I suddenly had a reason to stay alive, which was a new thing in my world. I damn well didn't want to miss my shot at happiness.

I was sitting at a café across from the school which wasn't very far from the Victorian. I knew Gabby had sent Sherlock to Arkansas on the jet with an assload of armaments, and I was relieved and grateful, not that I'd praise my cousin for his behavior. He was short-sighted, or so I thought, and maybe he needed a wake-up call just as much as me?

I was sipping a latte as I watched the comings and goings at the school when a *very familiar* face walked into the cafe and went straight through the place and up a flight of stairs, luckily not seeing me as I sat at a table pretending to read a book.

I'd made the drive out to Queens to check out Frankie Man's house, but there didn't appear to be anyone at the compound at all, which was troubling. Usually, a few guards were left to look after the property, but it was desolate, which was unusual.

I'd tried to find out information about the occupant of the suite at the St. Regis, but, of everyone in Manhattan who worked at a pricey hotel, that place had the only front desk staff who couldn't be bribed. Casper had hacked into their system and found Frankie Man's credit card on file, but the room was being used by someone else… a man named Marco Rialto.

The name seemed strangely familiar, but who the fuck knew why? The guy could be a goddamn rock star I'd read about in the news feed on my phone for all I knew. Since I kept hitting dead ends, I went back to my kid detail to help out the stupid fucker I was coming to hate, Duke Chambers.

Chambers was sitting in the SUV down the block to watch the school from the other direction, but I had a sneaking suspicion there was something afoot I'd never considered. I walked up to the counter and smiled at the pretty woman. "Men's room?" I asked, using my thick Italian accent.

The woman pointed down the hallway, so I went in that direction, seeing the restrooms behind the staircase. I looked around to see the area was isolated, so I quietly headed upstairs, finding an office I hadn't thought about being up there. It had half-walls of windows, but I couldn't see who was in there aside from the person I'd spotted entering the building earlier. Whatever was going on in that office couldn't be good news.

"Look, asshole, I'm tired of this. I want to see Marco right now. I've been waiting for him at the St. Regis for five hours. He told me he was coming here for a business meeting, but that was this morning. Where the fuck is he? I demand to speak with him right now!" my cousin, Lucia, snapped at whoever was in that office with her. At least I knew who was staying at the hotel now, my cousin and Marco Rialto.

I wished I could record it without being seen because my cousin could turn totally psycho on a dime—just like her sisters, and dare I say, my Zia Graciela. I didn't know who was in that office with her, but I was pretty sure the person was in for a rough fucking ride if he pissed off Lucia Mazzola.

I crawled to the corner of the landing outside the office and slowly rose on my knees, seeing the outline of a man sitting behind the desk while my cousin blocked his face from my sight. "Lucia, he had to catch a flight somewhere last minute," the man told her.

"Rico, my family goes away on business all the goddamn time, but they're still *available* ON. THE. FUCKING. PHONE!" Lucia shouted as she waved her cell phone in the air. I wasn't sure who the poor bastard was behind the desk, but I felt fucking sorry for him because she was only going to get more torqued up.

Lucia turned to pace, so I ducked and held up the top of my phone where the camera lens was located and snapped a photo before hurrying downstairs and out of the café, seeing it was nearly the end of the school day.

I walked down the block and noticed Duke still in the Escalade just as the last bell rang. I ducked behind a tree to see how long it took the fucker to get out of the vehicle to go greet the kids outside the building. It was then I had an idea to test a theory that suddenly occurred to me.

I hurried around the back of the school and picked the lock on the back door, making a note to tell Dexter he needed to talk to the school about securing the back of the building. I proceeded down the hallway to the office and walked inside, seeing the school secretary, Mrs. Jarrett, who smiled at me.

Dex had told me the names of all of the important people at the school when I first started watching out for Dyl and Searcy, so I was sure I was right. "Good afternoon. How may I help you?" the woman asked, obviously thinking I'd been let in through the front door of the building where there was an unarmed hall monitor.

If Searcy and Dylan were going to continue to attend school there, we needed one of our own to act as security. "I'm Mateo Torrente, Dylan and Searcy's uncle, Mrs. Jarrett. I'm here to pick them up for dentist appointments. I'm afraid Dexter's teaching a class at his studio, but you can call Gabriele to get permission for me to take them. Do you need the number?" I asked the woman, offering a kind smile.

As I expected, the old woman caved immediately, reminding me the Torrente charm still worked on the opposite sex. "If you give me a minute, I'll summon them to the office," she told me as she pointed to the chairs against the wall. I nodded and sat down in an ugly, orange, plastic chair, pulling out my phone as I remembered the photo I'd snapped.

When I pulled up the picture, I was surprised. Sitting there in all his glory was Vinnie Pezzoli who was apparently going by the name of Rico according to what I'd overheard my cousin call him.

Vincenzo "Vinnie" Pezzoli…*Rico*…was Frankie Man's consiglieri. How the fuck had my cousin become hooked up with the goddamn Mangello family without any of us knowing it? *Who in the name of hell is Marco Rialto?*

Unfortunately, before I had time to consider any answers, the office door swung open and in walked Duke Chambers with a Glock-19 semi-auto aimed right at my head. That fucking mag held fifteen with one in the chamber. When he saw it was me sitting in the office, he didn't put it away. The mother fucker bashed the side of my head with it, sending my ass to the floor before the lights went out.

8

SHAY

A hard, two-beat knock on the door of the motel room I was sharing with Danielle that Tuesday night startled me. Jonah and Mathis were in Jonah's room, waiting for word from someone regarding our backup's ETA. Dani and I took turns pacing, both of us nearly at the end of our ropes. We'd been told not to move forward with the rescue until reinforcements showed, so against my better judgment, we waited. Every minute was another opportunity for my cousin to suffer, and it was going to give me a fucking ulcer.

We'd spent the day on the verge of panic, all four of us. Dani and Jonah had gone to get food and other supplies earlier in the afternoon while Mathis and I had distractedly played cards. Hell, I didn't even know what the game was we were playing. I'd thought it was five-card stud until Mathis called, "Rummy," and put down all of his cards but one… the discard. I knew he'd cheated, but I'd been unable to figure out how. *Unbelievable.*

Mathis had demanded all of us turn off our phones for no reason I could determine so we had, being good little lemmings. When Dani and Jonah had returned, they'd brought a bag full of cheap, prepaid phones we were to carry with us so we could stay in contact with each other without anyone "tracing our whereabouts."

Dani and I had both laughed at Mathis' suggestion. "I'd be surprised if our entire family, collectively, could conjugate a verb, much less trace our cell phones to track us down," Dani had stated, which made me laugh that much harder because it was spot on.

Mathis smiled for a minute before he'd said, "Maybe not, but wouldn't it be fucking awful if one of them had a moment of genius and googled it to find your signals pinging off these towers and moved the kid before we got a chance to get to him? We take no chances." After that, we'd put our phones in a drawer and had watched television to waste time, just trying to keep our cool until we had some word for what to do next.

I knew it wasn't good for Dani's tiny passenger that things were so on edge, but getting her to go back to Memphis had turned into a fool's endeavor. Chase was her little brother, and she was freaked out, both of us wondering what our family could be doing to the kid while we were in a holding pattern.

I'd suggested to Mathis maybe we should try to get a bead on how many of my brothers, cousins, uncles, and their twisted friends were at the cabin. Maybe we could get an idea of how many people were there so we were better prepared? Mathis had said we couldn't chance going in without adequate supplies and backup, so we'd sat, and I'd tried to keep from being a paranoid harpy. I was fucking scared, but Mathis had seemed to have a calming effect on me, for which I'd been grateful.

I hopped up from my bed and opened the door to see Mathis, Jonah, and a handsome man I'd seen over more than once at various Torrente parties. "Hi," I greeted, not sure of his name. The men who worked for Gabe weren't ones to introduce themselves.

"Sorry we're late, but Sherlock got lost, the dumbass," Mathis stated with a smirk.

"Hey, jackass, you weren't very fucking precise in your directions, you barmy git," the man snapped back in a distinctly British accent, catching Dani's full attention. We loved British accents, both of us having fallen in love with James Bond movies when we were young because of Sean Connery.

The handsome Brit turned to my cousin and smiled. He took her right hand and lifted it to his lips, offering a soft kiss. "Everyone calls me James Bond at the office. What might your name be, you gorgeous creature?" he asked her, offering her a sexy wink. Hell, it made *my* heart flutter.

Mathis sniggered, but Jonah Wright moved forward and pushed the man away by his forehead as he took Dani's hand and wiped the kiss away with his t-shirt. "That's enough of that shit or dude, you'll find my fist up your ass, and not in the way most of you guys like," Jonah stated.

"Joe, Sherlock isn't gay," Mathis stated.

Jonah laughed. "Coulda fooled me," he stated as he led Dani further into our room and sat her down on the bed, speaking quietly to her. I saw him hand her a small gun and show her how to use it. The fact she pretended like she didn't know anything about guns made me want to laugh. Bitch was a better shot than me.

"Sherlock, this is Shay, a very good friend of *Mateo's*," Mathis introduced with an emphasis on the name of the man I was coming to care for more than was healthy, I was sure.

I saw the Brit give me the up and down for a second before he grinned. "Ah, I get it, now. I've heard rumors he's quite smitten with you, *kitten*. He was giving Dexter a pop quiz on you the other day. Well, good on you. I know Mateo pretty well, and he's a decent fellow. If you need advice," he began before Mathis cleared his throat.

"We can play Mystery Date later. Now, Dani, please stay here and wait for us to contact you… you have your burner?" Mathis asked. My cousin held the small phone in the air and nodded. "Give us an hour, and if we're not back or we don't touch base, call the police and report you heard shots fired. Give them the address to the campsite, trash the phone by dunking it in water, and get the hell out of here," Mathis instructed as he handed her the keys to the vehicle he'd rented at the Little Rock airport.

"Hopefully, that'll bring somebody out to the compound to check on shit. Hang onto that gun, and if someone tries to get in here without being invited, use it," Mathis explained. My cousin nodded again and hurried over to give me a hug.

"Be careful, Shane. You know they'll hurt you, especially if they see you with these guys. Remember, they have a lot of guns out at the camp," Dani whispered before she stepped away, referring to the fact they hunted out there during the seasons.

Jonah turned to her with a very serious face. "We'll return Shay and your brother unharmed, I promise. You think about what I told you earlier." Without explaining it to the rest of the class, he kissed my cousin on the forehead, and we were out the door.

Once we were in the SUV the Brit brought with him, we headed to the entrance of my family's property. Sherlock smirked at me before he addressed Jonah in the front seat. "Why didn't you piss on her leg to mark your territory, mate?"

Jonah chuckled. "I didn't have to, *mate*. She already agreed to see me again after this fucking mess is cleared up. Did she give *you* the time of day?"

Sherlock grumbled a little and sat back, which made me laugh. "So, you're Mateo's latest conquest? Is he really hung as all the girls and boys say back in Italy?" That stopped my laughter.

I turned to look at the Brit, seeing his face turned up in a big smile. "*Gotcha!* Seriously, mate, I love Mateo, and as far as I know, he's not a slut. Doesn't have the time, really. He's a good man, so enjoy it while it lasts because he's not really the 'settling down' kind of bloke. Luckily, I'll get credit for bringing you back safe and sound. I'm going to London soon to see my new nephew, and Mateo has a right nice flat there I'd like to use. Put in a word, will ya?"

I was a bit stunned at what he'd said, wondering how someone could be so lacking in self-awareness to say the things he'd just said about Mateo not being the settling down 'kind of bloke.' It shouldn't affect me at all because I hadn't known the man long enough to make a determination if he would be the kind of guy I'd consider for a permanent partner, but based on the Brit's comments, it was a fool's mission to try to pin the man down.

That moment wasn't really the time to consider what I was to

Mateo, anyway. I needed to concentrate on my cousin, but I couldn't lie and say I wasn't worried about the future. Or the lack of a future.

At least Dani knew who to call if anything went wrong and she didn't hear from us within an hour, but I prayed it wasn't necessary. I wanted to be home in one piece to talk to Mateo. We were only just beginning… or were we? Was I just a fling? Why the fuck had I let my heart get involved if I was just Mr. *Right Now*?

We arrived at the metal gate to the property, and just as I predicted, my oldest brother, Brett, had parked his old Chevy truck in the woods. What I wasn't prepared to see were ten other vehicles parked next to his. A lot of trees had been cleared out since the last time I'd been to the lakeside complex, and if those vehicles were any indication of the number of people at the camp, we were most certainly outnumbered.

"I think we have a major problem," I whispered as I looked around, using the glow sticks Sherlock had brought with him to see they were all Arkansas tags, though I only recognized my brothers' trucks and my father's, which sadly, didn't surprise me.

I saw Jonah take in the area before he smiled, shirking off a backpack and pulling out some road flares. "I think we can narrow the odds," the cop stated as he explained to us how to proceed.

We quietly made our way to each truck, removing the batteries and placing them on a stack deeper into the woods where there were a lot of downed trees, which we quietly dragged into a circle to make a pit for the batteries.

I was grateful Sherlock knew how to unhook the batteries from the vehicles because I was clueless regarding anything that involved cars. Once we had them all in a stack, Mathis turned to me. "Is there anyone else adjacent to this land who could be affected if we light this bitch up?"

I thought for a minute, remembering the nearest neighbors were about three miles on the other side of the lake. "No, and they've had a fair amount of rain over the summer—or so I've read in the online newspaper from down here—so it's not going to become an inferno. We just need to make it large enough so they can see it from the cabins," I whispered, not sure why, but it seemed appropriate.

Mathis nodded. "Sherlock, you stay behind and light up that stack of batteries with the flares while we go in. Go back to the cars and wait for us. Have the SUV ready to go when we come running, 10-4?" Mathis directed.

Sherlock rolled his eyes. "Whatever *yes* means in American copper speak, I'm all over it. I'm giving you thirty minutes before I come in, jackass. Everyone has enough firepower?" he asked. We nodded before we took off through the woods.

Thankfully, the land hadn't changed much since the last time I was there, and the moon was visible, even though it was a bit overcast. It was bright enough so we could see fallen trees, but not bright enough to expose our movements to anyone who might be taking a piss in the woods. We'd all decked out in black clothes and goddamn stocking caps, mine making me sweat, totally fucking up my hair because it was hot as hell in Arkansas in August, but all of the discomforts would be worth it if we found Chase and got him out of there.

We hiked for ten minutes until I heard the water lapping at the shore of the lake which gave me my bearings regarding our location, so I stopped us just outside the camp. The place was lit up with lights powered by a generator I could hear behind the main building. There were a few more cabins than I remembered from my last visit, but it didn't surprise me. They'd always loved going to the camp, and seeing it again made my blood run cold. I couldn't move for a second as the memories swamped me.

"Uncle Brett, how we gonna do this?" *my brother Brett, who the family called Buck, asked the Right Reverend Brett Barr while they stripped off my pajama pants and tied me to a chair.*

"You boys bring that cattle prod from the bed of my pickup?" Uncle Brett asked. That scared the hell out of me. I was a fucking teenager, and they'd taken me from my bed while I was asleep. They'd put a burlap bag over my head and taped it around my neck so I couldn't see where we were going. My

wrists had been bound with duct tape in front of me, and all I could fucking do was cry. I had no idea what they were doing or why, and I couldn't catch my breath very easily, fear seizing my throat.

"Yeah, Uncle Brett. What's gonna happen?" Elvin, my other ignorant brother, asked eagerly as Corbin, another ignorant brother, laughed maniacally next to my right ear. They eventually removed the hood from my head, and if they thought I didn't know where I was, they were fucking inbred morons.

We'd been going to the cabin since I was about three, which was when I had my first memories. I also remembered that my dad, Uncle Brett, and Grandpa Joe used to go out to the lake house with members of my uncle's church, and Mom and I weren't allowed to go along. I was grateful I didn't know what they were doing.

"We're gonna show the little pervert some pictures of men's privates, men engaging in sodomy and other filth his kind likes. When he gets excited, you zap him with that cattle prod. It's called aversion therapy. I heard about it at a convention this spring out in Colorado. I have a lot of other remedies up my sleeve, and your daddy told me we're not takin' him home until he's cravin' pussy, so let's pray," my uncle stated.

"Shay… Shay…" I heard next to me, opening my eyes to see Mathis standing in front of me with his hands on my cheeks. Tears were leaking from my eyes, and my harsh breaths echoed through the air. I wanted to puke in the worst goddamn way but getting my cousin out of there was even more vital as I processed those horrible memories.

"Yeah, I'm fine. Sorry. Uh, let me go up to the big cabin and look in the windows on the back side. I'll stay away from the lights, and I'll be back once I see what we're facing with how many of them there are and how many kids they have. It's best if we can figure out where they have them, especially Chase, right? Stay here," I told them.

Mathis pressed a pistol into my hand. "You know how to use this, right? We hear a shot, and we come running. Don't get yourself killed —Mateo will take it out of my hide." I doubted it, but I simply nodded and began making my way toward the back of the cabin I remembered all too well. I wasn't about to let those haunting memories of my time at the compound keep me from finding Chase. He needed me, and I was going to come through for him like nobody had come through for me.

Moving quietly through the woods, I headed toward the back of the main cabin where I recalled the bedrooms were located. The rest of the area was lit by battery-powered lanterns because they hadn't extended the electrical lines to the newer cabins. I was hoping that might go in our favor because the entire woods behind the cabins was dark, and we could move about without being detected.

I saw the old outhouse had been replaced with a much larger one built from cinder blocks instead of the shitty cedar plank job we had to use as kids. It had a tin roof, and it also appeared there were a few shower stalls, which surprised me because when I was a kid, we bathed in the lake with a bar of cheap soap.

I went behind the outhouse and circled to the north side of the main cabin which was hidden from any light by the other buildings and the slant of the moonlight through the trees. I looked into the window of what used to be the room I shared with Corbin when we were kids. There were four beds in that room where there only used to be two, and I could see three boys tied to the beds, which wasn't anything I expected. Thankfully, I held the gasp as I tried to recognize them, seeing none of them was Chase.

I made my way down the side of the house and looked into the bedroom that had been Brett and Elvin's when we were kids, seeing four more beds in the room. There were three boys tied to the beds in that room as well.

I crept around the other side of the cabin and rushed behind the one next to it, which was new since the last time I'd been there. I saw my mother, Carol, and my Aunt Judy, sitting in the living room with two women I didn't recognize. There were two girls tied to two chairs, both of them crying. It was much worse than I imagined it could be.

I knew Dani would get upset when she learned her mother was a part of it, but they were all religious fanatics, as Dani and I knew far too well. We should have anticipated something so fucking crazy from them because we knew them better than anyone. I had no idea what to do, but I needed to know more, so I stooped down and crawled around the cabin to where there was a bonfire burning in a pit in the middle of the circle of buildings.

I found my cousin Chase and another boy tied to benches, both naked and on their bellies. I could see my fucking brother standing between them with a hickory switch in his hand as Uncle Brett knelt by their heads.

"Do you rebuke this demon inside you that has taken over your soul and convinced you that sodomy is part of our Lord's plan for your lives? Don't you see the Devil's hand leading you astray into the forbidden land of deviance? Don't you want to be right with God?" he asked the boys.

When neither of them responded beyond anything but tears, my brother hit them, first Chase, and then the other boy, with the switch, wearing a big grin. Hearing the *swish* before the screams made me want to vomit again, but I didn't have time. I took a quick count of the men sitting around the fire with Bibles in one hand and a beer in the other as they watched what was happening and did nothing. We needed to get involved as quickly as possible, so I rushed back into the woods, cutting back to where Mathis and Jonah were waiting.

"It's worse than I thought," I told them as I tried to catch my breath. I explained to the two with me what I saw, and then I waited for anyone to have any idea of how we could get those kids out of there. I had no clue what we'd do with them once we had them, but I couldn't let what was happening to them—or going to happen to them —continue. *Not again.*

Based on what I'd seen as I hid on the edge of the woods, my uncle had refined his technique from when he was trying to 'cure' me, and it meant those kids were in for a hell of a lot of pain for the next several days. Mathis and Jonah listened to what I quickly explained, both of them seemed to be stunned by my words. "I thought that shit was made up. I didn't realize it was real," Mathis hissed, shock evident on his face. It was definitely a wake-up call for the city boys.

Jonah shook his head. "Dude, my family is from Alabama. I've heard about these conversion camps over the years and know that shit ain't no fucking joke. We gotta help those kids," he pleaded with so much compassion in his voice that it surprised me.

Jonah turned to me and offered a tender smile. "I'm not as closed-minded as most people think, Shay. This shit right here is why I became a cop in the first place, but whatever happens in Arkansas can stay in Arkansas as far as I'm concerned. I'm on vacation, and I don't gotta remember what happened down here, so let's make this shit right," he explained as he squeezed my shoulder and brought out a Glock, checking to see the safety was off before he slid it behind his back.

Sherlock suddenly stepped up, scaring the shit out of us. "Sorry, mates, but I got worried. I followed Shay and checked out the scene as well. This has to be a quick job. Give me about five minutes to get back and light it up. When the explosions start, get in and get out as quickly as you can. They'll come running this way, but I'm ready for them," he stated as he pulled a gun from behind his back and held it in his hand. It was some sort of thing I'd never seen, not that I was well-versed in firearms. While I didn't condone gun violence, I condoned torture even less.

Pain was exactly what the adults were inflicting on those poor kids inside that encampment, and it had to end. I also planned to burn down that entire fucking thing at some point in time, but I'd need more participants for that party than I had with me at the moment. I could wait for the right time, but I planned to see it happen before I died.

We all solidified the plan and took the time to gather our nerves before we began making our way back to the camp, stopping just inside the shadows. I pointed Mathis and Jonah to where I'd seen kids in the rooms, and thankfully, the windows weren't locked. They slid them up without waking the boys in the two rooms, so I made my way to the main cabin where my mother, aunt, and two strange women were sitting with the two girls who were tied to the chairs. I didn't know them, but I saw my mother with a Bible in her hands as she read to the girls, and I could only imagine what they were in for if we didn't get them out of that place.

I couldn't let it happen again, even if I didn't know them, so I slipped in through the back door of the cabin, hearing my mother's voice for the first time in years. She was reciting Bible verses from Romans, chapter one, which my self-righteous family believed addressed homosexuality.

I could see those girls were inconsolable. They appeared to be only sixteen or so, and they were scared to death because of what they could hear happening outside the door, and I couldn't blame them. There were screams on the wind, which was something I remembered far too well in the deepest part of my mind.

I engaged the magazine of the gun I had, hearing the sound echoing off the wooden walls which alerted everyone to my presence in the room. "Don't anyone move," I whispered as I crept behind my mother and my aunt. The girls looked up at me, both continuing to cry as they had been. When I looked into their eyes, I could see total confusion, but it wasn't fear of me, which was good.

The other two women started to move until I placed my hand over my mother's chest, holding her in her chair as I pressed the gun against her neck. "You told me I was evil. You said I was the demon from your loins, and you said you'd rather I died than manifest into an angel for Satan. Do you seriously think what you're doing to those girls is the right thing? Do you think what they're doing to those boys out there... what they plan to do to all of those boys is the right thing?" I asked as I used the scarf around her hair to gag her.

I then held the gun to Aunt Judy's head and whispered, "Don't shout unless you want your brains to cover the walls of this new cabin." She held up her hands, dropping the Bible.

I hurried around her, taking out the old pocketknife from my childhood to cut the girls loose. "Go out the back door and run toward the road." They nodded, not asking any questions, just taking off as quickly as they could.

My face was covered, and I shouldn't have let on to my mother that it was me, but I couldn't help myself. When I heard the explosion of the batteries, I glanced out the window to see the men running toward the vehicles, shouting at each other as a few rifles were raised into the air. Thankfully, no shots were fired. I was guessing they were so shocked at what was happening, nobody stopped to take aim.

I rushed to the closet and grabbed clothes and shoes for the girls, though they'd at least been allowed to remain in their bras and panties, and I rushed out the cabin door and cut the boys loose, offering instructions. "Come with me. Just run," I told them as I led them around the cabins and into the woods in the north.

I saw more boys running toward us with Mathis and Jonah leading them, carrying clothes as well. I looked around for a moment, trying to memorize the place so that when I came back and burned it down, I could rest assured no other person, man, woman, boy, or girl would ever come to harm there again.

My family had desecrated that land with their misdeeds, and from what I remembered of their religion? Only fire could sanctify the land once again. That was something I wouldn't forget.

We regrouped north of the battery fire, and after we gave Chase, the other boys, and the two girls the clothes Mathis, Jonah, and I managed to snag from the closets in the cabins, we ushered all of the kids into the back of a very large SUV after we put down the seats. We heard sirens in the distance as we quietly drove back to the highway, and for a moment, I took a deep, cleansing breath knowing we'd been able to get those kids away from the torture they were enduring in the name of religion. The sound of those batteries exploding as we drove away actually made me smile. I knew my father, uncle, brothers, and the others would be pissed. As far as I was concerned, they got off lucky.

The night sky had cleared, and the moon was brighter, which was helpful because we were driving without lights. It was as if the heavens were offering us a beacon in the night to get the hell away from that awful place, and I was grateful for it. As far as I knew, nobody would figure out who had come to rescue those kids… well except my mother. Maybe she'd betray me, but I'd be ready for anything that came my way. How could a woman's heart harden against her own child? It was something I was sure I'd never be able to comprehend.

We drove those kids straight to the hospital in Hot Springs, letting them out just outside the cameras at the ER entrance. We didn't offer them any explanation regarding why we'd done what we'd done or who we were. We'd simply directed them toward the hospital and told them to report what had happened to the doctors and nurses. Once we were certain they were safely inside, we drove away.

We had Chase with us, and I could see the kid was teetering on the brink of going into shock, so I needed to assure him that he was in good hands. I removed my knit face mask and pulled him closer to me as he sat in the back of the vehicle, crying. I reached for a soda from the carton someone had forgotten to bring into the motel, and opened it for him, remembering sugar helped defer shock. I'd taken a first-aid/CPR class so I could get a discount on my business insurance at the shop. Who knew it would come in handy under the circumstances?

"You might not remember me, but I'm your cousin, Shane. I'm so sorry they did that shit to you, but Dani's waiting for you, Chase. We'll keep you safe," I whispered to the poor kid, hearing his soul weeping. I remembered that feeling far too well.

I had seen stripes on his back which weren't unlike the ones I'd had on my own years ago. I didn't know if he'd ever get over the pain suffered at the hands of people who were supposed to be Christians and were supposed to love him, but I prayed it was easier for him to find a new life than my experience. It hadn't been easy for me in the beginning, and I made a lot of bad choices. I prayed Chase would allow Dani to guide him so he didn't repeat my mistakes. I wasn't a role model for anyone by any stretch of the imagination.

I wanted someone to release the pain inside me because the guilt instilled in me since childhood at the disappointment that I was to my parents—the unworthiness of being their son—would once again consume my soul, and I'd go into the darkness again. I had substituted rough sex for cutting when I started working in Manhattan because I became ashamed of the scars. Unfortunately, I was too far from

Brooklyn to get my usual relief… a spanking followed by a hard, rough fuck, but as soon as I got there? I knew I'd go back to that club and find someone to do it. I needed to clean the slate once again because clearly, I was the deviant they'd accused me of being so long ago. It was sad they won that argument. Maybe I should have let them kill me back then. *Then we'd have all been out of our misery, wouldn't we?*

9

MATEO

I was sitting on an examination table in the emergency room at Presbyterian Hospital in Brooklyn while a doctor put five stitches in my left temple. "I'm sorry, Mateo. I just didn't recognize you when I rushed into that office. Mrs. Jarrett called me and said someone was trying to kidnap Dylan and Searcy, so I acted on instincts," Duke stated with a smirk as the mother fucker watched me wince while the doctor dug into my head again with that fucking needle.

Duke, the prick, had told the doctor I was allergic to lidocaine, and I could see that nasty, mother fucker was challenging me to ask for the numbing agent. I stupidly nodded in agreement with him and took a deep breath while the doctor finished the last stitch and began tugging the thread which shot pain through my fucking skull. I was going to show Duke Chambers how it felt when we left the ER.

I had a hell of a fucking headache, but I couldn't forget the goddamn bone I had to pick with Dexter and Gabby. I didn't know I wasn't on the call sheet for Dylan and Searcy at the school. Sherlock and Chambers had been listed, but when Sherlock rolled off, and I rolled on, nobody told the school. That fucking secretary had called Chambers instead of Gabby, so he got there in record time. When he saw it was me, he still didn't hesitate to clock me with his gun as I sat in the waiting area of the goddamn grade school principal's office. I'd get him back.

"Uh-huh. How long do I have to have the stitches? Why didn't you use that liquid suture shit?" I asked the intern who had his tongue sticking out of the side of his mouth the whole time he stitched me up. He looked twelve.

"Oh, your friend said you were allergic to that stuff, as well. I got to stitch you up because I need the practice. Does it hurt too much?" the kid asked me. I wanted to grab his nuts and ask the same question, but I took a deep breath to relax.

"No, but I'd strongly urge you to ask the fucking *patient* about allergies in the future," I hissed at the child who believed he was about to be a doctor. When he finally tied off the knot and snipped it, he stepped back and appeared to be proud of his handiwork.

I knew if Shay saw the stitches, he'd be upset… well, I hoped he would. I really wanted to talk to him, but he was busy with that fucked-up family shit, so I was waiting for Sherlock or Mathis to call and tell me when they were coming back to New York. I missed my man… or the man I hoped could be mine.

"Okay, Mr. Torrente. I'll send the nurse in with the paperwork so you can leave. Be careful when you're riding a skateboard in the future. Maybe a man of your advanced age shouldn't try to do tricks any longer?" the doctor-wanna-be offered before he used the chart to salute the two of us as he left the room.

I turned to Duke, girding my loins for battle before we ever walked out of the fucking hospital. "I rode a skateboard and did what?" I didn't even know how to ride a fucking skateboard.

Duke chuckled. "Rode it off a rail trying to do a trick from your childhood. I was there to watch it because I tendered the dare, but you cracked your head on a flower box when you fell. Of course, I brought you here immediately." The fucker laughed, and I could barely hold my temper. It was time for a serious discussion because the man had an ax to grind with us… or maybe just me, and I sure as fuck wanted to know what it was so we could deal with it once and for all.

"How'd you square that shit with the school after you smacked me in the head with your fucking gun?" I asked, really shocked at his tenacity. If I didn't hate him so much, I might actually like the bastard. He did have a brilliant quality about him.

"I told Mrs. Jarrett you were a mentally unstable cousin of Gabby's who wanted to hang out with the kids. I might have mentioned you're on the sex offender list." I'd have choked the mother fucker if the nurse hadn't come in with a list of things to worry about in the event I had a concussion. I didn't, but the hospital was doing a CYA, and I got it.

I thanked her before we walked out of the building toward the large SUV. "Where are the kids?" I asked as we both got inside and took off.

"Dominic picked them up and took them to the Victorian. I didn't give him details about what happened to you. You want me to take you home?" Duke asked with a smirk after we were inside the vehicle, him turning us toward the street from the hospital parking lot.

I reached over and grabbed the prick by the ear, digging in my thumbnail as hard as I could. Duke squealed a little before making a quick turn into a neighborhood and shoving the SUV into park. He reached up and slapped my hand away, grabbing his ear. I was proud I'd drawn blood, which I wiped on his nice white shirt.

"You're a stupid jackoff. What's your goddamn problem?" Chambers snapped as he reached into the console and pulled out some fast-food napkins to hold up to his ear, which made me laugh.

"What's *your* goddamn problem? You seem to have it in for me, and I demand to know why," I demanded.

"I got it in for all self-important pricks. You're not special, trust me," he answered, that smug smirk never leaving his face.

I decided it was best to ask something more relevant than continue a schoolyard finger pointing campaign. I really didn't give a shit why he didn't like me. I had a job to do. "Do you know anything about Vinnie Pezzoli? You know who he is?" I asked, feeling the pounding in my head intensify as I considered the ramifications of what seemed to be solidifying in my mind in a fashion I wasn't expecting.

Duke turned to me as he held the napkin to his bleeding ear. "You fight like a fucking six-year-old-girl, you bastard."

I chuckled. "You're right. Searcy taught me that move. Anyway, do you know Pezzoli?" I asked a second time.

"Yeah, I've heard shit about him when I was in Italy working for your father, why?" Duke asked.

"He's set up shop at that coffee spot across from the school. He's got an office upstairs, and guess who showed up today looking for a dude named Marco Rialto, who also happens to be staying at the St. Regis in Manhattan?" I challenged.

"How the fuck would I know?" Chambers asked with a look on his face that said he was done with me.

"My cousin, Lucia. She's Gabe's older sister. She's affiliating with the consiglieri of the Mangello family while she's looking for a man she's been dating. That man has a suite at the St. Regis on Frankie Man's credit card, and apparently, my cousin is staying there with him? Now, how the fuck do we proceed with that shit?" I asked, because I really didn't know.

I definitely didn't count Duke as a friend, but maybe he could be an ally? I was beyond knowing how the fuck to handle the current predicament, and I couldn't go to Gabe about it yet. It was his sister for hell's sake. I was out of ideas, and since it seemed Duke hated all of us, maybe he was the best one to assess the situation as an outsider? *Fuck if I know?*

"You haven't found Sally Man, yet, correct?" he asked me, and for once, it wasn't with a judgmental edge to his tone.

"No. I've had Casper looking for him everywhere, but the asshole has gone dark. You were a Marine. Any tricks of the trade you care to share?" I asked him.

Duke turned off the vehicle before he looked my way, not exactly extending an olive branch, but I could tell he was concerned. "I need more background on the family. Mr. Torrente, and I mean your father, gave me basic intel, but I need more. I know none of you like me, but I'm an effective operative. I might not get along with you, but I'd never let you come to harm," Duke stated. It was the first positive thing I'd heard from the man since he started working for Gabby.

We sat in the parking lot for half-an-hour as I explained to him the basics of the organization, surprised my father hadn't schooled him as he'd done all of the operatives in the past. It was Giuseppe's thing to torture us with details, but somehow, Duke had been able to escape them. I honestly wanted to know why.

I finished and looked at the man, seeing his eyes were glazed over. I pushed against his arm and waited for him to turn to look at me. "I didn't realize that was what... that's not what I expected. All of those people aren't family?" he asked, referring to the entire organization, I was guessing.

I laughed. "They *are* family, but not all by blood. I mean, we have paths that cross, and there is the Italian organization which is different from the American organization, but Papa and Gabriele are the two men in charge, really. They work together, as I'm sure you know since you came to New York from Italy. Seriously, why do you dislike me?" I asked again. Apparently, it was bothering me.

Duke looked at me and smirked. "Why do you think I have any emotions regarding you at all, Mateo?"

I sat in the SUV and considered it before concluding the fucker was probably playing me for a fool. "Petra? You took her to London. Did you turn her over?" I asked.

"Yes. I surrendered the woman to a guy named Ace Hampton when he showed up with the codeword from MI6. He was an American, from what I could tell, but I didn't know him. When I called your father about it, Giuseppe told me he was legit, so I didn't follow up after Hampton took her from the drop site. Have you heard anything to the contrary that I was wrong and she came to harm?" Duke asked, seeming worried.

Ace Hampton made me smile. He'd worked for Papa in England as a gun-for-hire, but I knew him to be a hell of a good fuck, even though we didn't actually fuck. I didn't know most of his background, but I did know he was one sexy mother fucker.

I'd met Ace Hampton when I was still in London about six-months after a bad breakup with a guy I'd thought could be my happily-ever-after. He was called back to Pakistan by his family, and I got a stupid note not to try to contact him, so I was down in the dumps when I'd met Ace Hampton, the perfect pick-me-up.

Ace always had rumors swirling around him, everything from him being an American Green Beret to one that he'd worked for a mobster to another one that he was an operative for the CIA. In our world, everyone was surrounded by many myths and legends. Nobody ever discounted them, but nobody ever confirmed them.

"You ever meet him?" I asked Duke.

"Not really. Hampton was in the shadows when I took Petra into that restaurant. So, we clear here? We're both looking out for the kids and allied to destroy the enemies?" Duke asked.

"I'm good with that, but don't hit me with that fucking gun again or I'll shoot your ass, *fatto*?" I demanded as Duke laughed and started the SUV. We'd reached some sort of detente, though it would take me time to figure out what and why, but I believed I had someone willing to fight *with* me, not *against* me, and I didn't hate it.

Yes, I was used to working alone because that was what I did best, but I'd never had such sweet kids to protect, so I was willing to work with a man I disliked more than cooked cabbage. That shit was gross.

The pounding on my door at three o'clock in the fucking morning brought me with my Tan and a bad attitude as I looked through the peephole to see Shay and a young guy standing next to him. I quickly opened the door and welcomed them inside, taking Shay into my arms.

"God, I missed you," I whispered to him. He hugged me and kissed me with passion before he pulled away and wrapped an arm around the cutest young guy I'd seen in a while. He looked a lot like Shay, but I could tell he was really young.

"Who's your mini-me?" I asked as I closed the door, placing my gun on the table in the hallway before I turned on the light and led them toward the kitchen. I reached for a pitcher of filtered water and grabbed three glasses, filling them and handing one to Shay and his companion.

"This is my cousin, Chase, and I need to hide him for a little while. He's seventeen, and he'll swear he's a runaway if he gets picked up, but I was able to get him out of that camp. Do you have anywhere…" Shay began.

I could see Shay was upset and the kid was scared as fuck, not surprisingly. I wanted to know why, in detail, but first, we had other things to discuss. "You want him in the U.S. or outside it?" I asked, seeing the kid's face light up.

"Okay, uh, I don't want either of us charged with kidnapping, but I need to make sure his family won't find him for now. They'll probably find me, and I'm ready for them, but I need to keep him away from them. I don't want to say anything more than that right now," Shay explained.

My mind was racing because I could hide the kid anywhere in the world, but at seventeen, he'd need someone to watch over him and keep him out of trouble. A question popped into my head. "What about school?" I asked, knowing it was time kids should be in school. I had five stitches in my head to attest to it.

"Yes, he needs to finish school," Shay explained.

"Actually, I skipped a year, so this would be my senior year. I can do it online," Mini-Shay explained.

I looked at Shay and smirked. "He's not yours, right?" The boy cracked up, which caused me to laugh as well. The screwed-up look on Shay's face was hysterical.

"No, he's not, you ass. He's my cousin, okay? You met Dani. It's her little brother. My family will come here looking for me once Dani tells them where I live, but Chase can't be anywhere they can find him right now. I'll explain it more when…" Shay began before the boy stepped forward and extended his hand, where I noticed he had purple nails.

"I'm Chase Barr. My sperm donor and Shane's are brothers. They were holding about eight or ten of us at the family campground outside Hot Springs. I guess they were intent on beating the queer out of us, or they were going to kill us," he stated as he turned around and lifted the white t-shirt he was wearing, showing me the mangled, raw stripes on his back which took my breath. *How the fuck could a family torture a seventeen-year-old kid like that?*

"Look, uh, I'm not sure what to do, but he can't be anywhere near me when the family comes looking. I don't want to get you in trouble, but I need him not to be where they can easily get to him until I sort some shit out," Shay whispered. I turned to see the pleading look in his pretty, amber-colored eyes. I couldn't deny him anything.

I took a deep breath. "Again, *amore mio*, do you want him in the U.S. or out of it?" I asked, knowing I could easily get the kid out of the country.

Chase giggled. "Oh, he called you *his love*. He's so hot," the kid gushed as he grabbed Shay's arm and jumped up and down just as I would expect a teenager to do.

I couldn't help but smile as well. "How about you guys stay with me tonight, and we address this tomorrow in the clear light of day after we get some rest. Everyone come home in one piece?" I asked, changing the subject.

"Yeah. Mathis' friend, Jonah, has a thing for Dani, I think. Anyway, Mathis was incredible in this whole thing. His friend decided to go back to Memphis with Dani for the rest of his vacation. The other kids we rescued—we took them to a hospital to be checked out," Shay explained before gulping down some water.

He signed and looked into my eyes. "It'll probably take my family a few days to regroup, so yeah, if we can stay here for a day or two while we figure out what to do, I'd appreciate it. I need to go to my apartment and get some clothes and check on my cat. I'll be back in an hour. Stay here Chase, and don't be a pain in the ass, please?" Shay instructed as he quickly hustled out of my apartment before I could offer to take him to his place.

I turned to his young cousin and smiled, trying not to be creepy. "You hungry? I have a pan of my brother's lasagna in my freezer, but that'll take about an hour to cook," I suggested. It was too late to call Blue Plate to get something else for him.

The kid smiled and then glanced at my wild bedhead. "I can make something if you have food in the fridge. You know, you need a trim, handsome," he told me, sounding very much like Shay Barr. He sashayed over to my fridge, pulling open the door and jutting out his ass, which was a move I could imagine Shay doing, but it was totally inappropriate for him to do it in my direction. My heart was taken by his cousin. I needed to ensure the kid knew it before I was *really* on the sex-offender registry.

"I'm going to let Shay trim my hair when he has a chance, thanks. Knock off the sexy shit because you're far too young for me, and that behavior will get me into too much trouble. Find a cute guy your own age and blow his mind as I'm sure you can. Tell me what happened at that stupid camp," I requested, seeing his bright green eyes light up.

"O-M-G! It was like an action movie," the kid began his tale. "See, my parents… well, our whole family… are a bunch of illiterate Bible-thumping, assholes. Now, I'm not just saying that because we live in Arkansas. I mean, they don't value education, but that's because they're too damn stupid to learn, really. They use the Bible to find fault with anyone and everyone they meet, and they love torturing people they believe to be on the queer spectrum. They treat it like they're saving someone, but all they're doing is satisfying some sadistic need inside them to harm people they don't understand." His explanation made perfect sense to me. He could have been talking about any sadist I'd ever met.

"So, Charlie, a kid I know from school, and I were tied to these old, oak-split-log benches that have been on the property since before I was born. They stripped us off buck naked, which is really a weird thing for a bunch of grown men—who are supposedly straight and trying to save our souls—to do to queer boys, but…" Chase continued. The story was shaping up to be so fucking gruesome, but the kid was telling it like it hadn't actually happened to him, which had me equally intrigued and worried.

Once Chase got to the part where they'd taken an electric prod to his genitals after they showed him porn, I'd heard enough. How could anyone do anything of the sort to people they cared about? I couldn't begin to imagine it.

I'd tortured spies and terrorists in the past in the name of justice and safety, but it was non-contact techniques…sleep deprivation, bright lights, complete darkness, loud noises. I didn't really like doing it but considering my profession at the time, those were the least offensive things for me to be judged by whatever waited in the great beyond. That was all when I was in the *Carabinieri*.

Since I'd been out and working for Papa, there were harsher things I'd done which would warrant judgment when my time was up, but nowhere in anything I'd ever done had I laid a harmful hand on a child, which was what those fucking religious fanatics had done to those kids. Of course, I had no problem gutting a sick fuck, so maybe I wasn't the best judge of normal behavior?

I supposed I never believed that conversion therapy bullshit really existed because as far as I knew, it didn't happen in Italy, which was where I'd spent most of my life. Unfortunately, a sweet boy was standing in front of me offering living proof it was a real thing and the most tragic event I'd ever encountered. He'd shown me his back, and it sickened me.

I almost told Chase to forget about making food, but he seemed happy to pull together some sort of stir-fry from the stuff he found in my fridge as he animatedly detailed the events of the weekend. Me, a hardened killer, couldn't believe what I was hearing. Fuck, I was tongue-tied.

"Are you okay? Do I need to get a doctor to check you out?" I asked as I sipped the water I had, wishing to fuck it was something much harder.

Chase took a spatula he found in my drawer and continued to stir the food in the large skillet. He didn't look at me for a moment, but then he turned off the skillet and turned to look at me. "Shay doctored me at the motel before we flew back with his friends. That English guy was funny," Chase offered as he dished up three plates and set two at the table while slipping one into the microwave over the stove to stay warm.

I dug in, tasting a damn good stir fry of mostly veg and some ham I had in the fridge for sandwiches. "This is great," I offered.

"It's better with more seasonings than salt and pepper. Did you know Shay's a fantastic cook? Aunt Carol used to talk about how natural it came to him until Uncle Bobby would get pissed at finding him in the kitchen in one of Aunt Carol's aprons at the stove. Bobby would storm out, and Aunt Carol would get yelled at later. Our family is truly fucked up, trust me.

"My father's a hellfire-and-brimstone preacher, and he's a crazy bastard. I'm worried about Dani if they ever figure out she and Shay planned this together. I know they'll go to her place first to look for me," Chase told me. I could see he was worried about his sister, and I'd met the sweet woman, liking her a lot.

I would send someone to Memphis to look out for Dani if that was what Shay wanted from me. I needed to make a call, and based on the food the kid had made, maybe it wasn't the worst idea I'd ever had. I'd run it by Shay when he came back, and I hoped he agreed. There were risks, as always, but I believed it to be the best option. I just had to convince that little spitfire who had my cock hard all the time and my heart in his hands. He would be my savior or my demise, but I'd do anything I could to protect him and anyone he loved. I had the feeling he could be my soul mate, and if he wasn't? I'd still put down my life for him.

10

SHAY

"No!" I snapped. There was no way I could send Chase to Italy. First off, that kid would be fucking lost in a foreign country because he had grown up in the heartland and didn't know shit about living in a place where people didn't speak English. Second, it would be a goddamn international incident if my seventeen-year-old cousin was discovered in Italy.

Nobody in Hot Springs, Arkansas, would give a flying fuck what the family of the Right Reverend Barr had done to his little queer son, nor would they approve of us taking Chase to hide him from being further harmed by the family. A family that would do anything to get him back and make me a memory due to my part in the raid on the camp would be seen as great parents, not the criminals I believed them to be.

I made the mistake of succumbing to my own anger at the time of the raid to ensure my mother knew it was me at the compound, which was stupid. I was sure she told my father I was one of the men who invaded the camp that night, and I knew he'd take delight in finding me and making me pay for the fact I was still alive. If we sent Chase to Italy, they would have no rest until we were all in prison, and I wouldn't allow it.

It had taken me an hour and a half to get my shit together and grab Mixer to bring with me to Mateo's place. The sexy man hadn't officially sanctioned our move, but if he was my big, bad protector, then he knew we needed him... for however long he'd entertain the thought.

When I got back to his place, Mateo helped me carry my things from the entrance of the building to the elevator, including Mixer's cat cage. I could see the sexy Italian wasn't exactly comfortable about having the cat at his place, but he didn't seem exactly opposed to the prospect either.

I saw that while I was gone, he'd emptied drawers in his dresser to make room for my things, which I appreciated. He sat down on the side of his bed and watched as I pushed my stuff into the four available drawers before I turned to look at him.

Finally, Mateo exhaled. "Okay, if you don't want to send him to Italy to stay with my family, how about we take him to Long Island? No evident trail leads from you in Brooklyn to Long Island.

"You've spent time at Grace and Tomas' house for the wedding and a few parties, so you know he'll be very safe. Tomas and my father taught us how to use guns when we were young and used to go skeet shooting. They'll look after Chase for a few weeks while we sort this out, Shay, I promise," Mateo offered as he let Mixer out of the cage and picked him up, petting the cat who began purring immediately, the fickle bastard. That stupid stray was drawn to the sexy man like me. I wondered which of us was the bigger slut!

"How do you even know Graciela and Tomas would allow this unknown kid to stay with them for weeks? Won't they ask about his parents and why he's not with them?" I countered. I knew the couple was wonderful and welcoming to everyone, but taking in a kid they didn't know? That was a hill too high to climb, I was sure.

Mateo reached for me, pulling me onto his lap after he dropped Mixer on the floor. I looked at the cat and saw he wasn't too happy, but a part of me wanted to stick out my tongue because I had won Mateo's attention over that stupid feline.

"Listen, Shay, I can keep a close eye on Chase in Long Island, and I can have very effective people keep an eye on him in Italy, but I don't want the two of you together in Brooklyn because if they come looking as you predicted, I fear they won't hesitate to do damage to both of you. I can't allow that to happen, but I doubt you want all of your relatives to die in one fell swoop," the man pointed out. As I thought about it, I wasn't so sure.

"I'm going to keep you from them, Shay. I can't look out for both of you because you, *amore mio*, are the most important thing to me. Chase is a great kid, and I know he means a lot to you, so I'll make sure I have someone more than capable of doing what's necessary to keep him from harm's way. It's you I have to protect because I have plans for *you*," Mateo told me as he gently kissed my lips, showing me more tenderness than I believed he had inside of him and was in direct contrast to what the Brit had told me. *Shame on me for underestimating him!*

I pulled him close as our tongues continued to tangle in a way that had me lit on fire. We'd fucked before, and I wanted to do it again so I could get my mind off the total disastrous possibility facing me. If anything would distract me, it was the handsome assassin looking into my eyes.

I knew my family would find us eventually, but I didn't want to consider it. I didn't want to think about anything at the moment. I simply wanted to feel, and I needed to feel something in particular, though I was afraid to ask him. Unfortunately, if I didn't ask, my lesser angels would have me considering going back to that goddamn club the next night seeking the release I needed instead of following my heart to be with Mateo.

I broke the mouth-watering kiss and pulled away, looking into those gorgeous brown eyes. "Can I ask you for a favor?"

Mateo assessed my body language for a moment, not surprisingly since I was sure it was a tool he used a lot in his job, before he kissed my cheek and nuzzled my ear. "I know what you need, but I have to know why. I need you to explain to me why you need it, Shay," he whispered as he kissed my temple and pulled me, so I was resting my head on his shoulder as his hand gently trailed up and down my back.

It was time to tell him one of my darkest secrets or walk the fuck away. God knew I didn't want to do either, but keeping him in my life was a bigger draw than leaving him behind, so I gathered my courage. "I grew up in that fucked up family, and I was in church every Sunday morning, Sunday night, and Wednesday evening since I can ever remember.

"My Uncle Brett preached about hell more than he ever preached about heaven. All my life I've heard about everything that will condemn me to hell, and even though I didn't believe it was true, I was weak. I craved my parents' attention and love, so I listened, and I prayed to be normal again when I figured out I wasn't," I confessed, fighting like hell to keep the tears at bay.

Mateo nodded, so I continued. "I guess the guilt over never being able to be what my family wanted me to be altered something inside me. I've known I was different from my brothers since I was about thirteen, and I'm sure my parents picked up on it as well, which didn't win me any favors in the family.

"In order to try to deal with it, I began cutting when I was about fourteen. I got a pocketknife for my birthday that year, and one day I was sharpening it in the tool shed because I was hiding from my brothers who always wanted to use me as a punching bag. I wanted to see how sharp the blade was, so I sliced the knife over my forearm and watched as it split my skin with no effort at all." I could practically feel it as if it was happening right there, again.

"I watched the drops of blood roll down my arm toward my hand and remembered something Dani told me about the Garden of Eden and how Eve sinned by taking a bite of the forbidden fruit. Eve's actions condemned all women to bleed monthly for her sin. Dani's mother told her that when Dani got her period the previous year, but it made me think if women had to bleed for their sins, then maybe I could bleed for mine and be forgiven for being queer. It took me until I was in my early twenties to dislodge that twisted bit of logic.

"The scars have faded…well, most of them, but some of them are pretty ugly… which is why I usually don't take off my shirt when I have sex," I told him as I whipped off my t-shirt to show him the underside of my upper arms where the thin lines looked like silver stripes on my pale skin. I had to remind myself I was the person in control of my life now, and I didn't need to bleed for my sins any longer. It was at least seven years ago that I'd stopped.

"Even after all of these years, I can't help feeling guilty for the draw I have for men because it's been beaten, electrocuted, and burned into my mind that it's wrong, Mateo. All my life, I've been told my instincts, my reactions to things, are all wrong, and I just can't get it out of my head no matter how many self-help books I read or how much I meditate.

"I don't want to cut myself, but I need to feel the punishment… the pain for being filthy, sinful trash as I've been told I am since my family figured out my sexuality. I need to be able to release the feelings of being beyond redemption. Spanking helps a lot because it allows me to feel like I'm being punished for the sin of being gay," I explained, too afraid to look into his eyes.

I didn't want to see the judgment on his face, and there *should* be judgment because what I was feeling… what I needed… was absolutely ridiculous. I shouldn't need to be beaten to accept myself. I should just admit my family was fucked up and rid my mind of those sick monologues running through my head from growing up in the house where Bobby and Carol didn't believe I was good enough. I shouldn't need it… but I did, or I'd go back to cutting, which wasn't something I ever wanted to do again.

Mateo placed his hand on my cheek and turned my face to look into his gorgeous, brown eyes, seeming to have sensed my uneasiness. The tenderness I saw there was surprising, nearly taking my breath. "Shay, tesoro, I hate that's how you feel, and I want to try to help you see it's not necessary because you're perfect as you are. Until I can make you see it and accept it, I'll make a concession. If you disagree with me, we have a problem, but I want us to work it out. I want us to work out a lot of shit," he told me, not sounding like the man Sherlock described to me when we were in Arkansas.

Mateo leaned forward and kissed me gently before pulling away. "So, here goes. These are my ground rules for this until we can come up with another way for you to cope. I absolutely refuse to use anything but my hand to spank you, Shay. We'll figure out how much pain you need to feel as if you've been sufficiently punished, but we're going to discuss this further. I won't beat you the same as you've been hurt in the past, but if you need the sting to feel peace, then I'll do the best I can. By the way, it's not as uncommon as you seem to think that people want a little pain with their pleasure," he offered as he pulled me closer and offered a soft kiss before he held me in his arms like I was something precious.

Mateo, the man I knew who was capable of taking a life, was worried about hurting me? It was an odd dichotomy to contemplate, but he dipped me back as he continued to ravage my lips while he opened my pants before he flipped me onto my stomach over his lap. It was a surprise, but it wasn't a bad one. "How many to start?" he asked as he pulled my jeans and briefs over my ass, rubbing his hand over both cheeks.

I swallowed. "Ten… multiples of ten," I whispered as I braced my hands on the floor. I wasn't sure how hard the blows would be, but hopefully, they would be enough to set my mind *straight* because I needed it to be with him again. I remembered how great it felt when we'd last been intimate, and I wanted it again.

"I'm going to start with ten, slowly warming up your ass. Look, I did some research on this shit, and you need a safe word, Shay. I don't want to do any damage, okay? I need you to promise you'll stop me if it becomes too much," Mateo whispered.

I thought about what he'd said, and I knew he was probably right. It needed to be something that would get his attention if he got lost in the punishment like with the alleged Dom at the club—the guy Mateo had killed at my salon—so I racked my brain, finally finding a word. "Mullet." It was the worst fucking haircut in the world as far as I was concerned, and nearly all the male members in my family had one. Thinking anything about them was like throwing a bucket of ice water on me, so it would do the trick.

Fortunately, my little cousin Chase was enough like me he'd never allow himself to sport that embarrassing, chopped up, disaster of a haircut. I could tell Chase cut his own hair into a very fashionable bilength with shaved sides and longer hair on top that he could style many different ways. He was definitely my younger mirror.

I heard the beautiful man chuckle as he rubbed his hand over my ass. "Okay, Shay, what's your safe word?" he asked again.

"You fucking heard me…" I began as I felt the crack of his hand on my right ass cheek. It stung, just as it was supposed to do.

"My safe word is…" *smack* … "mullet," I whispered as he smacked my left, ass cheek. It stung, but something flooded through my body as it had done in the past, calming me. It was fucked up, for sure, but it was what led me to that awful club in the first place. The pain helped me release the guilt about my sexuality such that I could act on my feelings of attraction. God knew I was attracted to Mateo Torrente. God also knew I was so totally fucked in the head that he might leave me, but for now, he was there, and he was everything I needed.

After ten strokes, Mateo pulled me up and looked into my eyes, no nonsense showing on his face. "You realize this is something we need to work through together, right?"

I nodded as I dried my tears. Mateo pulled up my underwear and jeans before he stood from his seat. "I really want to fuck you, Shay. Is that okay, or should I take a cold shower?" he asked as he actually picked me up and held me in his arms, nuzzling into my neck and inhaling deeply.

I could see what he'd just done had affected him as much as it had me, but not in the same way. He had guilt on his handsome face, while I had bliss. We needed to figure that shit out for sure. He had no need to feel guilty. I'd been fucked up many years before he ever came into my life, and if he left as Sherlock predicted, well, I'd probably be fucked up again.

Mateo looked at me as we stood in the shower the next morning. He'd buried his cock inside me three times, and it had been ecstasy, but as I stared at him that morning, I could see he needed something from me.

He needed absolution for the part he'd played in my fucked-up sexual needs. There was no reason for him to feel bad about spanking me, and he needed to know I wasn't holding it against him. I'd give him what he needed just as he'd done for me.

"You did nothing wrong, Mateo. It's not your fault I'm as screwed in the head as I am, you know? The shit that happened to me years ago has nothing to do with you, and I shouldn't have involved you in this mess.

"I appreciate what you did for me last night, but I'll get Chase and Mixer, and we'll leave," I told him, meaning it with every fiber in my being. He might be a killer, but he wasn't a bad guy. He had a heart under all of those muscles, and he felt remorse he shouldn't. That was my fault.

Mateo poured shampoo into his large hands and began shampooing my hair, which felt incredible. "You think it's that easy for me to just let you go, amore mio?" he asked as he massaged my scalp. Hell, he could rival me when it came to giving a good scalp massage.

"What's that mean?" I asked, referring to his Italian. I wanted him to put words I could understand to the feelings he expressed. I needed the words.

Mateo moved me under the spray and worked the shampoo out of my hair before he gently wiped the water from my face as he moved me closer to him, wrapping his long arms around my body. "My love. It means 'my love.' I do believe I love you, Shay. You don't have to..." he began before his cell on the counter began sounding.

Mateo opened the shower door and reached out to pick it up, scoffing at the name on the screen. *"Che cazzo?"* Mateo snapped before he stepped out of the shower and grabbed his phone, cursing and shaking his head.

"What?" he snapped as he answered. I rinsed off and stepped out, taking the towel from the counter to wrap around myself. Based on the look on his handsome face, Mateo was angry, and I didn't want to draw his ire, so I kept my mouth shut and simply observed. His body language gave off the appearance that he was ready to rip off someone's head, so I slipped out of the bathroom and sat down on the side of the bed to wait for him.

Whatever had angered him wasn't anything I wanted to deal with that morning. I wanted to have sex again before we both started the day, but it didn't seem as if that was going to happen because something had the man quite upset as he stormed back into the bedroom to dress, seeming to ignore me as he shouted into the phone in Italian.

I hurried into the bathroom and closed the door to brush my teeth and shave before I went to get dressed, as well. I needed to get to the salon, and I was going to take Chase with me. I could hide him in the backroom for the day and make him read a book between visits with the people who worked for me because I knew they'd all want to get to know him, and hell, books never killed anyone.

After I was dressed and had finger styled my hair, I walked into the bedroom, finding it empty with the bed made. I heard noise in the kitchen, so I hurried down the hall to find Chase singing along with Gaga playing on his phone. The kid was stirring something in a sauté pan, spinning around and singing into a spatula about his "Poker Face," which made me laugh loud enough to catch his attention.

"Oh, I thought you two were getting down, again. The walls are thin, my friend," Chase offered with a devious smile before he giggled.

I puffed up my chest like an idiot. "Jealousy is such an unbecoming color on you, Chase," I joked as I poured two coffees and doctored them accordingly before I left him to take one to Mateo to test the water before the two of us parted ways for the day.

"Don't be too long. The eggs will get dry," Chase called after me before he began singing again.

I knocked on the door to Mateo's office with my foot so as not to spill the coffee, and when it opened, the man offered an apologetic smile. "Sorry about that call. I need to get going, but Duke's coming to pick up the two of you. Chase can go hang at the Victorian if you want while you work today. Dominic can keep him occupied," Mateo suggested, reminding me of Gabe's handsome nephew, Dominic. I'd seen the kid at family functions, noting he'd seemed to be kind of shy, so I wasn't sure about allowing my flirtatious cousin around the good-looking nephew.

"I'm not sure that's the best idea, Mateo. Chase might be a little too much for Dominic to handle. That guy's very attractive, and my cousin is a walking hormone," I reminded him, bringing a great laugh from Mateo.

"Yeah, but Dom can keep him occupied, and maybe Dex can talk him into helping out with shit at the yoga studio until you decide if you'll let him go out to the beach. He'll be safe there," Mateo promised.

I needed to consider it because I did have commitments to my clients and my staff. "Let me think about it and call Dani to get her take on it. I'm sure Aunt Judy has called her by now to see if she knows anything about what went down. I need to check on her," I explained.

"Ask her if Mathis' friend, Joe, is still down there. If he's not, I'll get someone to go to Memphis to look out for her. Not too closely, but near enough to see if anyone's connected her with that camp shit. I'll text you later. Duke will call when he gets here to pick up you guys. Don't forget, Sweeney, I love you," Mateo told me, lighting me up inside as he offered a quick kiss to my lips before he rushed down the hallway, his tie flying loose around his neck. *Maybe Sherlock was wrong?*

"Grazie, kid. Later," I heard him call to Chase before the front door slammed.

I knew our family would come for us, but I was beginning to believe maybe we had a chance to survive it, Chase and me. I honestly thought we had more of a shot than I'd have given us just a week ago. Plus... I was in love with an incredible man who I would cling to until he told me to go, though based on his actions the previous night and that morning, I wondered if that would happen. That was a great surprise, but I was hesitant to trust it. I'd experienced disappointment in my life. It wasn't pretty.

11

MATEO

"Are you fucking coming into the office today, or what? You got anything on Sally Man for me?" Gabriele roared over the line, the crabby asshole.

I understood the urgency he felt at finding Salvatore Mangello, but I couldn't help the fact the man had become a fucking ghost. I knew Gabe wasn't happy Sally Man was still in the wind, but it appeared the mobster wannabe was playing hide and seek. I knew Mathis was once again on kid duty since he'd returned from Arkansas, and Duke was his co-pilot since school was back in session, so saddling either of them with Chase wouldn't work.

I needed to consider who I could trust to keep the kid safe and occupied because Shay had a business to run, and I wanted no shit started at the salon. Unfortunately, Gabe was pissing me off.

"I'll be there in thirty, asshole. You need to watch your blood pressure, what with all that extra weight you're carrying around. When was the last time you had your cholesterol checked, Gabriele?" I teased, knowing it would piss him off and force him to hang up on me, which was the goal.

"*Fuck you, Mateo!*" The line went dead, which made me laugh. I hurriedly shaved, brushed my teeth, and dressed, stepping into the office in my apartment to grab my briefcase when Shay brought me coffee. We shared a few words about Long Island before I kissed him, reminding him I loved him and rushed out. He seemed to be a little troubled, but I'd address it with him that night when we had time. As I headed past the kitchen, Chase handed me a sandwich wrapped in a napkin.

"*Eat!*" the kid called after me. I thanked him and headed out, happy to see Smokey waiting for me on the street.

"How'd you know?" I asked as I hopped into the front seat, seeing coffee waiting for me.

"Eh, had a feeling. I remember how it is in the beginning, love and kisses. Anyway, you're going to need to get a company car. I doubt you'll fit into Shay's little roller skate," he explained, referring to that dinky-ass Prius. It was still at Shay's apartment building, which made me happy I'd hooked up a ride for him with Duke after he dropped the kids at school.

"Gabby call you this morning?" I asked him.

"Yep. I've been watching the store since Nemo's in North Carolina. His new man, Benjamin Hoffman, won the election to Congress, so Nemo will be back to work soon. He's going to split time between New York and DC for the next year while the Congressman rides out the term.

"Thankfully, he'll be back in charge soon enough, and things will go back to normal. I hate having to do the admin shit. I'm not cut out for it, and scheduling jobs and operatives? Not my strong suit," Smokey admitted, though it seemed like he was talking to himself more than me.

"Sherlock said he wants to go to London for a visit with his family since he finished up that job with Mathis in Arkansas. He's been too busy to go home over the summer, so I think it's important he gets the time off. His sister had a new baby a few weeks ago, so Dex made Gabe give him a few weeks of vacation." Smokey looked at me and grinned. "How's it going with you? Any word on Sally Man?"

I took a swig of the coffee Shepard Colson brought along for me and swallowed a large bite of the egg and bacon sandwich Chase had made for me. "Vinnie Pezzoli has taken up residence at the coffee shop down the street from the kid's school. What do you think Frankie's consiglieri is doing here in town while Frankie's in Venice? Giuseppe has eyes on him over there," I relayed.

"Why doesn't Giuseppe take the fucker out and be done with all this shit? If he took out Frankie, Sally would surface for sure, and we could get him before he starts more horseshit. His soldiers will splinter off and go their own ways while someone in Italy gobbles it all up."

What Smokey suggested was actually something that should have made me curious. Why wasn't Giuseppe handling Frankie? Why was he just keeping eyes on him, and why didn't Gabriele speak up about it to my father? He wanted the whole fucking Mangello family dead, and Papa had to know it, right?

I was being tugged in too many different directions to concentrate on one thing, so I needed to consider what was the most important issue at the moment. I owed allegiance to my family, for sure, so if I could find Sally Man and take out his surly ass, I'd be able to watch out for Shay myself. I needed to speak with my father, and quickly.

"You guys have any new operatives who could provide protective duty for Shay and his cousin? Mathis fill anybody in on the shit that went down?" I asked.

Smokey shook his head, which disappointed me. "We need guys. Giuseppe pulled Tommy back to Italy after the shit with Nemo and the Congressman was settled. Rafe is off-and-on, but Parker tells me he's gone more than he's around, so he must be picking up some of your old work?" Smokey offered with a cocked eyebrow.

I had pretty much checked out on everybody for sure, but it made me chuckle a little that Smokey even brought it up. The guy sweated red, white, and blue, and he'd been dealt a raw hand for sure when he was in the military. Smokey was a good man, undisputed, and when he worked with us in Italy, we kept him out of some of the work Papa undertook. I was usually called to do the wet work, to which I'd grown accustomed over time. I was assuming Rafe was handling shit in my absence.

Nemo took on some of those assignments back in the day because the guy had a lot of anger issues, as I recalled. He would tirelessly research a case before he acted, but he wouldn't hesitate to extract the proper level of justice when necessary. Raleigh Wallis was great at his job, and he was honestly one of the good guys. I was happy he'd found someone to love, even though the man was an American politician.

I was surprised to learn he was gay, but we all kept our secrets, didn't we? There was a rumor floating around GEA-A that Nemo was HIV-Positive, but I didn't give a shit. He was someone I'd gladly welcome to watch my back, and I'd watch his without hesitation.

"Yeah, uh, I need to make some calls," I told Smokey as he pulled in front of the Victorian and parked his truck.

I hopped out and hurried inside, noticing only Dominic was at the desk. "Where's your companion?" I asked him, offering a smile.

"She left a message for Uncle Gabe saying she's in San Francisco with her grandmother. She'll be back next week," Dom explained. I was pretty sure the last-minute notice would piss off my cousin, so I wasn't looking forward to talking to him.

I hurried upstairs and walked down the hallway, slipping by Gabe's office so I could talk to Casper first. "Hey, man, do me a favor and check on Sierra's location. Dom said she's in San Francisco, or so she said in the message, but I want to know where. Something's not right with that chick." Casper nodded before he made some notes. He then reached into a drawer of his desk and held up his hand to offer me a folder.

"What's this?"

"It's something I can't show anyone else except you. I think I have the connection to Francesco Mangello… or the family at least, but I'm not sure what to do with it. I trust you'll look into it and tell me whether I should shred the file?" Casper asked.

If Casper stumbled onto an old copy of the birth certificate listing Dino Mangello as the father of either of those kids, he'd definitely want to make us aware so we could do something to destroy the record. We'd kept it under wraps so Frankie Man didn't find out and come after his grandchildren, and if it was out there somewhere, we needed to get on it.

As far as Gabby had guessed, Frankie didn't know those kids were his grandkids, only that Dexter's sister was their mom, which wasn't even true in Dylan's case. It was totally fucked up, but we'd need to quash anything that led to the truth coming out.

Unfortunately, that wasn't what I saw when I opened the file that contained a birth certificate I wasn't expecting to find. It wasn't Dylan's or Searcy's. They were the connection to the Mangello family we all tried to keep a secret, which meant not many people knew about it.

What I had in my hands as I stood in front of Casper? The implications of it actually took my breath. I glanced up to look at the computer guru, only one question circling my brain. "This is real?" I asked as I stared at that piece of paper, feeling shock settle into my bones. I was pretty fucking sure the disbelief on my face wasn't hidden.

"I found it during a search of the *Archivio di Stato di Sienaon*, the public records registry for Siena. It came up when I was performing a worldwide search of the 'Torrente' family name. I narrowed it down to your immediate family, and lots of hits came up, so I set the parameter to the last one-hundred years," Casper stated with a look of regret on his face. "I swear, Mateo, I was only trying to help you find Sally Man. I guessed maybe something else might be going on, which is why I did the search in the first place."

I sighed because the guy had good instincts, and what I was seeing had me speechless. "Can you get me on the next flight I can make to Rome. Also, could you track a guy named Ace Hampton and get me a contact number for him, please? I'll take this from here, and thank you, Lawry. For now, this all stays between us."

He nodded, and I went to drop my shit in a vacant office… hiding the folder in my briefcase to take with me. It was in the office Sherlock usually used when he was in town, and since he wasn't in, I had the place to myself.

I pulled my phone from the breast pocket of my suit jacket and dialed my father. I looked at the clock to see it was nine in New York, which meant it was three in the afternoon in Siena. Papa would be done with lunch and should answer. When it rang through to voicemail, I left a message. "It's me, and I'm coming over. I'll be there tomorrow morning. Make time for me. We need to talk."

The time for keeping secrets was over. It never should have happened in the first place.

I called Rafael to meet me at my house that evening before I left town. I needed to pack and get to the fucking airport, but I needed him to look out for Shay because of my fucking cousin, Gabe. It was all I could do not to crack the fuckwit in the head with my Tan.

"What the fuck do you mean you're going to Italy? I'm trusting you to find Sally Man and take him out. Disposal isn't shit we do here, Mateo," Gabe snapped at me when I met with him after I'd solidified my plans to go home to deal with a pressing issue.

I couldn't hold the laugh. "Just a little too dirty for you, Gabriele? How the fuck do you think your problems go away when you run into some of this shit? That fucking brother of Dyl and Searcy's foster mom? How do you think he ended up dead? What about the General who killed Parker's father? You think that asshole just happened to pull the trigger because he felt bad? Smokey called in a ticket," I confessed, unable to hold my anger any longer.

"I seem to remember you walking into a warehouse and putting a hole in Dex's sister's head and watching several other of Dino's goons be gunned down, along with the man himself who St. Michael ended. If the DEA guys hadn't cleaned up that shit because they were looking for the cocaine, you'd have done what? You'd have called Papa, and you know who would have had to take care of your mess? Definitely not you because you're squeaky clean, right? How about Giancarlo Mangello? You think he just fucking disappeared? He was a threat to your kids, just like Sally and just like Frankie, Gabby," I reminded him.

"Your hands are dirty, just like mine, Rafe's, and lots of the other guys who work for Papa. Just because you don't pull the fucking trigger all the time doesn't mean you are without sin. I love your family, but the rest of us have fucking lives, and sometimes, we need support for the ones we love, as well," I snapped at the selfish prick.

I started to storm out when Gabe yelled at me, "Hey! What the fuck is this about, Mateo?"

I turned around and walked back into his office, closing the door. "Your sister's in deep with Frankie Man's consiglieri, who has set up an office right down the street at the coffee shop across from the kids' school. She thinks his name is Rico, and she's looking for someone named Marco Rialto, who doesn't exist as far as I can confirm.

"I've had Casper looking into that shit, so how about you talk to Lucia about what the fuck is going on? She's in town, you know," I growled out before I walked, leaving him with that information, but not the most important news that was taking me to fucking Italy. For that, I needed more of an explanation from dear old dad.

I walked into my apartment and wasn't surprised to see Rafael sitting on my couch with a glass of wine. "Make yourself at home," I joked as I strolled over and sat down, seeing he'd collected my mail and had actually opened all of it.

"You pay that much for cable? That's a sin. You don't even have porn," he chided. I smelled something delicious in the air, so I filled the other glass he had resting on the coffee table and picked it up.

"Saluti!" I toasted as we touched glasses. I reached for my old-school briefcase, opening it and holding out the file he needed to see, pulling it back when he reached for it to get his attention.

When Rafe looked at me, I decided to rely on my brother for help because Gabriele was blinded, either by love or stupidity. Damn if I didn't understand it more than I ever had in my life because I now had someone in my life I loved.

"This is something you can't unsee. It's not anything I ever expected, and I'm leaving in a few hours to go to Rome to confront

Papa. I need you to look out for Shay and his cousin, Chase. They're at DyeV Barr right now."

I let go of the folder and saw my cocky little brother's face turn white as he flipped through the papers, looking at me with shock. "This can't be true."

I took a gulp of the red table wine he'd opened before I looked at him. "I wouldn't have believed it, either, but I saw Lucia at the coffee shop down the street from the school the other day. She was questioning Vinnie Pezzoli regarding the whereabouts of someone named Marco Rialto," I offered.

"Who the fuck is Marco Rialto?" Rafe asked.

"I don't know. I have a sneaking suspicion he's an acquaintance of Sally Man's, but I have no proof. Suddenly, that takes a back seat to this," I told him as I pointed to the folder.

"Yeah, I get it," Rafe told me as he downed his wine and poured the two of us another glass.

"You'll look after Shay, right? I need to pin Papa down on the details, not just the highlights," I explained to my brother. We needed to eat before I got on the road, so I stood from the couch and took the wine with me to the kitchen.

"You're sweet on the hairdresser?" Rafe asked as he walked into my kitchen and pulled out a small pan of his sausage and cheese stuffed shells in a rosé pepper sauce, which was my favorite of everything he ever made. My brother was a celebrated chef, as his two Michelin stars and that James Beard would attest, but I remembered when we were kids and Mama used to make dinner for us. Every dish Rafe made took me back to our childhood, and I appreciated the reminders.

"I'm starved. Come on. I'm catching a flight from LaGuardia at seven. We need to discuss this shit because I'm not sure what to say when I get to Rome," I instructed.

We ate a meal together, discussing everything I needed him to know so he could watch out for Shay, Chase, Dylan, Searcy, and Dex…plus Rafe, himself. "You got it?" I asked my brother as we stood at the curb of my building, me waiting for an Uber.

"Christ on a cracker, Teo, are we the only people who are competent enough to keep the family safe? What the fuck are the rest of the operatives doing?" he asked with that signature smirk.

"Looking for… You know what the fuck they're doing," I snapped as a vehicle pulled up, and Rafe opened the tailgate of the monster.

I started to get in before I walked back over to my brother who was standing on the sidewalk. "Watch out for Chase because he's a seventeen-year-old horndog. He's cute, and he's underage, which is a recipe for disaster. I do love you, little brother," I told Rafe as I hugged him.

I knew our lives were about to change, and I could see Rafe felt it as well. What we were facing wasn't anything I'd ever anticipated, but I trusted my brother above anyone else. He trusted me to handle the situation with our father, and I would. How it would all play out? Who the fuck knew?

The cabin lights in the plane came on and woke me. I was fucking surprised I could even sleep in first-class knowing I hadn't called Shay to tell him I was leaving the country because I couldn't tell him why and I wasn't going to lie to him. I was relying on my brother to keep him safe in my absence and maybe smooth shit over, and I was acting on blind faith everything would be fine. I knew for certain Shay would be pissed at me, but I'd romance him, and hopefully, he'd forgive me.

"*Siamo sul nostro approccio finale. Si prega di inserire i vostri tavoli vassoio...,*" the flight attendant announced over the speaker. We were on our final approach to da Vinci airport in Rome, and it was time to put away the tray tables and put our seats upright. I'd heard it a million times.

I'd texted Tommy to see if he was in the city to pick me up. I wasn't in the mood to rent a car and fight traffic out to Siena, and I damn well wasn't going to take a cab that far from the airport. After I addressed things with my father, I'd leave it to him about how he'd deal with the rest of the family.

As I considered the news I'd discovered... Casper had discovered... I couldn't really say it wasn't anything that surprised me, but the ramifications of it could be earth-shattering for the family. I also didn't want to rat out Casper because he'd been the one to unearth that clusterfuck. He was good at his job. No need to shoot the messenger.

I followed the herd through the airport, dragging my wheeled bag behind me to the security exit where I saw Tommy waiting for me. I hurried toward him, embracing him with both arms and kissing both of his cheeks.

We had a history, Tommy, Rafe, and me. Gabriele was included in it so far as Tommy living with Tomas and Graciela for high school, but the three of us? We had grown up together like brothers. We were family, and I wanted to ensure the family remained the same regardless of what came of the news I'd found. I hated it had been kept a secret from us for so long, but Giuseppe's orders were respected by his brothers and everyone under his command. For me? Papa had some explaining to do.

"It's good to see you," Tommy offered in Italian.

"Don't be too quick to be happy to see me. You have no idea why I'm here. Did you tell your father I want to see him, as well?" I asked in our native tongue.

Tommy nodded and took my bag. "So, you look happy," he said in English, which made me smile.

"I was until I found out some shit. I met a great guy, though," I told him, unable to keep my face somber at the thought of Shay. I needed to call him and explain the reason I'd left so quickly was due to my family's bullshit, which I was sure he'd understand. I'd finish up as fast as I could and get back to him. That was the most important thing I had to tell him, but that would have to wait… not too long, though. I didn't want to leave him hanging. He meant too much to me.

12

SHAY

Sonya walked over to my station and touched my shoulder. "That famous chef, uh, Rafael Bianco? He's in the lobby asking to speak with you. Please, give him my number," she begged as I was cutting Angela Spires' hair.

Angela was the daughter of Randolph Spires, the mogul of Manhattan. I didn't hold her father's misdeeds against her. I liked her and her younger sister by another mother, Ainsley. Hell, how could I judge them when I had the fucked-up family I was born into? We didn't have a choice about the family into which we were born, only those we chose to make a part of our family.

I knew Rafael Bianco was actually Mateo's brother, though it wasn't advertised. I was anxious to meet him. I'd heard of him all over the place, but I'd never had the pleasure of eating in any of his restaurants, nor had I ever met the man in person. I'd been on the fringe of the Torrente events, but for the man to be in my shop had me a bit stumped.

"Sweetie, I need to take care of something. I'll be right back. Can I bring you anything?" I asked as I weaved my fingers through Angela's lovely blonde hair. She shook her head and picked up her phone, tuning me out, so I followed Sonya to the front, seeing Rafael looking at shampoo. His hair was gorgeous, and I wanted to ask who cut it. *Maybe I could entice his stylist away from their job?* I could use someone with that much precision at the shop.

"Hi, I'm Shay Barr," I introduced as he turned and looked at me, offering a quick smile.

"God, he's too damn lucky. I'm Rafael Bianco *Torrente*. Can we speak in private?" he asked quietly.

I nodded and led him to the kitchen where Chase was painting his nails. He was blowing his fingers while he was reading a magazine he found in the waiting area. I'd tried to get him to pick a book from Mateo's bookshelf, but he'd waved it off… not surprisingly. At least he was occupied and keeping himself out of trouble.

"Chase, this is Mateo's brother, Chef Rafael Bianco," I introduced as I closed the door to the kitchen area.

My cousin glanced up and smiled brightly. "I've heard of you. I saw an article on the internet that included one of your recipes for some great meatballs. I don't remember what they were called in Italian… pol-something," Chase began before Rafe smiled at him.

"*Polpette*? They're the meatballs my Nonna taught me to make when I was a little boy. Did you like them?" Rafe asked. I had no idea Chase even knew of the chef, but I shouldn't have been surprised. He was an extraordinary kid… nearly a man.

"They're incredible. I had a hard time finding fresh basil, and when I tried to talk my mom into letting me plant it in the yard, she called it a weed. I used the dry stuff to make the meatballs, but they were still really good, so I can only guess they'd be better if I had fresh herbs. Well, my father said they were fat hamburgers, but he ate them," Chase told the two of us.

Rafael chuckled. "A compliment I'll gladly accept. You guys should come to Blue Plate here in Brooklyn tonight, my treat. I'm taking the night off from Mangia, so I'd like to take you out. We can get to know each other," he suggested, and my inner cheerleader did a cartwheel.

"I, uh, I'll have to check with Mateo to see if we're free. Are you working at Blue Plate instead of Parker?" I asked as I grabbed three bottles of sparkling water from the fridge, handing one to Chase and one to Rafael before I sat down, pointing to an empty chair next to Chase.

Rafael sat down and opened the water. He held it up to his mouth, and I suddenly remembered I was a horrible host. "Wait, would you prefer a glass?" I asked as I started to hop up to grab one from the cabinet.

The handsome chef chuckled. "It comes in a glass, Shay," he offered with a wink. If I didn't know better, I'd swear he was flirting, and it kind of made me shiver, but I needed to shut him down.

"I'm sort of dating your brother, though we haven't exactly defined what that means," I explained to him. I didn't want to assume Mateo and I were something we weren't, but he'd told me he loved me, and he'd seemed sincere at the time. It wasn't my place to tell his brother about Mateo's lovelife.

Rafael chuckled. "Haven't you ever heard of brotherly competition? You're a hot guy, and my brother's not very good in the romance department, so how about you give me a shot?"

I laughed, maybe a little *too* high? "You're not gay, Mr. Bianco," I suggested, feeling my lashes flutter without my control, really. *You're a whore for a handsome flirt.*

Chase started laughing hysterically as he watched us. "This is cute, but seriously, he's been photographed with tons of chicks. He's just testing you, and honestly, Shane? You're not coming off as a loyal boyfriend in this whole scenario."

I turned to my cousin and saw the signature "Barr" scowl on his face just as I'd seen on Dani's for years. I chuckled at him, seeing he had a point. "Yes, I see your point." I turned to Rafael. "I see the Torrente family is full of flirts, but I've picked out the one I want. Anyway, you're not gay, so it's not an issue, is it?"

I glanced at Rafael to see him smirk. "Well, I'm not exactly straight, but I get your point. So, can I take the two of you to dinner tonight? I'm not cooking there. My executive chef has the place well in hand," he requested with a genuine smile.

Before I could answer, Chase giggled. "We'd love to." I could only shake my head. That kid was just like me in more ways than I could ever imagine, and none of them would be good for him, I was sure.

"Have a great week, Edward," I called after my last customer of the day, Edward Bower. He owned a large real estate company in Brooklyn, but his face was on the side of buses throughout the five boroughs. It was my responsibility to ensure his hair looked as perfect as I could make it, and I damn well made it look beyond perfection.

"Thank you, Shay. I'm holding an open house for a beautiful building in Williamsburg that would be perfect for you if you decide to expand," he pitched. Edward was always trying to get me to move my shop from the building I shared with Maxi Partee. Maxi was my dear friend, and he was a good landlord, so as long as he owned the building, I was staying put.

"I'm great here, but that's good to know. Feel free to leave some flyers on the counter," I told Edward as I cleaned up my station while he went to pay. I was sure Sonya would toss the flyers without me saying a word. My girl knew me like a split personality.

After I had everything swept and my station ready for the next day, I took my combs, brushes, and scissors to the back to sterilize. Chase was sitting at the table, looking at my laptop. I'd loaned it to him so he could do his classes online until we could figure out what to do about his school situation.

Chase's birthday wasn't until November, so technically, he was a runaway. I hated the idea of that because that meant his parents could get the authorities involved if they so desired. I prayed they'd let it go because they definitely didn't love that sweet kid like they should.

"You about ready to leave? We need to get back to Mateo's place to change. I'd like us to go over to my place tomorrow to see if anyone in the family has been snooping around. Have you seen anything on your social media that leads you to believe anyone's looking for you?" I asked as I tossed a load of towels into the dryer to run overnight.

"I haven't checked my social media because I don't want anyone to know where I am, so I'm staying off everything for right now," he told me, leaving me speechless. I figured he'd be the type of kid to be tied to his social media pages, but there he was showing mature restraint. *Who knew?*

Just as I was about to lock the door for the evening after all of the staff had left, I saw Parker's fiancé walking from a large pickup truck parked in front of the place. He glanced up and saw me in the window, smiling and waving before he entered the building. I heard him on the stairs, and I was nervous about why he was there. I didn't know the man very well at all, though he was really good looking. I prayed he wasn't there to give me bad news about Mateo.

When he opened the door to the salon, he had a worried look on his face. "Hi, Mr. Colson. What can I do for you? You need a trim, or are you here with bad news?" I asked, relieved to see the blush and slow smile on his face as he looked at me.

He dipped his head a bit before he laughed. "I should come by and see what you can do with this mess, but I'm here for more of a social call. Rafe called and asked me to pick y'all up. I'll take you to Mateo's place to change, and then we're all having dinner at Blue Plate. Rafe and Parker were having a meeting this afternoon, and since Mateo was unexpectedly called out of town, Rafe asked if I'd pick you guys up. You ready to go?" Shepard asked.

We both heard loud noises from the kitchenette at the same time, which brought a gun from under Shepard Colson's jacket-covered shoulder that honestly scared the fuck out of me. "Stay here. Whose back there?" he asked quietly.

"My cousin, Chase," I whispered. There was a back entrance to the shop, and the door was supposed to be locked. All of the staff had left for the day, so if there was someone in the kitchen, I was sure it was a member of my blood relations who were there to take the kid. "Shoot them if they're hurting him," I whispered to Shepard.

He pushed me to hide behind the reception desk and slowly made his way to the kitchen door, kicking it open with his gun drawn. I heard a loud, high-pitched scream, so I made myself as small as possible.

After a minute, Shepard came out of the back, laughing hard. "Shay, it's okay. Come out," he told me. I hated that my first reflex was to hide because that wasn't very manly, but I knew what the members of my family were capable of doing, and I wasn't about to sign up for that shit again anytime soon.

I crawled from under the reception desk, trying like hell to salvage my dignity as I brushed off my black jeans and looked at the huge man sporting a tender smile. "Everything okay?" I asked, noting I hadn't heard a gunshot.

"Yeah. Come talk to the little hottie in the kitchen. I think I scared the piss out of him," Shep suggested as he placed that huge gun back under his shoulder before he ushered me into the kitchen.

Chase was under the kitchen table with my laptop in his hand as if he was about to use it as a shield. I could see Shep trying not to laugh. "Come out, Chase. This is a friend of mine. His boyfriend is the chef at the place Rafael invited us for dinner. It's okay," I told the poor kid as I knelt down to address him as he still shuddered under the small table.

"He's not going to kill me?" Chase whispered loudly.

I turned to see Shep "Smokey" Colson squat down and offer his hand. "I'm so sorry, cutie. Let me help ya up."

I watched as my cousin took in the handsome man for a few seconds before he took the man's hand and allowed Shep to pull him out and help him to his feet. I saw the look on Chase's face, and I had to stop him. He was adorable, but Parker was one of my dear friends, and he and the bodyguard were planning a wedding in the spring. Hell, I'd already been enlisted to do hair and makeup.

Of course, my cousin's flirtatious nature took over, his big personality eager to make an appearance. "Aren't you just stunning? It's a *pleasure* to meet *you*," Chase offered with a wink.

"Hang on, Chase. This is my friend's *fiancé*, as in, he's taken. Shepard Colson, this is my cousin, Chase Barr. He's, uh, he's…" I trailed off, trying to figure out how to explain Chase without hurting his feelings.

Shepard laughed me off and turned to Chase. "Sweetheart, if you were about ten years older and I wasn't engaged to the man who captured my heart forever, I'd definitely be happy to take you out on the town. Maybe we'll have the privilege of meeting again in another life? Let's go to Mateo's, shall we?" Shep deflected his advances in the politest way I'd ever heard.

"Shame for me, but I'm looking forward to meeting Mr. Howzer. Mr. Bianco told me he's an incredible chef, and I'm a total foodie. I'd love to be an undercover food critic," Chase explained, which surprised the hell out of me. I had no idea that was the boy's ambition, but I'd do anything I could to help him… if I was given a chance.

We had to go by my place so I could grab some things for Chase and me to wear and sustain us at Mateo's apartment. Mixer was still there, and he'd grown to think of it as his domain. I wasn't sure what we'd do when Mateo returned, but when I tried to convince Shepard to allow us to stay at my place, he wouldn't hear of it. Mateo was gone, as in *gone* without a word for me, which had totally pissed me off because the man hadn't even sent a fucking text to tell me.

Rafael had sort of explained it to me earlier in the day, but he'd asked that I reserve my anger until Mateo was back in New York, and then he asked if I'd call him to come over so he could witness the punishment I'd levy on his brother. I didn't explain to him it was honestly the other way around with us, Mateo wielding his heavy hand on my ass, but I knew he only did it because I told him it was what I needed. That realization eased my anger considerably.

"So, maybe it's just better if Chase and I stay at my place since Mateo is gone. I can get my cat and the rest of my things out of his apartment, and we'll be fine. I'm not sure I feel comfortable staying there with him gone, and since he didn't tell me he was leaving, maybe we're not as serious as I thought," I mumbled, thinking about everything that had happened since I'd actually met Mateo.

Shepard quickly disagreed with me. "Mateo wants you at his place. The building has a first-rate security system because Gabby owns it, and the kids are there sometimes with Mrs. Henry. Gabby, nor Mateo, wants to leave anything to chance when it comes to safety. I gave Mateo my word you'd be there. I think Rafe is going to spend the night at the apartment as well," the cowboy enlightened. Of course, based on his tone of voice, I wasn't really given a choice.

I nodded in concession and headed to my closet to pack more clothes. Poor Chase had absolutely nothing with him, really, so he was stuck wearing my things, but they fit him quite nicely. The kid was definitely going to be a force once he hit eighteen. Keeping him out of trouble until then was going to be a full-time job, and I guessed it was mine.

We arrived at Mateo's apartment about thirty minutes later. I knew it used to be Dexter's because I'd met him right after those awful people had tried to kidnap the kids. I knew Dex and Gabe had bought the building and refurbished all of the apartments, so I was assuming it was the family connection that had Mateo living in his cousins' old place. He was as devoted to his family as much as I *wasn't* to mine… well, except for Dani and Chase. Those two, I'd do anything to protect.

"Okay, uh, pick something from the clothes I brought over and go shower because Shep's waiting for us. We need to be ready in about thirty minutes, so don't be a diva," I instructed Chase. Shep was in the living room watching some sports show and having a beer. I didn't want the man to have to wait for us too long, and I had a feeling Chase could take forever to get ready.

"Ick. Seriously? Whatever possessed you?" Chase hissed as he berated the clothes I'd offered him.

"Hey, Pee Wee Hormone! Look at what you're wearing and then what I'm offering. You have something better? By all means, don't lower yourself to *borrow* anything from me. We're only going to a four-star restaurant as guests of the chef," I reminded the ornery little shit.

I held up a teal-blue shirt in front of him and glanced up to see it made his eyes pop… his crying eyes. "What's wrong, Chase?" I asked as I tossed the shirt on the bed and took his hand. He'd been through hell, and I wondered when he was going to crack. Looked as if it was time.

"I've missed you so much, Shay…that's what *they* call you, your friends? I love it, by the way. I'm really not trying to be a pain in the ass. I want to impress you, and I'm not sure how," he confessed as he sniffled before wiping his eyes with his fingertips.

I wrapped him in my arms, seeing we were the same size. He wasn't done growing, and I envied him because he would be tall with long legs, a gorgeous face, and a tight body. He'd have all the boys in the yard with that milkshake, no doubt. That thought actually had me a bit worried as I remembered my own history at that age.

"You don't need to impress me, Chase. You're a beautiful person, inside and out. As long as you remember the inside's the most important part, I'll be impressed. Now, let's get ready for what I'm sure will be a delicious dinner and some really nice company," I told him.

He smiled brightly before he picked up the shirt I'd offered and grabbed a pair of black slacks from the stack I'd brought. He winked before he sashayed out of the room, and I knew the kid would be a force when he finally came into his own… that was if my family didn't get to him and wreck him as they'd almost wrecked me. That would be a travesty, in my opinion.

We were shown to the Chef's Table in the kitchen of Blue Plate where we were met with people I actually knew, including Maxi, my best friend. He didn't look happy with me at all. "Hi, everyone. This is my cousin, Chase Barr. Chase this is…"

"Introduce yourselves. We'll be back in a minute," Maxi snapped before he grabbed me by the arm and dragged me to the hallway by the restrooms. I should have known I wouldn't get by with anything. He'd been busy with weddings, so I hadn't exactly been able to clue him in regarding what was going on in my world, but clearly, my time was up.

"I was going to call you," I began before Maxi opened the door to a storage closet across from the ladies' room. I had to wonder if Parker and Shep got busy in there as Maxi pulled the string to turn on the overhead light, illuminating boxes of carryout containers.

Snap...snap. "I have to hear about you traipsing off to Arkansas to do battle with your family from my *fiancé*? We are *closer* than this, Shay," Maxi chastised. He was right, but he'd been very busy. It wasn't as if I hadn't returned calls. There hadn't been any calls.

"We are, *Maxim*, but we are both busy. You've got your business and Lawry, and I've got my own issues. Let's meet for coffee in the morning so I can explain what's been going on, okay? Mateo's out of..." I began, seeing his eyes light up.

"You and Mateo Torrente are *something*?" he asked. We were, but I didn't know what, so I shrugged my shoulders.

"Right now, I'm just trying to keep my family of religious fanatics from taking Chase back to Arkansas and damaging that sweet kid out there simply because he's gay. That's what they were going to do to him, Maxi. They run their own conversion camp thingy, and they were dead set on torturing the queer out of him. I was lucky to get him out of there when I could. He's hiding with me right now," I explained, finally realizing we were rude by keeping the others waiting to order.

The door swung open, and Lawry Schatz, Maxi's fiancé, came into the closet with us. "Just so you know, I got the short straw out there. What's going on, gentlemen? We'd like to order food and drinks, but you're holding us up, and I'm fucking starved," Lawry stated before he pulled Maxi into his arms and kissed his lips, dipping him a little. When Maxi was standing upright again, his face was flushed, and he giggled, which made me laugh as well.

"I'm just reminding my best friend that I'm available to talk to him in the event he needs me, even if I'm busy. His family is horrible, babe, and I just want to remind him we have extra rooms at the brownstone if he needs to hide," Maxi told me with that wicked eyebrow. I snickered as I nodded in understanding. It was incredible to have people who would walk through fire with, and for, me. It was new, but it was more than welcomed.

13

MATEO

I walked onto the terrace of the villa the entire family shared. My mother and father were sitting under the shade of a large olive tree, having their evening wine before dinner. I took one last breath because what I had to say wouldn't go over well, I was sure.

"*Mama, Papa, it's good to see you both,*" I offered in my native tongue. Tommy had opted not to stay, which was probably for the best, the lucky bastard. What I wanted to talk about was better kept contained.

"*I got your message, Mateo, and I didn't like the tone of it. You should know better than to threaten me,*" my father barked, spitting out the words like bitter wine. My mother looked totally unaffected by his tone, but that was nothing new.

I'd seen my sister sitting in the garden with her paints when I arrived, so it was a typical Torrente event that nobody really cared about anyone else's life as long as it didn't interfere with their own. The only exception was Rafael wasn't present to make wisecracks as was his usual contribution. Papa would scold him, but it was in jest. Rafe was his favorite.

I couldn't hold the chuckle at my father's attempt at putting me in my place. I sat down and looked at him without breaking at his alpha posturing. "*And you shouldn't lie to us, Papa. I found this,*" I challenged as

I handed him the folder Casper had given me with the printout of the old birth certificate that was probably an original long-since having been doctored by someone in the family. There were also the court papers that had used the birth certificate as an exhibit, giving me a clear view of what had taken place. I was anxious to see how my father explained it away—or attempted to.

I watched as Giuseppe Torrente took the folder and opened it while my mother poured me a glass of wine. *"We've missed you, Mateo,"* she whispered, not looking at what my father seemed to be studying without much emotion. At first. Then, he exploded, just as I was betting he'd do.

The litany of curse words brought my sister running from her spot in the lush garden, which was in the end-of-summer bloom. *"Oh, Teo,"* she smiled as she hugged me.

"Hi, Allegra, my love. How are you?" I asked switching to English as I kept a close eye on my parents.

Teresa, my mother, stood and offered a cool look at me. "Allegra, darling, let's go change for dinner. Mateo's staying," Mama told my sister before the two of them went into the villa, leaving me with my father who was staring out on the vineyard, Uncle Luigi's pride and joy.

"What do you want to know?" my papa asked in English, sounding just about as overwhelmed as I'd ever heard in my life.

"Why weren't we told?" I asked, sipping the incredible red table wine from the previous year's harvest. It was a blend, which I loved as much as Papa. We were alike in many ways, but we were different in one way—I didn't keep secrets from him. I could see he'd kept a big one from me and likely many other people in our family.

My father sighed and gulped the rest of his glass, tossing the empty crystal into the firepit to shatter. The mood wasn't promising, but it was time for him to enlighten me. I hadn't exactly expected him to be happy about what I'd uncovered, but the destruction was a shock. I knew the glasses were from my grandparents' wedding set, so I was surprised he'd broken one.

"Luigi, Tomas, nor I knew how to tell any of you, Mateo. Hell, we've stewed over this for years. Accepting the fact Lorenzo, our father who we looked up to more than anyone, wasn't faithful to our mother? It was unthinkable," my father began.

"Frankie was one of our best friends growing up, and to find out we shared a father with him broke our hearts and shattered our friendship. As boys, Frankie and I were closer than I was with Tomas or Luigi because we are the same age which meant Papa had fathered us at the same time. It was an unimaginable turn of events.

"Papa and Carlos Mangello had been the very best of friends since they both took Catechism, so it made sense I would become best friends with Carlos' only biological son, Francesco, when we were boys. We all grew up around here, and we had a wonderful life, or so I believed until everything went to hell." I could see a million emotions race across my father's face. It was the most conflicted I believed I'd ever seen him in my life.

"Back then, Frankie's mother, Alexa, turned up pregnant around the same time as Mama. Carlos touted it as a miracle provided by the Blessed Mother because he'd been told he was sterile after an injury in WWII where he lost a gonad. The Mangello's never believed they'd have biological children, so they adopted a war orphan, Pietro, Frankie's older brother who lives in Venice. When Alexa told Carlos she was pregnant, they were very happy.

"Of course, everyone in the village celebrated it as a miracle, though I'm sure they talked amongst themselves about the resemblance between myself and Francesco. Mama, however, figured out the boy was my father's bastard son right away. Francesco's christening was the last time Mama spoke to Alexa, or so she told me before she died. My parents never slept in the same room again, but Mama wouldn't shame the family by saying anything against my father, but the two of them lived separate lives, together," Papa continued.

"Wait, you lived in the same village and you looked just like your best friend, but nobody put it together that you shared a father? Carlos never put it together that Frankie wasn't his?" I knew the disbelief in my voice was clear. Did they live with their heads up their asses?

My father scoffed. "Carlos was dumber than everyone figured him to be, or he didn't want to accept Frankie was Papa's son for so many years until he could no longer deny it. Carlos threw Frankie out of the house when he was eighteen, but Frankie didn't know why until his mother, Alexa, died." Papa looked sad as he said it. I couldn't fathom why.

"Frankie had had to learn to make his own way in the world after that, so he fell in with a bad crowd, going to work for a boxing *allibratore*…uh, bookmaker. Frankie would ride his bike all over the village collecting the money from Mr. Collette's soldiers to return with cash after the matches sponsored by the man. Frankie made his way up the ranks until he became a soldier for Nicola Collette, and then he branched out on his own after he killed Nicola Collette and his sons, taking over the family business.

"Carlos eventually drank himself to death, and when Alexa passed, Frankie was given a letter of explanation and his original birth certificate with my papa's name listed as his father, which only fueled Frankie's hatred for our family.

"When Lorenzo died, Frankie wanted his share of what Papa left us, claiming his birthright and an equal cut of the vineyard and the family assets. Of course, we fought him and convinced the courts he'd made it all up, so they dismissed his claims. It only added gasoline to an already roaring flame of hatred, and he's been seeking his revenge on our family since it all came about. I'm just glad Mama died before Papa, so she never had to live with the shame of it all," Papa concluded.

I sat there gazing over the vineyards along with my father. The idea that Frankie Man had been cut out of his share of the Torrente holdings was definitely a reason for the man to hate us with such passion.

Papa turned to me and shook his head, extending his hands to me in pleading fashion. "I realize Gabriele wants him dead because he believes Frankie to be a threat to his family, but the man's my brother.

He was very hurt because my father would never acknowledge him as his son, and I can only imagine how that must feel. His hatred has grown and now it rules his life, and he's seeking his retribution for many, many years of inequity, I'm sure.

"Now, here we are with another connection that makes us vulnerable to his *rabbia*. Gabriele's son and daughter are actually related to him nearly as much as they are to Dexter. It's a cruel twist of fate, but I believe its destiny. Our families are destined to have this fight one way or another," Papa reasoned.

"It's un-fucking-believable is what it is," I mumbled, unable to come up with anything else that made sense.

"I also cannot forget or forgive the fact that Giancarlo is the boy who gave my baby girl the drugs that harmed her. That was why he had to die. Family is family, but some things cannot be tolerated," my father explained as if he was telling a story that had no relevance to our lives. *It means everything to our family, goddammit!* I was stunned, but what the hell else could I be? We were related to the Mangello family? Frankie Man was my father's half-brother? I never saw it coming.

I drank my wine and refilled my glass because I had another thing to report. "Does Salvatore know of the connection he has to our family? Do you think Frankie knows we killed Giancarlo and Dino?"

"Not for sure because if he did, he'd have already made it known. I also don't think he knows Dylan and Searcy are his grandchildren…*yet*. Dino was ambitious and wanted to take over the family from Frankie, and it pissed off the old man such that they didn't speak often. I'm sure if we hadn't taken out Dino, Frankie would have done it himself after that cocaine went missing," Papa decided.

"I believe as far as Frankie knows, Dino's only child was stillborn, which was what Dino told the family back then. I don't believe Dexter's sister ever told Frankie about the fact she'd been the surrogate and had given birth to Dylan, who is alive and well. I also don't believe they'd mentioned anything about little Searcy in the mix when Frankie and Giancarlo took Imogen to Utah and held her captive while they tried to get the truth from those two dead men she knew from that cocaine deal.

"Never forget, Mateo, dead men tell no tales. The fact Frankie wasn't able to be linked to the cocaine Dexter found in Staten Island might have saved us all at the time, but the retaliation is coming, make no mistake," my father determined, not without reason.

Man, I have a doozy for you, Papa. "Have you ever heard of Marco Rialto?" I asked.

"That's Sally Man's alias," we both heard behind us. I turned to see Lotta standing on the terrace with a big smile. I stood to hug her because I'd missed having her and her sense of humor around. She was a dear, dear friend, and she'd saved my ass more times than I could even count.

When we were on the job, Rafe or me, Lotta was our only contact. We went dark before and after, and she kept us connected in the event anything went off the rails. I couldn't begin to guess the number of times she'd prevented us from ending up in a gutter somewhere. I loved her as much as I loved Allegra.

I hugged her and helped her take a seat, pouring her a glass of wine. We all toasted, and I turned to her. "How do you know that? Casper wasn't able to find anything on him, anywhere. You have proof?" I pressed her.

Lotta placed her glass on the table and leaned closer to Papa and me. "Don't get me wrong. Gabriele's organization is good for its purpose, but by proclamation of the Prince, they don't go dark. Gabe doesn't want to point any of the American authorities their way, so he keeps Lawry on a short leash… well, mostly," she commented. It was uncharacteristically bold of her to say it, and that bothered me a bit. When she spoke of Gabe, there wasn't kindness in her tone as there was when she spoke of others. That had me curious.

After another sip of her wine, Lotta looked at the evening sky for a moment before she spoke. "I respect them because they're able to do their jobs quite well without any of the extreme measures we have to employ on occasion, but let's face it, we do the things people need done but don't want to ask anyone to do. It provides a balance between good and evil, or so I tell myself when I put my head on my memory-foam pillow at night. Who does Gabriele call when they run into a problem that needs to be terminated or a mess that needs to be cleaned up? He calls us."

I gave it some thought, and I knew she was right, but the way she said it sounded a bit venomous. Gabby had been a soldier in the American military, which was far different than what I did in the *Carabinieri*, and it was what allowed him to sleep peacefully at night, I was sure.

Our organization was comprised of operatives who would make the kill. Gabe's was comprised of men who did their best to avoid it. It was an equilibrium I finally understood, and I suddenly realized how thin that line was Rafe and I walked between the organizations.

"Yes, well, it seems that Lucia, Zio Tomas' oldest daughter, has been keeping company with Marco Rialto, who is really Sally Man. If they're related, that shit needs to stop immediately. I only talked to Rafe about it because Gabriele will lose his mind when I tell him, so I'm not in any rush to stir the pot." That was a fucking understatement, I was sure.

"What should we do about it? Sally's cell phone is pinging in San Francisco, which is where I'm heading after I leave here tomorrow. Are we still on target to remove the problem?" I asked. People always said the truth was stranger than fiction. The shit I was facing was stranger than science fiction, to be sure.

"*La cena!*" My mother was calling us to dinner from the balcony over the terrace, and she refused to tolerate lollygagging.

"Let's meet in the morning before you leave, Mateo. I need to consider this unexpected turn," my father offered as he left Lotta and me.

I turned to look at her, offering a smirk. "What else do you know, *Bella Carlotta*?" I joked as I took her hand and looped it into the crook of my arm, the two of us heading into the house with our wine glasses in tow.

"I'm looking into something I'm not ready to discuss yet. I'm pointing no fingers until I have my ducks in a row, but if I'm right, things are worse than I suspected," Lotta stated before we walked into the formal dining room. She'd left me with more questions than answers, but it was her way. That was why she was one of the best.

The trip home was turning into a lot more than I bargained for, but it was family business I needed to know. I'd handle it, now that I had the truth, but I wouldn't lie and say I wasn't shocked about the whole thing. I almost couldn't wait to give Rafe the details because I knew he'd be blown away as well. As for who would tell Gabriele? *Not it!*

After dinner, Lotta retired to one of the rooms on the other side of the villa which were Tomas and Graciela's rooms when they were in Siena, likely taking Gabe's room, which she seemed to favor. I was still stewing over learning the news that Frankie Man was my father's half-brother. Dino, Giancarlo, and Salvatore were our cousins, and we'd already killed two of them... well, St. Michael had killed Dino and Rafe had hit Giancarlo, but they were family, and they were dead at our hands. It seemed very wrong, considering I'd never lift a hand against Gabriele, his sisters, or Tommy. We were all cousins, and I loved them like brothers and sisters... although Gabby's sisters drove me up a fucking wall when they were all around.

I went to my father's den and found a bottle of grappa and a glass before I went back to my room and out onto the balcony where I spent most of my time when I was in Siena, taking a seat on the bamboo lounger with my phone. Lotta had offered to get me a flight to San Francisco the next day so I could see what the hell was going on with Sally Man. She was planning to trace Sierra's cell phone to see where she was on the West Coast and if it was relevant to the things we were learning about the familial connection. I told her I'd handle it, but she insisted, so I finally relented.

I retrieved my cell from my pocket to call Shay. It was two in the morning in Siena, so it was only eight in the evening in New York. I needed to hear his voice and make sure he was okay, plus I owed him an apology.

"Hi, Mateo," I heard a voice answer after a couple of rings.

"Shay?" I asked.

I heard a giggle, but not Shay's. "No, it's Chase. Shay's talking to Maxim and Parker. We're just finishing up a really nice dinner. Where are you?" Shay's cousin inquired. I liked the kid, which had me even more concerned about his and Shay's safety.

"I'm at my family's home in Siena. Is my brother there? Who's with you guys?" I asked, worried about where they were and who was along to protect them.

"Hang on," I heard Chase say.

"Hello?" I heard from a familiar voice.

"Smokey? What the hell is going on?" I asked, puzzled as to why he was with them.

The background noise went quiet, leaving to think he'd walked away from the crowd. "Mateo, Shay's family is fucked up, man. Casper's been looking into some shit, and when he told Gabby, it became one of those all-hands deals, but we got it, so don't worry. You okay, man?" Smokey asked.

I felt a hell of a lot better learning that my cousin was finally taking something serious outside his own orbit. "Yeah, I'm fine. Shay and Chase are okay? Is Mathis in touch with his friend in Memphis? Is Dani safe?" I asked.

"I'll have Mathis reach out to you when he has a minute, but I know the kid talked to his sister earlier, and she was fine. Any leads on Frankie or Sally?" Smokey asked quietly.

"Yeah. Frankie's in Venice with Pietro. Sally's still in the wind, but I've got a lead on him. Is someone, maybe St. Michael, available for a few days? I don't want to ask Giuseppe for backup. I'd like to keep him out of this," I requested, knowing London St. Michael had no qualms about taking down a member of the Mangello family, unlike others in my father's organization if they learned the truth that Frankie was Papa's half-brother. People got weird when taking out family members was involved.

Besides, the Mangello's had fucked up St. Michael's grand exit from the DEA when that coke wasn't able to be linked back to Frankie Man, who walked away without so much as a slap on the wrist, much less a fucking drug charge.

"I'll mention it to Nemo and have Narc call you if it's a go," Smokey responded, making me laugh as I remembered the scowl on St. Michael's face when anyone called him the nickname. I was just glad our office didn't do that shit, though I knew Gabriele's employees had codenames for all of us. I just didn't want to know mine.

"Thanks, man. I appreciate it. Is Shay back yet? Is Rafe there?" I asked.

"Here's Shay, Mateo. Be safe, and bring us back some wine... oh, will you bring me back a couple bottles of that prosecco your uncle makes? Parker loves it," he requested. I promised I would, and then I heard the voice I needed.

"Hello, Killer." Shay's seductive tone resonated through the phone which had me hard in a nanosecond.

"Hey, don't let those assholes hear that nickname, or I'll get stuck with something stupid like Balls of Fire. Makes it sound like I have an STI, so I don't need that to catch on. How are you, *tesoro*? I'm sorry I didn't have time to call you before I left, but it was spur of the moment. You okay?" I asked him as I sipped my drink, determined to visit Uncle Luigi to bring home a case of Prosecco along with a few bottles of grappa to share with my man. It tasted like home... a home I was determined to bring Shay to as soon as some shit settled.

"Yeah, we're fine. Lawry says he's tracking my family, so hopefully, we'll have some notice if they come to New York or head to Memphis after Dani before they do anything stupid. I have something to discuss when you get back here. I mean, are you coming back anytime soon?" he asked, sounding quite unsure of our footing. I wanted to alleviate that worry immediately.

"I need to go see my Uncle Luigi tomorrow morning before I go to San Francisco for a thing. After that, I'll head back to New York. Hopefully, I won't be in San Francisco for more than a day or two. I'll text you when I'm on my way back to New York.

"Sorry I disappeared on you, but I have to deal with family business. I promise this won't be a regular occurrence, okay? I miss you too much, *tesoro*. Once this shit's settled, I'm looking to permanently move to the States," I offered, not convinced he was honest with his first *'we're fine.'*

I heard Shay clear his throat before he spoke. "I'm mad you left without even sending me a text about why you needed to go, but we can address that issue when you get back. I need to hang up because we're getting ready to leave. Take care of yourself, Killer. I guess I'll see you when you finally return to New York," Shay told me before I heard the buzzing of a disconnected line.

Of course, I was a dumbass for not calling to tell him I was going out of town for a few days and offering some sort of an explanation, but it was honestly something I wasn't used to doing… checking in with anyone. I was forty-two, and I'd never had a relationship where I had to seriously think about another person. Clearly, that shit had to change. A lot of things had to change. That was the last thought I had before I fell asleep on the balcony in the lounge chair.

When I finished the morning swim I always enjoyed while visiting Siena, I saw Allegra sitting on the terrace with her easel and paints, so I walked up to speak with her, watching her create what I thought would be a beautiful sunrise. My system was so fucked up since I hadn't slept well the previous night, but I still tried to talk with her, knowing she didn't understand much of what was really going on around her due to the brain damage she'd suffered at the hands of someone I had learned was a relative. Allegra still had her bright smile when she saw me, and I appreciated it.

What Giancarlo had done to her when he gave her the drugs that fried her brain? It was hell for our family, and it left Allegra much unlike the intelligent woman we knew and loved before that night. We'd never know if Giancarlo did it on purpose or if it was an accident, but as I watched her stare into the distance with a faint smile on her face as if she saw something I'd never understand, I wondered whether Allegra lived in a fantasy life we'd never experience together. I was sad she wouldn't get to have a husband, or a wife, or a family of her own. That was the cruelest cut of all.

I wanted to go back to New York and slice off a piece of that son-of-a-bitch if Rafe still had the remaining parts of the fucker in one of his freezers. I'd take it to Frankie Man, or *Uncle Frankie*, as I'd come to learn. I'd drop it at his feet before I put a round in his eye, hoping it fucking ricocheted around his skull and scrambled his goddamn brains as much as the drugs had scrambled my sister's. It was a debt I was more than happy... determined... to collect.

And that thought was one I'd need to discuss with Shay. Other than killing people or training people to kill people, I wasn't exactly sure I was fit to do anything else. My cover was as a salesman, but I was convinced all I ever sold was bullshit. I had no real profession... well, no real *legal* profession. Shay was doing much better at his life than me, and hell, I had a good twelve or thirteen years on him at least.

I could go all self-deprecating and say Shay Barr deserved someone better than me, and it would be true. However, I wasn't about to do anything of the sort because I loved him, and I knew he loved me. I wasn't stupid enough to let him get away from me because I couldn't imagine being without him, so we'd figure out our shit together. Hell, I'd be happy to sweep up around his salon for a job if he'd let me. I just needed to be with him.

My sister handed me the canvas, and when I focused on it, it wasn't what I expected. It wasn't a sunrise as I thought she was painting while she kept a close watch on me as I did laps in the pool. No, it seemed to be a wedding of some sort. Lights and candles were burning everywhere, and I was standing under a grapevine arch, looking toward the villa with a big smile on my face.

Allegra pointed to the other side of the canvas where a man was walking toward me with a smile on his face. That man... it was Shay, and I was breathless. She'd highlighted his smile and those amber eyes such that they shined like the sun. I was speechless for a moment.

I turned to her and smiled. "This, uh…" I started, unsure of what to say because I didn't think she'd ever seen him. Of course, I remembered my parents had brought her to the States for a party on Long Island a few years prior when Gabe adopted Dyl and Searcy. Maybe she saw him there? The painting I was staring at had a line of electricity racing up my spine, and the smile on my face could not be dimmed.

"You saw him?" I asked her as I pointed to Shay's bright smile. It was a bit distorted, but it was him, and he looked happy.

Suddenly, Allegra pointed me toward a painting on another easel I hadn't noticed. It was also Shay, and he was surrounded by dark figures. I had no idea which painting depicted my future, and it had my heart beating out of my chest.

Allegra kept pointing to the painting of Shay with the darkness around him, finally shrieking, *"Save him!"*

"I don't know what you…" I began before she started shrieking, which was far too common when she was upset.

I ran inside to find Mama because she was the only one who knew how to handle Allegra when she was that far gone into a meltdown. It broke my heart to witness it, but what she'd told me? That had rattled me to my core.

I jerked awake, breathing hard as I realized I was resting on sweat-soaked sheets. I felt my blood run cold as my heart pounded in my chest, not yet clear-headed enough to figure out what the fuck had happened.

I looked around my old room in Siena, seeing the sun was just coming up to shine through the open balcony doors, bringing me to the realization I was at the villa, and I'd had a horrible nightmare. I then remembered awakening in the middle of the night as I slept on the balcony and felt chilly. I stumbled into bed, stripping off at some point in time. It left me feeling unsettled and ready to get back home.

I wasn't one to believe in mystical bullshit, but I had the distinct feeling something bad was on the horizon, and it concerned the man I loved. I'd never had a nightmare of the sort, and I'd never been so scared shitless in my life than I was at the idea I might lose Shay to something like what I'd seen in that painting. Was it just too much grappa the previous night, or was the universe trying to tell me something?

I had no idea what any of it meant because I wasn't that fucking deep, but I knew how much I loved Shay, and the thought of losing him had me rattled. I needed to get back to New York because as much as I trusted Rafe and the others who worked for Gabe, I knew nobody would look out for Shay Barr like me.

14

SHAY

I was sweeping up the shop when my cell rang. Chase was actually downstairs helping Maxi with some last-minute Halloween decorations for a party for one of his clients, which was good because it kept Chase occupied and afforded me the time to do things at my own pace without Chase's constant complaints that I was slow as molasses. Keeping him busy was becoming a challenge, and I felt bad he didn't know any kids his age to hang out with, but it was too risky for him to really be out and about with anyone other than one of the burly men who worked for Gabe. We could take that chance.

I pulled my phone from my pocket to see it was Dexter, and I knew it was about the Halloween bash they were hosting. I hated to disappoint him, but I was sure it wasn't anything Chase would be interested in attending since it mostly catered to kids. I knew they'd have fun without us, but I still needed to be tactful about declining the invitation, so I didn't offend Dexter.

"Hi, Dex. How are you?" I answered, trying to sound like I didn't have a care in the world.

"Don't pull that crap with me, Shay Barr. I know you're not that happy. I talk to the same people who are watching out for you guys until Mateo gets back to New York. Please tell me you're coming over tomorrow night," he urged.

"What's going on?" I asked, worried about his tone of voice because Dexter was one of the happiest men I'd ever met. He was a walking Zen garden, which reminded me I hadn't taken one of his yoga classes in a while, and maybe I should talk to Chase about doing it with me. Maybe it would be something he'd enjoy, and we could both learn to relax a little?

"It's Searcy. She wants to be a unicorn, and she wants her face painted, which isn't anything I know how to do. I was hoping maybe you could come over early and help me out. I'm making a taco bar, and there will be plenty of drinks for all of us. Bring Chase with you. He can hang out here with Dom and hand out candy to keep the house from being egged," Dexter suggested.

My cousin, who was just getting his gay legs, and a sexy Torrente-related stud alone? That was a recipe for disaster if I ever saw one because Dom was drop-dead gorgeous and just a little too old for Chase, though I was sure my young cousin would disagree whole-heartedly.

"I'm sorry, Dex, but Chase has a big English assignment due, so we'll be staying in that night, but bring Searcy by the salon in the afternoon, and we'll fix her up. What about Dyl? What's he going to be?" I asked.

"Dylan wants to be Twisty the Clown from American Horror Story, and the costume scares the hell out of Searcy. Gabe found the damn thing on the internet and thinks it hysterical. I'm ready to ground them both because Gabe got Casper to download the damn show to his laptop, and he and Dyl snuck around and watched the whole season.

"Dylan's started scaring the hell out of all of us, and I've spent more time in Searcy's bed than my own. It's driving me fucking crazy, and I'm ready to pull out my hair. Anyway, I've missed you, Shay. You've been incommunicado for a while now," Dex informed me. It wasn't anything I didn't know.

"I miss hanging out with you guys, too, but Ari is doing great with your hair, right?" I confirmed. I'd requested Aristotle take over my Tuesday appointments temporarily, which pissed off Wren, another stylist at my shop. I didn't know why both of them were so wound up because there was definitely enough work to go around. Besides, when I came back, I'd take back my clients if it was their preference. I wanted to tell Wren if he wasn't so standoffish maybe he'd get his own book of regular clients instead of walk-ins, but I didn't want to upset him such that he quit. I needed him.

"Yeah, it looks fine, but I still miss you doing it. I'll be glad when we get back on schedule. I haven't seen Mateo in quite a while. Have you? Is he still mad at Gabe?" Dex asked. I knew about the fight in question, but I wasn't sure what to say because I didn't know what Dex knew about the reasons for the fight.

I sighed because I wanted to feel out Dex on a few things. If anyone would know what I was going through, I was sure it would be him. "I think the fight's a distant memory. I've only seen Mateo a few days here and a few days there. He's working on something that takes him to the West Coast a lot. San Francisco, mainly. That's where he is right now, as a matter of fact. How do you stand the absences?" I asked Dex as I loaded my tools into the tray to sterilize them, much like a doctor sterilized his instruments. *Okay, I'm overreacting...*

Dex hesitated. "Well, Gabe doesn't travel too much anymore, but when he does, he's not gone very long. What's Mateo working on?" Dex asked.

I was surprised he didn't know. "Some guy…uh, Marco Rialto in San Francisco. Isn't that where Gabe's sister still lives with her daughters?" I asked.

"Yeah, Lucia lives in Frisco. Who the hell is Marco Rialto?" Dex asked.

"I have no idea, but Mateo's been on his trail for a while now. Is Sierra back at work?" I asked, not having been to the Victorian lately.

"Yeah, why?" Dex asked, sounding very interested. Hell, I'd only overheard shit Mateo said to his friend, Lotta, in Italy. She was the computer genius for the Italian office, as Mateo had explained, and he often talked on speakerphone. My apartment was so small that Chase and I couldn't help but overhear him checking in with his office in Italy when he was in town and staying with us.

"I just heard Mateo telling his friend in Italy he believed there was something up with Sierra, but he wasn't mentioning it to Gabe yet. Mateo said something in Italian to Lotta about the last time they talked…uh?" I stalled, trying to remember what it was Mateo had said.

It finally came to me. "Oh, Mateo said, 'La donna è una fottuta traditrice!' and Lotta laughed at him and said he should calm down before he had a stroke. She said they couldn't say anything until they knew more, and Mateo was pissed when he got off the phone.

"I asked him what he meant because I don't speak Italian nearly as well as I speak Spanish, but he quickly changed the subject," I further explained, remembering him carrying me back to my bedroom and fucking me so supremely that I totally forgot about the conversation and anything else on my mind that night.

After that, Dex got off the phone, and the conversation hadn't come up again when he brought Searcy into the shop so we could do her up for Halloween… shimmer on her sweet face and temporary spray-on hair color which washed out easily. I'd tried it out on Chase before I used it for Searcy to be sure it would wash out, and Chase had laughed at me for not believing the instructions on the can.

That adorable, little girl looked so cute when she left my shop that afternoon with pastel rainbow hair and a headband Sonya had found in a shop. It had a silver, sparkly horn. Searcy was so happy with her look, she promised to share her candy with Chase and me since we couldn't go out trick-or-treating with them. I thought it was precious.

"Where's your *papi*?" Sonya teased as she stood in the doorway of my office while I was working on the schedule for the post-Thanksgiving weekend. There was a huge charity function at Spires Tower the Saturday after the holiday, and we were booked on Friday and Saturday morning to capacity for hair, makeup, manis/pedis, and various skin firming wraps.

Each of the departments would be buzzing, and nobody was getting the day off unless they died. We were opening early on Saturday morning—eight instead of ten—and I'd agreed to stay open until four that afternoon instead of two. I was closing the salon on Monday and Tuesday to give everyone a three-day weekend because they'd have earned it, for sure.

Paige, my makeup artist, had actually recruited Chase to assist her because she was back-to-back appointments on Saturday morning, and she'd been working with him to teach him how to apply the base coats… moisturizer, primer, foundation, and concealer so she could concentrate on the glitz and glamour… cheeks, eyes, and lips.

Paige caught me in the kitchen one morning and told me the kid had a knack, and he'd even learned to contour, which wasn't the easiest thing in the world as I'd come to learn. I'd watched Paige work with a bride to hammer out her wedding makeup, and I was truly surprised when she got done with the woman. The bride had a round face, though she was quite pretty. When Paige finished with her, she looked like she had just stepped off a runway with mile high cheekbones.

Paige was an artist in every sense of the word, and I was proud of Chase for taking things seriously since she'd taken the time to work with him. Chase had decided to go to cosmetology school after he finished high school, and it seemed as if he was quite invested.

Based on everything I'd witnessed with the kid, he was cut out for the business, and I'd told him if he did well with his studies and graduated high school with a decent GPA, I'd pay his tuition for cosmetology school, and he could work in the shop part-time. He really dug in after our discussion, and I was busting my buttons like a proud poppa at his progress.

"Mateo's in San Francisco for work, again. It's the holidays, so, of course, it's a wine salesman's busiest time of year," I explained to Sonya, seeing she didn't believe me at all. I couldn't blame her, really. I wasn't exactly selling that load of crap as wholeheartedly as I should.

I'd been so fucking mopey of late, and I knew Sonya was ready to hold an intervention because I wasn't giving up any details regarding what was going on between Mateo and me, but I missed the man and didn't know what was going to happen between us. Hell, I didn't want to talk about it because there were too many unknowns.

Whatever he was working on had him away more than home, but it was his job, so I couldn't really complain about it, could I? I made it my mission to enjoy him when he was in Brooklyn and deal with the rest of it when he was gone so I didn't come off as the clingy boyfriend.

Unfortunately, with his frequent trips out of town, I was left with a whole stable of handsome men watching me like a hawk... well, watching Chase and me. It was hard to shake them to even go to the bathroom, and while I loved Rafael Bianco's food and enjoyed Parker's company, I was tired of eating at Blue Plate. The food was divine, but sometimes a guy just wanted a grilled cheese or a bowl of cereal for dinner.

Dani was still in Memphis, though Mathis' friend, Jonah Wright, was back in New York at his job as one of NYPD's finest. Dani's parents had driven from Hot Springs to Memphis the previous week to check that Chase wasn't with her, or so she'd told me when we'd Skyped the previous night.

They didn't mention anything about the raid on the lake campsite, which led me to believe my mother hadn't yet spilled the beans regarding my involvement in the whole fiasco. I wasn't going to give false hope a place in my heart that maybe she'd had a change of hers and knew what my father and uncle had done to me when I was a kid was wrong. I didn't believe her to be strong enough to understand the difference.

My mother, Carol, had been sitting in that cabin with two girls who were bound to chairs while other boys were tied to bunks and my oaf of a brother was beating Chase and another kid with a willow switch. I didn't know why Mom hadn't told my father it was me who had orchestrated the raid to rescue those kids. She had to have a reason, and I was sure I'd find out what it was soon enough. I wasn't about to be caught unaware, but knowing my family? That was exactly what would happen.

I decided an attempt at a subject change was in order... from my love life to Sonya's. "You know what *Brown* can do for you, Sonya. Why don't you put Alonso out of his misery and go on a date with him? Hell, at the very least, meet him for a drink, will you? He looks so depressed when he comes in here," I taunted.

I'd been so busy with Chase that I barely kept up with anyone else. I was aware enough to know Maxi was busy finalizing plans for his engagement party to Lawry Schatz. We'd discussed whether he wanted to let his hair grow a bit and maybe change his highlights from the sunny blonde to a more golden blonde for the fall, but he hadn't made any decisions yet.

Their engagement party was the same day as the charity event... the Saturday after Thanksgiving. I knew I'd be late to their party because I would have a full day with the appointments for the Gala, but I wouldn't miss their celebration for anything.

The engagement party was being held at Blue Plate, which was convenient for all of us, and Maxi had assured me Rafe and Parker were working up a special menu for the event. I was thankful it wouldn't be the regular restaurant food I was becoming burned out on, even though the menu was delicious. I vowed I'd never tell another soul I was tired of it because it sounded horribly ungrateful of me.

The plan was for me to take Chase as my plus one to the engagement party because I couldn't count on Mateo to be back in town. I had my fingers crossed that the handsome man would find his way back to me, but I wasn't banking on it being in time for the party. It was a depressing turn of events, my quickly evaporating love life, complete with a vanishing boyfriend—if I could still even call him that.

Sonya flopped into a chair in front of me, catching my attention once again. "I went to brunch with Ari, Wren, Paige, and Ahn on Sunday, and I saw Mr. UPS, who was trying to get down on some slutty waitress. Attraction gone," Sonya recounted for me as she snapped her fingers, which made me laugh. I could see she was disappointed that he was a man whore, though she was too proud to admit it.

"Someday, your prince will come along, chica," I told her as I hit the print button for the schedule I'd worked out. I grabbed the document and handed it to her to double check to ensure I hadn't left anyone off the schedule as the front door rang, alerting us someone had come inside.

Sonya hurried out to the front desk as I waited for the second copy of the document to print so I could post it after Sonya signed off. My desk phone buzzed. "Yes, Mother Teresa?" I teased.

"*You have company,*" Sonya offered in a very sing-song voice, which made me laugh.

I hurried out, expecting to see one of my regulars with a colossal hair mishap, but I was pleasantly surprised to see Mateo standing there, brushing snow off his topcoat. I rushed him, happy he caught me when I jumped. "I've fucking missed you. Please tell me that you'll be home for the rest of the year," I whined as I hugged him. He pulled back and gently kissed me as he held me aloft in his arms.

The look on his face told me he wanted to lie and say yes, but I shook my head because he didn't need to lie. I wasn't a child. "I get it. I'm just glad to see you now," I told him as I kissed him again, this time deepening the kiss as I wrapped my legs around his body and held on like a koala, happy to be in his strong arms again.

The applause behind us brought me from my lust-induced fog, causing me to slowly slide down Mateo's body, feeling the heat in my cheeks as I glanced up at him. He had a cocky grin on his handsome face, which lit up my heart.

"Hello, all. It's great to see you as well," Mateo announced with a very royalesque wave and bow, which made everyone laugh before they went back to work.

It was close to the end of the day, so I led Mateo back to my office and took his coat, hanging it over my own on the brushed nickel coat rack in the corner. I pushed him to sit in my leather desk chair, and I plopped myself on his lap. "How long are you here?" I asked, afraid to use the word *home* in case he'd changed his mind and decided to go back to Italy.

Mateo gently wrapped his arms around my waist and pulled me closer, kissing the side of my neck. It felt so sublime, my dick hardened in record time under the pleather pants I'd chosen to wear that day. They were a tight fit and left nothing to the imagination, but they were also warm, and it was horribly cold outside for being about ten-days before Thanksgiving.

An early snowfall was coming down, and as I gazed out my office window, I wished we were back in my apartment snuggled under the blankets on my bed. It was definitely a fantasy I wanted to fulfill as soon as possible. Just looking into Mateo's sparkling brown eyes had me weak in the knees.

"These are far too sexy for you to wear without me around to appreciate them and protect you from predators. What do you have on under those?" Mateo teased as he bit my Adam's apple and smacked my left ass cheek before he gave it a squeeze. I couldn't hold the giggle, feeling joy sweep through my body all the way to my toes at having him back in New York.

"You'll have to wait until we get back to my place to find out, Mr. Torrente," I told him as I kissed his soft lips again. I was a silly slut for him, but I didn't care. With Chase's rescue and the subsequent care Mateo had taken with ensuring we were safe, I'd given up on questioning whether the lovely Italian man was right for me or not, and he'd been gone far too much of late. I needed some explanations, and maybe an end date to all the travel? It was making me crazy.

I stood and started to walk away to finish up for the day so I could take Mateo home and remind him he had someone waiting for him every night. He grabbed my arm and pulled me back onto his lap. "Not ready to let you go yet. How's it going here? I've talked to Mathis and St. Michael, who say there's no sign of your family anywhere, and Casper confirmed their cell phones are still pinging in Hot Springs," Mateo said. I would never know how to pay those guys back for all they'd done for us.

Mateo continued. "Mathis spoke with Jonah this morning, and he said he'd talked to Dani last night after the two of you had discussed the family. She mentioned her folks had come by but had only stayed overnight when they found out Chase wasn't with her. Why don't you invite her to New York for Thanksgiving? We can fly her up to keep her from having to make that long drive by herself. Dexter and Gabriele are hosting everyone for Thanksgiving dinner, and Mathis can bring Jonah so he can see Dani again."

I hadn't really thought about it, but it was a good idea. "I'll call her tonight," I replied.

"Rafe asked if we could help him on Wednesday night at the catering company. He's volunteered to cook for a homeless shelter, Our Shepherd's House, where Mathis' father is the pastor. I thought maybe we could help out for a few hours if you're up for it... if you and Chase are interested. The restaurants are closing at ten that night to allow everyone to pitch in.

"Reverend Nathaniel Sinclair, Mathis' father, said they feed about fifteen-hundred people at the place on Thanksgiving. He usually asks various organizations to donate food and help with the cooking, but this year, Rafe has volunteered himself and a group of cooks from his various restaurants to prepare the whole meal, and the church volunteers are helping serve the next day," Mateo explained, which touched my heart.

I was struck with an idea. "I could try to hit up some of my clients for donations to help with the costs, or at least make a monetary donation to Our Shepherd's House. They can afford to kick in a few bucks, and the holiday season is the best time to solicit donations. Does this mean you'll be in town? Maxi and Lawry's engagement party is that Saturday night. Will you be here to be my date?" I asked him, crossing my fingers behind his head in hopes I'll finally have a worthy plus one.

"*Sicuro, amore.* I'll be here to take you to the party. I'll need a trim, though," he teased, which made me laugh.

"I have a very special type of haircut in mind. You up for it?" I taunted back. I gave just as good as I got, and a naked haircut sounded like a lot of fun. I just had to figure out what to do with Chase because

I was sure the little horny toad wouldn't just do as I asked and stay in his room. Hell, when I was his age, they couldn't have boarded me in there if I thought there was a chance of seeing someone as hot as Mateo Torrente naked. God, my little cousin was far too much like me.

"Anything you want, Sweeney," Mateo offered before he kissed me stupid again. Ah, life was looking better every minute that passed in his arms.

I broke away and stood, kissing him again before rushing out to finish up for the day while Mateo made a few calls. After I had the shop closed up for the night, we stopped at Maxi's showroom to get Chase, who was happy as a clam with what he'd been doing that afternoon. We took him home, and we ordered Chinese while we listened to Chase regaling us with stories about the people who worked for Maxi and how he'd learned to make cornucopia centerpieces that afternoon with dried fruit and fresh flowers.

Chase wanted to volunteer to help Maxi's delivery people on Wednesday night until I explained to him about what we were going to do with Bianco Catering to help with Thanksgiving dinner at the shelter Mathis' father ran. His face lit up at the news like the Rockefeller Christmas tree.

After we were all full, Chase excused himself with my laptop to work on homework, making a big show of putting on my headphones and winking at us before he settled in the living room to work for a while. We hurried to my bedroom so the kid could make his bed on the couch, which reminded me how much we needed a bigger place to stay to give all of us privacy. My apartment was only a one bedroom, and my cousin deserved his space, as well, especially since he was going to be eighteen the week after Thanksgiving.

Mateo and I stripped each other in the bathroom to take a shower, me hurrying back to my room to grab condoms. I had another bottle of lube in my medicine cabinet because I liked to get off in the shower, and I didn't like to use soap when I fingered my ass. It would dry things out far too much, and that was painful.

Mateo broke away and looked into my eyes. "You told me we

needed to talk about something while I was in Siena and we were speaking on the phone. What's up?" he asked.

I wasn't sure how to address the situation but finally decided keeping my mouth shut about the living arrangements was stupid. "Would it be okay if Chase and I stay at your apartment for a while? When you decide to go back to Italy, I think I can afford the rent by myself, but I really need a two-bedroom, two-bathroom place, and my lease is up at the first of the year. Your place is two bedrooms and a den, so it's perfect for us if Chase stays with me," I explained, studying his features carefully to see any concern or fear at having Chase and I infringe on him.

Mateo grinned and leaned forward, nipping my lips as we stood outside the shower. "I've wanted you to move in all along, Shay. I'll gladly help you guys move your stuff. I'd be more than happy for you to move in with me... you and Chase, and hell, Dani can move in if she wants to come here to be closer to her brother," he offered, the handsome, generous man I loved.

It took a minute for the warm water to travel up the pipes to the bathroom, so I held my hand under the spray while Mateo ravaged my mouth and lubed up his fingers. They worked their way inside me just as the hot water spewed out of the showerhead. "Perfect timing," I told him as I removed his fingers from inside me and led him into the shower.

Mateo had a look of worry on his face for a moment because I hadn't asked him to punish me, but he suddenly smiled brightly. I knew he thought maybe I was over it, but I wasn't. At that moment, I was living out one of my fantasies when it came to him. The punishment could come after.

"Spank me later if I'm a bad boy," I teased as I slid a condom down his thick cock and slicked on a thin coating of lube. I wanted a little bit of the burn to set my mind free, and since we hadn't been together very much lately, he would definitely be able to provide what I craved.

I turned and braced my hands on the shower wall, smiling when I felt his cock rubbing against my eager hole. "You want slow or fast? I'm not going to jam it in if that's what you're thinking instead of the spanking, but it's because I'm selfish and want to do it again as soon as I can recover. I've fucking missed you and your gorgeous body, *tesoro*," he whispered as he slowly pushed inside me. There was pain, but it was quickly followed by the delicious burn I longed to feel.

Once Mateo was fully seated inside me, he nuzzled my ear and waited. "I love you, Shay. I'm so happy you'll move in with me," he whispered before he slowly withdrew and slid home again. It was inspirational.

One of the advantages of showering at eight in the evening was the hot water heater had all day to fill because Chase chose to shower in the morning. I washed and styled my hair at the shop in the morning, preferring to shower before bed, or better yet, a soak in the tub if possible. I'd have to plan that little party for Mateo and me when we moved into his place because he had a gorgeous, claw-foot tub in his master bath. There were many possibilities of things we could get up to in that tub threatening to distract me until the head of his cock began pegging my prostate. Oh, he had my attention then for sure.

Mateo whispered sweet things in my ear as he fucked me in the shower with my chest and cock pressed against the tile. I was about to come, and just as I told him, "I'm so close," he pulled out and spun me around. Before I could take a breath, Mateo picked me up and braced me against the wall, kissing me as he maneuvered me into position, his rod sliding back inside me without resistance. He held his position for a minute as he gently moved my hair out of my eyes.

"Tell me about the haircut you plan to give me," Mateo ordered as he started to fuck me, driving me out of my head in the best way as he held me in his strong arms.

"*Oh, God, Mateo*," I whispered, hoping Chase was still wearing the headphones. If not, Mateo's moans and groans would clearly let the kid know what we were doing, but I wouldn't stop the man for anything. I'd worry about what to tell Chase later.

"I'm not gonna last much longer, *tesoro*. Tell me," he pushed…*oh, yeah, he pushed*.

I was tempted to reach for my cock but decided it was safer to hold onto him because we were under the spray of the warm water against the slick wall of a shower without a rubber mat. "I'm going to trim the back first, then I'm going to strip both of us and sit on your cock while I trim the front. You'll want to stay very still so I don't fuck it up. I'm curious to see if I can finish the haircut before you lose control," I tormented.

Mateo stopped thrusting and kissed me hungrily. He pulled away and smirked. "Challenge accepted, Sweeney. Let's finish up. I've had a long day of travel, and I need to hold you in my arms before I wake you up again in a couple of hours for another round. I've missed you like *molto*," he whispered before his lips found mine and he began thrusting harder, tapping my p-spot quite handily with the thick head of his long prick.

I sealed my mouth over his, our tongues battling as I reeled in the wonderful friction his abs provided for my dick while Mateo held me tightly and took me to heaven. When I erupted between us, I felt him pulsing into the condom inside me. I wanted no barrier, but that was a discussion we needed to have between us before we ever went without. There was time, or so I hoped. I wanted a long time with Mateo Torrente. He had already moved into my heart and taken over. I wanted to feel him there for an eternity.

15

MATEO

I stared into the mirror in front of the treadmill I was standing on in the basement of the Victorian watching the activities around me. Ace Hampton had signed on to temporarily work for Gabe, at Papa's recommendation—after Casper found him and I suggested it, of course. Gabe told me he believed the guy was going to be a good fit and thanked Papa for sending Ace his way.

I saw Ace and Duke were spotting each other on the circuit as I started up the treadmill to warm up. They were laughing, and I wondered if they knew each other before Ace showed up at GEA-A.

I heard the barbell hit the iron stand over the bench and turned to see Ace stand up, pulling his long hair up into a rubber band as the sweat rolled down his body. Ace glanced up into the wall of mirrors, checking out Smokey, who was running next to me with earbuds in his ears. He was humming some of that country shit he loved, totally oblivious to the rest of us.

When Ace's eyes landed on my reflection, his face lit up with a huge grin as he walked over to me and laughed. He stood on the front of the treadmill and smacked me on the shoulder. "You mother fucker! I wondered when your surly ass would show up. Gabe told me you were on a job out of town when we talked about me helping you guys out for a while after your old man tracked me down. How the fuck you been, man?" Ace asked, seeming genuinely happy to see me.

I was pretty sure Gabe knew more about Ace's background than me because he'd have asked Casper to do a full background check before the two of them ever spoke. Based on what I'd witnessed in a bar fight or two when the man and I first met in London, Ace, (whose real name was Angel, though he hated it), wasn't afraid to fuck up someone with his fists before he was willing to go for a weapon. I could totally relate to that mindset back then, though I'd become more dependent on weapons that didn't cause me to fuck up my pretty face and hands.

I slowed the treadmill until it stopped, and I picked up the towel to dry my face before Ace pulled me in for a one-armed hug. "I'm great, man. I was on the West Coast for a thing, but I'm back for Thanksgiving, at least. You getting acclimated to the place? You're from the U.S., right?" I asked.

"Yeah, man. Grew up in Cali, but I haven't gone back since my mom died. After you and I hung out in London, I went to Brussels to train as a boxer. I wanted out of the *terminator* racket, so I thought I'd try something new, but boxing was too constricting for me because I still had the bloodlust. I finally looked into MMA fighting, and I found my home for a while," Ace explained. I took in his muscular physique and decided the man could definitely be a cage fighter.

Smokey stopped on the treadmill next to me and removed his earbuds, leaving them around his neck as he took in the sight of Ace. The guy was about Smokey's same height and build, though I was pretty sure he was younger than Smokey. Ace had a world-weary look about him, especially with the beard and long hair while Smokey still had that boy-next-door appearance.

"MMA, you say? What weight class did you fight in?" Smokey asked, not introducing himself. He appeared to be pretty interested, which made me worry a little.

"Light heavyweight. Ace Hampton, man. You're Shep Colson, right? Giuseppe told me Gabe had quite a collection of operatives, and he showed me pics of all you guys and explained your specialties.

Good to meet you, Demo-man," Ace offered as he held out his hand for Smokey to shake.

Smokey turned to me and smirked without acknowledging Ace at all. "I'm gonna guess this ain't the first time y'all met, is it? You met Mateo's boyfriend yet?" Smokey asked as he turned to look at Ace again, clearly putting me on the spot, the fucker.

Of course, Ace cracked up before looking at me. "Wait, you've decided to settle down? One guy, strings attached? Fuck no, I don't believe it," Ace challenged as I stepped off the treadmill, drying my sweat from the machine before I moved to the weights.

"Well, nothing's been set in stone, yet, but if I'm lucky," I replied.

"You wanna go a few rounds?" Ace asked. When I looked at him, I couldn't tell if he meant in the ring or in the sack, but I sensed I was in rough territory if Shay found out about the man's flirting. All the guys in the gym were looking at me, likely having overheard our discussion, and I knew all of them thought highly of Shay. I knew for sure those guys were just looking out for Shay. Honestly, I was happy to know they were so protective.

I was accepted into the group because of my familial association with Gabe and my father, but the majority of those men didn't really know me, or Rafe, for that matter. We hadn't earned their trust. I was pretty sure if I hurt Shay, they'd stand in line to kick my ass with the last guy having the privilege to put a cap in my dome.

Before I could say anything in response to Ace's request, London St. Michael approached Ace, smirk in place. "I'm your huckleberry," the former Narc offered with a slow drawl and a swagger I'd never seen on him. We all looked at each other because nobody knew what the fuck he meant by the comment, but it was clearly a challenge to Ace.

Smokey, our resident interpreter on Southern colloquialisms, stepped forward as if to narrate for the idiots amongst us. "It's a challenge. It's a quote from an old movie with Val Kilmer as Doc Holliday." He then bowed and gracefully exited the space between the men. I almost laughed at the shit I was witnessing. It was never fucking boring around those guys.

"Oh. Uh, well, sure. Style?" Ace asked Narc. I walked away before they began pounding on each other. They were both at least six or seven years younger than me, so let them beat each other to a bloody pulp. I was getting too old for that shit.

I walked over to Shep to spot him. "How the fuck did you know that?" I asked him as I held my hands about three inches beneath the bar he'd loaded with about two-bills of weight. It was effortless for him to pump it because his adrenaline was high, reflecting his anger as he'd observed the interaction between Ace and me that I should have quashed immediately but hadn't.

"It's from an old western movie. *Tombstone.*' My brother, Woody, loves the damn thing. Hell, he bought it on Blu-Ray, I think. Uh, Kurt Russell, Val Kilmer… don't remember the rest. You and Shay are still a thing, right?" Smokey asked, reminding me of my stupidity when Ace showed up unannounced.

"I think we've reached a new level in our relationship. Shay's agreed to move in with me, but until this shit with Sally Man is sorted, I'm worried about it. I don't want him to become a casualty of a stupid, unnecessary war," I confessed to Smokey. It was a worry all of us had, I was sure. Would someone use our significant other's to get to us?

The demo man did ten reps before he settled the bar on the cradle and sat up. "You *think* you're at a new level? Seems like somethin' you oughta be sure about before he moves in, don't it? Are you stayin' in the States? I don't remember hearin' anything from Giuseppe or Gabby about that," Shep pointed out, clearly not thrilled with me.

Guilt was a bitter bitch, and I was swamped with it. I definitely should have shut down the flirting and clarified with Ace that I had someone important in my life, but more than anything, I hated the accusatory tone in Smokey's voice, as if he expected me to cheat on Shay. I'd only ever been in one other committed relationship and it ended badly which had me hesitant to jump into another, but with Shay, I found I couldn't stop myself from doing just that. Still Smokey's interrogation pissed me off. "What's your point?"

Smokey, who was a bit shorter than me, got into my face, angrier than I'd ever seen the man since we'd met years ago when he came to work for Papa. "I happen to like Shay, a lot. He, Maxi, and Dex are my Parker's best friends. Those guys hang out and keep each other sane, so when we stupid sons-a-bitches get home from a particularly bad day, our better halves are there for us and love us, so we don't go crazy because of the goddamn job.

"If you're not serious about Shay, go back to Italy and take your side piece with you," Smokey insisted before he looked toward the center of the mats where Ace and St. Michael were beating the fuck out of each other with Duke as a ref.

I'd have to let Rafe know Gabe's people finally got serious about training. He loved to beat the fuck out of me when we were sparring in Rome. I couldn't wait to tell him it was time for him to find another punching bag, and Gabe's organization was full of them.

"I am serious about Shay, and Ace isn't my sidepiece..." I began defending myself before we heard pounding feet on the stairs. I turned to see Casper running with his tablet in his hands.

"I finally got something. Here," Casper told me before handing me the device. I glanced at the screen to see the last thing I wanted to see, Lucia Torrente Mazzola...Gabe's sister, standing on the sidewalk outside of a popular restaurant in San Francisco.

The fucker wrapped around her and kissing her neck? Marco Rialto, I was guessing. Of course, we knew that slimy bastard as Salvatore Mangello. It was twisted as fuck, but it was about time to get Gabe involved and tell him shit he didn't know about our connection to the Mangello family. He knew Lucia was involved with the Mangello family in some capacity, he just didn't know they were cousins. It was *his* sister, after all.

After I showered and dressed, I went upstairs and closed the door to the basement, just in time to see Sierra heading upstairs to the offices with a ring of keys in her hand, looking none too happy to be there.

"Hey, Sierra. You're in early," I announced as I stealthily approached her.

I was pretty sure she didn't think anyone was upstairs yet because she jumped and squeaked a bit. That was fine. She needed to be on edge around me because I believed I had her figured out. I was just trying to nail down the why of it.

"Oh, hi, Mateo. I thought you guys were all working out downstairs," she offered as she walked back down the stairs and behind the reception desk, sliding a keyring into her desk drawer. I'd been told by Gabe once that Sierra had the keys to all of the offices and conference rooms if I ever needed them. Hell, it would be stupid if she didn't since she was sort of the office manager. The keys, however, were pretty much obsolete, or so I guessed after a discussion with Casper regarding the new security he'd installed inside the Victorian over the last few weeks.

Gabe was the system administrator, so when he came into the office through the back door in the morning, his palm was scanned which released the master lock on all of the doors. The exception was Dex's studio. That one required Dexter's palm as well, but his studio wouldn't open without Gabe having scanned before or at the same time. I wasn't sure why, but it was what Casper had set up at my cousin's direction, and who the fuck was I to question it?

Apparently, our little sparrow didn't know the keys she had on that old keyring no longer worked on any of the doors in the building except the front door. It still used a key and had a keypad inside the door to disable the alarm, but it recorded the security code used to identify who had opened the door.

Another more complicated level of security had been added to the systems already in place. The offices would open with the occupant's palm scan, but only if Gabby was in the Victorian first. Nemo could override the system with Casper's assistance in Gabe's absence, but none of the rest of us had the capability.

The entire system reset itself automatically at 00-hundred unless Gabby manually locked it when he left, and nobody could get into the building until he scanned in the next morning. Each person's palmprint was his or her security code that even Casper couldn't override, so unlike a lot of shit that went on where nobody could tell who was responsible, we had checks and balances in place at the Victorian, and it would be impossible for anyone to do anything in that building without being detected and identified.

I quickly deduced that since Sierra had been out of town for several days, she wouldn't know anything about the upgrades that had taken place. The backdoor security scanner had been in place before she went out of town so she wouldn't notice anything unusual when she came into the office that morning. I had a feeling it was better to leave her in the dark until I figured out her game. "Gabe's already here, though I'm not sure where he is because he wasn't downstairs.

"You got big plans for the holiday? You have a boyfriend, right?" I asked, remembering the vague details about her last boyfriend, Perry. The gossip was he'd disappeared and left her with a hell of a lot of bills she wasn't expecting. Gabe gave her a raise to try to help her out, and the other guys tried to offer support when they could, what with buying her lunch and paying for Ubers to get her back and forth to work. One thing that struck me was she never seemed to appreciate their efforts. She almost treated each offer of kindness as a personal affront, which I couldn't comprehend in the least. The only people she was even really cordial to was Gabriele and Dexter, though she was more reserved with him. She flirted with Gabe something fierce when Dom wasn't around.

Unfortunately for Sierra, I was weighing her behavior against Angelina Bracco, the woman who worked in the same capacity at GEA-I. She'd been there for years, and she was trusted by all of us as we trusted each other. Mama didn't like her, so Angelina didn't attend any of the family functions. It didn't really matter to me. Angelina was good at her job, and she was loyal… much unlike I was coming to determine about Sierra.

"Uh, yeah, but he's out of town with his family for the holiday. We're going on a cruise for Christmas," she stated with a cocked eyebrow as if I had no business asking anything about her personal life, which she'd just lied about right to my face.

"That sounds fun. Where to?" I asked as I leaned over and got into her space where she sat behind the large desk. She began to squirm uncomfortably before she hopped up and offered a fake smile.

"It's a surprise. You want an espresso? I'm going to turn on that beast of a coffee machine. I can make you something, or I can let you know when it's warmed up," Sierra explained, seeming very nervous for no clear reason I could imagine if she wasn't guilty of something.

"I'll check back, but thanks," I told her as I stepped away and headed up the grand staircase, seeing the light on in Casper's office as well as Gabe's. I knew Casper was still downstairs, so I went to Gabriele's office and knocked.

"*In*," I heard called. I turned the handle, and when the door opened, I saw Gabe sitting on the couch with Dexter, the two of them having coffee.

"Am I interrupting?" I asked them, happy to see both of them smiling at me.

"No, come in, Mateo. When did you get back?" Dex asked as he rose and offered me a hug. Gabe shot me the bird, which wasn't a surprise. He didn't like Dexter hugging anyone else, and I was starting to understand it the more I ever thought I could since Shay Barr had entered my life. Possessiveness ran in the Torrente blood, and I respected it.

"Got back yesterday. We have some things to discuss, Gabriele. There are some issues we need to brief on regarding the family. There are also some things concerning the business. I don't care if we talk about family or business first, but everyone doesn't need to be present for the family discussion. I think we'll want to limit the operatives for the business shit until we have proof, *siamo d'accordo?*" I suggested.

"Agreed," Gabe answered. I nodded and left them to their morning coffee, hurrying down the hallway to the office I was sharing with Sherlock.

I considered calling my brother to come to the Victorian, but I knew Rafe was busy at the restaurant planning his Thanksgiving cook-a-thon at a shelter in Queens. I couldn't complain about being enlisted to help since I'd been the one to mention it to Shay. He'd truly liked the idea, so I was in. It could actually be fun because I'd be spending time with family and people I wanted to count as friends. *Hell, why not?*

We didn't celebrate Thanksgiving in Italy because it wasn't our holiday, but Mama would make a huge feast that Thursday at the villa and have everyone over to celebrate, anyway. There was never a turkey, but she still made a huge meal. Papa gave everyone time off and invited those in Rome out to the villa for the long weekend.

Little did I know, every year when we all got together, we were missing a whole other part of the family. We had an uncle and cousins we'd been kept from, and I wondered how things would change after I told Gabe the secret I'd been keeping after Casper gave me the news. Well, Rafael knew, but I couldn't keep things from him because he was my brother. We'd need to come clean with Gabriele, but timing was everything. How he'd take the news was anyone's guess.

At my suggestion, Gabe gave Sierra the afternoon off. We all met in the big fishbowl conference room next to Gabe's office after the phones were directed to voicemail, not that we expected any calls. Dex was teaching classes, so he was busy, and we had needed time without interruption.

It was time to explain shit to Gabe, Nemo, Smokey, and of course, Casper. Ace, St. Michael, and Mathis were out of the office on other cases, while Sherlock and Duke were on kid duty, so I decided to let Gabe determine who else he wanted to tell. I didn't want too many assholes walking around with concerned looks on their faces every time a pin dropped until we actually had something concrete so as not to alert others something was going on.

Once we were all settled around the table, I pulled the blinds and closed the door. Everyone had a drink with them, so after Gabe sat his ass down, I nodded to Casper who projected his laptop to the large screen at the front of the room. "I found this footage through security cameras at the building across the street from this restaurant. I've been following the woman since I got word she's been trying to find this man, and he finally surfaced," Casper explained as he sharpened the image.

"Ah! Sally-*fucking*-Man. You cagey son-of-a-bitch. We've got ya. Who's the…wait? Fuck, no," Gabe gasped as it finally dawned on him it was his sister, Lucia, on the screen.

"What's she *doing*?" Gabe asked as he stared at me. At the moment, it just looked traitorous, and I knew he wouldn't find the rest of it any more palatable.

"Before you lose your fucking mind, I have a theory. Your sister believes he's a guy named Marco Rialto," I offered my cousin after I took a sip from my bottle of water. I'd had a sausage and pepper sandwich from a shop down the street, and it was causing me to have indigestion… that or the fact I'd have to tell Gabe his sister was fucking our cousin? It was too soon to know which news was worse.

Gabe nodded but didn't take his eyes off the screen as the footage played on a loop, thanks to our cunning geek. "I believe *he* sought *her* out. The family lives in Jersey, except for when they're in Venice with Pietro, Frankie's older brother. Frankie's there now, and we all know I've been chasing that fucker all over the fucking country for the last several weeks. I believe he knows I'm hunting him, so he decided to take me on a fucking wild-goose chase," I reminded Gabe, handing him my airline ticket receipts to punctuate the fact I'd been all over the fucking place. He picked them up and looked at them before staring at me to continue.

"Let's not forget they didn't get their cocaine back after St. Michael and his narc buddies seized it, so they're planning some other sort of revenge. Lucia got divorced a while ago, and it's not hard to track down your family, Gabe. I seriously doubt she's the mole," I laid out for his consideration.

"Hell, Lucia's not in town that often since the girls go to school in San Fran. Besides, I don't believe Dominic would say a word about the business to his mother. We both know if your sister had an inkling of what you really do at Golden Elite Associates, she'd make Dom move back to Frisco in a heartbeat to keep a mother's watchful eye on her only son.

"Lucy thinks Dom's learning how to run a business from his favorite uncle, and I say let her live with that illusion to save the kid from his mother being a pain in the ass. Our problem is not your sister, directly. She's *your* problem, but we'll get into that later," I defended.

Gabe glanced up. "Goddamn! How'd she... If she's not the mole, who is?"

"Our problem is Sierra. I have reason to believe she's our mole. She came with the building, right? You never vetted her because she worked for the doctor before you bought that dude out, so you had no reason to know her background, but... Casper," I urged. He'd dug into Sierra's background, and it was better if he provided the proof before I offered my opinion.

"Sierra Michele Conti. Twenty-six. High school graduate and junior college drop out. Parents live in Montauk, but she's got an elderly grandmother who lives in San Jose where Sierra went to live after getting picked up for shoplifting when she was fourteen.

"Mom's a self-proclaimed psychic and astrologer... read that *hippy-dippy, coo-coo for cocoa puffs...* though she has a degree in sociology and formerly worked for a now-defunct marketing firm. Dad's a retired professor who graduated NYU Law, though he taught at Columbia. There's no record he ever actually practiced anywhere, nor that he ever even took the bar, so I'm guessing it's a classic case of those who can't, *teach*," Casper briefed everyone.

He took a drink of his coffee and continued. "Apparently, when Sierra got caught shoplifting, her parents sent her to live with Grandma on a ranch in San Jose and paid Grandma to keep the girl on the straight and narrow, probably so Sierra didn't put a stain on their social circle here in the city. The money stopped when Sierra turned eighteen, and Grandma's home was about to go into foreclosure not long after, so she sold it and moved into a pretty swanky retirement community," Casper explained as he flashed a picture of the place on the screen. It did look pretty posh.

"First five years, the proceeds from the sale of Grandma's small ranch paid the way, but for the last two years, someone else has made the payments for Grandma's apartment by wire-transfer, twice a year. Each payment comes from a different bank with a dummy corporation as owner. No money has been transferred into Sierra's known checking account, so I'm looking for another one outside the U.S.

"Still checking out the corporate names used for Grandma's rent to see if I can get anything on her benefactor, but so far, no luck at all. The only activity on Sierra's local account involves her rent, utilities, and normal expenses. Based on what goes in and what comes out, she doesn't have a lot of extra cash, so she's not paying Grandma's rent, especially not lump sums, twice a year," Casper surmised before looking around the room for questions.

Everyone seemed a little stunned, so I pointed to Casper and nodded to continue. "For undisclosed reasons, Sierra moved to the East Coast in the fall of 2014 after she turned twenty-one. She met Dr. Westphal when she worked at the BMW dealership where he took his car for service. She was the receptionist in the service department, and when the economy took a dump, she approached Westphal about a job.

"He told me he liked her, and she was very nice to his patients, even if she was quite young. She told him about taking care of her grandmother, and the guy had a soft spot for grandmothers, so he hired her without any references. Sierra worked for him for three years before the practice with Dr. Foster dissolved. He mentioned he's very grateful you came along, Gabe, so he wasn't hung with this building," Casper passed along.

He then hit some buttons on the computer and another image flashed on the screen. "Sierra's boyfriend, Perry Sanders, twenty-nine. A drug dealer who liked his product just a little too much, according to what I could trace out. He owed someone a lot of money, likely one of Frankie Man's soldiers since they run drugs in this part of the country, so to try to make up for the shortfall in his drop, he suddenly became very clumsy on the job where he worked for a moving company. He got hurt… a lot… seeming to accumulate scripts for oxy and various other delights to sell on the side because he had a powerful taste for the heroin he was supposed to sell for Sally Man. I found five aliases for the guy after only searching for fifteen minutes. Perry went missing about nine months after you set up shop here, Gabby," Casper spelled out, putting up a picture of Perry's record on the screen for emphasis, I was guessing.

"We can't know if she provided information on our organization to pay back the debt or if she worked it out another way. I don't know who's taking care of her grandmother, but she's been visiting a lot more lately. I also found a brother she's never mentioned around me. He's in the Air Force, but I can't get anything else on him without hacking into DoD. You told me not to do it unless it was a last resort. I can keep digging if you want more, Gabby," Casper pointed out.

I cleared my throat. "Sierra's been taking off a lot from what I've noticed, and her wardrobe has definitely improved since the other times I was in town, even though her income hasn't gone up significantly since her last raise. That points to cash transactions that can't be tracked. Casper's been able to track her whereabouts, and not surprisingly, she heads to the West Coast a lot, not renting a hotel room under her name during her stay. Either she's staying with Grandma at the retirement community, or she's got a host when she's there."

Casper nodded before he continued. "Sally Man, a/k/a Marco Rialto, has a suite at the St. Regis here in New York and another in Frisco, both under his father's name. Must be racking up a lot of free nights with the points, right? I mean, it can't just be a coincidence for all of this shit to line up?

"I'm gonna go out on a limb and speculate that Sally's romancing Sierra and Gabe's sister at the same time. He's keeping Lucia on the hook until he can figure out the best way to use her. If he's milking Sierra for information about the business and our comings and goings, then we need to feed her some bullshit information and catch her in her own web. I'd bet a nut neither woman knows about the other one," Casper hypothesized.

"But, Sierra's met Lucia more than once. Hell, she sits next to Dom for about eight hours a day, so I'm sure she knows all the family secrets. How the fuck can she not put together that the guy she might be dating is dating my sister," Gabe began, working himself into a fit over the news. I couldn't imagine what he'd say if he knew the guy was our cousin. Hell, I didn't want to even consider the ramifications of it.

"Yeah, true. What if Sierra runs back to Sally with every morsel of information she gets from Dom and the gossip around the office? Then what? Sally Man uses the scant information Sierra gives to romance your sister for one reason or another, without Sierra's knowledge?

"Dom told me a few weeks ago Lucia had met a guy, and he said the man's name was Marco Rialto, but he didn't want me to mention anything about it because he was sure you and Zio Tomas would go nuts over the news. I'm sure it was based on Lucia's history with Gio, that fucking punk, and the fact you and your father never liked him and tried to talk her out of marrying him," I reminded my cousin.

"Dom told me he believed his mom should have a shot at a new life. I doubt this is the life he'd have chosen for Lucia. I'm speculating Sierra knows nothing about Sally's alias, and I don't think she's smart enough to put together some of the shit Dom tells her that might point to Lucia's new love interest being Salvatore Mangello, the guy she might be selling our family secrets," I pointed out.

It was Gabe's job to put it together and decide what we should do about it. Myself? One flick of my wrist and she wouldn't know what hit her. I was the family Grim Reaper, after all, which was something I still needed to discuss with Shay. Full disclosure was the only way to proceed, especially if he was moving in. He needed to go in with eyes-wide-open.

"That fucking two-faced, backstabbing cunt! I'm going down there and…" Gabriele began as he stood and sent the chair into the wall. He was working himself up into quite a tantrum, but it was the holiday season, and I wasn't about to have his heart attack or stroke on my hands.

Nemo stood and grabbed Gabe after he pulled away from me,

dragging me half-way across the conference table as I tried to hold onto him. "You'll get your sister killed. Sally knows she's your sister, but she doesn't know anything about the business, so she has no idea she's being conned, Gabby. *Think about this.*

"If you're gonna kill Sierra, then make it clean and get a crew to dump the body, but you'll risk tipping off Sally we're onto him. I'd bet he'll go after your sister when he has her alone. Then what? What are you gonna do? What will you tell your family about Lucia's disappearance? We need to give this some thought," Nemo reasoned as he shoved Gabe back into the chair.

If anyone could keep the idiot from doing something rash, it would be Nemo or Smokey. They had a lot of respect between the three of them, and I was pretty sure there were only two other people Gabe would listen to over them… Casper's brother, Bull, and their other Ranger buddy, Hawk. Those guys didn't work with us, so it was best to keep them out of things. They had legit jobs, and each man had a family. If we couldn't handle it without them, we all deserved to be dead. Hell, I might end up dead anyway after I told Sweeney one of my new co-workers was a guy I used to blow…

16

SHAY

"Okay, Ainsley, you're all set. Are you having a big party for Thanksgiving?" I asked. I'd just finished touching up her roots for the holidays, listening to all of the latest gossip from the younger set of New York social climbers.

Ainsley Spires was a really sweet girl, though most people held her family against her. She worked in the front office of the *New York Spires* baseball team because she wasn't exactly a member of *Mensa*. Her father, the biggest asshole in Manhattan, was the only person who could guarantee she wouldn't be fired for any reason because the poor girl was dumb as a box of rocks, but I liked her, and she tipped hella well.

"I'm going skiing in Jackson Hole with my new boyfriend. I'm the black sheep, you know, Shay. New Mommy doesn't want me around, so I get my check to stay away, and then I go about my life," she explained with a giggle that made me laugh as well.

New Mommy was the Greek goddess, Athena, who was thirty years younger than Randolph Spires. He'd married her not long after he'd divorced Ainsley's mother, Cheryl (who went by Cher). She was a former beauty queen, and she'd been the one to break up Randolph's second marriage to a Polish woman, Paulina, who was the mother of Angela and her two older brothers.

I lost track of how many wives and kids were in the family because the man didn't seem to hold the sanctity of marriage in high regard. The poor kids were hated by almost everyone in New York because of their old man, based on what I read in the gossip pages. Eh, I wasn't close to my family, either, and for a lot less glamor-filled reasons.

"That sounds fun. I guess you're not going to the *Thanks for Giving Gala* on Saturday, then?" I couldn't help but ask. It was then I noticed the shop was dead silent. I glanced around seeing we had everyone's undivided attention, and I knew I should be ashamed, but Ainsley only laughed.

"Got a ten-grand kicker to stay away, and I'm taking it. I'll see you in six weeks, Shay. Happy Thanksgiving," she told me as she peeled off ten Benjamin's and handed them to me.

"Ainsley, that's…" I began my protesting.

"Give the extra to the shelter where you're going to make food for the Thanksgiving dinner. Daddy can afford it," she told me as she offered me an air kiss on each cheek. I obliged, and after we all saw she was gone, the place erupted in chatter.

I laughed and walked out front to Sonya's queendom, handing her four hundreds for the bill and an extra hundred. "Make change and tip out Inez and Chase, equally, for dealing with her. How many more?" I asked as the door buzzed. We both turned to see my cousin, Dani, enter the shop, and to say she looked like shit was like calling a skunk a kitty cat.

"I'm sorry but…" Sonya started.

"This is my cousin, Danielle. Dani, this is my right hand, Sonya. What's going on with this?" I asked, waggling my freshly manicured, bronze nails at Dani's hair and clothes. She was wearing a pair of jeans that were held together with a rubber band because she was definitely showing. The blouse she was wearing was only buttoned half-way, and she had dark circles under her eyes.

"What's wrong? I thought you were going to call and let me know when you were getting in so I could arrange for someone to pick you up or come get you myself. Come with me," I demanded as I took her hand and led her to the kitchen, which was thankfully empty.

Dani started sobbing, immediately causing the hairs on the back of my neck to stand up. "Dani, talk to me." She grabbed a tissue from the box on the table and wiped her eyes before she dried her hands, which were chapped and red. Her cuticles appeared to have gone through a meat grinder, and she wasn't wearing any makeup.

Danielle wasn't wealthy, but she was a proud woman and always looked her best. The woman I was looking at wasn't the woman I was used to seeing. Something had gone horrifically wrong, and I wanted to know what it was immediately.

Dani looked around the kitchen before standing to get a drink of water from the sink faucet after picking up a glass on the counter. "Put that down," I snapped as I grabbed her a bottle of purified water from the fridge. "God knows who used that thing and didn't wash it," I told her as I took the glass and put it in the dishwasher.

"Where's Chase?" she asked.

"He was helping Inez with the rush, but I'm pretty sure he's downstairs with Maxi by now. They're making up small centerpieces to take to Mathis' father's shelter for tomorrow's Thanksgiving dinner. We're going to a friend's place tonight to help make the food. You remember Mathis, right?" I asked as I urged her back into the chair after taking her too small coat to hang on the rack behind the door.

"Mom popped in yesterday unannounced and saw I'm knocked up and due next May. Of course, when she didn't see a wedding ring, she freaked out and called for my father to come to get me. I told her I had to go to the drugstore for prenatal vitamins, and I drove straight here. I have no other clothes, and I don't have any cash. I spent the last of my money on gas so I could get here," she told me before she started crying again.

"Fucking hell. Do you think she knows you came here?" I asked her.

"I don't think so," she told me. I reached into the fridge and pulled out two yogurt cups, offering both of them to her with a spoon because I was guessing she hadn't eaten since the previous morning.

I had to do something about all of this shit quickly because if her dad called mine, and mine had spoken to my mother, they'd put two-and-two together and likely get five because they weren't exactly beautiful minds. Eventually, they'd figure out Dani and I were in cahoots, and they'd head to New York. When they arrived, they'd find Chase, who wouldn't be eighteen until the Tuesday after Thanksgiving, and everything would just go to hell from there, no doubt.

I needed help immediately. The problem was bigger than I could handle, but first, I needed to get Dani situated. "Did you stop to sleep at all?" I asked her.

"I stopped at a rest area in Northern Virginia and slept for a while before I drove the rest of the way today. I'm fine, Shay. I just didn't know what to do about Chase," Dani told me as she devoured the yogurt and finished the water.

I held up my finger and walked out to the reception desk, seeing Sonya, Wren, Ari, and the twins, Posey and Olson Green, in a deep discussion I was more than happy to break up. The Greens were twin masseuses. They were good at what they did, and even though they had a strange, bordering-on-incestuous, relationship, I liked them. "Good, you're all not busy. I need help," I began before I dispatched them with tasks.

"Posey and Olson, can you check the towels to be sure there's nothing left in the washer and fold whatever's in the dryer to get ready to go on Friday? Wren and Ari, will you finish sweeping the salon, and ensure Paige and Ahn are done with their customers for the day? Also, shut off my laptop and lock it into my desk, please?" I requested as I tossed my keys to Ari, who happily nodded before the two of them took off.

I then turned to my Sonya and handed her my credit card, pulling her with me toward the stairs. "I don't care how much it costs. Will you please buy Dani enough things for at least a week? Ask her sizes, and then send her down to Maxi. He has couches all over that joint, and she needs a nap. I'll go talk to him," I informed her as I hurried down the stairs to Maxi's studio where I heard lots of laughter. The speakers were blaring Christmas music, which was annoying considering it wouldn't be Thanksgiving until the next day.

I saw Toni standing next to Chase, the two of them tying raffia around the tops of old-style canning jars they were using for centerpieces, so I walked up to the table and touched Chase on the back. He turned to me and smiled. "Hey, Shay. How *is* it upstairs? You need me to come up and help with anything?" he asked with the sweetest smile.

I took his hand and led him to Maxi's office where my best friend was on the phone laughing with someone. "I promise, Jewel. I already made you an appointment with Shay, who just walked in. Let me call you back, Sissy. It seems like he's upset. I'll come by and pick up you and Maureen to come help out tonight. Gene, Lawry, Hank, Reed, and Brock are going to do boy things, whatever that means, while we decorate the shelter. Can't wait to see you, honey. Tell your mom and dad to make themselves at home," he told her before they said goodbye.

I'd forgotten Lawry's family was coming for Thanksgiving and the engagement party. I started to turn around and leave when I heard Maxi's throat clear behind me. "What's going on? You look like you're about to launch into outer space," he observed as he walked around the desk and placed his hand on my shoulder.

"My cousin, Dani, is here," I told Maxi before I looked at Chase. "They found out about the baby, and they were going to take her back to Hot Springs. She got in the car and drove straight here. She's upstairs," I told Chase, who immediately ran out of the place. We could hear him pounding his way up the stairs.

"What can I do?" Maxi asked, just like the true friend he'd been since the day I met him.

"Can she come down here to take a nap? I've sent Sonya to get her some essentials. She came with nothing, and she slept in a rest area last night. She's exhausted and upset, and that can't be good for the baby, can it?

"Our family is going to come here for her and Chase, I'm sure. They're a bunch of radical religious freaks, but they'll eventually put it together about me heading up that damn raid in Arkansas, especially now that Dani's disappeared. My mother won't forget to report I was there that night, of that I'm sure. Frankly, I don't know why she hasn't told them yet," I explained rather haphazardly.

"Back up, sugar. What the hell are you talkin' about?" Maxi asked, allowing his southern drawl to make its way to the surface as he often did when it was just the two of us.

I hadn't told Maxi much about the trip except I'd brought my cousin to New York to stay with me from the family camp in Arkansas. I neglected to go into detail about what we'd found there because I didn't think I could get it out without becoming very emotional. I didn't want someone asking a lot of questions because I didn't want to explain what I'd experienced at their hands. I didn't want to have to explain why it was important I go down there and get Chase… and save those other kids in the process. I didn't want people to know what the fuck had happened to them, much less what happened to me because I was over it… *mostly*.

Nowhere in the explanation for my best friend had I mentioned the fact I'd made myself known to my mother as I was kidnapping Chase. I hadn't told anyone I'd succumbed to the temptation of gloating at the woman who turned her back on me when I needed her. I was just grateful I'd been able to get the kid out of there before any real damage was done. I'd been stupid and prideful, which made me weak. I wasn't eager to share those shortcomings with anyone.

I quickly made my revelation as I paced his office while Maxi cleared papers off his couch and went to a closet, returning with sheets, a pillow, and a blanket. I looked at him with curiosity. "I've had to pull all-nighters more than once. I refuse to sleep on an unmade couch where people put their asses all the time. So of course, I have linens and proper pillows. I'm not a barbarian, Shay. Help me make this up and then go get that poor woman," Maxi ordered.

I felt I owed Maxi more of an explanation because I knew he had no family, and if I had members I still loved, I was sure he would judge me for not helping them out sooner, especially when he saw her. "I don't call her a lot because she has a lot on her plate, and I don't want to put her in the position where the family finds out we keep up with each other because I'm a demon. If there is any truth to that shit Mathis said about them googling how to trace cell phone calls, I don't want to give them any help," I offered, seeing Maxi cock his eyebrow at me as if he didn't understand.

"Talk to Lawry about it, okay? Anyway, what can I do?" I asked him as he changed the case on the pillow and unfurled a gorgeous patchwork quilt. I looked up at him and saw his smile as he gazed at it.

"It's not a family heirloom. Lawry and I went to one of those country-fair things upstate for the weekend before Halloween. I bought it from a nice Mennonite woman. Anyway, Cousin Dani can nap here. I'll vacate and help with the centerpieces in the showroom. What time are we supposed to go to Shepherd's House?" Maxi asked.

"Uh, Rafe and Parker aren't off until ten, but Rafe is sending all of the food over this afternoon. He told Mateo there would be a refrigerated trailer there with everything for the meal, so we can probably start washing vegetables and peeling stuff until he arrives. Call Parker for precise times and let me know, will you?" I asked, unable to keep from wringing my hands.

"Yeah, I'll call. I'll come up when I know more. Calm down, Shay. You're not going to help Danielle if you're pacing like the expectant father. Where is *he*, by the way?" Maxi asked.

"God only knows. If my family found him, he'd be nothing but a memory. He's African-American," I told Maxi, not really needing to elaborate on how my family would feel about that turn of events. Maxi grew up in the *deep* South. He knew the story all too well.

I hurried out, waving to everyone in the showroom before I shot back up the stairs. We needed to make some plans and fast. Dani drove the whole sixteen-plus hour trip alone, and Aunt Judy wasn't stupid. When Dani didn't show up at home after an hour and didn't answer any calls, they'd start working the phones. She maybe had a four- or five-hour lead on them, but that was a hopeful guesstimate. Things were looking very bleak.

Dani was downstairs napping in Maxi's office after he ordered her something to eat and gave her a pair of his sweats to change into so she could wash up in his private bathroom. Chase was down there helping pack one of Maxi's vans with the stuff to take to Queens that night, and he was as worried as me about Dani and what we both knew was likely coming our way.

I planned to pamper Dani with the full regimen, but she needed rest more than anything. I could smother her in spa treatments Thursday morning if she wanted. Right then, I needed to take her to my place, but I was afraid they'd find her there. Chase and I weren't moving to Mateo's place until Sunday, but we'd been packing up, so my small apartment was a disaster. It just felt as if everything was crashing down around me, and I didn't know what to do about any of it.

Dani was about four months pregnant, having told me she was due in the middle of May. I damn well didn't want anything to happen to her baby. As far as I knew, she was yet to learn the sex of her child unless she'd recently gone to the doctor to find out. I thought I read it wasn't easy to tell before twenty weeks, but what the fuck did I know?

I heard a commotion at the front of the salon, so I rushed to the lounge to find Mateo, Gabe, Dex, Mathis, and Jonah Wright, who was dressed in full police regalia. Mateo stepped forward and pulled me into his arms. "Maxi called Casper. Tell me what we can do," he demanded, making tears pool in my eyes. *Man, you need one protector—you get a handful!*

"I need to stash Dani and Chase somewhere," I suggested.

"I'll take them to our house. Max and Lawry have Gene, Maureen, and Jewel, so they don't have room, but we do," I heard Dexter assert. I looked to see Gabe nodding.

"Why can't they just go to *our* place? We have enough room, *tesoro*," Mateo reminded.

"We're not going to be home to look after them, and Chase and I haven't moved yet. If they find his stuff at my place, they'll just call the police because he's a minor, and they'll arrest my ass for kidnapping without hesitation," I reminded.

No way was I going to ditch on Mathis and his family for the prep for Thanksgiving. They were doing something wonderful, and Rafe was committing a lot to the cause. The least we could do was help out as much as possible.

"I don't live far from here. Let me take them to my house. They'd never know to come looking for them with me. It's not a mansion, but it's clean, and I have two bedrooms and a pull-out couch. I doubt your family would be able to track Dani and Chase to my place," Jonah suggested.

That was definitely true. Our hillbilly family would never know where Chase and Dani were if they were with Jonah Wright, the cop. That was a big plus.

Everyone began speaking at once, and suddenly, there was a very loud whistle I'd know anywhere. I turned to see Danielle looking much better than when she'd arrived at the salon three hours earlier. "How about everyone just calms down and takes a deep breath."

Dexter laughed and patted her shoulder. "Great idea. I'm Dexter, Gabe's husband. It's nice to meet you, Danielle. Let's all take a deep breath together and put some positive energy into this space," he instructed. *Yogi in the house!*

I half expected most of the big men in that lobby to laugh, but when I saw the murderous look Gabe had on his face, they merely took in a deep breath. "Slowly let it out… five… four… three… two… one," Dexter counted as he exhaled.

Dani finally had a smile on her face. "Thank you, Dexter. Now, what I think is the best thing is for Chase to go with you, Shay, and I'll go home with Jonah. That way, if they somehow find me, they won't find him. Keep him out of their hands until Tuesday," she suggested, which made sense because Tuesday was his birthday.

"Why don't you bring him to Queens to help us. They'll never figure out where you guys are in Queens," Mathis added, which also suited the purpose.

I walked forward to Dani and took her hands in mine. "Are you sure, honey? I'll get on a plane with the two of you right now, and we can go to Italy where Mateo's parents live. I'm sure they'll let us stay with them, however long it takes, and our family could never find us. Or, we can fly up to Quebec. Let's see the hillbillies try to navigate French," I offered, half-teasing.

Dani chuckled. "That all sounds like a dream, but I don't have a passport, and neither does Chase, Shane. Do *you*?" she asked.

I nodded, though I was embarrassed to admit why I had one. "I always dreamed of traveling to exotic places, so I got a passport when I moved here and established residency. Maxi and I both did, swearing one day we'd go to Tahiti or Fiji or London," I confessed quietly.

I felt a large hand on my shoulder and turned to see Mateo smiling down at me. Dani glanced up at him and smirked, damn her. "I have a very good feeling you'll get there, Shane. Now, I need to get my coat from Maxi's office, and then, Jonah, if you don't mind if I stay with you, I'll take you up on it. I get paid on Friday, so I can get some money and pay you back for…" she began as high heels clanked on the stairs, alerting me that my Sonya was back.

The door flew open as the woman bustled in with lots of bags and a big, happy smile. I couldn't begin to know the high women got from shopping, but there was something about it. I liked to shop, but to most of the women I knew, it was like a religious experience.

"I'm sorry it took so long, but the boutique I went to didn't have a few things I wanted in the right size, so I had to go into Manhattan. Anyway, this should take care of things for at least the weekend," Sonya offered as she placed the bags on the couch in the lobby seating of the salon.

Dani looked at me with a stern face. She was about to give me hell, but I wasn't going to have it. "What? You're going to walk around in Maxi's workout sweats for however long it takes before you can go home? That won't do for dinner at Gabe and Dex's place tomorrow," I told her, feeling my throat tighten as she started to cry.

"Get her out of here, Jonah, and all of you, go back to the Victorian. Chase and I will be there after we finish here for the day," I assured as they began filing out. I was either going to kick Maxi's ass for the reveille call summoning the troops, or I was going to buy him a very nice cashmere sports jacket for Christmas. He was the first friend I really ever had, and now I had people who would come to help me at the drop of a hat. It was a whole new world for me, and I was quite grateful for it.

Dani's car was in the parking lot of the building I shared with Maxi, which was fine. Maxi put a tag on it that it was okay to remain on the lot so nobody would tow it. It was a piece of shit, so I doubted anyone would try to steal it, but if they did, they'd be doing her a favor and hate their poor judgment in one fell swoop.

"You ready?" Chase asked as he bundled up in my office. I shoved the money into the safe, having decided to wait to go to the bank until after the busy Friday and Saturday morning. The money I would make in those thirty-six hours would pay my taxes and allow me to give my people a nice bonus for the holidays. It would be long days, but we'd get through it with happy smiles on our faces, even if it killed us.

I handed Chase my keys. "Will you go down and start my car? It's cold outside, and I'd rather not get into a cold car," I complained like the spoiled queen I'd become. Chase laughed and hurried down the stairs. I heard the front door slam, which made me laugh. I'd kill for the kid's energy.

I did a final walk-through of the salon to ensure everything was turned off in all of the rooms, and I was pissed when there was a candle still burning in Posey Green's massage room. I hated having to continue to remind the woman about fire safety, but it had been quite a day, and I was sure she'd just forgotten it in all the confusion. I wouldn't give her hell because I needed her at the spa, but I'd tattoo the candle thing on her fucking palm if I had to so she didn't do it again. Of course, I'd do it in the kindest way possible.

I ran downstairs and locked the front entrance, then the door to my shop at the top of the stairs before I went to the door of the back stairwell leading down to the parking lot. I glanced out the window as

I searched for the key, ready to get changed and head to Queens. I was looking forward to the work we would do that night and the day off that followed.

I heard yelling, so I checked out the window to see someone was holding onto Chase's arm and dragging him toward an old, black pick-up truck, and the kid was struggling to get away, which had my heart pounding as I took the stairs as quickly as possible, nearly taking flight out the back door.

I ran over to the man in the wool cap and jumped on his back, taking him to the ground. *"Run, Chase!"* I yelled the command as I used my fists to hit the man as hard as possible to distract him from my cousin.

I tossed Chase my phone, and he nodded before he hopped into my car and sped off. He was smart enough to know to call the cops or Mateo. I didn't give a shit who showed up. I just wanted Chase to have a fighting chance at a good life, and I wasn't going to let some asshat take it from him.

I used everything inside me to keep the guy focused on me until he threw me off his back, and I landed on the asphalt parking lot, taking his stocking cap with me. The fight drained out of me quickly as I recognized my assailant. *My time was up!*

17

MATEO

I stopped to grab a hamburger before making my way back to the Victorian after the false alarm at DyeV Barr. My phone rang as I was getting out of one of Gabby's big-ass SUV fleet vehicles in the parking lot behind the building. I glanced at the screen to see a number with a New York area code I didn't recognize. I worried something might have happened after we all left the salon, so I answered, "Torrente Vineyards, Mateo Torrente speaking."

"Teo, it's me, Lotta. I have some unexpected news. Someone's been hacking into my network and looking around at our employee files for both GEA offices. They also copied files relating to the vineyard and your father's holdings. I'm afraid they're coming after the family, and when I traced back the IP address, it led me directly to the servers at Gabe's office. You've got a mole, and not a very good one, so I don't think it was Casper because he would have been a lot more sophisticated in his approach," Lotta told me, not that it was news to me.

We'd been digging for anything tying Sierra to Sally Man but had come up empty. I was sure Salvatore would be back in New York anytime now, and I wanted to get Lawry to start watching the airports to give us notice when he landed, hopefully *not* with Lucia Mazzola.

I seriously doubted Sally Man had balls big enough to show up at

Gabe and Dexter's house as Lucia's date since the whole family was congregating for the meal, along with several of the guys who worked for my cousin.

"Yeah, we know. We're just trying to catch her in the act. What number is this? Did you trash your phone again? Hell, it's nine o'clock at night. Why aren't you home?" I asked Lotta.

"Her? It's not a woman, Teo," she began, which stopped me dead in my tracks.

"Who the fuck is it?" I asked as my phone beeped, Shay's name and photo lighting up my screen. I ignored it because I really needed to hear what Lotta had to tell me. I almost couldn't believe my own ears, and I couldn't help myself, interrupting her to refute the news she was giving me rapid fire.

"My personal theory is he's pissed at Gabriele over something, and he's going to report him to the U.S. authorities as soon as he can dig up enough dirt to make it worth their time. I'd bet he's found out about Giancarlo Mangello, and before he turns Gabe over to the Feds, he's going to sell the information to Frankie Man, thus taking out the whole family. I've found international accounts in his name, Teo. You need to stop him," Lotta informed me, making my stomach turn at the idea of a traitor among us.

After we hung up, I stood at the back door, completely stunned by the news. I finally snapped out of it and placed my hand on the reader to enter the Victorian. "Just me," I called out in the event anyone gave a shit.

I walked up to the office I'd been sharing with Sherlock, who was probably still getting the kids from school. He was going to London to meet his new nephew that weekend, claiming he wasn't a fan of the American Thanksgiving holiday. Shay had mentioned Sherlock helped him out with Chase's rescue, so when Sherlock asked to use my London flat, I relented and gave him the key.

I'd known the guy for several years because he worked for Papa in Italy before he came to the U.S. to work for Gabe. He'd been with MI6, and he was instrumental in bringing Lotta to work for GEA-I. She was a huge asset to the operation in Italy, and I knew she'd been helpful to some of the guys at Gabe's organization without complaining. After the news Lotta had given me, I wondered if any of us would be left standing once the smoke cleared.

I sat down at the desk and plugged in my phone, seeing the key I'd given Sherlock had fallen on the floor beside the trash can between the facing desks. I bent down to pick it up and heard a strange sound under the desk across from mine. It sounded like a ticking clock… the old kind I remembered my papa used to wind up and put next to his bed at night.

I crawled under the desk to see a digital display ticking down with only one-hundred-twenty seconds left on the display. It took a good ten of them for me to figure out what the fuck I was looking at before I began yelling as I ran out of the office and found Smokey in the kitchenette. *"Come with me! Quick!"* I hissed as I pulled him down the hall behind me.

I actually tackled him to the ground and shoved him under the desk, listening as he started cursing. For a good twenty-three seconds, Smokey laid on the carpet and studied the stupid thing before he reached into his pocket and pulled out a Swiss Army knife. For the next forty-seven seconds, he worked the device, finally cutting something and letting out a loud breath… a sigh of relief? The clock showed forty-seconds on the display.

"Should I evacuate the building?" I asked Smokey as we both slid from under the desk.

"You stupid fucker, that should have been your *first* thought, not dragging me into this shit. I'm gettin' married in seven months, asshole," Shepard snapped at me. *He has a point.*

"What should we do?" I whispered, not one who loved surprises. Surprises brought the unknown, and the unknown was deadly. I was the one always in control. I was the assassin in the shadows waiting for my target to make that deadly mistake so I could do my job and fade away. What the fuck was wrong with me that I stayed in the room? Had I lost my self-preservation instincts?

"We do nothing right this moment until I get a minute to check this shit out. Go dissuade anyone from getting nosy and coming in, okay? You were sharing with Sherlock, right?" Smokey asked. I nodded, unsure of what else to say or do.

I got up from the floor and went down the hallway to the kitchen where Nemo was sitting with Dexter, the two of them discussing Nemo's new husband. "How is the Congressman? Happy to get a few days off?" Dex asked with that bright smile.

Neither seemed fazed by the commotion I'd caused, which was a relief. Suddenly it dawned on me there were a bunch of innocent people in that building I should have considered instead of panicking, which was something I'd need to give more thought to when I had time in the future. Dex held classes on the main floor, and his students didn't deserve to die just because they wanted to stretch. It wasn't just me on this mission. There were many lives at stake inside that building.

"He's doing great. I'm picking him up at JFK, and then we'll come over to Shepherd's House to help out. Benji's excited because he really wants to get to know everyone, but with the limited amount of time he can be in town, it's not easy. We're flying down to North Carolina on Saturday to see the families, and we'll each fly to our respective homes on Monday," Nemo explained to Dexter. Dex nodded.

"By the way, did you and Gabby leave the front door unlocked? When I came downstairs after you all left earlier, the door was actually open. Maybe I need to talk to…" Nemo continued until we all heard thundering footsteps on the stairs, along with giggles.

I walked to the door to see Duke and Cyril with the kids. "Hey, you bloody bothers, give me a hug. I've got to get to the airport. I need to find what I did with the…" Sherlock began before I tackled yet another co-worker in the hallway.

"*Whoa!*" Duke yelled as he tried to pull me off of the Brit.

I swung an elbow around to bust him in the mouth as I twisted Sherlock's arm up behind him. "Move, *ti sfido, cazzo*. Go ahead. I'll fucking break it off," I hissed in his ear. I heard Dexter scrambling the kids to get out of the way, and I felt Nemo trying to pry me off Sherlock.

"I'm going to kill him, so you'd do right to just move along," I snapped at Nemo. I didn't want to fight with the big man because I liked the guy a lot. He was truly an honorable man, and I respected him. It didn't mean I wouldn't knock his ass out if he got in my way.

"Bloody fuck, Mateo! You've gone off your nut!" Cyril snapped as he actually headbutted me, tossing me off his back as my nose exploded. It was bleeding like a fucking faucet, but that asshole was trying to blow up the fucking building and had to be stopped.

Just then, Smokey ran into the kitchen and grabbed Cyril, strong-arming him back to the office before he pinned him on the floor on his belly, knee in the middle of his back. Of course, Nemo and I followed—me holding a roll of paper towels to my nose—and entered the room in time to see Smokey with that big ass Smith & Wesson hog leg pointed at Cyril's right ear.

"Was this supposed to be a prank?" Smokey snapped as he rolled Cyril onto his back and held up what looked like modeling clay with wires hanging off it, closely resembling a spider's body.

"What the fuck is that? I have no idea what... get the fuck off me," Cyril snapped as he began pushing before Smokey cocked the revolver and held it up to Sherlock's right eye.

"Smokey, man, what's going on?" Nemo asked as he held up his hands and walked further into the room until Smokey offered his attention. I could see the look wasn't exactly friendly.

"This is PE-4, isn't it, *mate?* It's what you Brits use in place of C-4 to blow shit up, isn't it? It was hooked up to these," Smokey explained as he gently placed the clay on the desktop and held up what appeared to be a battery of some sort and the digital clock with the display still flashing forty.

"I don't have the slightest... you've gone bleedin' barmy. I'm not a demo man, and you fucking well know it. I don't appreciate..." Sherlock began before Gabe waded into the mix looking none too pleased.

"What in the actual fuck is going on?" Gabe asked as he pulled Smokey up and took the S&W pistol from his hand, uncocking the fucking thing.

"This *cazzo di stronzo* was trying to blow the place," I snapped as I pointed to the makeshift bomb Smokey had thankfully dismantled.

"Except for the fact the goddamn thing was totally wired wrong. It's a wonder the asshole didn't blow himself up with that piece of shit," Smokey snapped as Gabe put the gun behind his back and pushed Smokey out of the way.

My cousin then helped up Cyril and turned the Brit to look at him. "Are you the one? Are you trying to get all of us killed by selling intel to Frankie Man? Are you his inside man?" Gabe asked.

I saw Casper look at me with worry on his face, so I waved him off. It wasn't the time to tell anyone what we knew until Lotta confirmed one more thing for me. I wasn't ready to tell Gabe about dear Uncle Frankie and his desire to kill off the whole bunch of us… his estranged family. Until we had proof, I wouldn't tell Gabe I believed Frankie Man had enlisted one of our own to help him. It was disgusting to think you could work with someone and become friends with them, only to learn they'd turn against you on a dime.

"*Frankie Man?* What the fuck is that crack supposed to mean? I've been the butt of many a bloody joke, but I've never been called a fucking traitor by any of you lads. I don't appreciate being looked at as if my underpants are hanging out with a big shit stain, which they probably are after this brilliant display of blaming the wrong bloke for something I couldn't possibly have done.

"I was with Duke, picking up the kids from school, and as I was about to get into my car to go to the airport, I realized I didn't have the key for Mateo's flat in London which he said he'd loan me. I came inside to look for it, and then I was jumped by these two plonkers," Cyril stated as he pointed to Smokey and me.

I held out the key. "I found it on the floor in our office, and when I reached down to get it, I heard the ticking. I looked under the desk and found the fucking bomb, so I grabbed Smokey. How did I know you didn't know shit about making a bomb?" I cracked at the asshole.

Just then, the phone on my desk buzzed. "*Mateo, you have a phone call,*" I heard. It was Dexter's voice, so I hurried over and picked up the phone.

"Mateo Torrente," I answered, not sure who the fuck it was calling me at Gabe's place of business.

"Mateo, it's Chase. How do I get to the Victorian? Someone has kidnapped Shay. The guy was trying to grab me, but Shay came to my rescue, and the guy got him instead. I was told to take the car and call the cops, but I thought I should call you first. What should I do? Where are you?" Chase asked, sounding as panicked as I'd ever heard anyone before in my life.

We all heard a noise downstairs, so Gabe and Nemo went to check it out while Smokey and I stayed with Cyril in the office. "Tell me where you are, Chase, and I'll talk you in. Don't you have GPS on your phone?" I asked.

"Yes, but since I don't know the address…" Chase definitely made his point.

Casper walked over to the speakerphone and shoved me away. "Hey, Kid. It's Casper…" he began, giving Chase the address.

Suddenly, Shay appeared in front of me with ripped clothes, a small bruise on his handsome face, and his hair sprouting in ten directions. The man with him didn't look much better, though he did look a lot like Shay.

I rushed over to my man and pulled him into my arms. "Are you okay?" I asked as I picked him up and held him to me, grateful he was there and appeared to be okay.

"Yeah, but Chase is out there somewhere, and I'm worried…"

"I've got it. I'll be there in a few," we all heard over the speakerphone before the line went dead.

Casper turned to look at me. "He's on his way. What the fuck is going on with all of this? Who the fuck are you?" Casper asked, pointing to the guy with red hair and a busted lip. He was about four inches taller than Shay, and he appeared to be very anxious at being in our company.

The man looked at Shay, who shook his head in what I believed was disgust before he moved for me to put him down, which I did, though not happily. "This is one of my worthless brothers. Corbin. He was at the compound the night… well, you guys know what happened. Anyway, he showed up at the brownstone and tried to grab Chase, but I tackled him, and we had a fight. Chase got away, though.

"My brother swears he's on a humanitarian mission… here to keep Chase safe, not that I believe it," Shay snapped as he stepped away from me and crossed his arms over his chest, looking none too happy with his brother after questioning the reason for the visit.

I'd never seen the man, but I could see a resemblance between the two of them… not that I was about to mention it. I could tell Shay was aching for a fight, but it wasn't going to be with me. I loved him too much to fight about anything related to his family.

We all heard a throat clearing, so we turned to see Smokey still had Cyril's arm wrenched up behind his back and another, smaller pistol aimed at the back of the man's head. It was Cyril who spoke. "This is touching, really, but can I get this arsehole off my fucking back? I didn't try to blow the goddamn place. I'm an intelligence agent, not a goddamn explosives expert. I couldn't make that thing with a goddamn diagram designed by a bomb expert," Sherlock protested, which brought a laugh from the three men now in the doorway of the office.

Gabe cleared his throat. "Let him go. He's right. He's not smart enough to have designed anything like that, even if it wasn't done right," my cousin demanded as he looked at Cyril. Clearly, Gabe read him and believed the man to be truthful. I trusted Gabby's instincts, but not more than my own, and until I had more information from Lotta, I wasn't looking at anyone cross-eyed.

My desk phone rang again, and since Casper was closest, he answered. "Mateo's… Oh? Well, yeah, we'll be right down. Thanks, Dexter."

Casper looked around the room and smiled, turning to glance at Gabe. "Bull and Reed are here. What do you want me to do? I can take them for a drink or… actually, I won't, but you can," he explained, reminding us of his recovery status. No one commented because the guy was doing well in his sobriety, and we were a supportive group of assholes… until we had a reason not to be.

"I'll have Dex take them to our house. They can stay with us, especially since Searcy and Dyl love spending time with Brock and you've got Maureen, Gene, and Jewel at your place, Casper. It'll be fine.

"Sherlock, if I get so much as a sniff you had anything to do with this IED, I'll cut off your dick and…" Gabe began before we heard someone on the stairs again and turned to see Chase rush inside.

"Whoa! That sounds harsh," Chase joked as he walked into the room and up to Shay, offering a hug. "Your car is crap," the kid told him.

Chase turned to look at his redheaded cousin and growled. "What the hell were you trying to do to me, asshole?" he asked Corbin.

"I was trying to help you because the family is on the way to Brooklyn to get you and take you back. Dani's car had a tracker on it. Aunt Judy put it on there when she got to Memphis in case Dani tried to take off exactly as she did. They're going to take the two of you back to Arkansas and try to finish what they started at the camp," Corbin explained.

I grabbed Dani's keys from Shay and handed them to Casper, who nodded in understanding. "On it. I'll stash it and meet you guys in Queens. What are you going to do with that guy?" Casper whispered as he pointed to Corbin Barr who was in the process of getting his ass reamed by Shay and Chase.

I'd seen enough, so I turned my back and addressed Casper. "I'm going to strip him to his underwear, take him to the ammo bunker, and handcuff him to anything I can find. I'll lock him inside for now and deal with him later," I responded quietly. Casper smirked before he left to handle Dani's car.

I'd treat Corbin Barr with kid gloves for now, but the jackoff had beaten the shit out of the man I loved and apparently, caused the whole mess Shay had dealt with in Arkansas earlier in the summer. I wasn't the type of person to let any of that go unpunished. Everything was converging into an imperfect storm. I needed to get my head together, *pronto*, and take care of business before it had a chance to get too messy.

Shay and Chase were still arguing with Shay's brother when I snuck up behind Corbin and put him in a sleeper hold until he was out, no permanent damage done. I carried him down to the basement of the Victorian with Shay following behind. I directed him behind the locker room to the ammo bunker where weapons were stored under impeccable security, thanks to Casper. I put my hand on the reader, and when the door opened, I nodded for Shay to go in first. I dropped Corbin onto the floor and retrieved a gurney from the corner of the room, securing Corbin to it before he woke.

I then turned to Shay and smiled, gently caressing his cheek. "Do me a favor and forget what you see in here. Your brother will keep his mouth shut about this shit, right? Or I can just get rid of him," I half-joked as I pointed to the man with a knife I pulled from the waist of my slacks. I wasn't sure it might be our only option, killing the guy, but I wasn't ready to approach Shay with other scenarios, none of them turning out too great for Corbin.

"He's not the brightest bulb, but I'm sure he has a desire to live, so he'll keep his mouth shut," Shay assured. Five minutes later, Corbin jerked his head up from the bed, thrashing a bit because I'd blindfolded him as well. "Who's there?" Shay's brother whispered, his voice trembling as he turned his head in every direction because the room was totally silent except for our breath.

"It's me, you fucking idiot. I've got someone with me, so don't get any bright ideas," Shay told him. I smiled and winked at my handsome man because he was offering a very compelling bad cop impression. It was cute on him.

I pointed to a chair for Shay to be seated and quietly walked behind the top of the bed where his brother was secured, seeing Corbin flinch as he sensed my presence near his head. I nodded for Shay to begin talking. "What the hell were you trying to do? You show up at my salon with a stocking cap over your face and try to take Chase *for his own safety?* What the fuck does that even mean, Corbin? You were at the compound along with the rest of those assholes before school started," Shay began.

I saw his brother's head perk up. "The compound? You mean at the lake camp? How do you know that, you little bastard?" Corbin asked. I smacked him on the side of his head because he was getting mouthy, and I didn't like it.

"Who the fuck is here?" he snapped angrily as he struggled to get his hands free from the cuffs on the rails of the bed.

"Someone who really wouldn't mind killing you unless you tell me what the hell you know about what's going on with the family. Y'all had Chase and a bunch of other kids at the lake compound, and you were doing to them what you all did to me," Shay reminded.

I bent over next to Corbin's ear, smirking when he jerked in fright. "Speak up," I prodded in a menacing voice.

"I-I-I... I wasn't supposed to go with them that weekend, but I was afraid they'd kill some of those kids without me there to stop them. Uncle Brett and Dad have lost their fuckin' minds when it comes to fa... gays. I don't know why, but Buck and Elvin got off on tryin' to torture the queer out of those kids. This is the third conversion weekend they've had over the summer. When school was out, Chase told Aunt Judy he's gay, and she tried to pray it away. After she figured out it wasn't gonna work, she told Uncle Brett, and then he set up one last camp for before school started for Chase and some of the other kids. The others were from congregations in other towns.

"Other pastors send their gay kids to Uncle Brett to make them straight, and he scares those kids so much I'm sure they never think about sex again, much less who they want to have it with. I'm tired of people thinkin' he's doin' God's work. He's mean, and he gets off on the power he has over those kids. It needs to stop, Shane.

"I don't understand about bein' gay, okay? I've been taught all my life it's an unforgivable sin, just like you, just like all of us. Last spring, I met someone... a new friend at work. He's gay, and he's been talkin' to me about it for a while now. Tells me he didn't pick bein' that way any more than he'd picked to be born in that ignorant town where we live, but he's lookin' out for his momma because his dad and brother are mean to her. He doesn't feel like he can leave her alone," Corbin explained.

I saw Shay's mind going a mile a minute before he slapped the table where he was sitting, scaring the shit out of his brother once again. I was pretty sure the guy was going to piss himself if we kept startling him, but I didn't really care. I'd rather just shoot him and be done with the whole mess.

"It's Derek Hines, isn't it? Dani said Drea told her Chase had a crush on him and wanted to ask him out. He did it, right?" Shay offered.

I saw his brother shaking his head quickly. "No, it's not Derek. I'm not sayin' who it is, just that what he says makes a lot of sense, and I don't want the family to keep hurtin' people who might not have a say in who they wanna fuck," Corbin told Shay.

I slapped him in the head again, because I didn't like his tone. Shay winked at me before he shook his head that I shouldn't hit his brother again. "He doesn't know any better, I promise you," Shay said with a sad smile. I crossed my arms over my chest and nodded in understanding. I had my fair share of bigots in my own family, and while I might like to put a bullet in some of the cousins' heads, I wouldn't… unless they gave me a compelling reason.

"It's about a hell of a lot more than fucking, but let's move on. Whose idea was it to put a tracker on Dani's car?" Shay asked.

"Uncle Brett. He's gone off the deep end, and he's takin' Dad, Buck, and Elvin with him. Aunt Judy keeps her mouth shut most of the time like Momma, but Uncle Brett sent her to Memphis to see if Dani was lyin' about Chase not bein' there with her. I heard Uncle Brett tell Dad he only has until next Tuesday to convert Chase. They made plans to bring him from Memphis to the lake camp over the holiday weekend. We were all ordered to be available to help out, and Momma was gonna bring all the stuff to make a big meal for all of us out there since we would be stayin' the whole weekend for an intervention," Calvin outlined. Good lord, what kind of people were these?

"Uncle Brett and Aunt Judy have Wi-Fi at their house so he can use the internet for spiritual outreach and research, or so he says. He bought a tracker off a website and gave it to Aunt Judy to put on Dani's car when she went to Memphis. I don't think any of them imagined she'd come to New York, but Buck called to tell me what was goin' on and he told me all about the thing, sayin' Dani's car was in Virginia, likely for the night.

"I took off as soon as I hung up with him. They think I'm on a parts trip to a junkyard in Tulsa and won't be home until tomorrow afternoon. I'm supposed to meet them at the lake. *This is serious, Shane,*" Corbin emphasized.

"I told Buck I didn't believe they had that kind of technology, so he gave me the unit number for her tracker. I found it by using my phone, and I drove here as fast as I could. They're all coming, Shane, and they'll find you, too. I'm afraid they'll kill you. Dad says you're a demon, and he'll kill you hisself if he ever gets a bead on ya," Corbin told Shay.

I shook my head because no fucking way was that going to happen. I checked my watch to see we needed to get going. "Let's wind this up for now. We have somewhere to be," I reminded Shay, seeing Corbin jump again. The man had no self-preservation instincts at all.

Corbin suddenly became incensed at the idea we were going to leave. "You can't leave me strapped to a bed with a blindfold around my head. I'll need to go to the bathroom, and I'll need somethin' to eat. What if the place catches on fire?" he demanded. *Not unwarranted concerns.*

I held up a finger and walked over to a locked refrigeration unit in the corner, working the combination to open the door. I pulled out a bottle of diazepam and a fresh syringe, drawing enough to keep the guy out until the next morning.

"You're not going to kill him, are you?" Shay asked after he rushed over to me. I opened the packaging for the syringe, holding it in my right hand as I wrapped my left arm around him. He was shaking, and I didn't want him scared. Without his permission, I wouldn't lay a hand on his brother.

"No, no. He'll sleep like a baby," I explained, showing Shay the bottle. He sighed and walked away, though I could tell he wasn't exactly happy about the turn of events.

I gave Corbin a quick jab, and as soon as he was knocked out, I unlocked his wrists and opened the door to a small toilet room with a sink. "I had no idea that was in there," Shay said as he looked inside while I covered Corbin with a blanket from a drawer in the corner. I wasn't heartless. There were MREs inside the cabinet over the fridge, and there was plenty of water. Corbin would be just fine.

The truth of the matter was if Sleeping Beauty wasn't related to the man I loved, Corbin would already have a nine in his thick skull, and I'd be calling in a clean-up team to take care of my mess. I had better places to be.

After I was sure Corbin had all the comforts of home, I stripped him down, grabbing the man's clothes and cell phone before I turned to Shay, offering what I hoped came across as a genuine smile. "I'll come in tomorrow morning and take care of him," I offered, seeing the look of apprehension on Shay's face. "Not *that* way, *tesoro*. I'll drug him again after he's dressed, and I'll drop him off on a park bench somewhere without his cell phone. I'll put some cash in his pocket so he can get somewhere.

"It'll take him a while to figure out where he is or how to get back to where he came from, but I promise you, he'll be fine," I assured Shay as I flipped the switch for the lighting strips along the floor of the bunker and locked the door, securing the safe room with my palm scan. It made me the only one who could let him out, or so I believed if I understood Casper correctly. I went to my locker in the gym and stowed his clothes, taking Shay's hand to feel it shaking.

I gently kissed the top of his knuckles before I wrapped my arm around him and led him upstairs so we could collect Chase, and the three of us went to Shay's apartment so they could clean up. I had clothes there as well so I changed while Shay was in the shower, resisting the urge to join him and ravage my man.

I was out of my rhythm… had been since I'd met Shay Barr if I was telling the truth. I needed to talk to him about several things—Ace came to mind immediately—and I needed to learn to compartmentalize my relationship with him because if anyone found out he was my weakness, they'd use him to get to me. In my job, I couldn't have it hanging over my head, and it wasn't fair to Shay at all.

I needed to consider the best way to handle Corbin Barr to ensure he wouldn't lead the rest of those deranged hillbillies to my man with the intent of doing him harm, but they were easy to handle in my mind. I'd have to threaten Corbin nine-ways-to hell for his silence, though. I had a distinct impression, however, that Corbin had some secrets he didn't want coming out, either, so perhaps I could simply blackmail him to keep him quiet? It was another way to go.

Of course, the incident had brought up worst-case scenarios that were now circling my brain about Shay's vulnerability to other dangers in my world. I was a ruthless killer who had suddenly grown a heart and a weakness, which others would exploit to get to me if they found out about Shay. I knew Gabe and the crew would keep him safe from his family, but the rest of the mean and ugly in the world that had become my specialty? That would take a more drastic step to keep it from him. His safety was the most important thing to me and being with me would be highly detrimental to it.

1 8

SHAY

Mateo called a car service to take the three of us out to Queens to Our Shepherd's House where we were meeting everyone. We were going to prepare the food for the Thanksgiving dinner being held at the shelter the next day after the morning service, and I could see Chase was excited. The church choir was supposed to be practicing, and while religion wasn't my thing, I loved a choir. Mathis mentioned there were speakers in the shelter cafeteria we could turn on to listen to their program, and I was looking forward to it.

I wasn't exactly thrilled my brother was locked in a vault in the Victorian, but at least we knew he was safe and not calling my family to alert them where Chase and Dani were hiding in case his whole story was bullshit. I was pessimistic about my brother's change of heart and alleged new-found acceptance of LGBTQ folks. Too many nasty, hurtful names had been shouted in my direction when I was growing up with those three asshats to make me believe there was any way for one of them to develop understanding and empathy for anyone who was different than them.

We couldn't take any chances with the situation because Chase and Dani were at risk, so I agreed knocking Corbin out and locking him up was probably the best idea for all concerned. I didn't want to consider my own ass was on the line right with them because my parents would likely hold me responsible for the whole mutiny they were witnessing in the family. I chose to believe I could take care of myself.

The black sedan stopped in front of the massive red-brick building next to an ornate, white-stone church designed in an English Gothic style. It had impressive detail, and I made a note to go see it in the daytime because it appeared to be beautiful at night, so I could only imagine it during the day.

The three of us got out of the car, but I saw Mateo lean back through the door to communicate with the driver. The man nodded before he drove away and stopped down the block. Mateo looked at Chase and smiled. "Can I talk to Shay for a minute?" Chase nodded and left us in the parking lot.

Mateo walked us over to the steps of the church, and we sat down next to each other. "You're going to be mad at me, but I can't stay, and I'm not sure when I'll be back. Something has come up that I absolutely have to handle, and I hate that I have to go. I love you, Shay. This shit tonight with your brother is penny-ante compared to what could happen to you if you are with me. Having something happen to you is absolutely the last thing I want to happen, so I'm afraid I need to try to take care of some things before they become detrimental to your safety," Mateo stated, sounding rather cryptic to me.

I felt like I'd been slapped. "Wait… a hot minute ago you asked me to move in with you, and you told me you were happy about it. What the fuck happened, Mateo?" He had to be fucking kidding me. He was gonna dump me on the steps of a church?

"I talked to Smokey and Nemo while you were showering, and they've promised to look out for Dani, Chase, and you until I can come back. I think if you talk to your brother, Corbin, you'll find out he's not so different from you. I believe he feels guilty for feeling the way he feels, much like you, which is why you like pain before pleasure. I think the two of you could benefit from going to a therapist to talk out the issues and unlearn the shit those religious fanatics taught you. Having someone beat you so you can have fulfilling sex isn't the answer, *tesoro*, and I want you to think about that while I'm gone," Mateo suggested.

So the Brit was right? He'd told me Mateo wasn't the settling down kind, but I had the audacity to think I could change him. I thought he'd just be pleased as punch to settle down with me? I was a fucking idiot. Once again, I was expendable. I should have seen it coming, shouldn't I? Well, it wouldn't be the first time I'd been tossed aside, and I was pretty sure it wouldn't be the last. I wasn't the best judge of character as I'd learned over and over again, so being left behind was a position more familiar than not.

I nodded, accepting my fate. "Sure, I get it. What about my brother, Corbin? You're not going to kill him, are you?"

Mateo gently cupped my face and leaned forward, brushing his lips softly over mine before he pulled away and looked into my eyes. "Ordinarily, I wouldn't hesitate to handle him in a manner we both know I'm used to, but for you, I won't do anything. As I said, I'll drop him somewhere before I leave. He's smart enough to get around, right?" Mateo asked.

"Yeah, he'll get around, but I can't guarantee he won't go to the cops and tell them everything," I realized.

"I'll handle it. Corbin won't go anywhere near the cops I can promise you. If he doesn't take my words seriously, he *will* regret it. He'll probably contact you in a few days. Call Nemo or Shep immediately and give some thought to the type of relationship you want with your brother in the future, but be careful," Mateo warned.

I nodded. "I'm glad Chase and I had you to depend on to get through this shit. I guess we should go back to my place…" I began.

"No, you'll be moved into my place tonight. I hired someone to move my shit out and your shit in. I paid the rent for six months, so you have time to decide what to do. Everything will be as it should be for you, *tesoro*." Oh, a do-gooder? That was novel, wasn't it? Getting me into a better apartment by asking me to move in with him and then moving out of it and leaving it with me. That was a no one to me. I couldn't even respond.

"Remember to talk to Nemo or Smokey if anything happens and

you need help. They'll do anything to help you, Shay," Mateo insisted as he stroked my hair.

I knew just as sure as I was sitting on a cold, concrete step numbing my rump roast that once the pain of losing him settled into my heart, it would be all-consuming and rip me to shreds. There was only one way to relieve that kind of pain, and it wouldn't be me going to a BDSM club to find someone to beat my frozen ass, just as Mateo had cautiously done when I needed the pain to keep my self-loathing at bay. My relief would come in a much less dignified form, and it would feel like an old friend coming back into my life to eliminate any personal growth I wanted to tell myself I'd achieved.

All the work I'd done to get over that need would just disappear, but what the fuck did I care? After I ensured Dani and Chase were safe and on the road to a beautiful future, what the hell did I have to lose?

I watched as Mateo motioned for the town car to come back, hopping inside with a grin and a kiss to his fingers which he aimed at me, the mother fucker. I'd never felt lonelier in my life. I sat in the cold for a few more minutes before I decided to go inside and help with the meal prep. I could fake it for a few days, and after the holiday weekend, I was going to disappear for a little while and do my best to maintain my sanity.

I walked into the shelter and saw people busily washing vegetables and chopping things. There were a lot of helpers there, which was a good thing. It was a *more-the-merrier* situation, and many hands made light the work, or so I remembered my mom saying when I was a kid.

All I had to do was disengage my brain and get through the tasks with a smile on my face. I took off my coat and my scarf to hang them on a coat hook in the foyer before I walked over to a table where a bunch of aprons were folded, grabbing one.

Chase came sliding over with a big smile. "Hi, I'm Chase, your cruise director. Where do you think you'd be most useful? You can set up tables, iron linens, peel vegetables, wash dishes as the chefs dirty them, or you can help make setups. If you have something more specific in mind, let me know. Mr. Bianco asked if I minded acting as coordinator when he arrived a few minutes ago," the kid explained as his face flushed with excitement. Obviously, Rafael Bianco had another admirer in my cousin.

That reminded me of something Mateo had said before he left after handing me that envelope. "Where is Mr. Bianco?" I asked.

"He's in the cooler outside with his cooks. They're moving food into the kitchen in the order of necessity," Chase told me with an infectious smile.

I nodded and hustled out the back door of the kitchen to the large trailer where people were carrying in waxed boxes of produce along with carts full of other ingredients. I was nearly mowed down by Parker who was wheeling out a dolly with a stack of turkeys on it as he pushed it down a ramp. "Holy Shit! Sorry, Shay. Are you okay?" he apologized as he stopped and hugged me.

"No worries. Is Mr. Bianco inside? I have something for him from his fuckwit brother," I explained.

Parker studied me, and I saw his stance become a bit rigid. "What's wrong, Shay?" he asked. I cursed myself for getting so close with that group of men and women... that group who knew me better than anyone, especially my own family.

I took a deep breath. "I don't want to talk about it right now. Lunch next Tuesday?" I invited, knowing I had no intentions of attending lunch with my friends that day. I couldn't handle the scrutiny of all of those happy people. They were living the life I'd never have, and I really didn't need the reminder.

"Yeah, sure. Are you okay?" Parker asked, a look of concern written on his handsome face. As much as I wanted to hide from them, I was grateful for the friends I had because they were genuine. It was a shame I couldn't say the same about Mateo Torrente.

I offered a smile which I attempted to make as sincere as possible. "I'm always okay, Parker. Chop, chop," I joked as I walked up the ramp and stood outside the trailer, watching the precision with which Rafael Torrente executed his job.

When the last person left the trailer with a box of small pumpkins, I walked inside and held out the envelope I was instructed to give Rafe. "Oh, hi, Shay. Where's Teo?"

I cocked an eyebrow. "Mateo has a nickname? He didn't like the one I gave him, so I was sure he hated all of them. Yet another thing I wasn't allowed to learn about him," I told the man as I shook the envelope at him.

Rafe took it and quickly opened it, reading the paper which only had one sentence on it from what I could see through the back of the sheet. Rafael looked at me for a moment before he became angry. "He left?" I could only nod. "Are you okay?" Rafe asked. Again, I nodded.

Rafael wadded up the paper in his fist as he turned his back to me for a moment. *"Fottuto idiota!"* I wasn't sure what the first word meant, but I knew 'idiot' when I heard it. I couldn't have agreed more.

"I'll deal with him tomorrow evening. This isn't the end, Shay. Teo gets inside his head and does stupid things, but I know he loves you more than he's ever… well, that's not for me to say, but don't let this bother you because he'll come to his senses, I promise you." Ten minutes ago, I'd have believed the man, but now? No, it was all lies. Lull the Arkansas hick into a false sense of security and then rip that fucking rug right out from under me. *God, I was a gullible fool.*

"Now, what would you like to do? Chase is my kitchen manager, and if he was out of high school and wanted to go to culinary? I'd find him a place in my organization and put him in school to train, but I get the feeling he's more suited for your line of work," Rafael told me as he dragged a large bag toward the front of the trailer and turned off the light inside the huge, freezer-on-wheels.

"What's that? I can help you carry it inside. I'm stronger than I look," I offered with a flex of my flimsy arms. Rafe laughed at me as he put his arm around my shoulders and steered me down the ramp. We lifted the metal thing and pushed it inside the trailer before Rafe closed the doors. He guided me toward the back entrance of the massive commercial kitchen where everyone was working happily, and I almost wished I'd fallen for him instead of his brother. Rafe had roots in the U.S. He planned to stay. His brother never had the same intentions, though I had never asked him, had I?

"It was just trash. I'll get someone to move it to that big dumpster, no problem," Rafe told me as he gave me a hug before we each went our separate ways inside the large building.

I walked out into the dining area, seeing Maxi orchestrating the placement of long tables with the assistance of Smokey, Nemo, Mathis, and Ace, the newest employee at Gabe's company. I saw Searcy, Dylan, and Casper's sister, Jewel, opening folding chairs for the other men to place at the tables, and it immediately lightened my mood.

I walked over to Jewel, knowing she would be in my salon chair on Saturday morning. "You're Lawry's sister, Jewel, right?" I asked. "I'm Shay. Not sure if you remember me. We'd met at Gabe and Dex's wedding, and I remembered her persuading Searcy to walk down the aisle when the little doll got stage fright.

"Hi. It's good to see you again. I like the color of your hair," Jewel told me as she reached up and gently touched it. I'd had Ari give me highlights a few weeks ago while Mateo was gone because I was trying to look like I belonged with him... so I looked worthy of being on his arm. There was no need to try to look my best any longer. The outside trappings didn't make up for what was lacking on the inside... the things lacking Mateo had picked up on and rejected.

"Why are you so sad?" Jewel asked as she pulled two chairs over and sat down, patting the other for me to join her. Maybe the young woman had some advice for me? Hell, any outsider could probably see the flaws in the relationship I had with Mateo clearer than me. Maybe Jewel could see something about me I didn't recognize in myself? It was worth a conversation.

I sat down and reached for her hand as she studied me with a sweet look of concern. "I just got dumped," I told her, feeling the tears come without my bidding. Before I could blink, she ran over to Maxi and whispered to him. He turned to look at me and handed her something from his pocket.

Jewel ran back over to me and sat down in her chair, moving it closer to me. She touched my bicep and handed me a white handkerchief with the letters, *MP,* embroidered in gold on the corner. It was so sweet of her. I knew the story behind the hankies, and it had touched me deeply.

I dried my eyes and touched the hand she had on my arm. "Tell me about your music," I coaxed. I wasn't going to rain on anyone's parade. It was a night to give thanks for many reasons. As I sat with Jewel Schatz and listened to her tales about school and how she was going to take her driving test again in the spring because she didn't pass it the first time, I realized the simple things that made her happy were much more important than the shit I was allowing to stress me. It was time for a priority realignment.

"So, Shay, you're the hair expert of the group?" Congressman Ben Hoffman asked as we sat preparing silverware at Maxi's direction. I'd pushed my troubles down after I had my little meltdown with Lawry's sister, and I felt better. Well, I felt better for the time being, but I wasn't sure what the morning would bring.

"I've never been called an expert before, but I'm closer to an expert than these clowns, Mr. Hoffman. If you ever need a trim when you're in town to see your husband, call me. I'll make time for you," I offered as we continued to polish the utensils before we sent them down the table to Jewel, Searcy, and Dylan to actually roll in the thick, paper napkins.

"Please, call me Ben. Raleigh talks about all of you, and I've wanted to spend time getting to know you, but I'm in office until December of next year. After that, I'm not sure what I'll do," Ben offered. Shepard Colson was sitting next to Ben, but I could tell he wasn't exactly comfortable talking with us, so I decided to put the man on the spot to include him in the conversation.

"Shep, you know the city pretty well. Can you offer Ben any suggestions about job opportunities for him in New York after he's out of office?" I taunted, seeing the man actually give me the stink eye for drawing attention to him. It made me laugh.

Shepard finally laughed as well. "Shay, we both know the Congressman will have many doors open to him if he and Nemo decide to settle in New York once his term is over. I'm sure any number of firms would love to have a former representative with such a great record fighting for LGBTQ issues at their firms. Hell, I'd guess the lobbying firms in D.C. would lose their minds if they could get you," Shep suggested as he turned to Ben Hoffman and smiled, which was something I hadn't thought about. *Kudos to Shep for thinking outside the box.*

Not surprisingly, Lawry's little sister moved so she could sit next to Mr. Hoffman. "I'm Jewel. What's your position on the rights of people with emotional and physical disabilities?" she asked. The table was quiet for a moment before Ben Hoffman offered his hand to shake Jewel's, which made her smile.

"It's a pleasure to meet you, Jewel. Regarding the rights of our citizens with challenged abilities, I believe we all have challenges, and I don't see anyone as really having disabilities, though a lot of people tell me that's a condescending assessment for me to make regarding some of our fellow citizens. I disagree, by the way.

"Some people have challenges harder than mine, but the goal should be success for everyone. Would I like to offer more programs for people in my district who have physical, mental, and emotional challenges? I would, but I want to ensure my constituents who could benefit from such programs would be treated with dignity.

"I think it's sad it has to be spelled out, specifically, but as we've learned from history, we can't allow ambiguity to be the order of the day because there are people who will use it to take advantage of others. I want to be one-hundred-percent certain everyone is treated fairly and with respect, and after I'm no longer in public office, I hope to find a position somewhere to allow me to continue to fight for those rights for everyone," Ben explained to her. When Jewel started clapping, hell we all did.

Raleigh Wallis walked over from where he'd been placing chairs around the various tables in the large room and leaned forward, kissing his husband on the cheek. "No politics tonight, Benji. We're here to have a good time and for you to get to know everyone," he whispered into his husband's ear, but we could all hear it, and it warmed my heart. The two men definitely loved each other very much. It was inspiring to witness, but it broke my heart at the same time because I would never have it. Goddamn Mateo for walking away without really giving us a chance.

The rest of the evening, I got to know a lot of people, including Mathis' parents, who were lovely. They thanked us for being kind enough to help them provide a meal and some basic hygiene essentials which Rafael Bianco had collected at his restaurants over the last month, offering discounts to his customers for a donation. His employees had gotten together to make the care packages for those who would be attending the dinner the next day, and I felt humbled I hadn't considered doing something similar at the shop. I did, however, donate a thousand dollars of my own money because I'd forgotten to collect from my customers. I slid the check into a donation box next to the front door and hoped it would be found in time to do something for the people who came to the shelter on a regular basis.

I felt a deep disgust for anyone who wouldn't want to help provide a meal for people who were homeless or in poverty and needed a helping hand. Hell, I was on board. Instead of allowing my heart to break and mourn Mateo Torrente? I'd turn the pain into something constructive. I didn't know what, but I'd figure it out.

"You're not coming for dinner? Shay, Mateo's not going to be here. He's leaving the country," Dex assured, and I knew he meant it to be supportive of me, but I damn well didn't feel good about going to their home in light of Mateo's disposal of me like so much dogshit on his shoe.

Dramatic much? No, they all knew he'd dumped me, so being

humiliated at a Thanksgiving gathering wasn't exactly what I was hoping to do that Thursday.

Chase had opted to spend Thanksgiving in Queens with Dani and Jonah Wright's family, and I supported it. I'd helped him pack up his things to take with him, both of us deciding it would be for the best that he wasn't in Brooklyn where Dani's car had probably been traced by the family.

I didn't know what had happened to Corbin, but I believed Mateo to be an honest man, even if he was a cold-blooded killer and a complete fuckwad when it came to me. He'd given me his word he wouldn't hurt my brother. Why I cared wasn't anything I wanted to consider, but when I thought about what Mateo had said, it sort of made sense.

"I think if you talk to your brother, Corbin, you'll find out he's not so different from you. He feels guilty for feeling the way he feels, much like you. I think the two of you could benefit from going to a therapist to talk out the issues and unlearn the shit those religious fanatics taught you."

I knew Mateo was spot on in his assessment of my brother's situation, and I would never forget he was the one who pointed out something that was apparent… had been most of my life. Corbin was either gay or bi, and he was scared to death about it, much as I'd been for most of my life. He didn't know how to live his truth, and maybe it was my job to help him figure it out. That was likely a much nobler endeavor than taking a razor blade to my thighs as I'd planned to do at first.

I needed to find Corbin before he was irreversibly harmed by our family as I'd been. Maybe he hadn't been my champion when I was growing up, but I had to imagine he was as scared as me when it came to the hatred we'd witnessed for anyone who was the least bit different from our parents. I could support Corbin, even if he couldn't support himself.

I was at Mateo's old apartment by myself, seeing he'd kept his promise as he'd mentioned. Everything that was his was gone, and all of my boxes were stacked in the living room. I felt as if my heart was broken in half at seeing any traces of the man I loved having been erased from the apartment.

When I'd been dropped off at the building the previous night by Gabe and Dex, I only picked up a blanket from one of my boxes and slipped off my shoes to sleep on the couch. I had no idea what to do next, and when the phone rang that morning, I listened to Dexter's prodding for me to attend the big dinner they had planned, even though I didn't exactly welcome it.

"I'm sorry, sugar, but I'm currently nursing a migraine. Tomorrow and Saturday are full days at the shop, stem to stern. I need to get over this to be ready for work because there's the Gala and then Maxi's party. I appreciate the invitation, and you make sure to have fun with your family and friends. I'll see you at Maxi's party on Saturday night if I feel better," I offered before I hung up my phone.

I was taking Thanksgiving Day to mope, and I wasn't going to allow anyone to make me feel guilty about it. I needed time to process the pain from the end of a relationship I had hoped would be permanent so I could move forward. I'd decided after my full weekend of clients and Maxi's engagement party, I would take myself somewhere to regroup and get my act together. I hadn't really taken a vacation in years, so maybe it was time? Fuck a stranger? Rework my life's plan? The possibilities were endless.

I knew I could leave the salon in Sonya's more-than-capable hands, and Ari and Wren could handle my clients while I was gone. I would make certain Dex and Parker had the haircuts of their dreams before I left, and then I had a month to disappear. It sounded decadent and just what I needed. Heaven to me had consisted of spending time with Mateo, but that wasn't going to happen ever again, and I needed to mourn it and get over it.

I went to the freezer of the stainless monster in the kitchen, not surprised to see Mateo had left food inside. Everything had a date scribbled on it, and I was actually happy there was a pan of stuffed shells dated the prior week. Unfortunately, it reminded me of a conversation Mateo and I shared in bed one night after he gave me a delicious spanking before we made love.

"So, can you keep yourself alive, or do you depend on your brother to feed you?" I asked Mateo as we settled into my bed after eating the food the handsome man had brought from Blue Plate. It was the Thursday special... spaghetti and meatballs... and it was incredible. Chase had ordered the filet tips and penne pasta in a garlic cream sauce, and he'd passed out on the couch in my apartment about an hour after we cleaned up the dinner dishes.

"Well, Mama always wanted us to find a nice wife to cook for us, but when Rafe took off on his culinary adventures, and I went into the Italian police force, I never had to worry about being fed, and I'd already addressed the 'wife' issue with my parents, so I was on my own.

"Now, that's not to say I didn't sit with Rafe at our Nonna's knee to learn to make pasta and her meatballs, as well, but he was much better at it. I'd just need to call him to get the recipe, and I firmly believe I could make Nonna's meatballs for you. How about you? Any favorites you like to make?" he asked with a cocky grin as he settled onto his back and pulled me onto his muscular chest, my arms crossed as my chin rested against my forearms.

I chuckled. "I can make a mean fried chicken, mashed potatoes, and bacon-laced collards. My mother's a southern cook, and she used to let me stay in the kitchen when my dad and brothers were out doing manly things. She'd say, 'You're more of a gentle soul, Shane, and there's nothing wrong with that. You can be my little helper.' I guess she was trying to keep my father from figuring out I was never gonna be his budding sports star...'" I remembered our discussion. Mateo had smiled at me, and my heart had been lost to him. I'd have to figure out how to get it back.

I was pulled from my hunt for food as I considered the idea that maybe my mother hadn't totally disowned me. She might have been trying to protect me back then by keeping me near her? Maybe she tried to stop Dad and Uncle Brett from inflicting the pain they'd seemed to delight in when I was younger, but she didn't know how to keep them from going against their better angels? Hell, maybe she *didn't* tell my father I was part of that raid, after all.

I needed to talk to her, but I had no idea how to get in touch with her without alerting my father and brothers… other than Corbin. I started to call Parker so I could talk to Shepard, but I decided to try Mateo's number first, praying he hadn't changed it.

I understood what he meant when he told me we were done. His job didn't allow him to have a relationship, blah-blah-bullshit. I wasn't a hanger-onner. But, maybe Mateo would allow a favor for an old friend? It was worth a try.

I called his number, not surprised it went directly to voicemail. It was just the standard, pre-programmed, automaton voice. *"Please leave a message after the tone."*

I took a deep breath. "Killer, it's me. I'm sorry to bother you, but I need a favor. After this, I won't ever call you again."

I hung up and hoped he was the honorable assassin I believed him to be, and he'd return my call. Yes, the man had taken lives, though I didn't know how many, and yes, I'd seen him actually kill a man in my salon. I wasn't condoning it, but I was sure there were instances where someone had to do a job they might not like to do, but it was necessary, right?

Who wanted mercy for the pedophile in the neighborhood the cops couldn't seem to get enough evidence to put behind bars? If someone killed that sick fucker when people weren't looking, I doubted any of the neighbors would set up a floral tribute in his front yard. They'd hold their children a little tighter at night and thank their god for the silent avenger who had handled the problem. I wasn't making Mateo into a saint by any stretch, but I couldn't condemn him for his job, either. That was what I'd keep telling myself, anyway.

19

MATEO

Late Wednesday night...

I sat in the back of the town car down the street from the church and watched as Rafe moved the frozen remains of Giancarlo Mangello to the front of the trailer while he spoke with Shay, which meant he was ready to give up torturing our *cousin's* corpse. I didn't know if he was ready because he'd learned Giancarlo was family or if he was trying to turn over a new leaf for Papa's sake. I hoped it was the latter.

Rafe was definitely one to hold a grudge and the shit that happened with Allegra... Giancarlo hooking her up with those drugs until she overdosed and was left with traumatic brain injury... was unforgivable in my brother's opinion. It was complicated as fuck, but it seemed as if Rafe was at least done with delivering pieces of his quarry to the man's father. Well, I hoped he was finished because it was fucking twisted.

After everything was emptied from the trailer, I saw a crew pull up to it to haul out Giancarlo's worthless body before a truck stopped to hook up to the white monster emblazoned with *Bianco Catering* on the side in red, white, and green letters, hauling it back to Brooklyn to Rafe's catering company. One thing I noticed was the *moles* were missing from the mix of attendees that night, which had me a bit concerned.

Once I left the church parking lot, I went by my old apartment in Gabe's building since I had my shit moved to a storage facility not far away, and Shay's remaining boxes moved into that apartment to get him out of that fucking pit where he lived. I was relieved he was willing to move in because it was bigger than his little apartment and had a security system I knew I could rely on to keep him free from harm. I was just heartbroken I wouldn't get to live there with him.

Regardless of that *merda* excuse I'd given Shay earlier in the evening to explain why we couldn't be together, I loved Shay Barr and wanted him to have a fantastic life because he deserved the best of everything. Yeah, I was a *cazzo* for the way I'd dumped him. I hadn't said when I'd be back because I couldn't bring myself to say it out loud that I never planned to come back. I left it open ended, which was probably cruel if he held out hope that I'd come back. I prayed his hatred for me was strong enough that he'd get over me quickly. I still wanted him happy.

Some of my things were still in the basement of Gabe's apartment building, and I'd need to retrieve them before totally vacating the premises. After the movers delivered Shay's stuff, I went to the basement and found a particular leather case containing some tools I would use as props for my next stop. I was going to the Victorian in the morning to deal with Corbin Barr before I left town, but I was pretty sure the man would sleep like a baby until I got there. I had time to dump him out at Grand Central with a couple of bucks in his pocket before I finalized my plans for handling Sally Man. Then, I'd disappear for a long while.

I drove to the building where Dom lived in Gabe's old condo and picked the back lock, surprised to see Casper hadn't changed it to something high tech because Dom lived there alone, but I decided to ponder it later. I took the stairs to the third floor and picked the lock on the stairwell door to get into the hallway.

It was a nice building, to be sure, and if I honestly had the desire to live in a condo, I might buy into the whole multi-dwelling lifestyle myself, but I wasn't interested in buying a box stacked on top of other boxes. I was a temporary quarters' guy. No roots and no teary-eyed goodbyes.

I made my way down the hallway and quickly let myself into the condo without drawing any attention before I slipped off my shoes. I heard sounds coming from the back of the unit, but I decided to let my little cousin have his fun because when I got done with him, he'd be too scared to fuck anyone for a very long time. If he were with the person I believed he might be, I'd have to break the awful news they were over forever, and I hoped I only had to take out one of them.

I went to the kitchen to get myself a drink of water, but I saw a bottle of the Torrente *Chianti* was open on the counter. It had always been one of my favorites, so I poured myself a glass, took off my jacket, and made myself comfortable.

"I'm almost there… fucking hell," It was the familiar voice of Dominic that I'd expected to hear.

"Let go for me, baby," was the response from an unfamiliar voice, but it was likely who I'd been expecting.

The keening sound wasn't anything I wanted to consider, and the ramifications of the coupling were fucked up, but weird shit happened every day. I'd have never imagined I'd fall in love with a flamboyant hair stylist, but there I sat, wishing the sounds I was hearing were being made by Shay and me. Unfortunately, that couldn't happen again, and it was my stupid fucking fault.

As I considered what I needed to do, I decided I'd clean up the mess I was about to make before I went to the Middle East to regroup. There was always something to do there, and I was actually looking forward to the solitude of being away from everyone in my life. I needed time to get over Shay… though I had the feeling it would be nearly impossible to do based on the pain in my chest.

I sipped my wine as I listened to the two men in the shower, honestly happy there was a lot of laughter for them before I brought the harsh enlightenment of justice into focus. I hated what I was about to do, but it was a necessary evil.

"You hungry?" I heard after the bedroom door opened. I pulled out my Tan and screwed on the suppressor before placing it on the sofa next to where I sat, praying it all didn't go to hell. I was hoping it would be quick and easy without a lot of problems.

"I could eat. What do you have? I know you don't cook," I heard from a softer voice. The two men came down the hallway, not seeing me sitting in the dark living room. I watched as they made their way into the kitchen, but it seemed best to keep my presence unknown until I had a handle on the situation.

"Do you want more wine? I thought we had more than this? I'll get another bottle. Uncle Gabe left most of his stuff here when he moved in with Uncle Dexter," my cousin said as he held up the nearly empty bottle of *Torrente Vineyards* finest.

"You can have it, though it's really good, and I don't generally like wine. I'll have a beer. What do you have to eat?" the mother fucker I planned to kill asked. I picked up my Tan and the glass of wine I'd been sipping, heading into the kitchen where they were kissing passionately.

"Isn't this cozy?" I offered, seeing the two men jump at the sound of my voice. I watched Dom's companion hold up his hands while the blood drained from his face. His appearance wasn't what I expected at all, but his sniveling certainly fit the bill.

Dominic, well, he was more shocked than his friend. "Mateo? What's this… Wait! He's a good guy," the kid offered.

I lifted my gun to put one in the other asshole's skull when Dominic stepped in front of him. "No, Mateo. You can't hurt him. I think we can get him out of his current situation, and I'd like to see him again. We need to help him, and you can't tell anyone about him yet," Dom told me, which made me hesitate.

Hesitating was something I'd never done during a kill before in my entire career, and it wasn't settling well in my gut. I acted first and analyzed later. I was a killer, but I had a feeling Shay, *my Shay*, had changed me without my knowledge or consent. That wasn't promising going forward because I couldn't do the job I needed to do if I had any compassion. *Hell, I'm fucked.*

"How about you tell me what it *is*, Dominic?" I snapped at him as I placed my gun on the counter, so the two of them didn't have meltdowns and piss themselves.

"Either of you strapped? Drop the towels and turn around," I commanded as I kept my hand on my Tan while they both did as I asked, spinning around and then both covering their junk with their hands. I almost laughed.

"Dominic, go get the two of you some sweats or shorts, and if I think you're trying anything, I'll gut him like a fish," I told my younger cousin as I pulled the knife out from behind my back and used it to point to the burly soldier who looked like he was about to go into convulsions.

Dominic rushed down the hallway and was back in a few seconds. His companion hadn't moved an inch, still covering his junk as he watched me carefully. Something just wasn't adding up for me.

Lotta had called to tell me there was an account in Dominic's name and another in Sierra Conti's name where money transferred from one to the other before it was wired to a third, anonymous account in a bank in Switzerland and disappeared. What the fuck had I missed?

It was finally dark on Thanksgiving evening, so I wrangled the lovebirds to leave the condo, and I'd made them leave their phones behind in the event someone was tracking them. We'd eaten Chinese from the only place open on Thanksgiving, and after, we took a nap to kill time because I needed darkness to go forward with my plans.

I'd sent Sherlock a text to meet me at the Victorian before he went to London because I'd given him the wrong key. It was a thinly disguised ploy to buy myself some time. Sherlock's plane wasn't leaving until ten that night anyway, so he could wait. "Where are we going?" Dominic asked as we sped to the Victorian.

I felt as if my skin was crawling. Too many things were going down at the same time, and I hadn't even brought up the Lucia shit. Maybe that was an avenue to explore?

"We're going to the Victorian because Sherlock is meeting us there. What do you know about your mother's new boyfriend? Did she come to New York for Thanksgiving and did she bring him with her?" I asked.

"I, uh, she should be at Nonna's on Long Island by now, but she was only bringing the girls with her because she's not ready for Marco to meet the family, or so she told me. I'm sure I'm in the doghouse because I missed lunch today at Uncle Gabe and Dex's, but I had a crazy man holding a gun on me, so what could I really do?" Dom taunted, which made me laugh.

I hadn't actually held a gun on him, but I didn't let either of them leave. I needed to put an end to the suspense, and either of them leaving that day had the potential to throw a little more gasoline on an already volatile situation.

"I'll explain to Gabriele and Lucia later. How much do either of you know about computers?" I asked. I couldn't call Lotta because I was beginning to worry I had been given some less than truthful intel about what was actually going on.

Lawry had his family visiting, and his engagement party was on Saturday night, so I was trying to keep the drama to a minimum. Only if I couldn't handle shit on my own would I call him. I prayed the two in the SUV with me could pull enough intel together to give me an idea of what the fuck was happening so I could formulate a plan.

"I worked in intelligence before I was discharged. I was in a relationship with an officer, and we got caught together by a General who wanted his picture taken in front of an F-16. We were fucking behind it.

"Of course, they wanted to cover it up because the officer I was with was from a well-known family and is a decorated squadron leader. What would it look like if an O-6 got caught fucking an E-4 in a hangar? They had to get rid of me, and quick. To keep from being arrested for conduct unbecoming, I was given the *opportunity* to sign an NDA and receive a discharge, honorable thank hell, and he was busted down to an O-4.

"The man got to stay in and keep his happy life, and I got fucked, and not in the good way I just did," Nick, the kid with Dom, responded. I glanced at my little cousin to see him with a cocky look on his face, which made me chuckle under my breath.

"Okay, well, I'll get you into Casper's network, and you can do some searches for me. I need to know online activity for a couple of people for the last twenty-four to thirty-six hours. I think Casper has all of the shit on everyone's phone and provider or whatever it is, you just…" I started.

Nick cleared his throat from the back seat. "I got it. I could do it from any laptop. I don't need to be in your network," Nick explained.

"Yeah, you do because I don't want you getting caught hacking in another way. Better to do it from our place. Can you make it look like it's coming from…?" I started to ask.

"He wants you to mask your presence so they don't know it's our network. We got it," Dom decided. *At least he's got more Torrente than Mazzola in him.*

Sierra still wasn't off the hook as being the mole, but if the Nana story held true, at least I had a good idea why she was doing what she was doing. I needed to know about the other two, and I needed to know now.

"You got a sick Nonna?" I asked the kid.

He glanced at Dom, who rolled his eyes. "He's asking about your grandmother in California. Yeah, she fell and broke her hip, and she has shitty insurance, so they're trying to help her out with expenses. Tell him about your parents," Dom said to Nick.

"Nana is my father's mother. He was killed in Kosovo. Navy pilot. Mom took us to live with Nana and then took off with one of Dad's brothers. Sad story, blah-blah-blah. I want to help out with expenses, but Sierra and I have distinctly different ideas of how to make money," he finished.

I knew all of that was bullshit because Casper had come up with Sierra's history for us. I knew her crazy parents lived on Long Island, but I kept my mouth shut and pulled into the lot behind the Victorian to see the lights were on, which meant either Sherlock beat me there, or someone else was in there nosing around.

I knew for sure Corbin was still downstairs because only I could release him from the bunker unless Gabe had shown up, which was doubtful. I looked at my companions, and even though I'd had every intention of shooting both of them previously, I couldn't let Dominic become collateral damage in such a fucked-up scenario because I knew in my gut that kid was innocent.

I reached into my pocket and handed Dom a small revolver, pulling a nine from the other pocket and handing it to his boyfriend, though it wasn't loaded. "Sit in the car. Watch for flashes. If you see them, get the fuck out of here. If anyone comes out of that building that's not me, shoot, but don't make it a kill shot in case it's my brother or Gabe. I'll let you know when it's safe to come inside," I told them, praying to fuck I wasn't trusting a lovesick fool and a fucking degenerate. I had to remind myself I didn't know Nick Conti, and well, Gio Mazzola, that worthless piece of shit, *was* Dom's father. There was the possibility he was like his old man.

I quietly slipped out of the large SUV and glanced at my watch to see it was 23:30, so I could still get in through the back door. I made sure to leave the keys to the vehicle in the event they needed to get away. I slid behind the car and up to the back of the Victorian, remembering if I used the back entrance, the lights would flash and alert whoever was inside I'd entered the building.

The front entrance, however, didn't work the same way, so I rushed back to the car and knocked on Dom's window, seeing Nick had moved into the driver's seat. The car was idling, so Dom powered down the window. "Yeah?" he whispered loudly.

"You got a key to the front door, or do you always come in through the back?" I asked him.

"I left my keys at home. Dex always forgets his, so he has an extra key to the front door stashed inside a green frog in the front planter box on the porch. The combination to the frog is twelve-twenty-four," Dom whispered. *Leave it to my cousin-in-law to use his wedding anniversary for a goddamn find-a-key.*

"Does Gabe know about that?" I asked. I couldn't believe my security-fanatical cousin would be down for that shit.

"Oh, God no. He'd lose his mind," Dom told me.

I nodded as I rushed around the side of the Victorian and to the porch. *Of course, a fucking frog doesn't stand out at all in November,* I told myself. I rarely came or went by the front door, so imagine my surprise when I looked in the planter box and found five fucking green frogs. My luck had severely turned for the worse.

Ten minutes, and four broken, plaster frogs later, I had the fucking key. I also knew what I would be buying Gabe and Dex for Christmas. Something better than a fucking frog-shaped, hide-a-key.

I quickly inserted the key and listened to hear the security system begin to beep. That was the thing I'd forgotten. You had thirty-seconds to enter your personal security code once you were inside or the cops were on the way. If I didn't have a fucking hostage in the basement, I might have just let it go. The more, the merrier.

I heard someone on the stairs, so I crouched down, thrusting open the door before I rolled into the room, gun drawn. The security lights flashed on, illuminating one of the people I needed to find. "Fuck's sake, Mateo. I could have shot your stupid arse," Sherlock snarled at me as he lowered his gun. I didn't take the chance he'd change his mind. I fired first.

20

SHAY

Thanksgiving afternoon…

Since Mateo had probably already left the country without calling me back and I couldn't get Rafe on the phone either, I called my mother's cell from a payphone at a shitty gas station down the street from the building Gabe and Dex owned. Before he flew the coop, Mateo had moved me into his place. At the time he'd suggested I move in, I had hopes we would have a great life together. Of course, that wasn't going to happen, as I'd learned when I got home the previous night to see all of his things were gone and the rest of my things had been moved in while I was in Queens. That was *Dear Diary* shit, right there, but I had a bigger problem at the moment.

The phone rang twice before it was answered, though no one spoke. I decided it was worth a shot. "It's me. I need to talk to you. Meet me at *Bud & Freda's Diner* at eight in the morning," I told the person, praying it was my mother. I heard a whispered, "Okay," before I hung up.

I walked back to Gabe and Dex's building and let myself inside, hurrying to the elevator and inserting the key I had for it so it took me to the third floor. I leaned back against the wall and closed my eyes for a minute, trying very hard to forget what Mateo had told me.

"You're going to be mad at me, but I can't stay, and I'm not sure when I'll be back. Something has come up that I absolutely have to handle, and I hate that I have to go. I love you, Shay. This shit tonight with your brother is penny-ante compared to what could happen to you if you are with me. Having something happen to you is absolutely the last thing I want to happen, so I'm afraid I need to try to take care of some things before they become detrimental to your safety."

What the hell did he mean about something being detrimental to *my* safety? The only reason I could come up with for his blow-off comments was that he'd fed me a line of bullshit from the start and like a fool, I fell for it. Hot, slick guys like Mateo Torrente were always juggling things, and I was sure I was just one of many. I knew he wasn't really a wine salesman, but he had to at least put up a front to support his cover, right? Was I part of that cover, as well, so he could do the things he did and maintain a "normal" life for the viewing public? He loved me? We had a very different definition of what love meant, me and the bastard who broke my heart. *Fuckitty-fuck-fuck.* I was losing my mind, one lonely, little fragment at a time.

I didn't sleep at all Thanksgiving night. I hadn't eaten anything all day because I was too twisted up inside over everything going on, and when I finally laid on the couch to try to sleep that night, I couldn't close my eyes without seeing Mateo's handsome face and sexy grin.

Finally, at three-thirty on Friday morning, I gave up sleep in favor of unpacking my shit. I vowed I wasn't going to wallow in self-pity, and when I remembered Aunt Judy always saying, "Idle hands are the devil's workshop," it pissed me off all over again and gave me the energy to do something constructive to make the time fly.

Unfortunately, my cat, Mixer, didn't agree at all and disappeared down the hallway, likely to Mateo's bedroom where he liked to ensconce himself in Mateo's soft comforter. The cat would probably give me hell when I tossed that damn downy dream to the trash in a few days, I was certain.

I prayed to fuck Mom didn't bring Judy with her to meet me later that morning because Chase and Dani's mother was as self-righteous as her husband, Brett. I had no idea how many of the family had driven to Yankee Central, and I honestly didn't know if I'd spoken with my mother earlier, but I needed shit to come to a head one way or another. I couldn't live in the land of *'what-if.'* Not my style at all.

I broke down the boxes I'd emptied and decided to put them in the hallway to take to the trash the next morning. I unchained the door and opened the lock, surprised to find a familiar man asleep on the floor in the hallway of my apartment. I walked over to him and poked his shoulder, seeing his eyes flash open and a gun in my face faster than I'd ever seen a cowboy draw in a western movie. It was pulled back equally as fast.

"Sorry, Shay. Reflexes. We have an all-hands situation right now, so I came to check on you. What are you doing up at this hour?" Mathis Sinclair asked me with a worried look on his handsome face.

Mathis was about five-nine, but he had a very muscular body which made him seem much larger than life, in my opinion. He was handsome and had soulful, green eyes. His father, Nate, was from Nassau, Bahamas and had moved to the States with his parents and sister when he was fifteen.

Nate met Mathis' mother, Minnie, in a police station in September of 1979 after they'd both marched in an anti-nuke protest in Manhattan. Minnie had been a poly-sci student at the time and told me it was love at first sight. She fell in love with his laid-back vibe *and* his Bahamian accent, and they became inseparable. They were still adorable when I'd met them, and they'd raised an incredible son.

"Why are you sleeping out here? You can come inside," I told him. I stepped closer and held out a hand to help him to his feet, unsure how long he'd been asleep and wondering how I hadn't heard him.

"You can take the couch. I was trying to sleep there, but I've got to be somewhere in a few hours, and my shit isn't going to unpack itself," I told Mathis.

"Who'd you call from the gas station?" Mathis asked as he engaged the safety on his gun and placed it on the table next to the sofa. He took off his coat, tossing it into one of the chairs Mateo left behind. I needed to get rid of the furniture in my old apartment because the shit Mateo left, be it out of charity or his convenience, was better than anything I had at my old place.

I was surprised Mathis had been following me to the gas station and back without my notice. "My mother, well, I hope it was her. I called her cell phone, and it was answered, but I don't know for sure it was her. I asked her to meet me at Bud & Freda's this morning at seven. I know, stupid, right?" I asked because it was how I felt at that moment. *Stupid.*

Stupid for hoping Mommy didn't really think I was a worthless, demonic piece-of-excrement she wished she'd never given birth to in the first place. I was sure I was an example of why the religious right might question their stance on abortion. Which was worse? Giving birth to a queer son or aborting it? If they figured out how to test to see if a kid was going to be gay, I wondered how many people would take the test and terminate the pregnancy if they learned their child would be anything other than straight? I feared that sort of scenario wasn't too far in the future. The world was a fucked-up place.

What did it say about his parents when they called him an abomination to God and a spawn of the devil? It said they were the abomination to the love their God allegedly had for his children. Further, if he was conceived in love, which was what his parents always touted when they held youth Bible study to promote abstinence among the kids in our church, then shouldn't he be a symbol of that love? That was my take on it, anyway.

Mathis looked at me and reached for my hand, pulling me close enough to hug me, which felt nice… but wrong. "Right now, everything is for shit, but don't doubt yourself. You're a wonderful person, Shay Barr, and I think you're an ass-kicker. We'll go to the diner and scope it. If it's not just your mother, then we skedaddle," Mathis told me, which made me laugh.

"Is that a Bahamian term or Korean? I don't believe I've ever heard that word before," I joked as I hugged him. He wasn't Mateo, but I felt his care and concern through that hug. That had to be worth something, right?

We both heard sounds in the hallway, so Mathis released me. "Get in the coat closet, and I'll lure them down the hallway toward the bedroom. When you hear me whistle, get the fuck out of here and get to Gabby's place," Mathis instructed.

I nodded and hurried into the empty coat closet. I wished to fuck I'd gotten around to hanging up my shit because I could have hidden behind it. I backed up until I heard a soft *bang* behind me. I reached up and felt a metal door which belonged to a wall safe that was the same color as the paint in the closet, making it ostensibly invisible. The door to the device was cracked, and as I felt inside the unit, I found a flashlight and… a gun. *Thank you, Mateo!*

I heard the front door open before Mathis laughed. "Dude, what the fuck? You scared the shit outta me. What are you doing here so damn early?" he asked.

The door closed before the closet door opened. "Come on out, Shay. It's just Jonah, Dani, and Chase," Mathis explained as I looked out to see my cousins and the cop standing next to Mathis. I turned to quickly stash the gun and close the safe, not locking it. I might need the damn gun, so there was no need to tell the cop I had an unlicensed firearm at my disposal.

Chase pointed at me and laughed. "I thought you came *out* of the closet a long time ago, Shay."

"Ha-fucking-ha! What are you doing here so damn early?" I asked, repeating Mathis' question to the trio.

"Mathis told us you made a call from the gas station, and he was coming here to check on you, so we got here as fast as we could. You're not going to do something self-sacrificing for us, Shane. I know that's what you're planning," Dani told me before she tossed her purse on a chair and sat down on the couch, moving around a bit before she reclined and promptly fell asleep.

I turned to see Jonah Wright smiling as he walked over and took the blanket I'd tossed into the floor, covering her before kissing her forehead. It was nice to see a man treat her with respect and kindness.

The men in our lives didn't even know how much it meant to us because we hadn't experienced it previously.

I motioned for all of us to go into the kitchen and proceeded to make coffee for us. "So, what's the plan for the morning?" Jonah asked.

"He called his mother," Mathis offered, not waiting for me to answer.

Chase looked at me as if I'd lost my mind, which I probably had. I needed to explain myself before they locked me in a psych ward for a seventy-two-hour hold. "Look, I want *you* safe. I want you and Dani to be able to live without constantly looking over your shoulders. I want to find out what Mom knows about all of your dad's conversion therapy bullshit, and I want to know if she told anyone I was there when you and the rest of those kids went missing."

I then turned to Jonah and Mathis. "We need to buy time until his birthday on Tuesday, and if Mom told Dad and Uncle Brett what really went down, I want to get him and Dani out of town and into hiding at least until then," I explained.

Chase stepped forward and hugged me. "I can't ask you to do that, Shay. You've already done so much for me, and I don't want you to put yourself in danger. Hell, maybe I should just go back to Arkansas and report my parents to Family Services? I should tell them the shit my dad tried to pull before I turn eighteen and let them figure it out while I'm in foster care, right?"

I looked at him and felt tears come to my eyes, though I fought them like crazy. "I understand what you're thinking, and maybe it would work in a perfect world, but you're too important to Dani, and you're too important to me for us to take a chance like that. I believe the best course of action is to keep you from them for now and go after them for this shit another way. I'll go talk to Mom, and we can see what is going on with the family. Hopefully, she'll be honest with me," I offered as I kissed the kid's temple. He was truly a gem, and I wanted to protect him at all costs.

"I'm going with you," Mathis commanded. I turned to see he wasn't going to be swayed, so I nodded. It couldn't hurt to have a backup.

Jonah and Chase pitched in to unpack my kitchen after sending me to shower and change so Mathis and I could get ready to go meet my mother. I quickly showered in Mateo's master bathroom, finding his products still on the shelf. The fucker had left things that would remind me of him, and I wanted to kick him in the nuts before I hugged him for doing it.

The beautiful assassin didn't want me anymore. Mateo had fucking kicked me to the curb, but the man had gone out of his way to make sure I couldn't forget him. He was a fucking sadist, just not in the same way as the late Mr. Franzl. That man's punishment was quick and dirty. Mateo wanted to fuck me up for the rest of my life, one day at a time.

I finished dressing and opened the door to see Mathis sitting on the bed. He was scrolling through his phone and looked a bit upset. "What's wrong?" I asked.

"Uh, nothing too bad, I guess. Let's get going. We can…" Mathis began. I wasn't stupid, I could see the man was upset.

"We go nowhere until you tell me what's wrong," I ordered.

"We, uh, we had a mole at the company, and it seems it was Sherlock. I don't have all the details, and I need to concentrate on this right now, anyway. Let's go." I nodded and followed Mathis, refusing to ask him if Mateo was okay. I shouldn't fucking care. *Keep telling yourself that, sweet cheeks.*

I followed Mathis out to the kitchen to see it was finally daylight, and Dani was awake, sipping water and eating crackers I didn't know I had. "You okay?" I asked her.

Dani could have set a land speed record down the hallway, and I smiled when Jonah went behind her without question. Hearing the violent retching coming down the hallway would have sent me in a totally different direction, but Jonah didn't come back.

It amazed me the man didn't seem to give a shit the baby she was carrying wasn't his. I could see he was in love with her, whether they knew it or not. I'd seen him look at her with the same look on his face

Mateo had… *Goddammit, he loves me!* He might have been making excuses to be away from me, but I couldn't let him get away with that shit. We could work it out. I just had to convince him why he couldn't live without me.

Mathis smiled and took my arm, leading me toward the closet door where I'd hung my coat after I found that safe. Chase grabbed his coat from the hook in the hallway, pulling it on to follow us out, so I turned to him and took his hands, squeezing them in mine. "You're not coming, Chase. I need you somewhere out of sight. I need you right here with Dani," I told him as I released his hands to get my coat from the closet, covertly grabbing the gun without either of them seeing it. I pulled on my coat after the gun was secured in my pocket and turned to see Chase was pissed off. I braced for the coming battle.

"It's my family and my future, dammit. I want… no, I *need* to be a part of this, Shay. I deserve to have my say in this whole goddamn train wreck, and I need to make certain my parents know they can't torture or scare or hate the gay out of me or any other kid like me. I'm a person of value and who I love is the least important thing about me. They need to hear it from my own lips," he stated with authority, which made me proud of him.

I looked at Mathis and saw his slow grin. "He's right. Chase *should* have his say, Shay."

I considered Mathis' comment and looked at my cousin, finally conceding the two of them were right. Chase deserved to tell his parents his thoughts on the whole, ugly situation. He was attacked by our family, just like me. We *both* deserved a say. "You got a gun for him, just in case?" I asked, knowing Chase had as much training with using firearms as me. The kid was a good shot, and he should be able to defend himself if necessary.

Mathis bent forward and lifted the leg of his jeans, revealing an ankle holster with a small Ruger .357 revolver, checking to see the safety was engaged before handing it to my cousin. "Only if necessary, okay?" Mathis instructed, to which Chase nodded.

We went downstairs to Mathis' Jeep, the three of us climbing in without speaking. I had no idea what we would be faced with when we arrived, but I was ready for anything. I turned to see Chase checking the revolver before he put it in his pocket, looking at me and smiling. "You and me, Shane. I got your back," he stated.

"You and me, Chase. I got your back, too," I offered as I squeezed his knee before he sat back and buckled into the back seat.

We drove to the diner, and Mathis parked down the street to allow us a bit of anonymity to check things out before we walked into a trap. Mathis turned to me with a look of determination. "What's your mother look like?" he asked.

I glanced at Chase, seeing a smirk before he spoke up. "She looks like him, but she has long hair and wears it half up and half down. You know... sort of country style. Anyway, she looks just like Shay. My mom looks like me with the red hair, and if you see her in there, come running because it means my dad and Uncle Bobby are hiding somewhere," Chase told him. I could only nod.

We were likely fucked, so I held onto the gun Mateo had left in the safe. I glanced around to see if my crazy brothers, Dad, or Uncle Brett were anywhere within eyeshot, but since I hadn't been home in a long time, I didn't know if the cars and trucks on the parking lot should be familiar. I needed to see faces to be sure.

Mathis nodded and tossed me the keys to his vehicle before he reached into the driver's side door and pulled on a pair of glasses that looked perfect on his handsome face. "Gimme five minutes, and if I don't come out, book it back to the condo, get Dani and Jonah, and fucking disappear," he stated as he checked another gun before replacing it under his shoulder in the holster.

I took a breath at his words, but I decided we weren't going to run scared just yet. I turned to Chase in the backseat and handed him the keys. "Get up front. Five minutes. If we're not back, get back to the condo and get Jonah and Dani. Don't stop driving until you're good and lost." He nodded, so I hopped out and headed in Mathis' direction.

After Mathis went into the diner, I decided to play it cool, just as I'd seen Mateo do more than once, and followed him. I shoved the gun into the back of my pants and pulled down my coat before I walked to the front of the diner, looking through the window to check for my mother. I was actually surprised to see her sitting at a booth in the back, alone.

When I entered the diner, I glanced to where Mathis had taken a stool at the counter, seeing he wasn't happy with me for ignoring his instructions. I winked and walked over to the table, not sure what the fuck would happen when Mom realized it was me.

I sat down across from the woman… the mother who had tried like hell to keep me safe as a little boy. The woman who used to chastise my brothers for giving me a hard time and send them out of the house so we could finish cooking dinner. The woman who would get angry at my father and not speak to him because he wanted me to be tough and used to slap me around to teach me to fight back.

Carol Barr had been my champion until the day my father and his crazy, fucked-up brother decided they could heal me from the queer disease. That night when they pulled that hood off my head, and I looked at my mother crying in front of me, I waited for her to save me again, but she closed her eyes and walked away.

I flipped my coffee cup and looked at Carol… my mother. "Why?" I needed to know what the fuck she thought when she allowed my father, his brother, and my own brothers to do those things to me. *Did she think what they did was okay?*

Like when they took an electric cattle prod and held it against my genitals to zap me when I refused to say I wasn't a fag. To take turns shouting Bible verses at me as they took a rope on a pole and wrapped it around my dick and balls, turning it until they cut off the blood flow to bring enough pain so I'd tell them anything they wanted to hear to get them to stop. Incidentally, they didn't stop until I passed out. Carol didn't step in to save me from any of that, did she?

My mom started crying. "I'm sorry. I'm so sorry, Shane. I just didn't know… I didn't know what to do. Your father promised me you wouldn't be hurt badly. He swore you'd be in intense counseling, and he said when they were finished with you, you'd meet a nice girl and get married. He said eventually you'd have children, and we'd be a happy family again. I believed what he told me, Shane. I thought it was for the best, my beautiful boy, because I just couldn't understand that side of you. I still don't."

I must say I was proud of myself for not cracking. I didn't say a word or make a move. I just stared at her, and then she kept talking. "I have no idea what I've done wrong as your mother to make you believe you should be attracted to men and not women. I don't understand why you refuse to accept the way Our Heavenly Father intended life to be. You should be marrying a young woman and planning a life. I just don't understand what I did wrong," my mother whispered as the tears fell.

Hell, I wasn't surprised at her comments, and honestly, I wasn't pissed at her response because she just couldn't comprehend anything that wasn't the way she'd been raised. She'd never get it. It was too late to try to convince her, and it was time to cut the tie, permanently.

"Aunt Carol, you didn't do anything wrong except listen to the bullshit my father told the congregation about the evils of gays and lesbians. He decided he could rid the world of us, and you all listened to the venom he spewed from his pulpit. You're supposed to be intelligent adults. Why would you believe that crap?"

Apparently, Chase listened to me as well as I'd listened to Mathis. I felt a lump in my gut when I glanced around to see him standing there.

"According to the Bible you believe in, chapter and verse, we were *all* made in the image of God or so you all used to say to us in Sunday school and summer church camp. If you believe that so passionately, you have to believe God is gender neutral, and he or she loves all of us. We are all children of God," he said as I felt a gentle hand on my shoulder. Chase, my seventeen-year-old cousin who was so much like me, stated as he stood next to me.

I didn't hesitate to scoot over in the booth, happy to have his support even if I was worried about his safety. I glanced to my left to see Mathis was paying very close attention to us, ready to snap into action at a moment's notice if he needed to protect either of us, so I smiled at him and turned back to the three of us at the table.

The waitress approached the booth, happy smile in place. "Welcome to Bud & Freda's. My name is Melynn. Can I bring coffee, tea, orange juice, or something else?" the young lady asked.

I heard the door of the diner open behind us and turned to see my Worst. Fucking. Nightmare. My father and Uncle Brett walked into the diner, both smirking. They confidently strolled over to the booth and pulled up chairs from a four-top to the left of us. Brett placed his hand on the back of Chase's neck, squeezing such that Chase's shoulders shot up under his earlobes in pain.

"You sit up in that booth, *boy*, and you enjoy this little bit of freedom before I take you to hell and back so I can get rid you of this demon. What I just did is nothin' compared to what I'm gonna do to you when we get back home. You sit here and look happy because we're all leavin' in a few minutes. Shane, you won't speak out, and you won't act up unless you want me to take it out on Chase," Uncle Brett hissed at both of us.

Chase took a deep breath and looked at me. "I'm not going back. I'd rather die than go back there," he stated as he pulled the gun from his pocket and placed it against his right temple. I shrank back against the booth in horror.

Chase's voice was clear and strong so everyone in the diner could hear him. "Now, you get to decide whether you really want to follow up on the threat of torturing me until I'm not gay anymore. I'm telling you after what you've already done to me, I'm not going back for more. If you insist on doing it, I'll end it right here and now. I'm not going back to Arkansas with you, and you're not going to run my life anymore," he stated as he turned his head to look his father in the eye. I was paralyzed with fear at that point.

"You just assaulted me in front of all of these people. Right now, if I pull the trigger, everyone's going to know it's your fault, and all of these people in this restaurant will tell the police what I said. My death will be on your hands, Daddy, but I'm not going to let you hurt me like that anymore. You feel like taking a chance they'll all lie for you the way everybody does back in Hot Springs?" Chase snapped at his father.

Make no mistake, I was proud of the kid for taking a stand, but there was no way I was going to allow him to take his own life. Out of my periphery, I saw Mathis get up from his chair to head in our direction, so I reached up and pushed the gun away. Chase pulled the trigger before anyone could move.

Life was too short, for sure, but when confronted by a fucking bully the likes of Brett and Bobby Barr? What was the right thing to do? Was there a way to right size it? I didn't know, but one thing's for certain, Chase had fired a shot, and the sound was deafening.

21

MATEO

"You fucking shot me in the arse!" Sherlock shouted. He was fucking lucky I didn't shoot him in his goddamn head, but I had him debilitated, which was the goal. He'd turned to run up the stairs when he saw me draw on him, so I took the shot, hitting his ass instead of the back of his melon. If he was a fucking traitor, he was lucky I didn't just end him. I wanted goddamn answers before I made the decision if he'd breathe another day.

I didn't respond to Sherlock, grabbing my phone to call my cousin, Tommy, in Italy, finally having come to some conclusions about a few things. Not surprisingly, he answered because it was afternoon in Siena. "Teo? Do you need more wine?" he asked with a smile evident in his voice. He and I got along very well, and when I needed more wine, I called him, and he'd send it without question.

Tommy was the general manager at the vineyard, and he was extremely good at his job. Uncle Luigi was the vintner, but Tommy ran the other pieces of the operation, and even Uncle Lu would admit his son made the place a success. Tommy was the type of person who stayed on the fringes of family issues, but when we needed him, he always stepped up to do what was necessary.

I admired my cousin for his unwavering support of our family, though he never actually voiced his opinion regarding anything he found out or anything we asked him to do. He did what was necessary without comment, which was exactly what I needed. I respected Tommy, so I made a practice of not soliciting his help unless it was absolutely necessary, but this time, I needed him to do something for me to keep the current mess from spiraling out of control.

I'd considered everything that had happened in our family of late, and it became clearer to me there was more at play than any of us ever anticipated. The fact Lotta came up with her theory that Dom was the mole had left me uneasy because, while I liked the kid, I didn't see him as the *mastermind* kind of guy.

When Lotta called me from a New York area code and began telling me she'd found shit on Dom, I had a hard time believing it, but she'd never steered me wrong in the past, so I bought it. That was the reason I'd shown up at Gabe's old condo and held Dom and his lover hostage. I believed her.

Nemo's off-handed mention about the front door being open when he came downstairs on Wednesday had stuck in my mind, and when I considered things, it all came together in a way I didn't want to consider, initially. Then? It just pissed me off. She hadn't responded when I asked why she was calling from a phone I didn't recognize, and at the time, it didn't actually register. Now it was a big fucking flag waving in the breeze with fireworks exploding around it.

I needed to get Casper to look into whether she'd traveled to the U.S. recently, though we might never know if she used an alias for the trip. Something told me that IED had more to do with Cyril than the rest of us, but I didn't believe he made it. Things were slowly converging into a very, very ugly picture.

"I've got a situation I'm not sure about, but my gut says I need Lotta contained until I can get to the bottom of things. No access to our family, and no access to her computers. Can you handle it?" I asked, hoping he was up to the task.

"Sì," I heard before the line went dead. *One less problem for right now...*

We were treading unknown waters as a family and an organization because to date, I'd never heard my father mention anyone in his employ who was disloyal. It would be a hard blow to the family because Lotta was like a daughter to Papa, but it was even worse for our organization because, in order to do our job, we needed to trust those with whom we worked. Faith had been broken by two people we counted as trustworthy, and when word got out, it would rock all of us.

None of us would really know who we could trust. I couldn't begin to understand how we got to that point because as far as I'd ever heard, both Lotta and Sherlock loved their jobs and those with whom they worked. When had the tide turned against us? That was the great unknown.

I was trying like hell to ensure the family survived their betrayal, especially since I had no idea why they'd do it or how deeply it ran. Were they the only two involved? I was the eldest member of the next generation of the Torrente family, after all, and it was my responsibility to get to the bottom of things and ensure the family prevailed.

I finally turned to Sherlock after Tommy disconnected the call. "Me shooting you in the ass is the least of what I'm gonna do to you if you come down on the wrong side of this shit. Let's go downstairs where you can meet the asshole who is probably going to die after I kill you unless you can offer me some redeeming reason not to do it," I taunted, trying to calm my anger. He would die a slow, painful death if I found out shit I didn't like.

I picked up Sherlock by the collar of his shirt and dragged him behind me to the basement, smiling as his body hit every stair. He moaned and groaned, but the pain he was experiencing was minimal compared to when I got done with him. The mother fucker would beg to die.

I quickly secured his hands with a zip-tie, followed by his feet before I squatted down next to where he was leaning against the wall of the ammo vault, patting him down to find another gun aside from the one he'd dropped on the stairs, a switchblade, and a pair of brass knuckles, which made me want to laugh. I took a sobering breath, readying myself to do what I did best, extracting the truth by any means necessary.

"Tell me, and be convincing, what do you have against the family? Why on earth would you go to the Mangello's and sell us out? What did you tell them?" I asked as I pressed the button on the side of a silver, pearl-handled knife that bore his initials in black on the bottom. I waited for his answer, not happy to be in the position of facing someone who had betrayed the family, as far as I could tell.

"I didn't go to that slime, and I didn't tell them anything, mate, I swear. I would never go to the Mangello's with anything about the family or the company. I love those kids as much as if they were members of my own family. I could offer you a long explanation, but you do what you're gonna do. I know Lotta's a member of the family, so I doubt you'd believe a word I say. Make it quick if we were ever friends at all," Cyril asked as a tear trailed down his cheek.

I wasn't a sap, but something surprised me, so I pressed him. "Tell me the long explanation. Lotta's not a member of *my* family, and you can buy yourself some time."

Sherlock lifted his shoulder and wiped his eye. "Look, mate, Lotta's brassed off at me, and I believe she's manufactured a shambles to make me pay for cocking it up with her. I was able to hack into the computer network in Italy, and I printed off the accounts *she* set up in the names of Dominic and Sierra. I hesitated to mention it to anyone in the event Giuseppe was directing things behind the scenes in case he was trying to put Gabby on a leash. That's why I couldn't come forward until I was sure Giuseppe wasn't involved.

"To be honest, Mateo, Lotta and I were seeing each other off and on for a few years after I joined you blokes in Italy. I didn't kill Harry, my old partner, and I didn't set the bugger up like my superiors tried to claim. Harry did that shit all on his own by taking that bribe from his contact at SVR and offered the bloody list of agents in their organization, but that's neither here nor there.

"Lotta offered proof to the Service regarding my innocence after she did some snooping into Harry's life and found his communiques with the Russian agent who killed him, so I took her out for dinner as thanks because she'd been brilliant with it all. We stayed in touch with each other because we had no bloody clue if we were targets of the Russians or even MI6, and we were trying to cover each other's arses," Sherlock began his long explanation. I took in the information, waiting for the fucking punchline.

"Along comes your father who hunted me down and offered me a job, promising he'd watch out for me. I jumped at the chance, and that's when I met with you prats. When the jobs picked up and required access to intelligence faster than we were able to uncover it, Giuseppe asked me if I could get the agent who saved my tea-and-biscuits to join us. I talked Lotta into coming to work with us, and we settled in Italy and did our jobs. She even stayed with me when she first moved, and yeah, we shagged on a regular basis back then, but I didn't believe we had any feelings for each other besides friendship. Because of the job, we spent a lot of time together, but we were never exclusive.

"Lotta moved on from me and started dating another bloke in the organization, and I thought I was luckily rid of her because she was mad as ferrets. When things didn't work out with him, she was gutted, and I felt bad for her, so I tried to be a friend. I even went along with it when she insisted we start up again, but I declared it casual. That was my clanger," Sherlock stated. I truly didn't know what he was talking about half the time, but then again, I didn't give a fuck.

I studied him for a minute. "Okay, so?"

He rolled his eyes at me, not for the first time, and continued. "Unknown to me at the time, the previous tosser was the one who shattered her, and he did so with a fatal blow where she totally lost the plot and became unhinged. Mate, that bird's gone barmy. She's out for revenge over that broken heart, and she'll take down all of us to prove the point.

"Make no mistake, Teo, she's brilliant, but she's as sinister as a merry widow. I broke it off when I got the chance to come to America to work for this office, and I've tried to maintain a friendly distance from her ever since. I thought I was out of the crosshairs until Lotta got wind I was dating someone. Fuck it, I started seeing Sierra. When

Lotta found out, she set on her path again, this time determined to take us all down.

"Sierra and I talked a lot when we first moved into this building before Gabby clued her into the skinny about what we *really* do here. She had questions, and I had time, so we got to know each other. She called me one night after Perry beat her bloody and asked for a ride home from the hospital. It happened time and time again, so after the last time she called me from the hospital, I paid a visit to the bleedin' bastard. Just so you know, he's taken up residence with a lot of other blokes at the bottom of the Huddy, and she won't be going to the hospital again anytime soon."

I nodded in understanding, not shocked by what I'd heard. It wasn't a new story, and while it was sad, I was ready to get to the part where everything had gone to hell. *Why had Lotta targeted our organization?* That was the answer I was seeking.

"So, why did she go against us? Who was she dating in Italy who broke her heart so badly she turned against the entire family?" I pressed.

Sherlock ignored me. "After Perry disappeared, one of Sally's soldiers paid Sierra a visit at her flat to collect on Perry's debt. The man threatened to kill her, mate, and I can't let that happen because I fell arse-over-appetite in love with her. I've turned a blind eye to her selling drugs out of the Victorian for about a year now, and I'm not proud of it, but we couldn't figure out a fix.

"Why the hell do you think Dex's yoga studio is doing so well? He's got more fucking junkies in those classes and has no idea about any of it. You blokes are bloody daft to the shit that happens around this place, for sure," Cyril pointed out. He likely had a point with that shit.

"Fuck. So?" I pressed.

"Sierra requires her clients to take yoga classes before she sells them their drug of choice. She says at least they're doing something healthy by taking the class, plus she likes Dex and says his business was failing which was why she was constantly sending out those bleedin' mailings. She honestly wants to help him.

"Her brother, Nick? That smarmy bastard showed up about six

months ago and began acting as the errand boy between the supplier and Sierra. He got kicked out of the Air Force for drug abuse, and when Dom saw him continuing to come and go from here, Nick pretended to be interested in Dom to get him off the scent," Sherlock explained as he leaned against the wall. That made sense, but I still had a hard time thinking of Sherlock as the mole. I thought I knew him better than that, but apparently, I was *fottuto pazzo...fucking crazy!*

I could see the man was in pain from the slug in the ass, but it wasn't my first concern. I needed to give his explanation some time to settle so I could decide if I believed him. The fact Sierra was dealing, and Sherlock had helped her or ignored the activity and didn't disclose it to Gabby, showed his alliance was to Sierra, not us. Her brother showing up and leading on my little cousin pissed me off substantially.

Sierra and her brother were behaving in a way which could get law enforcement looking at us, and we couldn't have it. We had too many skeletons rattling around for the cops to start investigating us. Thankfully, Rafe had just gotten rid of the latest problem. I needed time to determine who the fuck was telling the truth and what to do about it. Just then, my phone buzzed, and I saw it was a text from Mathis.

We have a huge problem. Are you still in town?

I quickly hit the screen to call him. *"Where?"* I asked when he answered.

"Bob & Freda's, then the 68th Precinct," Mathis responded.

"Ten minutes." I opened the door to the bunker and dragged Sherlock inside to deal with later. I turned to see Corbin Barr was still asleep, which was a relief. I'd have to figure out what to do with him, but I still had time, well, until the next morning.

I sent a text to Rafe to meet me at the diner because I needed his help. My head was spinning for sure, but it was apparent my cousin, Gabe, had his head up his ass regarding the shit going down at GEA-A, and I needed to get to the bottom of things before we all ended up in a fucking jail cell or worse. It had all tumbled into a snake pit, and I didn't like the idea the man I loved might be in danger because we were all fucking distracted by worthless shit that never should have happened.

I still saw Shay as mine, though I doubted he saw things the same way because I'd been an awful prick to him. I knew Gabe was only worried about Dex, Dyl, and Searcy, and he was too busy enacting a goddamn Rockwell painting of the perfect Thanksgiving to pay any attention to what the fuck was going on. I got it. He was a happily married man with a loving family. He'd lost his edge, but that wasn't necessarily a bad thing as long as someone minds the store. I prayed to the saints Nemo and Smokey had shit under control.

At the moment, I had more important things with which to concern myself. I loved my Sweeney, and I couldn't get him off my mind no matter how hard I'd tried. If Shay were in trouble, I would be there and give my life for his, gladly, regardless of the bullshit I'd told him. How I'd reconcile my words with my actions was something to worry about later.

I went out to the SUV and opened Dom's door, holding my gun on him and Nick Conti. "Both of you, out. I need to deal with something more important than your bullshit right now. Give me your guns and come with me. I will shoot either or both of you if you don't do as I say just so we're clear. Come on," I told them.

They both handed over their guns and walked in front of me to the Victorian, Dom continuing to look over his shoulder in an attempt to judge if I was serious with my threat. I took them downstairs and opened the safe room, again, forcing them inside. "You boys stay put. I expect the three of you to have a straight story when I come back, *comprendere*? Also, Sherlock has a slug in his ass, so find the first-aid kit and see what you can do to help him out because I'm sure he's in pain. I'll be back."

I heard a lot of protesting as I closed the door and secured it with my handprint so only I could let them out. I needed to call my cousin because he and his husband could be implicated in the drug trafficking if it were true. The man needed to remove his head from Dex's ass and take a look at what was going on around him. Hell, I didn't know what the fuck was true anymore, so he was more clueless than me. *Che cazzo!*

I parked down the street from the diner to see the place crawling with cops, which made me shiver even though I'd been a *polizotto* in Italy for several years. It was funny how knowing I'd just committed a crime by holding four people as veritable hostages at the Victorian had me feeling a bit excited as I stared at a hell-of-a-lot of cops milling around.

There was crime scene tape along the parking lot, and I could see Rafe and Mathis in front of the dry cleaners across the street. I stowed my Tan under the seat of the SUV before I got out and crossed to where they were both nervously pacing. "What the fuck happened here?" I asked.

"Chase accidentally shot his father in the ear," Mathis explained, which made no fucking sense.

"Where'd he get a gun?" I asked quietly, staring between the two of them.

"I gave him one of my unregistered ones, but he claims he found it in his father's pickup truck," Mathis confessed. I wanted to deck the moron for giving a loaded gun to a virtual child.

"You were a fucking cop, dude! *Merda!* How the hell are we going to get out of this shit without seeing the inside of a jail cell?" I pointed out. As far as I remembered, we tried to keep gunplay under the radar. Thankfully, I had a suppressor on my Tan when I shot Sherlock in the ass, so the neighbors weren't alerted. We were getting sloppy, and it was making me jumpy.

I saw Shay talking to a cop off to the side of the frenzied activity, so I sauntered across the street and snuck around the police barrier to get to him. "*Bello?* You okay?" I asked as I walked up to him, seeing he'd been crying. I quickly pulled him into my arms as the cop I thought to be a detective stood next to him, eyeing me very carefully.

"Mateo? I didn't expect you'd be here," Shay whispered as he curled into my body, letting me hold him. My arms had felt so empty before that moment, and I hated myself for my stupidity. I wasn't sure if it was because I pushed him away in the first place or because I was there with him now. Either way, it was too late. I didn't have the strength, nor the will, to pull away from him again.

"What happened?" I asked the cop.

"I'm Detective Gurley, Mr. Torrente," he greeted me by name, shocking the fuck out of me.

"Have we met?" I asked, trying to keep my face neutral. If the American authorities were onto me? I needed to get back to Rome where I could disappear for a while, but I was taking Sweeney with me.

"I know a relative of yours, Gabe Torrente. You guys are spitting images. His husband, Dex, helped me out on a case a few years ago, and a friend of mine represented the couple in the adoption of Dylan and Searcy. You might want to contact him for this shit show, but that's off the record." *Gabe is sidling up to locals? Has he lost his mind?*

"What's going on? Where's Chase?" I asked as I looked at Shay.

"How do you know Shay and Chase?" the cop questioned, which almost made me regret going to the scene at all.

"Mateo's my boyfriend, and he was there when Chase showed up at my place after he ran away from that camp I told you about," Shay stated. It then occurred to me Sherlock was on that trip to Arkansas to rescue Chase and those other kids, and if the authorities went looking for Sherlock for his statement, we were all fucked based on what the Brit told me earlier about his tie to Lotta.

I turned to see Shay's imploring look that I should corroborate his story, so I nodded in support, not sure what else to say. The cop was looking at me expectantly, so I cleared my throat. "Yes, Shay and I were together when Chase showed up at our place," I responded.

Gurley looked at Shay with a cocked eyebrow. "You said it was *your* place, and *you* didn't live with anyone else," the cop stated, obviously waiting to catch us in a lie.

"I misspoke. We live together *now*, but when Chase showed up,

Shay was still in his apartment. We've just recently combined households. What's the charge here?" I asked.

"Thus far, we haven't been able to sort through enough of the statements to verify exactly what's going on. Reverend Barr says he came here to take his minor child home because the boy had run away after a family run-in regarding an unsanctioned party his son hosted at the family's lake property in Arkansas. Obviously, that's out of my jurisdiction," the detective stated.

Shay, my little spitfire, cleared his throat and stepped out of my arms, quite pissed if the cocked hip and head tilt were any indication. "And I told you that's a load of horseshit. My uncle, father, brothers, aunt, and my mother all conspired to take Chase to that lake campsite to perform what they call *'conversion therapy,'* which is code for making him regret being his authentic self because he's gay. They did that same shit to me when I was around his age, and just like Chase, I ran away. I didn't have anyone to go to for support back then, but a stranger was kinder to me than my own family had ever been.

"I'm just paying it forward, and as soon as his sister gets here, she'll verify Chase didn't come to her place in Memphis because they both knew their parents would look for him there first," Shay snapped at the man.

I was an expert at reading body language and seeing the cop stiffen when Shay mentioned Chase was gay told me volumes about the man. I stepped forward to touch Shay, so he knew I was there to support him. "I've been a witness to Chase discussing it, and Shay has shared with me some of the shit he went through at that same campsite. Let's not forget, Chase is still a minor.

"I'd think the American authorities would want to investigate any sort of torture of a minor, especially at the hands of his own family?" I added in a heavier accent than usual as I reached for Shay's hand. He slotted our fingers together and squeezed my hand, which I believed was his way of offering me his appreciation for my support. I'd definitely always be there for him, even if it meant only in spirit because he sent me away.

An hour later, I was outside the police station where most of the Barr family, including my Shay, was being questioned. Gabe and Nemo had shown up, and Rafe had gone in search of Shay's brothers, Elvin and Buck. Shay swore there was no way the family didn't bring them to New York, so it was for the best if we knew where they were hiding.

None of us bought the story that Chase, the most vibrant, loving, and kind person I'd ever met, intended to take his own life as Mathis had explained to us. Shay's quick action to move the gun at the split-second Chase pulled the trigger had caused Chase to accidentally shoot his father in the ear, though Mathis said it was almost as if the two of them had choreographed the move it went so smoothly.

We were all sitting in Gabe's Escalade, and we had Casper on the phone. "I've got the CCTV-feed outside the diner that shows you, Jackass, getting out of your POV first, then Shay, and finally, Chase. He walks over to a large pickup just inside the view of the camera and opens the passenger-side door before reaching inside. When he steps away from the truck, the camera shows him tucking something into his jacket pocket. I can't make out what it is, even if I sharpen the picture. It could be a gun, or it could be a phone. Hell, it could be a teddy bear for all I can make out.

"If I can't tell what the fuck it is, I doubt the cops can tell when they look at it, so they'll probably take Chase's word for it, considering the other guns they found inside those two trucks. Also, I had the city tow Corbin's truck to impound. It should take about a year to track it down," Casper offered as we looked at the feed on Gabe's phone.

"How the fuck did you let this happen, Mathis?" Gabe snapped, which pissed me off immediately.

I cleared my throat because there was definitely more to the story than my cousin could imagine. "Okay, Gabriele. How about the fact there are three people in the bunker in the Victorian who have implicated each other in betraying the family, along with two others who aren't in our custody yet? Your organization is crawling with people looking to sell your *culo* to the highest bidder," I informed, seeing the surprise on his face.

Gabe looked at Nemo who hopped out of the vehicle and pulled out his phone, putting it to his ear. I opened the passenger door and got out to join him. "Do *not* call Lotta because I've got her tucked away in Italy. I'll let Gabe handle his business *here*, but after I'm sure Shay's in the clear, I'm going to Italy to deal with Carlotta because she's the mastermind behind at least one of the betrayals in your organization. A romantic triangle could put all our grapes in the press. Deal with your boss, Nemo.

"I know your husband is a politician. It won't look good for him if Gabriele's lack of attention to the business we're in takes down the whole fucking organization," I told Raleigh Wallis, just offering a hint of what I thought was to come.

Without looking back, I headed into the police station to see what the fuck was going on with Shay. I needed to be in front of Lotta to speak with her so I could tell if she was the one orchestrating the current chaos at the Victorian. All signs pointed to her, and I definitely didn't think Sherlock was smart enough… or devious enough… to pull it together himself. I also wanted to be certain Shay was safe, so I was torn in about thirty different directions, still unsure of the clear path.

"*Mateo!*" I stopped and turned to see my cousin lumbering in my direction. Gabe was as pissed as I'd ever seen him, but I was ready to do battle. He needed to answer some questions whether he liked it or not, and I was ready to ask them.

He came at me with fists cocked, so I stepped to him, not stalling for a second. "Is it wise to do this on the front steps of a police station? We can go to the Victorian and beat the *cazzo* out of each other in the gym before we open the door to the bunker and pull out those *stronzi* to get their take on things. You can interrogate them right there, and we can figure out how this disaster seems to be settling on *you*, Gabriele.

"You *do* remember interrogation techniques, right? I mean, we learned them in…" I started before he grabbed my arm and pulled me with him back to the SUV. I went because I didn't want to cause a scene, but if he didn't unhand me, I was going to show him I was the better man, despite my age.

"I fucking know interrogation techniques. I want to know what this has to do with Lotta. Nemo was going to call her, but you told him not to do it. *Perché?*" Gabe stood there expectantly after asking me why.

I took a deep breath and decided to shoot for the moon. "You had a relationship with Lotta how many years ago? You broke her fucking heart," I proposed, remembering what Sherlock had mentioned about her dating another operative back in the day.

I saw my cousin's face pale as my comments settled on him, and I knew I was right. "Don't lie about it. She's got a fucking ax to grind with you and Sherlock, and you need to find your balls because the two of them have enough information to bring down the family, *Cugino*," I reminded Gabe. I could see he was torn, but we all had to atone for our indiscretions. Gabriele was no exception.

"I, uh, I didn't know she'd told anyone about us. We only saw each other when I had time off from the Army and went to Italy. I just thought we were having fun. It wasn't anything serious," Gabe stated.

I could see my favorite cousin was worried, so I gave him the advice I'd give anyone in his position. "To her, it was serious. You're bisexual, and you're a good-looking man, though not better than me. There was a time when you fucked women, and I'd bet you fucked *over* a bunch of them.

"This one is carrying a grudge, and it's ugly as hell. Talk to your husband because it's going to come out. You and Sherlock are why Lotta is trying to destroy us. Don't be a coward about this shit because I believe she's about a day away from sending the Feds your way for retribution, Gabe. That's why I had Tommy take her into his custody. Oh, by the way, the Victorian is nearly a crack house," I told him as I headed back toward the police station to see where things stood with Shay.

Shay Barr and I had things to discuss because I had fucked things up so badly with him, but I knew for a fact I couldn't leave him again.

We'd need to get to the Victorian in a few hours to feed and water the captives, but first, I wanted my time with Sweeney. I walked into the station to see Shay was sitting in a chair in the corner while the rest of his family was scattered about the huge space where they were being questioned.

I walked up to the desk and offered my Torrente smile. "Hi, I'm here to pick up Shay Barr. Is he being held on any charges?"

The desk attendant looked down a list in front of her and looked up at me with a smile. "No, he's not. He's over there," she stated with a wink. I returned it before I walked over to Shay.

"*¿Vamanos?*" I asked, knowing Shay spoke more Spanish than Italian.

The handsome man glanced up at me and smiled. "Sure. I have a lot of questions for you," he told me as I took his hand and led him out of the station.

We took off in my rental, me driving us back to the apartment in Gabe's building and parking in the reserved spot underground. I felt my gut churning because I knew for a fact I had a long night of talking ahead of me.

I glanced over to see Shay wasn't happy, but what the fuck did I expect? He wasn't going to be happy with me because I hadn't given him any reason to be, had I? I'd been a fool, but maybe I could win him back. I'd damn well give it my best shot.

22

SHAY

"*¿Vamanos?*" the sexy Italian asked me. I stared at Mateo Torrente as he stood in the police station with an authoritative air about him. He'd asked whether I was finished, and when the lady at the desk said I was free to go, he stepped to me with a sexy smirk. I was more than ready to get out of there, but I wasn't really ready for the confrontation brewing between us.

Chase had been taken to NYU-Langone Hospital for psychiatric evaluation. He would be kept under surveillance for seventy-two hours and assessed by a medical team to determine if he was a danger to himself or others. He'd winked at me when the police detective on the scene had made the determination. I had the sneaking suspicion Chase knew exactly what he was doing when he pulled that stupid stunt…if it was, indeed, a stunt.

It seemed as if the kid was buying time until his birthday, and if that was the case? I was damn proud of him. I had questions for him when I could speak with him again. Why the fuck had he threatened to kill himself and had I caused him to accidentally pull the trigger when I shoved his hand away? I was feeling responsible, and I wasn't thrilled with the guilt.

The cops had confiscated the gun Shay had in his possession, along with several other firearms my family had brought with them to New York, so they were in a bit of a pickle because none of them were registered in New York.

The detective had told the social worker who came to the precinct to accompany Chase, a minor, to the hospital that Chase said he'd grabbed the gun from under the front passenger seat of his father's truck, which put Mathis in the clear. Chase swore it was a known spot for the pistol, and he grabbed it because he was scared of what his family would do to him since they'd found him. My uncle protested he didn't own any firearm not manufactured in the U.S., but he was the moron who had driven to New York with three unregistered rifles and a semi-automatic gun I'd never seen before, so they didn't give much credence to his claim. I'd heard the term "terrorist act," bandied about, and it made me smile.

Detective Gurley was instrumental in getting Chase into a decent hospital instead of a juvenile detention center. The man had given the social worker the name of Sister Florence from *Shepherd's House* as a potential foster parent after Chase was released from the hospital, and I was greatly relieved to hear the news.

Gurley had called Sister Florence to confirm she'd be willing to take Chase for a few days, having mentioned to her that he and his friend, Miller Downing, had stopped by the community center in Queens to meet the kids on a few occasions through Miller Downing's juvenile outreach law clinic. Sister Florence was more than happy to agree to help out, much against the outcries of my family as the news was relayed to them.

"*You can't take him away from us. We're his family, and we came to bring him home from this pagan hell. He needs to go back with us so we can save him,*" Aunt Judy had announced, showing her self-righteous ass for all of New York to judge. I was grateful for Cameron Gurley's help in the matter.

Uncle Brett was handcuffed to a bench with a bandage on his ear where Chase had winged him. I held the laugh at the lame injury because one would have thought Brett had lost a nut instead of a piece of his ear. He was still playing the part of God's messenger while he continued to inform anyone who would listen how he was continuing to pray for his son to come to Jesus and ask forgiveness for his sin of being a sodomite. I wanted to punch him in the mouth, but the fact he was sitting next to my father, who was facing a few gun charges of his own, was appeasing for the time being.

The charges against Chase had the potential to be serious if the cops were so inclined, but Detective Gurley had spoken with the waitress, Melynn, and a few customers seated nearby, and they'd heard the threats Uncle Brett leveled against Chase. The detective was leaning toward discussing the possibility of not charging Chase with gun possession, but rather with discharging a firearm in a public place. That was good news if it worked.

Chase would be released into the custody of Sister Florence and would be in foster care long enough to turn eighteen while the charges were being further investigated, though he would still be considered a minor if the assertion of the shooting being an accident didn't stand up. With the statements by the witnesses at the diner, I hoped my cousin would prevail. Gurley told me I wouldn't be charged with anything, which was a relief.

It also made me ecstatic the family couldn't fucking touch him until the cops finished their investigation. Chase had a fighting chance at a better future, and I'd do my best to help him with it. I knew the family would get released sooner than I'd like, which was sad because they'd just continue to push their hate-laced brand of justice on another unsuspecting kid who was trying to figure out how to survive in that closed-minded town. I prayed that boy or girl would have someone who would rescue them from that bullshit, just as I'd tried to do for Chase.

For the immediate future, my cousin was safe in a hospital with a backup plan to keep him away from his parents, and I was relieved. My own dilemma was staring at me as we stood in the police station… Mateo Torrente. What the fuck was I supposed to do with him? He'd dumped me, after all.

"Yeah, I'm ready," I responded. We left the building, and I climbed into the SUV with him, unsure what was going to happen next.

"I need to go to the Victorian. Your brother is still there, as are a few others. Do you want me to drop you off first?" he asked.

I was cocked and ready to unload. "You'd drop me where? A fucking *airport*? Oh, wait, that's where I should drop you, right? I'm not able to handle myself, or that's what you seemed to mean when you gave me that *it's not you, it's me* bullshit excuse earlier. Well, *Killer*, you can drop me anywhere, and then you go live your life without me interfering," I snapped at him, despising the words as they came out of my mouth.

I did not expect him to pull into a parking lot down the street from the police station. Mateo hopped out of the SUV and paced a bit before he came around and opened my door, pulling me close and wrapping his arms around me, smothering me with his large body. He didn't kiss me, but he tilted my head to meet his gorgeous eyes.

"I know I've been a *stronzo*...an asshole. I'm sorry I was a fool, and I beg your forgiveness, *bello*. I love you, and I realize you might not believe me right now, but it's the truth, and I'll prove it to you. I know we're meant to be together. The rest of this shit? It will fade into the ether, but you're *mine*, and I'm *yours*. I'm sorry I didn't realize it before," he stated before he kissed me the way I wanted to be kissed by him. *Slow... soft... hot... commanding.*

I wrapped my legs around his waist, and when he leaned into the open door of the SUV, I settled into his arms, feeling his body melt into mine. It was exactly what I needed, and I wasn't about to waste our reunion focused on bitter memories or anger. I was getting what I wanted, and I was going to embrace it… *for now.*

I pulled away from him after nipping at his bottom lip, happy to hear the sexy laugh from him. "Ouch," he stated with a smile.

"That's just the beginning of what I plan to do to you for your shitty behavior. You don't treat the person you love the way you treated *me*, Mateo. You owe me more than that," I told him as he held me in his arms.

He leaned forward and placed a soft kiss on my lips. "You're right, *tesoro*. I owe you much more than that, and if I get the opportunity to make it up to you, I'll do it for the rest of my life. I'm sorry. Can you forgive my stupidity?" he asked quietly, keeping the moment between us.

As I stared into his beautiful eyes, I had a feeling I'd forgive him anything. He was exactly what my soul had yearned to find, but we needed some boundaries before I surrendered. "Later, we need to talk about what is not acceptable regarding how we treat each other, and I need to tell you something about myself before you make a final decision. Right now, let's do whatever we need to do so we can get home? I've missed you, *sugar*," I offered, not curbing my Arkansas accent.

Mateo laughed. "That's sexy as hell. My little southern *bell-o*," he teased before he kissed me again, taking away my breath.

It didn't leave my mind he could decide to walk away from me again after I told him something I should have told him in the beginning. I had to make sure I'd survive if it were his final decision. I had people depending on me for many things, including the income to care for their families. I couldn't let a man break me, even if it was Mateo Torrente.

Mateo led the way to the basement of the Victorian where my brother was still locked inside. I hadn't paid attention to the large room housing the bunker, given the circumstances at the time, but there was a full gym with a boxing ring and many types of workout machines, along with a full array of weight-lifting equipment.

The large building was currently empty, or so I believed when Mateo put his hand on the glass box outside the large, steel door. An infrared scanner flashed, and the door opened, revealing the room where, with Mateo's vigilance, I'd asked my brother questions regarding why he tried to take Chase and fought with me. Corbin was still in his underwear, and I was sure he was pretty ripe.

"Gentlemen? Rise and shine," Mateo announced as he walked inside and flipped on a bright light. I stood in the doorway and noticed Dominic, Gabe's nephew, was inside, along with another handsome guy and Cyril Symington, who was sweating profusely.

"Huh?" I heard, which was my idiot brother, Corbin, so I stepped inside, seeing he was on the gurney but not tied down any longer. It was then I remembered Mateo had cut him loose before we left him there.

"What's up with them?" I asked as I pointed to Dominic, Cyril, and the other guy.

"They're really Gabriele's issue. Let's get Corbin and go. He's still a bit hazy so we can drop him off somewhere unless you want to take him back to the condo and talk to him. Up to you, Shay," Mateo told me.

I pointed to Cyril Symington, who looked to be quite ill. "He looks bad, Mateo," I suggested.

My handsome man sighed. "Have you three formulated an answer regarding who is responsible for this *fottuto casino*?" Mateo asked.

We all looked at him with raised eyebrows. "Ugh! Fucking mess. This is a fucking mess, and I need to know who instigated the idea it was okay to sell drugs out of this house? Did you three sell us out to Frankie Man," Mateo demanded.

Cyril looked at Mateo and took a breath. "Mate, I told you before you shot me in the arse. I don't know for sure if Lotta sold you out to Frankie Man, but I know she's behind this shit with Dom and Sierra. I don't know what she told anyone, but Nick could probably explain his connection to the Mangello family because he's the one dropping off the drugs for Sierra to sell," Sherlock stated as he pointed to the handsome man next to Dominic.

The guy, Nick, looked up. "Dude, seriously, I've never dealt drugs in my life. If my sister told you that shit, she was lying." That was a red flag for me.

Mateo walked over to him and knelt down to where the guy sat on the floor next to Dom. Mateo reached behind his back and pulled out a knife. He held it up to the soldier's neck and glanced at Dominic. "Do you believe him?" Dom swallowed but didn't answer.

Before I knew what was happening, Mateo had the knife at Dominic's throat and turned to the soldier-looking guy with a menacing look on his face. "If I think you're lying to me, I'll slit his throat, so choose your words carefully."

I looked over to see Corbin had nearly swallowed his tongue, which was good because I wanted to know what the fuck he really thought about Chase's situation and whether he was scared shitless. If he were, I'd likely get the truth out of him. Was my brother being honest when he said he came to New York to save Chase, or was he trying to be the fucking family hero and capture the rainbow flag-carrying queer?

I turned back to Mateo and swallowed as well. "Mateo, I'm sure Dom hasn't..." I began. The gorgeous Italian Stallion turned to give me the 'shut the fuck up' signal, so I did.

"Niente panico. Non ho intenzione di farti del male," Mateo hissed at Dominic. I saw a tear fall down the kid's face and wanted to throw myself over him, but I had no idea what was going on. I firmly believed Mateo had a reason for his actions, and I wasn't about to interfere, regardless of how much I wanted to stop it.

"What did he say?" the soldier asked.

"He said if you don't tell him the truth, he'll kill me and then you. Nick, tell him what's going on," Dominic whispered.

The soldier stood, as did Mateo. "Fuck you," the man stated as he lunged forward with his hands directed for Mateo's throat. The knife went into the guy's chest like hot butter. When he fell to the floor, I heard my brother dry heaving behind us, but I was more worried about Cyril, who appeared to be losing ground as we stood.

I felt the shock sink into my body at the second person who had been killed in my presence. I wasn't naïve. I knew there was evil in the world, but loving a *bona fide* killer? I wasn't sure what that looked like for me.

"I think you need to decide how Cyril looks in all of this because he needs medical attention, Mateo," I stated as I walked over to Cyril and touched his neck. His pulse was strong, so when he grabbed me and pulled me onto his lap, his zip-tied hands going around my neck, nobody was more surprised than me. He had his hands circling my throat, slowly cutting off my intake of breath.

"*Non sono un fottuto idiota. Sei disposto a sacrificare Shay per proteggere la tua famiglia?*" Cyril hissed in Italian.

"What did he say?" I gasped as I felt Cyril's hands move to my head and neck in a similar position I'd seen Mateo use when he killed Mr. Franzl.

"He asked if I was willing to sacrifice you for my family. *Non per un secondo cazzo, traditore,*" Mateo stated before he pulled a small gun from his jacket and shot Cyril in the head over my left shoulder… very close to my left ear. The man's hands fell away, but his arms had encircled me because of his bound wrists, prohibiting my ability to escape. Mateo quickly lifted me to my feet after he cut the zip-tie from Cyril's wrists, and I scrambled away from him, feeling blood and brain matter on my neck and shoulder. I then promptly threw up on the floor, trying to get my breath.

Mateo pulled me into his arms and held me tightly as he wiped my face and mouth with the sleeve of his shirt before he leaned forward. "My answer was no, not for a second. I wouldn't sacrifice you for my family because I love you. I want you for my family, Shay," he whispered as he held me.

"Uh, excuse me? I really gotta take a piss," we both heard from behind us. It was Corbin, and when I turned to look at him, I could see he had a fear of God in his eyes. I was sure, based on what he'd witnessed, he knew better than to lie. Obviously, he hadn't awakened while we were gone, so I was pretty sure he did need to piss.

"Come on, Dude. I'll show you to the locker room so you can clean up. I'll find you some clothes to wear as well. This shit doesn't involve us, really. I guess I was just being used, yet again," Dominic stated as he stood and grabbed my brother by the arm and led him out of the safe room.

"His clothes are in my locker," Mateo stated before they left the two of us alone.

I looked at Mateo, not sure what to say. "You know what I am, Shay. It's what I learned to do when I was a cop in Italy, and it's all I've ever known. I've never kept a count of how many people I've killed for one reason or another, but I always believed if my papa had given the order, there was a good reason.

"I'm going to do this less, okay? I never want to do this in front of you ever again, but this is my life. I can try to find another job, but Shay, I'm forty-two, and this is what I've done for a lot longer than I want to remember.

"For you, I'll give it up and become a fishmonger if it will make you happy. Hell, I'll sweep up at your shop, *mio amato*. I don't want to lose you," he told me as he led me from that room and closed the door, placing his hand on the glass box again. We heard the door lock before my man looked at me, waiting for an answer.

"What about them?" I asked as I pointed to the door.

"They're no longer our problem. I'll call someone. That's something I have…people to call who clean up after me. I know I scared you, and I hate it like hell. I don't want to be the man who scares you, Shay. I want to be *your* man. I want to be the man who can be honest with you when I have to leave town for a reason I don't want to share. I know it's a lot to ask, but do you think you could love a *salesman*? Can you forgive me for doing the job I need to do sometimes?" he asked as he looked into my eyes.

It wasn't anything I'd ever considered when I thought about falling in love with someone. Mateo would ask me to forgive him for his job? It didn't make sense to me. I cleared my throat and came up with an answer I never imagined. "Should I spank you when you're naughty?" The laugh that came from him brought a smile to my face I'd never imagined, considering what I'd just witnessed.

Mateo led me to the locker room and got me a towel. He helped me undress, throwing my clothes into a trash bag before he undressed himself and then went to a locker, opening and pulling out some sweats that were going to be way too big on me.

He then took me into a shower stall and washed me so gently it made me tear up—or maybe I was coming off the adrenalin high from all of the excitement. He found mouthwash in a dopp kit he'd brought with him, and I rinsed my mouth as well. All of the bad things that had happened in the last thirty-six hours washed away down the drain with the suds, or so I hoped.

Once I was wrapped in a soft towel, Mateo kissed me, making my eyes roll back in my head. Our tongues swirled together in a glorious dance, and I knew I'd forgive him anything. First, though, I needed to know if he could forgive me my own sins. "When I first moved to Little Rock after I turned eighteen and ran away from Hot Springs, I was homeless and turned tricks to survive. I only did it for a month, and I was always safe, even though I got slapped around for not giving a blowjob without a condom a time or two.

"I won't lie and say I wasn't tempted to do it again when I got to New York, but thankfully, I met Maxi, and he helped me find a place to live until I got on my feet. I need you to know I used to be a whore. I'm not proud of it, but it helped me survive. Can you live with that?" I asked, feeling my soul lighten for just a moment before the gravity of my confession weighed on me.

Mateo smiled and pulled me close, taking my face in his firm hands. "*Tesoro* means treasure, and that's exactly what you are to me, Shay. You're my treasure. I don't care about anyone who came before me. I just want to be the only one for the rest of my life," he told me before he gently kissed my lips. I felt the tears begin to fill my eyes again as I closed them to enjoy the love I felt flowing between us.

A throat cleared near the entrance, breaking us from our moment. I turned to see Gabe Torrente on the stairs. "Sorry to break this up, but Mateo, I need to talk to you." I could tell there were some pending issues, so I decided to take my brother with me to the condo to get him settled.

"After I'm dressed, I'll take Corbin and Dom home with me before I get to the shop. Sonya moved some of my clients around so I have a full day today. Do we know where my parents are right now?" I asked Mateo after I slipped my cell phone in the pocket of the sweats I was holding. They were Mateo's. I'd know his scent anywhere.

Gabe left us and we both dressed. Mateo cleaned up my loafers from the earlier mess and handed them to me. After he had his shoes on, he stood and pulled me with him. "I'm going to guess they're still at the police station, but I'll get Casper to check it out, ASAP. I'll call you, *tesoro*," Mateo stated as he handed me the keys to his SUV and kissed my forehead before he took me out of the locker room to the bunker again, placing his hand on the glass box again.

I ran up the stairs as Gabe rushed down before he began shouting at Mateo behind me in Italian. I didn't need to see the inside of that room again. That was a side of Mateo's life I didn't want to consider, though I accepted it. He was a trained killer, and he had no problem gutting one man and shooting the other without a second's hesitation.

Did they deserve it? What was my standard for who lived and who died, and how did I feel about the fact Cyril Symington, a man I knew had been close with my best friends, had no problem ending my life without any hesitation? *Far too many questions circling my head.*

The task at hand was to collect my brother and take him to my home... the home I would share with Mateo if he stuck around New York. Corbin and I needed to discuss our family issues, and I needed time to wrap my head around what the fuck had just happened. At the very least, Corbin was too fucking scared to even fart crossways. I finally had the upper hand, which for me, was a miracle. I would use my power for good... *probably?*

I'd been through enough shit at the hands of my family to know what evil looked like, and when I looked at the man I loved, I didn't see evil. Well, I didn't see an angel, either, but there were jobs to be done, and they weren't pretty. That was what my Mateo was doing. I could justify shit all day long, but I loved Mateo regardless of his *unorthodox occupation*.

Who was I to say his job wasn't as necessary a job as, say, a garbage man? Not me. I had a few people I wouldn't mind putting on a list for Mateo to look into and deal with accordingly. There were people in life who didn't deserve mercy, and I believed I knew far too many of them.

I had the feeling if anyone in my family believed they could hurt Chase or me, I had the man who wouldn't be afraid to show them the error of their ways. I had no doubt Mateo would look out for me and the members of my family who were important to me… Dani, Chase, and hopefully, my brother, Corbin, though that remained to be seen. Well, at least until he gave me a reason not to trust him. The fact Mateo *loved* me was icing on a very good cake I couldn't wait to devour.

23

MATEO

Gabe and I were standing in the safe room of the Victorian, him looking at me as if I'd been the one to screw the pooch. Nope. I hadn't been the one to fuck over a vindictive woman. That had been Sherlock, who was dead because he tried to kill the man I loved, and my dear cousin, Gabriele, who used Lotta and threw her away.

There were now two more dead bodies my Shay had been there to witness, and it was more than enough reason for him to run like the fucking wind, but he'd stuck around. In my opinion, that had to stand for something. His revelation of what he'd done ten-years prior when he was running from his crazy family hadn't fazed me. Hell, I'd gone through a period of time where I whored around a lot. I just didn't get the benefit of collecting money for it. It definitely wasn't a deal breaker.

I watched as Gabe walked over and touched Sherlock's neck before he turned to Nick Conti. There was enough blood to verify they were both dead. "Ask your questions before I get a crew in here," I told him.

"I can't believe it. Sherlock was… fuck, he was loyal, Mateo. He…"

"He got involved with one crazy woman and then got involved with another. Sierra is still out there, Gabriele. She was selling drugs at your front desk right under your fucking nose and you didn't have a goddamn clue. Hell, half of Dex's clients were high when they were taking his classes, so he's as blind as you, but this is your place of business. You don't want the police looking into drugs, Gabe," I explained.

He was dumbfounded, I knew, but I had more to say. "You need to find Sierra before she learns her brother is dead and goes to the authorities with wild stories about things that go on around this building. We both know what needs to be done. I realize you think these people are part of your extended family, but this mess? This proves people change, and you can't close your eyes to it," I reminded him.

Gabe turned to me and shook his head. "I don't get any of this. None of this makes sense," he stated as he went over to the table in the corner and took a seat. It was time for me to fill in the blanks for him.

I wanted to get back to the apartment Shay and I planned to share so I could get ready for the party later that night. I wanted a nap, and I wanted to hold my man in my arms, but I knew he had a full day. I just needed to feel him with me in some way.

"I've been withholding a little bit of information from you, but now I see I should have told you sooner. Rafe and I know it, and I'm sure Tommy knows it by now. It's been a family secret for a long time, and when I pushed Giuseppe on it, he told me the story. It's not pretty," I told Gabriele before I sat down with him, ignoring our silent companions.

None of it was really palatable for me. After I explained the history surrounding the fact Francesco Mangello was actually Nonno Enzo's son… our fathers' half-brother… to Gabe, I could see he was as overwhelmed by the information as Rafe and I had been. "And, let's not forget about Marco Rialto, a/k/a, Salvatore Mangello and your sister. Dude, that's her *cousin*," I reminded in case he'd forgotten the connection.

The cursing tirade was sort of comical, or it would have been under any other circumstances. It seemed we Torrente's were doomed to power through things which were unbelievable. It was why we needed the men and women we loved to anchor us. Otherwise, who knew what the fuck we'd do.

※

I walked into my brother's restaurant, not surprised to see many people hard at work to ensure Lawry Schatz and Maxi Partee had the engagement party of the year. Of course, the place was as elegant as I expected. I was looking forward to seeing Shay when he showed because I knew he had appointments all day that Saturday.

Friday, Shay and Corbin had gone back to the apartment in my SUV, so I called a car service to pick up Gabriele and me at the Victorian. Gabe was too shaken to drive, so I made sure he got home safely before I went to the apartment I hoped to share with Shay. I was glad my shit was nearby because I intended to move in again... if my sexy Sweeney would allow it.

Early that Saturday morning, Corbin was in the kitchen with a breakfast burrito and a stunned look on his face. "Where's Shay?" I asked the man.

"Shower. He's really going to work after what happened?" Corbin asked.

"He's got a full day, and your brother is very dedicated to his clients and employees. You okay after all of that bullshit?" I asked.

"I really don't know how I feel, if I'm honest. You actually killed those two people, right? It wasn't just to scare me?" Corbin asked.

I really wanted to say he'd caught me in a prank because the two men were both actors and I wanted to teach him a lesson, but Corbin witnessed two murders, and it was essential he believed I'd kill him as well if he opened his mouth. I didn't want to threaten the guy, but survival was a primal instinct, and it seemed as if he knew it was in his best interests to forget what had happened.

I decided to be brutally honest with him to hit home the point. "The Brit was someone I've known for about thirteen years. He turned on my family which wasn't something I imagined he'd ever do. That, I could have ignored, but when he grabbed your brother and threatened to kill him? That was unforgivable. I won't allow anyone to hurt Shay. You'll do well to remember that," I told Corbin as I left the kitchen and went to the master bathroom where Shay was standing under the warm spray of the shower with his head bowed.

"Tesoro, may I?" I asked, seeing him jump a bit because he hadn't heard me enter the bathroom.

"Please," he whispered. I quickly stripped and stepped into the large shower, pulling Shay into my arms to hold his trembling body. I wasn't surprised he was freaking out because it was a human reaction. If I'd been anyone else and witnessed what he had seen for the first time, I'd have been a fucking mess.

I leaned forward to whisper, "I'm sorry if I scared you, bello. It wasn't my intent."

Shay looked up at me and stepped closer into my body. "I realize it's your job, Mateo, but I need to see the man I love a lot more than the killer inside. I fell in love with you, the guy who is kind and handsome and good with kids. That's the man I want to come home to every night," he explained, which made sense.

I turned him to face the shower wall before I poured some of the coconut-scented shampoo I'd left behind... on purpose... into my hand and gently began massaging his scalp, happy to hear him softly moan at my ministrations.

We didn't make love, skipping the instant gratification for a much-needed nap. When I woke, he was gone, but he'd left a bottle of water on the bedside table and a note... "I owe you a tantrum for your disappearing act, but don't forget how much I love you." That was all I needed.

A blonde woman walked from the busy kitchen into the dining room and eyed me before she smiled. "You're Chef's brother?"

I stepped forward and offered my hand. "Sì, lo sono. Uh, yes, I'm Mateo Torrente, Rafael's older brother. Is he here?" I asked her.

The young woman shook my hand in a way that made me believe she was interested in more than my familial relationship with Rafe. "He's in the kitchen. I'll get him," she told me before she walked away with a little more wiggle than I expected or wanted. *Hasn't he told anyone I'm gay and taken?*

When Rafe barreled out of the kitchen, I could see he wasn't happy, but that was just another Saturday for him, the crabby bastard.

"You fucking *stronzo*… where've you been? I've been calling you," he snapped. I reached into the pocket of my jacket and pulled out my phone, seeing it was dead, yet again.

I turned it to him, but his hissing had me holding the laugh. "You need more wine? I've got some at the apartment," I offered, remembering the Reserve I had in a closet that had been a bribe from Papa and Zio Lu to stay in America and help Gabe with his issues which had mounted up to more than any of us ever anticipated.

Rafael looked at me for a moment before he grabbed me by the jacket, leading me to his office. It wasn't unexpected by me because my little brother had his own anger issues, which were worse than mine by a far stretch. He was well known as the one with the most volatile temper in the family. "Get your *culo* on a plane to Italy and deal with this fucking disaster, Teo. Tommy called me this morning. Lotta's screaming her innocence, and he's questioning your intel regarding her part in whatever the fuck is going on. I know you want to stake a claim here with Shay, but you need to clean up things back home," he ordered.

I wanted to protest my place in the mess because I hadn't started any of that bullshit, but we all knew I was the family fixer… though Rafe shared the burden with me when it was necessary. While I hated to accept his accusation that the current predicament was my problem, my brother was right. I needed to get to Italy and deal with Lotta in person. The likelihood she was responsible for the betrayal of our family to Frankie Man? Yes, it was something I needed to handle in person.

I sighed heavily as I stared at my brother and nodded. "This might cost me a nut, but my phone is dead. Can you please tell Shay I'll be back. By the way, where are Buck and Elvin?" I asked after Shay's brothers.

Rafe laughed, but he'd gone to look for them after the shooting at the diner, and I needed to know if I had to tell my lover they had disappeared. "They're at Rikers Island for indecent exposure and public intoxication. It'll be at least a day before they are with it enough to figure out what happened to them so they can ask for a lawyer to bond them out. Those two were entertaining as fuck," my brother told me as he pulled a throwing knife from his sleeve where I knew he wore an armband that held three and threw it over my left shoulder to sink into the mahogany door behind me. I looked into his face to see his crazy smile and laughed.

"You're a fucking psychopathic jackoff who thrives on other people's fear," I joked as I chucked him on the shoulder.

"You still love me, big brother. Get back soon, or I might steal your man," he told me with a waggle of his eyebrows. We hugged before I left the restaurant, headed for JFK. I booked myself on the next flight, which was much more of an undertaking than I'd previously realized. It was a lot more convenient when Lotta handled everything, but I no longer had that resource, and if I were right about what she'd done, none of us would have it in the future.

Of course, Papa wouldn't be happy about the turn of events because Carlotta Renaldo was his dependable information guru and someone he'd grown to love like another daughter. He'd need another geek, which would be the last thing on his mind when it all hit home, but I had someone in mind for him.

Maybe the kid needed to take a few classes, but it would get him away from his domineering mother who was a pain in the ass, and honestly, Dom could benefit from some independence. I had no doubt that someday, Dominic Mazzola could be at the head of the table for GEA-I and GEA-A.

I had no doubt the party for Casper and his Maxim would be great, and I hated I'd miss it, but my brother was right. I had a lot of *cazzate* to clean up before I could begin to make a life for myself in America with the man I loved.

Shay Barr was my priority, hands down, but I still had responsibilities to the family. I hoped when they met him, my parents would see I'd made the best choice for myself. My Sweeney was worth the change in the way I did business. With the amount of love I felt for Shay, I wasn't sure if I could kill on command any longer. That would be an adjustment for certain, but it would be one I'd happily make for the man who had set my heart on fire.

I walked out of *da Vinci* airport to catch a taxi to our house in Rome. There wasn't a car waiting for me as there had been in the past, but of course, that was my own oversight. Tommy had sent a text informing me that he'd taken Lotta to my parents' house in the city, and I was eager to speak with her. She had a lot of explaining to do, based on the things Casper had sent me regarding those accounts I believed she'd opened in Sierra and Dom's names.

Substantial amounts of money passed from unknown origin to Sierra and to Dom, only to disappear into what Casper believed were phantom accounts all over the world, but just as he got close to identifying them, the accounts would disappear. Casper couldn't verify beyond a shadow of a doubt that money actually changed hands, only that the accounts gave the appearance that hundreds of thousands of dollars had gone through each account on the first Monday of the month for the last three years… beginning in January after Dex and Gabby got married at Christmas. It was a damn good way to launder money if, in fact, any money was being transferred at all.

Dominic, who I was prone to believe more than anyone, had told Gabe that he had no knowledge of those accounts and according to him, Sierra and her brother had just disappeared or skipped town. He'd sworn to Gabe that he and Nick were only a fling and Dom wasn't heart broken, which I guessed was good. Gabe had called me earlier to relay the information, putting both of us at ease—especially me, because Dom hadn't told Gabe that I'd threatened to kill him or that he'd seen me kill Nick and Sherlock. There was no need to bring the kid into it, anyway. He'd been innocent in the whole fucking mess.

I also believed Sherlock when he'd said he had only turned a blind eye to what Sierra and Nick were doing with the drugs at the Victorian, but he'd confirmed for me that the woman had a connection to Frankie Man from her ex, Perry, who owed Frankie money. Sierra had been the real mole for Frankie Man in Gabe's office, and he had been too blind to see it. The woman needed to be dealt with, and I *would* find her. I needed to know what she'd already told Frankie

Man, and we needed to go on high alert when it came to the kids. I'd search the world over until I found her and ended her for her betrayal of my cousin who had taken care of her over the time she'd worked for him. I vowed on my mother's life that Sierra wouldn't get very far without me finding her and ending her.

I was in Italy because I wanted to have a conversation with Lotta in person. Casper had proof she was orchestrating shit behind the scenes, and I needed to confirm why—was it really because she'd been fucked over by Gabe and Sherlock, or was it because she, too, was on Frankie Man's payroll? Her body language would tell me everything I needed to know. Besides, she knew better than anyone when Rafe or I showed up to deal with a situation, things weren't going to end well for the person(s) involved.

I paid the fare and hopped out of the cab, grabbing my suitcase before I headed up the stairs of the house. When the door opened, I was surprised to see my mother had answered instead of Maria, the woman who really ran the house in Rome. "*Ciao, mamma. È bello vederti,*" I greeted. Teresa Torrente didn't look happy to see me at all, and my comment regarding how happy I was to see her didn't change a thing about her displeased manner.

"*What's going on, Mateo?*" she asked in Italian.

I knew she'd be unhappy with the truth, so I decided to lie. "*I can't come to see you because I miss you?*" I responded to her.

My mother scoffed. "Don't try to bullshit a bullshitter, *il figlio*. It's not very becoming." She spoke in English, which told me she was quite furious about the course of events.

I cut the shit and asked outright, "Is Lotta here?"

"Yes. Your cousin, Tomas, has her locked in one of the rooms upstairs in advance of your arrival, and your father's quite angry about these activities. Make this go away, Mateo. I'm tired of the secrets. There is more, you know, and it's going to divide the family someday. I used to hope it would be after I was *morto*, but I fear we don't have that much time," Mama stated before she walked away and disappeared into the house.

I walked up the stairs and took a deep breath because I was pretty sure I was going to do something I'd never wanted to do in my life… for the second time. Killing Cyril Symington wasn't great. Killing Carlotta Renaldo was an entirely different animal… gender. I hated killing women.

As I approached my father's office, I heard the gunshot, so I ran down the hallway after I let go of my suitcase. I made it to the door and jiggled the handle, finding it locked. *"Papa!"* I pounded on the wood.

The door opened, and I saw my father standing in front of me with a Ruger in his hand which was pointed at the floor. He was rattled, which was nothing I expected, but when I saw a female body slumped in a chair across from his desk where she was tied, I knew he'd cleaned up the mess himself.

I stepped inside and relieved him of the gun. "Are you okay, Papa?" I asked as I led him to a couch in his large office. I wasn't exactly surprised my father had handled the situation himself. I also wasn't shocked he was clearly upset by what he'd felt compelled to do.

Giuseppe Torrente didn't trust many people, but when he trusted someone, he did it with his whole heart. When my father found his trust was misplaced? Well, he was a Torrente, so he didn't take it lightly.

"She was trying to make events appear as if the family was turning in on itself. She was going to make us believe Dominic had betrayed the family in an attempt to undermine Gabriele. She has been gathering documentation for years to give to the authorities here and in America that would be the end of all of us, and I couldn't let it happen.

"You took care of the situation with Cyril for Gabriele and me, which was really my responsibility because I hired the man to work for us. It was only right I should handle this predicament. Lotta told me about Gabriele and how he broke her heart after she admitted Cyril had also jilted her. She was planning to send Frankie's people after Dexter and the children as well. I couldn't let it happen," Papa told me.

"Did she set up that shit with Salvatore and Lucia?" I asked. I should have known my father would take over when he found out

Lotta was only one of the moles in our organization. He wasn't one to shy away from betrayal, and based on what I could see, he didn't shy away from retribution, either. I didn't have the heart to tell him about the other one who was also orchestrating her own coup. I'd have to handle it myself and quickly.

"She claimed she didn't know Frankie was my half-brother, and I know for a fact she doesn't know the real parentage of Dylan and Searcy because that's been handled by another party. I asked if she set up Lucia and Salvatore, but I could see she was going to lie, so I didn't wait for an answer. She was set to take all of us down and hand us to Frankie Mangello without knowing why he hated us so much.

"Tomas found a shortfall in the vineyard accounts, so he went to the bank to investigate. He found unauthorized monthly draws from the vineyard's accounts and deposited into a series of accounts Carlotta had opened under Allegra's name. I spoke with the bank, and they described Carlotta as the person who had opened the accounts over the last few years… in person. To think she was using your sister's identity to bankrupt the vineyard is inconceivable.

"Anyway, from those accounts, funds were transferred to Sierra Conti, and then into Dominic's accounts here at a bank in Rome. The money returned to her through a series of other accounts under dummy corporations, seemingly without anyone's knowledge. It was Carlotta who paid for Raquel Conti's retirement home in San Jose twice a year… or I suppose the vineyard did. Check into it when you get back, okay?

"This is all my fault because I gave her too much free reign over the family businesses. She wasn't family, though I trusted her as I trust my own children. For not monitoring her activities, I suppose I got what I deserved. I'm sorry, Mateo, that I pushed you to figure this out without offering any assistance to you. It was always my responsibility, but I pushed it onto you. I hope you can forgive me," Papa whispered.

I scooted forward on the couch to hug my papa, finally realizing he looked so much smaller than I remembered as a young boy and then as a man trying to fill his huge shoes. Back then, my father was the king of the world. He was larger than life. As I looked at him sitting on the couch, he looked like a small, old man who was crushed under the weight of a deception purported on him right under his nose. I should have anticipated that Lotta's betrayal would hurt him because he trusted her with our lives. He believed he'd been wrong about her, but I couldn't let him blame himself.

"Papa, she wasn't exactly innocent. She was out for revenge, and it didn't matter who she hurt because she wasn't family. I think I might have someone who can take her place if you give him a chance. Dominic gives me every indication he's up for the task, and with you here to show him the ropes, he'll make a great operative," I suggested.

My father looked at me, and he smiled, gently patting my cheek. "Yes, I think you're right, my wise son. Well, that is if his mother will let go of him," he joked, which made me laugh.

"I think by the time Gabriele gets done with her and this Sally Man business, she'll do whatever he tells her. I want to bring home a guy the next time I visit," I told my father, seeing him smile.

"*It's about fucking time,*" Papa hissed in Italian as he hugged me.

I rose from the couch and walked over to Lotta's body, picking her up. "I'll take care of this."

"*No!* I'll do it," my father announced as he took her from me and left the room.

I called the airlines and booked my ticket home the next morning. I had a man to comfort, and we had decisions to make… together. Throughout my life, I'd learned to put certain things into their proper place—compartmentalizing things so I could live my life without regrets. I'd learned it from my father, and I was sure that was what he'd do with Lotta's betrayal. It was how the Torrente family survived.

Sometimes, bad things happened for a good reason. That was the only explanation I had to offer, and I'd stick with it because it worked for me. I was a *salesman* after all, and I could sell myself anything.

24

SHAY

"I look so pretty," Jewel Schatz gushed as I turned the swivel chair so she could see herself in the mirror at my station on Saturday afternoon. I smiled because she was a pure soul. She was always happy, and while I was exhausted because I had no sleep the night before, I was elated to see how thrilled she was with her hair.

I'd trimmed her brunette locks a bit, and her mother, Maureen, had allowed me to give her a few blonde highlights near her face to brighten it up a bit. She looked incredible, and the fact she believed she looked pretty, well, that made me smile. If only we all could be so honest with ourselves.

"You're always pretty. I just changed the color of the bow on the beautiful package," I told Jewel as I motioned for Paige. "Go light. Her mother's already going to have her hands full when the young men at the party see her," I joked, seeing Paige's friendly smile.

"You ready for a little sparkle? That's what Searcy calls it," Paige asked. Jewel shook her head gently like she didn't want to mess up her hair. The two of them disappeared behind the screen that separated Paige's area from the rest of the salon, both talking animatedly about the party that night. I walked out front to see Rafe Torrente standing at the desk talking to my Sonya in Spanish, which shouldn't have surprised me at all.

"You should come. It's at my restaurant, so I can invite anyone I want," Rafe said in Spanish. I could see the Torrente charm was working on my manager and knowing Sonya's affinity for being drawn to the wrong guy, I decided to step in before it was too late.

"Chef Bianco, can I help you with something?" I asked, glancing at Sonya and nodding toward the back of the shop so she could give us some privacy. I had a feeling I wasn't going to like the reason he was at my shop in person that afternoon rather than his restaurant where he should be making food for Maxi's party.

Rafe guided me toward one of the couches in the lounge and pulled me to sit down next to him. "Teo asked me to come…" he started.

I shot up from the seat to dramatically stomp away when Rafe grabbed my arm and pulled me back down. "Hang on before you get all hissy-pissy. He *needed* to go. Teo is sort of the caretaker of the whole family. There is still a threat out there, and he believes it's his job to diffuse it so the rest of us can be safe, plus I kind of told him to go deal with it to keep Papa from having to do it.

"He's been the caretaker his whole life, and I get the feeling he's about to diminish his role as such for you, so let him finish this one last thing before he figures out how he fits into things in his new position. Don't make him regret not doing what needs to be done. If someone in the family is harmed by those who are going against us, Mateo will blame himself for the rest of his life, and I know you don't want to watch him be eaten up with guilt," Rafe explained. It made sense. I didn't want to come between Mateo and his responsibilities to his family.

Rafe wasn't done making me feel bad. "All I'm asking is that you give him a chance to do this before you decide whether the two of you can make a normal life together. He loves you, Shay. I've never seen my brother care about anyone, other than family, the way he cares about you. Just give him a chance," Rafe asked quietly.

I wanted to stomp off in righteous indignation, but what he'd said was so heartfelt, I could only nod. "But I'm still going to jerk a knot in his ass over the fact he didn't have the balls to tell me he needed to go... where'd he go?"

"In his defense, his phone died when I talked him into going to Italy to deal with a situation. He'll be back in a day or so," Rafe explained.

I sighed. "So, I have to go to the party alone tonight?"

Rafe smiled. "Bring that beautiful Latina with you for your plus one."

I put my hand on his knee, feeling his larger one cover mine gently. "Sonya's special, Rafe. She's my dearest girlfriend, and I don't want to see her hurt," I whispered because I had a feeling Sonya was within earshot somewhere. Hell hath no fury like that woman when she was pissed.

"*Fratellino*, Little Brother, I'd never hurt her. She scares me just enough that I want to get to know her better," he stated a bit louder than necessary. From somewhere in the salon area, I heard Sonya cackling, and it made me smile.

"Okay, I'll bring her," I conceded.

"Good, I think I have a great guy for her to meet. He's not my type, but I think he might be right up her alley. He's the head chef at Solé, my restaurant in The Village. His name is Sanford Brenton, and he's very 'boy-next-door,'" Rafe offered with a bright smile, not unlike the one I saw from Mateo on occasion. His explanation that the man wasn't his type had me confused, but before I could prod him for an explanation, Dexter came in with Searcy and Dylan.

"We're a little early, but I hoped maybe I could get a quick trim?" Dex asked as Searcy jerked from his hand and ran over to me. I caught her in my arms and quickly swung her around.

"Guess who's still here?" I whispered.

"Oooh, I love guessing games. *Peppa Pig*? No, wait, *iCarly*? *Kate and Mim-Mim*?" she spouted off in rapid fire. I looked at Dexter, confusion on my face for certain.

He laughed. "Come on, Shay. Aren't you up on kids' television?"

Dylan stepped forward and offered me his fist. "It's stuff she watches on television when Daddy and Papa let us pick a show. They're boring, but it makes her happy. Myself, I like *Transformers, Ninja Turtles, Lego Avengers,* cool stuff like that," he explained as we bumped fists.

I turned to Searcy and winked. "Uh, no, none of them, but go look behind that screen," I instructed as I turned to see Rafe staring at Dexter like he was a juicy bone. Of course, they knew each other because Gabe was Rafe's cousin, but what I saw on Rafe's face was a whole lot of *'I don't give a fuck you're married.'* That only added to my confusion.

I looked at Dexter, seeing him staring at his son with so much love, it made my heart happy. "I'll do Dyl first. Sit down and relax. You want anything to drink? I'll trim Searcy next, and then I'll trim yours while Paige does her makeup," I instructed as I placed a hand on Dylan's shoulder and guided him back to my chair.

Once I had the cape around him, I took off his glasses and placed them on my station. "What'll it be?" I asked him. The child had gorgeous hair, and I suddenly remembered something Mateo said to someone on the phone one night. *"With my life, okay? I'll keep them safe until the day I die because we owe it to them. They should never know their biological father was a Mangello."*

I knew that revelation was significant. I just didn't know the details, but I felt in my gut those kids were at the heart of the matter, and suddenly, Mateo's job… salesman/killer… was less important than the fact he was protecting those he loved. That was something I could reconcile in my heart, and I planned to tell him so when he returned to me.

"How've you been, Shay?" Grace Torrente asked as she sat down at my table after the meal had been served. I was sharing the six-top with Sonya, Shepard Colson, London St. Michael, and Toni Williams, Maxi's second in command at Weddings by Maxim and Parties by Partee. Toni had spearheaded the party planning at Lawry's insistence so Maxi could enjoy the family visit and have a good time at the celebration. Based on what I was seeing, everyone was enjoying it, especially Maxi who had the biggest smile I'd ever seen as he worked the room with Lawry holding his hand as any dutiful fiancé would do.

"I'm good, Grace. I've been super busy this weekend, but tomorrow is my lazy day. I have a brother in town for a visit, but I've already informed him I'm sleeping in tomorrow," I told her as I sipped my Pinot Gris. I was surprised they'd decided to have alcohol available at the party since neither of them drank, but I didn't hate the delicious wine I was drinking. It was a Torrente wine, which made me miss Mateo, but that wasn't going to interfere with my fun.

A woman walked up and put her hand on Grace's shoulder, drawing my attention as well. It was Dominic's mother, but she wasn't alone. St. Michael jumped up and reached behind his back, as did Shepard Colson across from him. I felt a hand shoving me under the table, along with Toni and Sonya.

Suddenly, there was lots of noise, and people were scrambling for the exits. The next thing I heard was a loud thump, and when I turned toward the direction it came from, I saw the man who was with Lucia on the floor next to the table with a shiny, silver knife sticking out of his neck. Blood began to ebb toward us, so I pushed the women out the other side of the table to get away from it and hopefully keep them from seeing it.

"*Mio Dio! My God!* Rafael, what have you done?" I heard Lucia yelling as she crumpled to the floor.

Gabe rushed over and picked her up, hustling her and his mother away from the body as the restaurant quickly emptied. There were sounds of sirens just before there was a loud explosion from the back of the building. The next thing I knew, the place was filling with smoke.

"*Parker!*" Shepard Colson yelled as he took off toward the fire with Rafael on his heels.

I turned to my companions who were both in shock. "Come on, let's get the two of you out of here," I ordered as I began leading them toward the doors. When we got outside the building, there was nothing but chaos everywhere we looked.

I ran back inside to try to help anyone in need get to safety. That was when I saw Shepard cradling Parker in his arms a look of total defeat on his face. I saw my friend was bloody and unmoving. My heart was in my throat. *What in the hell happened?*

An hour later, I was sitting in the waiting room of NYU-Langone Hospital… the same fucking hospital where Chase was still finishing the seventy-two-hour hold in the psych ward. I'd given my statement to one of the policemen who was working the room to speak with witnesses, and from what I'd overheard, it was something akin to the nightmare situations emergency responders trained for during the lulls in activity.

Whatever had started the whole commotion, which I speculated was the dead man in the dining room, had taken a back seat in everyone's mind after the explosion. There were some injuries, though I hadn't heard how serious they were as yet. I also noticed nobody had mentioned the dead body in the middle of the party space, a far-too-common occurrence in my life of late.

Parker had been in the kitchen during the explosion. He was knocked out by something having hit him in the head, and he had shrapnel embedded in the right side of his body from the explosion behind one of the large stoves, or so I'd overheard a doctor telling Shep.

The police and fire departments were still working to find out if it was an intentional explosion or faulty gas or electricity in the building. Three other restaurant employees were injured in the blast, but a doctor came into the waiting room to inform Rafael none of their injuries was life-threatening. It was a relief to all of us who were waiting.

For reasons I couldn't exactly understand when I was interviewed by the policeman, I didn't mention anything about the events I'd witnessed that led to a man bleeding out in front of me just moments before the explosion. I heard Lucia Mazzola shout at Rafe, but I hadn't seen from what direction the knife came, so I kept my mouth shut. I didn't really remember much of what happened after I saw Shep carrying Parker out, so instead of saying anything to the cops I wasn't sure about, I talked about how we were chatting with friends when we heard a loud bang.

I couldn't be certain the explosion wasn't a diversionary tactic on Rafe's part to draw everyone's attention from the dead man, so I was keeping it under my hat. Thankfully, Toni and Sonya hadn't mentioned it, either, and I didn't see Grace, Tomas, or Lucia at the hospital. Gabe came, but Dex and the kids weren't with him. I couldn't imagine how there was no talk by the police or those in the waiting room about that dead body, but I wasn't going to ask.

Maxi sat down next to me, looking as shook-up as I felt. "Do you think this is a sign I'm making a mistake by marrying Lawry?" he whispered, likely to himself more than me. I scooted closer and wrapped an arm around his shoulders, hoping I was offering him some relief.

"Now don't be stupid, sugar. I think what you have to remember is that when the explosion sounded, Lawry tackled you to the ground and laid on top of you without a second's hesitation," I told him, having listened to Ace Hampton giving his statement to a policeman earlier.

Maxi reached up to wipe his eyes, looking at me with a tender smile. "Yeah, he did do that, didn't he?" I nodded and then glanced up when I heard the door to the waiting room open. It was Lawry, who rushed over to where Maxi sat next to me.

"What did the doctor say, Max?" Lawry asked. He'd insisted Maxi get checked out because of how hard they'd fallen to the polished concrete floor.

"Nothing's broken, but I'll be sore for a few days. Thank you for protecting me," Maxi whispered as he started to cry again. I scooted over to give Lawry a place to sit, but he smiled and sat on the other side of his fiancé, pulling him closer.

"Baby, without you, I have nothing. I'm gonna protect you with everything inside me," Lawry whispered to Maxi as a tear rolled down his cheek as well.

I left them to their privacy, unsure of what I should do. Mathis came into the waiting room and sat down in a plastic chair, so I walked over and sat down next to him. "You okay?" I asked him.

"Yeah. I gave my statement to an old friend on the force. He said they're going to wait to go into the restaurant until the morning. The fire chief wants to have some structural engineers check it out for stability before they inspect the damage and determine a cause. Uniforms are guarding the scene with the fire crew standing by in case there are any flare ups. God, I don't miss that shit anymore.

"I'm gonna go get some coffee for everyone. You want something else?" Mathis asked. I shook my head because I had something pop into my head that might be a way out for all of us.

When Mateo ended Cyril Symington, Cyril took the secret with him about that raid at my family's encampment in Arkansas and the twisted shit they'd hoped to accomplish, which saved Chase, Dani, and me from a lot of grief. If no one had gone into the restaurant yet, maybe that was why there had been no mention of an unknown dead man in the middle of the dining room?

If we could get to him before the cops, maybe nobody had to know? Mr. Franzl had disappeared without a trace. Why couldn't the guy who had been bleeding out on the floor as the building exploded? There had to be a reason he was killed. Nothing happened without a purpose, or so I was coming to learn, which was a bit bleak as I considered it.

I saw Rafe return from wherever he'd gone, so I casually walked up to him, gently coaxing him to the side where we could have more privacy. "Have you heard anything about your friend with the knife in his neck?" I asked quietly, moving closer to him.

Rafe glanced down at me and put his arms around me. "What friend?" he whispered in my ear.

"The one who was supposed to be part of the *murder mystery game* we were going to play after dinner at Maxi and Lawry's party for the whole crowd to enjoy," I offered, feeling him pull away and cock an eyebrow.

"If the cops and fire department aren't going into the building until they can get an engineer to come in and attest the building is structurally sound for the inspector to enter, there's time to get your friend out of there and circulate the story the guy's just fine and got out through the bar. He just needs to disappear," I whispered in return, amazed at the deviant detour my mind had taken.

"The only person who could possibly know it's a made-up story would be Lucia Mazzola. I'm sure you could handle the explanation for her, right?" I asked, trying to cover every angle.

Rafe pulled me forward into a hug and chuckled in my ear. "You are going to fit into our family *perfettamente*. I'll meet you at the ER exit to the parking lot in a few minutes. I drove here," he whispered. I nodded and watched him leave before I went to sit down by Mathis again.

He turned to me and smirked. "You and Rafe okay?"

I smiled at him. "Yeah. How's Dani? Still staying with Jonah?" I asked, changing the subject.

Mathis laughed. "Actually, she's doing just fine. He hooked her up with a doctor near his apartment, and she's talking about moving to Brooklyn. I'll give you Joe's number so you can call her. She's worried about you," Mathis explained, which made me smile.

"You think he's the kind of guy who would be in for the long-haul regarding Danielle?" I asked him, curious about his friend's intentions regarding my sweet cousin.

Mathis chuckled. "I've known Jonah for several years. He was my partner back in the day, and he knew I was gay, but he didn't say a word to anyone. He became my friend when nobody else gave a shit about me. He's stood by me through a lot of bullshit, and he is an honorable man. He has fallen in love with your cousin, and he'll take care of her as a friend. He won't push her into a relationship if that's what's worrying you."

"By the way, if you get bored anytime between the week before Christmas and the week after New Year's, feel free to come by Shepherd's House. It's a lot of fun, actually. A lot of those kids crave attention, and you're a very personable guy. I think they'd love to meet you," Mathis invited. I made a mental note to go there over the holidays when I had time. That church was doing so much work in the community, it deserved support.

"Thanks. I think I'm going to head home. I'll talk to you soon," I told Mathis as I gave him a hug before heading out. I waved to the few people who were still in the waiting room, glad to have witnesses to testify I was heading home alone.

I hurried out of the hospital to see Rafe in a bright blue sports car that was idling at the curb. I looked around to see some people outside smoking, which reminded me… "Where are my idiot brothers, by the way?" I buckled my seatbelt and turned to look at the man.

Rafe chuckled. "They're in Rikers for indecent exposure and public intoxication. They can drink a lot, you know? I stripped them off and took their clothes before I called the police and reported them as drunks. They were in the alley next to a grade school, which makes things a bit more troublesome for them." I laughed with him when he finished his explanation. It served those assholes right.

We pulled up to an alley behind a row of brownstones not far from Blue Plate… or what used to be Blue Plate… and Rafe drove into a garage that was opening about midway down the block. "I need to change into something less conspicuous and grab some gear. You can stay here," Rafe insisted.

"No. I'm going to help you. Mateo isn't here, so you'll need my help. Who was that man with Lucia Mazzola?" I asked.

Rafe pulled into the garage and closed the large door before he got out of the car. "It was Salvatore Mangello. It's a long story my brother can tell you, but if what you said is true and I can get his body out of there, well, *Ethel, Lucy* needs to get to work. It's messy, what I'm going to do, and I doubt it's anything you'd like to be involved in, so you stay here like a good boy. I'll be back soon," he told me.

I was determined to help him whether he liked it or not. I was going to bully my way into that family, one way or another. Of that, I was certain.

25

MATEO

I stood from my seat in first class after the plane landed and the seatbelt sign went dark. I was fucking exhausted, yet again, and I needed to get myself together because I had received a strange text from Rafe which left me confused and ready to beat my brother's ass.

Shay's my fucking hero, btw. You're not good enough for him, but he misses you. Get home, idiota. R

I tried to contact Shay after I received the text, but he hadn't answered my calls or texts. Rafe hadn't responded when I sent him the picture of my middle finger, and Gabe hadn't bothered to answer when I called to check on things. There was far too much shit going through my mind, and none of it was good.

I didn't know if something more happened with Shay's crazy family or was he pissed at me about taking off on him again and didn't want to talk to me? I was sure if that were the case, neither my brother nor my cousin would want to talk to me after Shay gave them an earful at the engagement party.

Forty-five minutes later, I hopped out of the taxi in front of the building where Shay and I were going to live together if I had any say in the matter. I didn't know if Corbin was still around or if Shay's other brothers had gotten out of Rikers yet, so I was cautious.

I went into the parking garage to my rental SUV parked in my spot so I could secure my Tan from the glove box. I wasn't going into that apartment unarmed, but I prayed I had no reason to be concerned.

I walked off the elevator and straight to the door to our unit to see it was cracked open, which was a huge concern. I dropped my luggage in the hallway and pulled my Tan, ready for whatever was coming my way.

I pushed open the door, noticing nothing unusual in the immediate vicinity. There were still a few boxes in the living room from when Shay's things had been moved in. I slid off my shoes by the door and crept into the kitchen to see the coffee maker was on with half a pot still in the carafe.

I started down the hallway when I heard the front door squeak open before it was closed and locked. "I don't know when I'll be back. Hell, I might not come back down there, but if I don't, then maybe you wanna come here?" I heard. It sounded like someone was on the phone, so I stepped into the living room and pointed the gun in the direction of the voice, just in time to see Corbin walk into the room and scream bloody murder.

The phone he held went flying into the air, and Corbin immediately fell to the floor. The man was taller than Shay, and his hair was bright red, not Shay's reddish-blonde, which I was coming to decide was a style choice, not his natural color. My man was hairless except for a bit of a beard when he woke in the morning. I had no carpet to judge from, but it didn't really matter to me. Shay was sexy as fuck. He brother was cute, though.

"What the fuck is it with you and shooting people?" Corbin hissed when he finally recognized me. I looked at the phone, which was a burner, to see it was obliterated from bouncing off the hardwood floor.

"Why was the front door open?" I asked as I walked over to help him up from his prone spot on the hardwood. I wasn't surprised to see the poor bastard had pissed himself. I wanted to laugh, but I didn't. I had, *yet again*, scared the piss out of someone. I almost grabbed my phone to take a pic, but that would be in poor form. *Hell, even I know that much.*

"I was taking out the fucking trash and carrying down the boxes Shane left in the hallway before the neighbors complained. I'm sure they didn't want to see them there for another day, and I didn't want them to complain to the building owner about it.

"Shane's not here if you're looking for him. He didn't come home last night, and I haven't heard from him," Corbin explained.

That news had me worried, for sure, but I wasn't going to give it away to his brother. I didn't know if I could trust him yet because I wasn't actually sure where he figured into the family dynamic. "Well, he isn't answering his phone, not that anyone else is. Have you heard from your family?" I asked him, curious if the older brothers were still in Rikers.

"Shane told me to keep my phone off. That's why I had that thing. He called it a burner phone," Corbin told me, which made me smile. My Sweeney had paid attention, and I was very proud of him.

"Ah, well, he's right. You go ahead with whatever you're doing, and I'll go look for Shay," I told him as we both heard a key in the lock. I walked over to the door and looked out of the peephole to see it was Shay and my brother.

I jerked open the door and scooped up my Sweeney, so grateful to find him alive and in one piece. "I missed you, *tesoro*," I whispered to him, feeling his arms around my neck and his legs around my waist.

I smelled his hair, but instead of my coconut shampoo, I smelled smoke. I pulled away and looked at Rafe, who had dark smudges on his face. I could see ash on the black sweater and black jeans he was wearing, and I noticed Shay's hair was a disaster and his face was also covered in grey smudges.

I released Shay and pulled the two of them into the apartment. Corbin had disappeared, not surprisingly, so I took them into the kitchen where I could get a better look at them. "What happened?" I asked as I reached up for mugs for the three of us and poured the coffee.

I handed each of them a cup and sat down at the small kitchen table. Shay went to the kitchen door and looked into the living room. "Where's Corby?" he whispered.

"Likely in the shower. Where've you been? Why do you smell like smoke?" I asked, not mentioning his brother's little accident.

Shay began talking a mile a minute as he took a seat on my lap. I caught snippets about an explosion and a murder mystery. Some people were in the hospital, including Smokey's fiancé. There was a quick mention of a dead body, but it all went by way too fast.

I looked at Rafe to see him smiling. "You've got yourself a go-getter, Teo. Don't fuck it up. I'm going home to crash for a while. I need to call the hospital to check on everyone, and then I've got to go to the police station to see what they found out during their investigation.

"Oh, by the way, Sally won't be a problem any longer. Tell Gabriele it's not done yet, but almost. Only Frankie's left, but Papa needs to give that order." I nodded and watched my brother place his coffee cup in the sink before he took off.

I then looked at the man I loved. "Whose clothes? What did the two of you do again, but slower this time?" I requested. My gut was churning because if he'd been in danger, I'd beat Rafe's ass at the Victorian the next time I got him on the mat.

"Okay, so Saturday night we were at the party, and everyone was having a good time. Rafe came into the shop earlier in the day to tell me you'd ducked on me again without the courtesy of a call or text, but we'll get into *that* later. So…" Shay went on, giving me a very involved story filled with lots of details but instead of being annoyed, I found myself fascinated.

We stripped off to shower as he continued to chatter. It was then I learned the sweater he was wearing was one of Rafe's, but the pants were his. Shay's hair was fucked because Rafe made him wear a balaclava so he wouldn't be recognized because they were sneaking into the restaurant while the joint was surrounded by cops.

They apparently went to remove Sally Man's body because Rafe made the decision to take the fucker out during the goddamn party. I balked at that one. "That fucking…" I began as I washed Shay's hair.

"Salvatore had a gun in his hand only Rafe could see from his vantage point outside the kitchen, and the man was aiming it at Graciela, Mateo. That's why Rafe threw the knife and took him out. As far as we can tell, only Lucia saw it, but I was the one who came up with the story about a murder mystery aspect for the party as an explanation. I need to schedule lunch with Maxi soon to talk to him about it so he can tell Toni it was a surprise he concocted for Lawry, you know, with him being former CIA," Shay explained. He was quick on his feet, my Sweeney.

"Anyway, we rolled that guy, Sally, in the butcher's paper Rafe had in the supply room, and we put him in the refrigerated trailer behind the restaurant, stacking a bunch of other stuff in front of him on one of the shelves. Rafe called someone to come to take it away, so we stayed until they showed up," Shay explained.

"Oh, for the love of… Now, he's got you doing cleanup work?" I complained. I was definitely going to kill my brother.

"No, no. I insisted because he needed the help. There was a minor altercation because the cops didn't want the trailer moved, but the guy, uh? I think his name was Sandy, but I'm not sure. He works for Rafe. Anyway, he said the supplies were being relocated to Manga con Me. He asked the cop if he wanted to be responsible for a hundred grand worth of meat and poultry going bad, so after the guy opened the door to the trailer and let the cop look around, he was sent on his merry way.

"I've never been so fucking scared in all my life, but it was exhilarating! I understand why you do what you do, and I figured out it was because these people, the Mangello's, are a danger to Dylan and Searcy. I swear, I'll go to the grave without ever bringing it up, and I'm not going to ask you to stop doing your job because I get there's a reason why you do it, Mateo. There are a lot of evil people in the world, and there are those who need to keep it in check," Shay reasoned. I wasn't sure where he was going with it, but I had hopes…

"I thought about it while Rafe and I were staking out the restaurant, and I can live with it… with your profession. Rafe explained how he felt about it, and I get it. I love you, and I know you may have to travel at times, so if you'd rather not tell me why you need to go, just give me a kiss before you leave.

"Don't send Rafe to tell me you needed to be somewhere else. If you can promise me *that*, I swear I won't nag you about things," my Sweeney rambled as he stepped out of the shower and wrapped himself in a large towel.

I felt a lot better at having the airplane grime off me, and while I tried to remain attentive to Shay's retelling of his adventures, I couldn't help but crave him. I led him to the bed and pulled back the covers, relieving the two of us from our damp towels.

"Sweeney, you're going to crash from the adrenaline rush in about an hour, and I'm guessing you'll be out cold for the rest of the day. I'd like to make love to my partner before that happens. We can hash it all out until the end of time, but I need to reconnect with you. I need to feel you in my arms so I can show you how much I love you," I whispered to him as I crawled into the bed and took his hand in mine, pulling him with me.

The kisses were just what I needed, and as I worked my slick fingers into his tight hole, I never wanted to get out of that bed. I loosened him and rolled onto my back so my bossy bottom could take control. "All yours, *bello*," I whispered as I pulled him onto my body. He had the condom between his teeth and ripped off the foil, whisking it down my rod in record time.

He leaned forward and kissed me as he slowly worked his way down my cock, driving me insane the whole time. "I love you."

"I love you, more."

"I owe you a temper tantrum."

"Yes, and I can't wait to see it, *tesoro*."

"Oh, god…"

After that, things got a hell of a lot more rigorous as Shay took me to heaven. "Baby, I'm not going to last," I gasped as he circled his hips around my cock, driving me *pazzo*…crazy.

"Okay, *Killer*, it's time," he told me as he began riding me hard, bracing his hands on my chest and getting exactly what he needed. He shot on my chest, and I shot into the condom. It was pure bliss being inside him, and when he leaned forward and rested his head on my shoulder, I wrapped my arms around him and pulled the sheet over his back.

"We're going to become welded together, you know," he whispered as he kissed my neck.

"God, I hope so," I whispered back as I slid out of him.

Sex felt different with him, and I knew it was because he was someone I loved, and I never wanted to forget it. There were hookups, and there was love. They were nothing alike, and that was a fantastic thing to learn.

Love made everything much more intense, and I never wanted to be without it again.

"So, you're not going to keep that *meat* in the trailer again, are you?" I asked Rafe as I sat in his office at Mangia in Manhattan. I knew Shay had helped Rafe remove Sally Man's body from the restaurant, and I wanted to ensure my crazy brother didn't start hacking off pieces of our cousin to taunt the man's father, yet again.

Rafe laughed at me as he sipped an espresso. "No, our cousin was laid to rest yesterday. We need to go to Long Island and talk to Lucia before she goes back to San Francisco. Do you think Gabe told her the guy was her cousin?"

"I've got a bigger question. How did you know the guy I killed in Shay's shop back in the summer was a trigger man for Sally Man? Do you have a fucking deck of playing cards like the soldiers had during the wars in Iraq and Afghanistan?" I asked my brother. It had been bothering me for months how he knew Mr. Franzl, Herman Geist, worked for Sally Man when I didn't. I hated that shit.

Rafe shook his head. "You've gotten sloppy like Gabe since you fell in love, Teo. I'll never make that mistake. You have to know the enemy and the enemy of your enemy, *fratello caro*. I know what every man, woman, and child in that organization or affiliated with it looks like, and their weaknesses. It's how you stay one step ahead of your opponent, Teo. You taught me that years ago. Very few changes happen in Francesco's organization that I don't find out. I'd urge you to do some research," he explained.

I wasn't sure what he meant by the comment, but I didn't have time to dwell on it at the moment. "Whatever. Maybe going forward, you could share with your inferiors? Anyway, what the fuck do you think Sally Man was trying to accomplish by showing up at that party?" I asked, having a crazy thought pop into my head.

I held up my finger to stop him before he spoke. "Is there any way he didn't know Lucia was his cousin? Do you think he just thought he was using Gabe's sister for information about our organization because his father didn't tell him we all shared a nonno? Could Lucia have been an unwitting mole?" I asked, thinking about Sherlock and Nick Conti who were no longer in the safe room of the Victorian, thanks to the crew Papa sent to handle it.

"We can drive out to Long Island and ask her. Have you talked to Dom?" Rafe asked.

I laughed. "Not yet, but Papa has an opening for a new tech person, and I mentioned Dom might be the perfect person to fill it without mentioning his name. Papa picked up on it right away. Tommy's pretty computer savvy and could help out until Dom gets up to speed. He won't be the hacker Lotta was, but he won't try to take down the whole fucking family, either. Casper can handle the hacking needs of the whole organization until we come across someone with Lotta's skill set.

"I guess we should all go talk to Lucia before she heads out to San Francisco again. Let's swing by and pick up Gabe. I want to talk to him, anyway," I suggested. Something was on my mind that needed clarification. It was something my mother said when I was back in Italy.

"Make this go away, Mateo. I'm tired of the secrets. There is another, you know, and it's going to divide the family someday. I used to hope it would be after I was morto, but I fear we don't have that much time."

What it meant I didn't know, but maybe Gabe had some idea? Or, maybe Gabe was just as much in the fucking dark as we'd all been before Papa told us about Francesco Mangello being his half-brother? Once again, there were more questions than answers.

It was time for us to dig into the secrets my mama referred to in that statement, and I was pretty sure Teresa wouldn't offer us any clues about what she meant. Whether Papa would give us the truth was something to consider, but I was starting with my cousin first.

Rafe and I drove to the Victorian in my rental SUV, which I needed to return sooner rather than later. I needed to buy myself a vehicle, and I needed to register my Tan in New York. I'd have to apply for a detective's license, that was, if Gabe would allow me to work for him.

Being a wine salesman had been my cover for several years, but it really wasn't my idea of a profession, and I had no intentions of going back to Rome. I had dual citizenship… well, Rafe and I both had it… because Mama was born in the US, so we could stay in the States for as long as we desired without worrying about being tossed out over a visa issue.

I parked, and the two of us hopped out, coming around the side of the building and up the front stairs. I looked into the windows of Dex's studio to see a bunch of women in some yoga pose. "You think we should tell Dexter about the junkies in his class?" I asked.

"What? I don't know…" Rafe asked.

Hell, I didn't remember who knew about the drugs and who didn't, but it was all about to come to an end. "Come on. I'll explain it to you and remind Gabriele at the same time. We have to learn to communicate better," I told my brother.

We both started laughing at my comment. We argued and fought more than we actually had heart-to-hearts, but with all the love coursing through my body for Shay Barr? I wondered if I could ever fight with my brother again. *Of course, you can, stronzo!*

Rafe and I let ourselves into the Victorian, seeing Dom at the desk alone. There was shouting from the second floor of the building, and when Dex came storming out of his studio, I almost laughed at the angry look on his face. "What the fuck is going on?" he hissed at Dominic.

"Ma's talking with Uncle Gabe," Dom said with a slight smirk. Dexter stormed back to his studio and closed the door. Apparently, he knew enough to understand there was a problem in the family.

"Hey, Papa asked if you'd like to work in Italy for a while? He's short a computer person, and he thought you might be able to help him like you helped me... uh, he wants to know if you'd like to train in Italy for a while?" I asked, not wanting to remind him of the previous week where I'd killed his latest fuckbuddy.

Dom chuckled at me. "Yeah, I'd like to go, but *you* tell Lucia. She's damn near on fire right now because of her missing *boyfriend*." He had a smirk on his face, but I held the laugh.

I saw Rafe glance at Dom, who nodded. "I know who it is, now. She didn't know, you know? She doesn't know anything about what goes on here. She still thinks we're a video and photography company, I swear."

Rafe and I both chuckled. "We'll handle it. Think it's safe to go up?" I asked. Since Lucia had seen Rafe take out Sally Man, she deserved some sort of an explanation, and I wasn't sure if Gabriele was equipped to explain it to her. We both headed up the stairs and toward Gabe's office, still hearing the screaming.

Rafe knocked on the door before opening it. The look on Gabe's face made me laugh, but his harpy of a sister was out for blood. "*You!* What the hell is wrong with *you*? We were..." she directed at Rafe.

"*Cousins*. You and Sally Man, or Marco Rialto as you knew him, are first cousins, Lucia. Think about that for a minute," I told her as I sat down on the couch in Gabe's office, seeing the relief on Gabe's face at our rescue.

"No, that's not..." Lucia began as she stared between all of us, not at all happy with the answer I gave her.

"It is, Lucia. His father is a half-brother to Zio Tomas and Papa. We don't know if he knew about it, but you shouldn't feel guilty for whatever happened behind closed doors," Rafe went on to explain in a very smug voice that almost had me laughing. He'd never liked Gabe's sisters, either.

The three of us looked at Lucia, waiting for her to respond. While she was stunned silent, I decided to toss out something else. "Did you tell Salvatore... Marco... anything about Dylan and Searcy he might take back to his father? Did you tell him about them not being Dexter's biological children? Did you tell him they were Dex's *sister's* children, and did you tell him her name?"

I saw the look on her face and knew it was the worst outcome. "I... I didn't know. He asked about the family, so I told him about all of us. I told him about the adoption... how great it was that Gabe adopted those two kids, and I mentioned Dexter's sister, Imogen, had disappeared. I didn't say she went into witness protection, but I thought we had a future, and I didn't want it to be based on lies," she admitted before the tears started coming.

I jumped up to grab Gabe before he got to her while Rafe pulled her out of the office. Gabriele had murder in his eyes, I could tell. "Listen to me. Papa, Uncle Tomas, and Uncle Luigi need to make the call on Francesco. He's their half-brother, and they all knew it after Enzo died. You know we won't make the hit until we get the word," I reminded.

Gabe looked at me and settled back into his desk chair. "When the fuck did all of this become so goddamn complicated?"

I sighed before I answered because he was right and wrong in the same context. "It's always been complicated, Gabriele. You've just been immune or blind to it," I reminded.

He looked at me for a moment before nodding. "Yeah, I guess I have. What's *your* plan?" he asked.

"I want to stay here and work with you if it's possible. I might have to do clean-up work for Papa on occasion, but I want to make a life here with Shay. Can you find a spot for me?" I asked.

Gabe chuckled. "Seems I'm suddenly short an operative, so I can offer you a job. Salary is..." he began.

I all out laughed at him, cutting him off before he got to the end of his sentence. "You *do* know I don't give a fuck?"

"So, you want to *volunteer*?" he asked with that Torrente smirk.

"I tell you what, fat man. Let's go wrestle for it?" I teased. Maybe Gabe had only gained five or ten pounds, but the fucker was vainer than any of us, and I had no problem aggravating the fuck out of him. He was my cousin, after all.

Gabe laughed. "Okay, Teo. Thanks for stepping in with Lucia. She might not be such a pain in the ass after your comments regarding Sally Man. You guys are…" he began before he looked away from us. I knew what Gabe meant.

We'd been close, all of us Torrente boys, and while we'd gone our separate ways as adults, we always came back together. It was comforting to have family who understood us, much unlike Shay's family. They were fucking crazy.

"I know, Gabriele. I know how it is. I'm a *salesman*, after all," I teased, seeing his smile. It was as I'd always remembered… ready for anything. That was us growing up. When Gabe was in Italy, the four of us… me, Gabe, Tommy, and Rafe as the youngest… we were always ready for anything. I still had my partners in crime. I also had a very hot man waiting for me at home.

Life was better than I ever imagined, and it was all due to Shay Barr. What more could I ever ask for? I had the opportunity to experience perfection sleeping right next to me every night. Someday very soon, I would ask for more from my man, but in the meantime, I was blessed with everything I could need in life. I had Shay Barr.

EPILOGUE

Shay

Two months later...

"That actually went well," I stated as Cal, Chase, and I walked to the Prius. We'd gone to court that morning, and Miller Downing had done a great job of working out a plea agreement to keep my cousin out of jail for negligent discharge of a firearm in public. Chase pled no-contest to the charge and received a fine of five hundred dollars, along with two-hundred hours of community service instead of jail time.

"I talked about it with Sister Florence when I stayed those few days with her, and she told me if I was lucky enough to get either probation or community service, she'd allow me to rent the garden apartment in her house which is three blocks from the church. I just need to get a job to be able to pay rent and stuff," Chase told us, surprising me. He'd actually thought about what he would do after the current crisis was over. That showed maturity, and it made me smile.

"Well, how about for right now, you stay with me and Mateo? You can work in the salon a couple of days a week, and after you finish school, we'll see about moving you to Queens and getting you into cosmetology school? We can go talk to Sister Florence about doing your community service at the shelter when we stop by tomorrow afternoon. I just need to get Sonya to move around some of my appointments so I can take you," I offered.

Cal cleared his throat from where he'd folded himself into the back seat of my car, which was quite a snug fit. "I don't want to go back to Arkansas. I'd like to stay here, as well, but I'll need to get a job, too."

Yes, I was surprised, but I tried to hide it. The fact Cal didn't want to return to Arkansas was shocking, but maybe he saw how big the world really was? I hoped to hell that was it. "Okay, well, I'm sure there are plenty of garages here in Brooklyn that would be grateful to get a seasoned mechanic. You should go on the internet to get an idea of who's hiring and then follow up," I suggested, wondering when I became the fucking career counselor in the Barr family. It was an odd turn of events, really, but I was actually grateful to have some of my own people around so I no longer felt totally abandoned.

Dani had gone back to Memphis where she had a job, but Jonah Wright had gone with her for a week to ensure she was fine and that her parents would leave her alone after she'd told him she needed to slow things down with the two of them until she had a handle on her future. I appreciated his attentiveness to her well-being, and his willingness to give her space. He was a good guy, for sure, and I hoped to be able to coax Dani to move to New York after the baby came. Whether she and Jonah pursued a relationship or not was out of my hands, thought I thought he was a great guy.

Casper assured me he'd keep an eye on our parents and my brothers' movements. My father and uncle had been released from police custody and given a ticket to appear in front of a judge in February. Mathis called an old buddy of his from the DA's office to find out what happened with them, and we were told the charges against Uncle Brett and my father had been reduced to failure to file for a gun permit in New York, which was truly bullshit.

The Lt. Governor of Arkansas, who was a friend of Uncle Brett's, interceded on their behalf and spoke with the district attorney in

Manhattan to ask for a reduction of the charges to misdemeanors. Dad and Uncle Brett would pay a fine after making a court appearance in Manhattan and pleading 'no contest' to the charges. It pissed me off they still got by with their bullshit, but at the end of the day, it was wasted energy to wish them harm. I just wanted them to leave us alone so we could live our lives in love and happiness. Maybe it was a stupid dream, but if we didn't dream, how boring would life be?

My brothers ended up getting released from jail after a few days in the drunk tank at Rikers Island, from what Mathis learned. The whole family returned straight to Arkansas, and we hadn't heard a word from them.

Corby disconnected his old phone number and carried a simple prepaid phone, so he called to leave a message on Mom and Dad's answering machine that he'd decided to go on vacation for a few weeks, and they hadn't called him back, which I believed was a good thing. All we could do was prepare for their return when their court date came up and wait to see what happened.

Fortunately, there wasn't much they could do to us since Chase was now eighteen, and any retaliation they attempted wouldn't go in their favor because of what happened at the diner. The police had a report on them, and Uncle Brett was seen as the aggressor in that situation.

As for me? I had a walking, talking, fiercely protective man who would fight anyone who tried to do me harm, and I had the feeling he'd do it for anyone I cared about, too. The conversation we had the previous night had left me feeling very reassured.

"So, I've got myself a shit disturber? I thought Rafe was the agitator in the family, but it looks like you have the same dangerous mind as my brother... sneaking into a smoldering building to retrieve a body and hide it from the cops. Sweeney, I see your demonic mind and raise you a guardian angel," Mateo told me as I settled my head on his chest.

My body was boneless because my gorgeous Italian stud and I had just sixty-nined. Mateo had rimmed me until I came a second time after he'd sucked the life out of me the first time, him holding off until after my second orgasm to shoot a healthy load down my throat. It was perfection.

I couldn't stop the embarrassing giggle because Mateo had a way of twisting a phrase that was quite entertaining. "Well, you can't say you weren't warned, St. Mateo. You knew exactly what you were getting into when you asked me to go to the Empires game back in the summer," *I reminded him of our first quasi-date.* "I think I'm ready to throw my temper tantrum now," *I told him as I felt the surge of anger coursing through me at his sometimes-careless treatment of my heart by disappearing without a word.*

"Okay, but first, I want to ask you a question. Will you go back to Italy with me over the Christmas holiday? I want to introduce you to my family. I told Papa I was bringing a boy... man... home for the first time, and he was pleased. I want you to see what you're getting into with the Torrente family because Gabriele isn't exactly a fair representation of the rest of our brood. Too much of a goody-goody. So, will you go?" *he asked with a child-like hopefulness on his handsome face. How could I stay mad or deny him anything?*

"Dammit, that look isn't going to work every time, Killer," *I informed him, forgetting all about my tantrum.*

"It doesn't need to work every time, Sweeney. It just needs to work right now," *he told me as he rolled us, so he was hovering over me, his hard cock rubbing against my hip.*

I laughed again. "I'm going to get laugh lines around my eyes and walk funny for the rest of my life if I keep hanging out with you, Balls-of-Fire," *I teased as I pulled him down for a quick kiss.* "I'd love to go on my first trip outside the U.S. with you to your bella Italia," *I told him, remembering some of the Italian words Rafe taught me when we were watching the restaurant to ensure the trailer was taken away before the cops looked into what was in all of the packages of meat inside. One large package, in particular, would be very terrifying, I was sure. It scared the fuck out of me, and I was the one who helped create it.*

"Well, I'll smile when I see your laugh lines, and I'll make damn sure to help you get around when necessary, tesoro. I love you, Shay, and I won't ever let anything happen to you or Chase or Dani, or even Corbin and anyone else who is important to you," *Mateo told me before we made love again. I slept with the biggest smile on my face, happiness flooding my soul.*

"I need to go back to Arkansas and get my stuff, I guess. I have some savings so I can find myself an apartment," Cal advised likely planning in his head more than talking to me. It was then I remembered Mateo telling me Dominic was going to Italy for a while to train with Mr. Torrente's organization, and that meant his apartment would be empty. It was worth an ask.

"Let's hold off on that until after the first of the year, okay? Let me talk to Dexter because I might have a line on a place you could sublet for a while. Anyway, I'll go with you to Arkansas after Mateo and I get back from Italy. You're not going alone," I told Corbin, suddenly feeling very much like the big brother in the relationship.

As I thought about it later, I came to the conclusion I really *was* the big brother to Corbin. He'd lived under the sheltering, *stifling* wing of our family his whole life, and Arkansas was a long way from New York.

Corbin told me he lived over the garage at our parents' house in the little apartment they fixed up to give traveling evangelists a place to stay when they came to town to hold tent revivals. Corby told me Elvin and Buck had each moved out not too long after I ran away, which was a surprise to me. Buck actually had a fiancé who was expecting their first baby, may God have mercy on that child.

I was trying to be the supportive brother, just as Mateo had suggested I should be, instead of being a pushy asshole to demand Corbin tell me whether he was gay. Everyone *should* get to come out on their own, as my handsome man had reminded me, but it was still killing me not to know Corbin's deal. He'd been an awful shit to me growing up, but if my brother needed my support, I'd be there… or so Mateo kept telling me.

I took Corby and Chase back to the home I shared with Mateo so I could get to the salon in time for Dex's regular appointment, grateful to finally be back in a rhythm, though it was a new one. Everything had changed since I met the gorgeous man for whom I'd fallen, and I was willing to adapt. My man was worth all the changes.

Mateo was working at the Victorian that day, and after I finished Dex's hair, the usual group was going to lunch at Watercress. I was looking forward to catching up on all of the gossip I'd been missing from the friends I'd come to think of as family over the years. I'd missed them, but I was also happy to have a few members of the family I'd grown up with in my life. I was a very fortunate man, and I would be grateful for those blessings every day.

For the next few weeks, our lives went on as if that explosion never happened, well, except Parker, who spent a week in the hospital and a week on bedrest at home. Rafe had scattered the uninjured staff of Blue Plate to Solé, his seafood restaurant in The Village, and Mangia con Me on the Upper East Side.

Rafe had been informed there had been a bomb rigged to the gas line in the basement of the restaurant which had a cell phone trigger device that set it off when someone called the number. It went off at the height of the party... just when all of the operatives were there with their families and dates. Rafe said the police told him it was PE-4, the same compound Mateo and Shepard found in the Victorian under Cyril's desk. It all scared the hell out of me.

The computer guru they used in Italy had taken off, or so Mateo mentioned in passing. He said Casper had learned the person had been in New York around the same time the bomb had been planted in the Victorian, and it would have been easy for them to plant another bomb at the restaurant, but there was no way to verify it, nor was there any way to figure out why.

Both, GEA-America and GEA-Italy were on high alert because it appeared there was still someone who wanted to do harm to those who worked for the organizations and those they loved. Mateo told me not to worry, but I did. One of my best friends was nearly killed in that shit show.

It was all very nefarious, and a bit unsettling, but I had more important things on my mind with holiday shopping and the salon being crazy busy as people booked appointments because there were always parties to attend in New York. It was all rumbling toward me, and I didn't feel ready, but my Mateo seemed to love the holidays.

The night before, we'd received three cases of wine from the family vineyard, one case of prosecco for Shep and Parker, and one case of prosecco for us. *"Why do we need a case of Prosecco? I mean, not that I don't love it, but is there a reason?"* I'd asked.

Mateo took me into his arms and kissed me passionately in front of Chase, who was peeling potatoes to make fries for his *homemade burger-and-fry-extravaganza*, as he'd labeled it. Chase's giggle broke our kiss, but Mateo looked into my eyes with such love, I nearly buckled to my knees to blow him in the kitchen. *"I want us to have prosecco around always because I believe every day I get to spend with you is a reason to celebrate. I love you, Sweeney,"* he told me. That sealed the deal for him after dinner. We fucked for hours.

The other case of wine was for Rafe to use for the Christmas Eve party he was planning for friends and family at Solé. It was an Italian tradition to have a huge seafood meal, and I was actually excited to attend. We were going to Long Island with Gabe and Dex for Christmas dinner with Graciela and Tomas, along with Gabe's sisters and their families, which I was sort of dreading because those women weren't exactly nice to each other, much less to strangers. At least Dylan and Searcy would be there to entertain me.

Rafe was heading to Italy on Christmas Eve to be with the family, but Mateo was content to spend time with my family because Dani had agreed to come to New York, and Mathis and Jonah Wright were coming over for dinner with Mateo, Chase, Corbin, and me on Christmas day. I was looking forward to hosting a big party. I usually spent Christmas by myself.

Corbin had just moved into the condo Dom rented from Gabe, and I knew they were giving Corby a huge financial break on the space… if he'd pay the utilities, they wouldn't charge him rent. They were holding it for when Dom returned to New York, and Gabe went so far as to offer my brother the job Dom did at the Victorian as Nemo's assistant until he could find a job as a mechanic.

I could tell my brother had no idea what that might entail, so he

SALESMAN MATEO | 317

asked for time to think about it. I admired him taking a step back to consider if he felt comfortable about something so unfamiliar, but he was older than me, and I'd decided he should make his own decisions about things.

I was going to try to keep my big mouth shut on the matter, remembering Corby had spent an overnight in that ammo vault downstairs where he saw Mateo take out two people right in front of him. I was certain it had made an impression on my brother, so I was giving him the time and space to decide things for himself.

At the salon, I'd relented on my past rules and allowed Sonya to play Christmas music instead of the smooth jazz we always had playing, even during the holidays. Ari and Wren had actually come into the salon the previous Sunday and helped with the Christmas decorations while Sonya supervised.

We had added gourmet peppermint hot chocolate to our available beverages, and we were in full swing with holiday spirit up to our eyeballs. I had to admit it was a much more upbeat atmosphere than we'd had in the past, and I didn't hate it.

I walked into the lobby to see it was empty, which was a surprise. "Are we done for the day?" I asked, looking at the large clock on the wall next to the armoire where I had products available for purchase. The armoire was a distressed oak unit I found at a Salvation Army store not far from the building, and I loved it. It fit in with the design Maxi helped me create for the salon when Kitty Rae rented me space, and it didn't violate her rules that I couldn't paint the place while I was a renter. Maxi didn't care if I painted, but I loved the vibe we'd created, so I was content to let things go for a while. It was familiar and welcoming, and with all the changes in my life, it felt good to go there every day where I knew what to expect. It was my sanctuary of sorts.

Sonya smirked at me. "You have one more appointment, and the guy has been trying to get on the schedule for months. He's on his way. After him, that's it for the day," she told me.

The clock showed it was just three-thirty, and with all of the people clambering for appointments all week, I couldn't believe I'd finally get a Thursday afternoon to myself, so I was planning to take the opportunity for a little pampering. "Okay, after I finish with him, can Posey give me a quick maintenance wax, and if Olson's available, I wouldn't mind a massage. I can't remember the last time I had a massage," I bemoaned as we both heard footsteps on the stairs outside the salon.

Sonya smirked. "I'll check with them. Go freshen up because the guy's a new client. I'll get him in the chair for you," she offered, which was rare. She was never that helpful, so I should have suspected something was amiss.

Instead, I nodded and went to the bathroom to see if I had shit hanging out of my nose or was there something in my teeth that prompted her to send me to check? I quickly finger-combed my hair and checked my teeth, taking a quick gargle from the bottle of mouthwash I had under the sink in case the salad I'd eaten for lunch had tainted my breath.

I dusted off my apron and checked to see nothing seemed out of place, so after a quick touch-up of my eyeliner, I walked back into the salon to see a very handsome man sitting in my chair with a smirk. "Hello, and welcome to DyeV Barr. I'm Shay, your stylist for today. What can I do for you?" I asked, keeping my face steady before I began running my fingers through his gorgeous, long hair.

"I think I want to shave my head," he told me as I turned him to face the mirror.

"Nope. A trim, and how about a razor shave? I can have Posey shape your brows, or I can do it myself. You say you've been trying to get into my chair for a while?" I teased, seeing Mateo sit forward in the chair with concern.

"What's wrong with my eyebrows?" he snapped as he studied himself in the mirror over my station.

I curled my lips between my teeth to keep from smiling. Mateo was as bad as Gabe when it came to being vain. "Well, if you're fine with rocking the unibrow, then go for it," I responded as I went to a drawer to pull out a fresh styling cape, whisking it over his black shirt to shield him from the small amount of hair I planned to trim. I loved his dark brown hair, and I wasn't going to cut it short. I loved to wrap it in my hands when he went down on me. Based on the moans I heard from him as he expertly sucked my cock, he didn't hate it, either.

"I don't have a unibrow, do I, Sweeney?" he asked with a look of concern.

"No, *Killer*, you don't. I'm just kidding you. How was your day?" I asked as I gently massaged his scalp while looking at him in the mirror, admiring his handsome face, yet again.

"Busy. I went all over Manhattan in search of something. I hate traffic, you know. Oh, I finally bought a car, and after the first of the year, we're getting rid of the Prius…or we can give it to Chase. He's the one taking eight trains to Queens," Mateo exaggerated.

I popped him on the shoulder. "Don't make plans for my Prius. It's the first car I ever bought, okay? There's sentimental value, Teo. Let me get Inez to shampoo you while I sharpen my straight razor," I teased as I took his hand to lead him to the shampoo room. When he dropped to the floor in front of me, I was immediately startled that something was wrong, but when I turned to see him kneeling next to me and holding out something in his palm, I lost the ability to move.

"I was kind of hoping you'd give me that haircut you promised before Thanksgiving, but you've been too busy to do it, so I actually had to make an appointment. I think this should ensure I don't have to get on your book again to get a haircut, right?" Mateo asked as I looked into his hand to see a white gold ring with a sparkling stone channel set into the center.

"No, no, no. It's not…" I began as I backed away a few steps before Mateo grabbed my hand.

"Don't walk away. It's not a wedding ring, it's just an engagement ring. You can take all the time you need to decide if you want to get married, but I'd appreciate it if you'd allow me to put a ring on it, as the song says. I do like it, and I want to put a ring on it," he quoted Queen Bey, taking my breath.

I suddenly noticed the salon was silent, and as I looked around all work had stopped. Hell, all of the people who worked for me and their customers were staring at me, but when I looked at the man I loved, I didn't see or hear anyone else. Just my Mateo.

"If you want me to wear that ring, you gotta ask the question," I stated as I stared into his gorgeous, brown eyes and saw that quick smile.

"Shane Barr, will you consider marrying me, unibrow and all?" he asked as he held the ring between his index finger and thumb, looking at me with those damn hopeful eyes he knew I was helpless to deny.

"You got me over a barrel, *Killer*. I'm a puppet to that look, and you know it. Yeah, I'll marry you, unibrow and all," I agreed.

Mateo jumped up from the floor and pulled off the cape, grabbing me to lay a kiss on me like I'd never imagined being decent in public, but fuck if I cared. I heard corks popping and lots of cheering, but I couldn't look away from Mateo. His huge grin was incredible, and as he slipped the ring on my finger and kissed me, I knew I had the promise of a life I only believed I'd see in dreams.

Mateo

"*Tesoro*, we're on approach," I whispered to the man I loved. We were on approach to the small, private airport in Siena, having skipped the stop in Rome. We'd go there for New Year's, but I wanted to take Shay to the place I really called home so he could meet all of my family and feel at ease.

I'd asked Ace to accompany Corbin back to Arkansas so he could clean up his life down there before he moved to New York. Ace easily agreed as long as he could be in New York for New Year's Eve. The two of them had met at the small engagement party Rafe had planned for us on Christmas Eve at Solé. When I'd told my brother what I was going to do, he quickly threw it together, calling it the Seven Fishes Feast and inviting all of our friends and family. While Mama and Papa couldn't... *or wouldn't...* come to celebrate our engagement, I was happy all of the important people in our lives were there to celebrate with us.

Christmas had been fantastic, and the best part was yet to come with Shay finally, officially, meeting my family. Papa had assured me they were pulling together a big dinner for us, and I was looking forward to it because I had the man I loved with me, and I was going to introduce my fiancé to the people who were important to me.

It was shaping up to be an incredible trip, and I couldn't wait for Shay to see the vineyard and the villa. I had hoped maybe we could have the ceremony there and have a small, civil service in the States, but I was leaving the wedding plans to him and his friends. Maxi Partee was as excited as he'd been at his own engagement, so I was sure the wedding would be perfect.

Shay stirred before his beautiful, amber eyes popped open. His eyeliner was a bit smudged, but he still looked stunning. He'd had a manicure before we left New York, *"so I can show off my ring,"* he'd reasoned. He looked incredible to me every day, but since we'd become engaged, he was glowing, and I loved it.

"We're about thirty minutes away, so if you need to go to the bathroom or anything, now's the time," I told him. We'd had prosecco early into the flight, and he'd fallen asleep, but I didn't because my mother's words kept circling my head. *"Make this go away, Mateo. I'm tired of the secrets. There is another, you know, and it's going to divide the family someday."*

I fully intended to press her on the meaning behind her comment because it was driving me crazy. It was distracting, and I never wanted to be distracted by anything other than the man I was going to marry. It was pretty fucking great to realize I'd finally found the one for me. I never anticipated it would happen in a hair salon, but life comes at you that way, doesn't it? Love hits you when you least expect it, and as much as I tried to run, I knew in my gut I wouldn't be happy without him.

The party my mother had planned was in full swing, and I could see my Shay was having a great time meeting people who worked at the vineyard and those who lived in the village. Uncle Luigi had insisted we have the party in the tasting room, and with all of the lights and candles, it was damn great.

Everyone had accepted Shay into our family, and I was just enjoying watching his reaction to their usual over-the-top behavior. Uncle Lu had hired a trio to provide the music, and there was lots of dancing. Shay was currently dancing with my sister, and the two were laughing, which made me happy.

I felt a touch on my shoulder and turned to see my father standing next to my chair. I stood and hugged him because I was so happy. "Can I talk to you for a moment?" he asked.

I turned to see Angelina Bracco had tapped Allegra on the shoulder, and everyone laughed at my sister ignoring the woman who was trying to cut in to dance with Shay. He was laughing and had pulled both of the women to dance with him while everyone was clapping, so I followed my father outside to the small firepit we'd lit after the delicious meal.

"This was nice of you to pull this together on such short notice. I'd like us to marry here when Shay decides he's ready, Papa," I told him.

We sat down on a bench made from an old wine cask. We had places to relax all over the property, and the smell of the oak casks reminded me of my childhood, running through the pressing rooms with my brother and our cousins. Those memories made me smile.

Papa handed me two grappa glasses before he poured us each some of the grappa he saved for special occasions. He placed the bottle on the table next to his end of the bench and turned to me with a smile. He was genuinely happy for me, and I couldn't help but gloat.

Papa held up his glass and smirked at me. "I want grandchildren, Mateo. Tomas doesn't hesitate to remind me of his fortune with his grandchildren, so please, give me something to throw up to him, will you?" my father asked, which made me smile.

He didn't wait for my response before he continued. "I like him very much. He can hold his own with your mother, and he's kind to your sister. He asked her to teach him how to paint, and it's made her very happy. I'm thrilled you found your happiness, so I want to give you something my father gave me when I married your mother.

"Well, he gave each of his sons a set when we got married, and I wore them for my wedding. I hope you'll wear these for yours, and then hand them down to your son someday," Papa told me as he handed me a small, black leather box that was aged.

I opened it to see a set of ivory cufflinks with a "T" inlaid in black onyx. They were beautiful, and I remembered seeing them in the picture from my parents' wedding. I was actually stunned.

"Thank you, Papa. What about Rafe?" I asked, worried my brother would be upset I got a family heirloom and he didn't.

Papa laughed. "I have no illusions your brother will ever settle down. Besides, I have the watch your mother gave me when we got married, so if lightning strikes twice, I'll give it to him. I'm very happy for you, Mateo," he whispered as he hugged me again. We toasted and sipped the grappa together as we talked about the recent events circling our world.

I finally asked him. "Do you think Lotta planted those bombs?"

My father sipped his drink and looked at the fire, giving it a lot of thought. Finally, he turned to me and shook his head. "The first one? Probably. The one at Rafael's restaurant? No, that was a professional. It might have been someone working for Frankie, but your brother's made his own enemies over the years. Tell him to consider if it was someone from his past," my father suggested.

I took a deep breath and looked at him. "Are you going to follow through with the order for Frankie?"

My father refilled my glass and his. "This isn't the time for such thoughts, Mateo. This is a time to celebrate. *Saluti!*"

I knew that was all I'd get out of him, but he was right. My life was looking up, and as I heard someone behind me and felt the sinewy arms around my neck and a gentle kiss to my ear, I knew I didn't need to sell anything to Shay Barr. He owned me lock, stock, and cock.

"Come on in. Is it done?" I asked Mathis as he stood in the doorway to Gabe's office at the Victorian on January 6. The New Year had been spent in Rome where Shay and I attended a party with Rafe and Tommy, the latter behaving jittery all evening. I was suspicious he had plans for the night that didn't include us, but when Rafe pressed him to come with us, he caved after he made a call. I was looking forward to finding out what really happened because I believed him to be just as much of a man-about-town as Rafael, though Tommy was very private about his activities.

"Yeah, it's done. I took video," Mathis told me as he looked down at his phone. A second later, my own phone—with my new, Brooklyn phone number--chimed. I pulled up the text and watched the footage of two men in full tactical gear pouring an accelerant around the various buildings at that camp in Hot Springs where my Sweeney and his young cousin had been tortured.

When the thing went up like a Roman candle, I smiled and put down my phone and pointed to the chair in front of Gabe's desk for Mathis to take a seat. "Who went with you?" I asked. I'd been the one to call him on New Year's Day to ask if he'd do it. I chartered a plane and told him to take people he could trust. The completion of the task wasn't something I planned to share with anyone but my Shay.

Mathis smirked. "Well, Jonah wanted to go with me, but I wouldn't let him. All I said was I had to go to Arkansas, and he knew why. I told him it would cost him the job if anyone found out he was involved, and then I reminded him about the lieutenants' exam he's taking in a few months, so he agreed to sit this one out.

"Don't tell Shay you heard it from me, but Jonah and Dani actually got married on New Year's Eve. She had said she wanted time, but when he went down to Memphis to see her after Christmas, they decided they were it for each other and got married. Dani said she's going to go to the salon to tell Shay and Chase in person once she gets settled at Jonah's place, so Shay will have his family here with him, and that'll be good for all of them I believe.

"The reason Corby couldn't start until today is that he and Ace went with me. When they went to get Corby's stuff in Arkansas, he took Ace out to the compound. Unfortunately, his family was there so he couldn't do anything before Christmas. Corbin actually begged to go when I asked Ace, so that's him and Ace spreading the accelerant. We got in and out in about three hours. Thanks for the private plane, by the way," Mathis explained with a cocky smile.

I smirked at him. "Now, you're not getting sweet on Shay's brother, are you?" I teased. Mathis and Corbin had talked a lot when we had everyone together on Christmas Day, but I still couldn't get a feel whether Corbin was gay or straight. It didn't matter to me unless he treated my fiancé poorly, but it bugged me that my gaydar was on the fritz.

Mathis laughed. "Right now, I'd say Coby's as confused about himself as anyone I've ever met. I'm just trying to be a friend. You might want to give it a try," Mathis told me as he stood to leave.

"Mom loves having Chase help out at the community center and the shelter. She says he's the sweetest kid she's ever met… well, aside from me," he joked. We both laughed, and Mathis left to start the new assignment I'd given him.

That was another change at GEA-A. Gabe and I were co-managing the American office. He missed field work and hated all the paperwork necessary to run the company, so we agreed he would go out on more jobs, and I'd take over a lot of the logistical planning and office work. The two of us would interview potential new clients when possible and have equal input into the cases we accepted. I believed we'd both be happy with the change, and maybe, Gabe could get his head back in the game? If not, at least I was there to follow-up on things.

I was still adjusting to having someone to come home to at night… along with having a giant furball, who had me wrapped around his tail, and I wanted to be there to enjoy Shay and Mixer, not out on some stakeout or guarding some selfish popstar like I'd just sent Mathis to do.

With Sally Man out of the picture, the only threat we had lurking in the shadows was Frankie, and Papa had him under 24/7 surveillance. We'd be prepared for him if he made a move, and I'd make sure it was his last, with or without Papa's permission.

The only thing that still kept me awake at night was the family secret Mama alluded to when the mess with Lotta came to a head. It felt ominous, but I was determined not to live my life waiting for the other shoe to drop. I was going to enjoy every minute I had on the earth and be happy about every bit of love and joy coming to me, and my Shay didn't hesitate to give those things to me every day.

Apparently, I wasn't the worst salesman in the world. I'd been able to sell Shay Barr on the idea of spending the rest of his life with me.

Mateo and Shay return in *A Lonely Heroes Holiday Story* - Bachelor Hero - which releases on December 26, 2021.

Read on for an exclusive extract from the newest series **On The Rocks**, which is set in the same universe as *The Lonely Heroes* series!

WHISKEY DREAMS
On The Rocks, Book One

By Sam E. Kraemer

WHISKEY Dreams

"I see him clearer with one eye than I ever saw anyone with two..."

On the Rocks - Book One

There was a huge deck and patio on the back that faced the Gulf, and it was full of scantily clad bodies drinking umbrella drinks and singing along to an acoustic guitarist who was performing country rock and beach-inspired songs.

A loud laugh caught my attention, so I walked forward to see Leo talking to a table filled with women as he delivered their drinks with multicolored silly straws topped with paper parasols. He'd actually cut his hair quite short, which was a surprise, but he still looked like a damn brick wall, just as he had in high school.

The hostess stand was in the lobby of the restaurant side where a window looked out over the bar that had a retractable door to bring the outside in. It was a damn nice setup. A perky young woman approached me with a glowing smile. "Welcome to On the Rocks. Would you prefer to sit inside or out on the patio?"

The hostess had a plastic covered sheet which appeared to be a menu, and she was wearing a pair of jean shorts and a black t-shirt with a beach shack on the front that had a neon sign next to a palm tree. *On the Rocks* was in dayglo pink, and the bright yellow sun—which was wearing black Rayban-style sunglasses—was setting into the water behind the building. It was really cute and not anything my brother would have thought of on his own, I was certain.

"Uh, I'd like to buy one of those hats, if I can," I requested as I caught sight of a display case housing baseball caps, t-shirts, tank tops, sweatshirts, keychains, and bandanas with the bar's logo on them. I wanted to sit outside, but on the off chance anyone noticed me—a short, skinny guy with long blond hair—as the lead singer for a moderately popular country band, I didn't want to embarrass my brother, much like I seemed to do to the rest of the family.

As far as I knew, Leo was always the live-and-let-live type, except when we were younger and used to aggravate the shit out of each other. Since I'd told my family I was gay, my brother hadn't made his opinion known on the matter one way or the other, but I didn't want to jeopardize the unspoken truce between us.

I handed over three tens for my purchase, glad I'd stopped at the bank on the way out of Tyler to get money. I shoved my braid up under the cap and pulled on my sunglasses before the young woman showed me to a seat at the outdoor bar facing the beach.

Leo had moved back behind the bar to mix drinks, seeming to laugh with a few guys sitting at the far end who I guessed were regulars, based on the easy camaraderie among them. There was a baseball game on a big screen television to my left, though the sound was muted, and one of the guys seemed to be humorously arguing with Leo about the projected outcome of the game, which made me chuckle. I knew my brother's savant-like memory for sports statistics. That guy would never win.

My brother glanced down the bar and held up his finger to ask for a minute when he spotted me, clearly not recognizing me. I nodded and picked up the menu that the waitress had left with me.

The young guy next to me had most likely been at the bar for a while. He seemed happily three-sheets-to-the-wind, laughing at whatever the lady next to him was saying.

There was a loud crash behind me, so I turned to see a big, bearded guy on his knees, picking up some broken bottles before he winced and held his hand.

My brother hopped over the bar and hurried to the guy who was wearing a black beanie, quickly grabbing the man's hands. It was then I noticed one hand was bleeding pretty badly.

There were clean bar towels on the end of the bar, probably waiting to be put away. I grabbed two and rushed over to Leo, handing them to him. "Thanks, man."

I took off my cap and pushed my sunglasses on top of my head, catching the quick look of shock on Leo's face. When I turned to the injured man, I registered a face I hadn't seen in years. "T-Tanner?"

Seeing that handsome face again caught me by surprise, but he appeared to be equally as stunned. "Kelso? Is that... I didn't know you'd... *Damn!*" he responded, his face mirroring my look of shock, I was sure. Something about him seemed different, but I couldn't place it. He didn't meet my eyes, which was odd, and he almost looked embarrassed at seeing me. *That* look I knew far too well.

I could remember Tanner Bledsoe's intimidating glare from high school when he used to visit our house to hang out with Leo. I admired him from afar back then because he was my dream man. Now, though, he seemed to be skittish, which didn't fit the Tanner Bledsoe I remembered at all.

"Thanks, Tanner. How badly are you cut?" I asked as I picked up a few pieces of glass from the floor, being careful not to cut myself in the process.

Leo glanced around, searching for someone. He waved when he saw the young woman who had greeted me at the door. I saw her smile grow as she approached my brother, but when she saw the blood, it morphed into a look of horror. "Oh, no! What do you need, Leo?"

"Dewanna, can you bring me the first aid kit from the office?" The girl nodded and rushed off without a question.

I looked at my brother and smirked at the interest the girl had shown in him before she figured out what had happened, seeing him chuckle. "Shut up. When did you get here?"

"Just a few minutes ago. I bought a cap. They're cool," I awkwardly pointed out as I put the hat on my head again, this time with the bill in the back, frat-boy style. It had been a long time since I'd last seen my brother, and I was still concerned about his invitation to visit him.

Leo chuckled as he helped Tanner from the floor. It was then I noticed one of Tanner's eyes seemed a bit off. I stood and glanced in question at Leo, who gave me a subtle shake of his head not to say anything.

We all walked over to a table where I pulled out a chair for Tanner, who turned his head at an odd angle before sitting down. Clearly, I was missing a piece of the puzzle.

Dewanna, the hostess, brought out a large white first-aid kit and placed it on the table, winking at Leo before she went to greet other guests who had entered the restaurant. Leo flipped open the lid and began gathering supplies to take care of Tanner's injured hand.

"After I fix up Tanner, I'll get the key to the apartment from my desk so you can settle in. Tanner's staying with me, but there are three bedrooms, so we should be fine. How long can you stay?" my brother asked.

"I, uh, I was gonna stay in Tyler for a week, but that wasn't exactly met with open arms. I won't stay here more than a few days. I need to get back to Nashville for practice, anyway," I lied to keep him from freaking out.

Leo and I weren't exactly what you'd call close, and I didn't want to put pressure on him to be "brotherly"—whatever that meant, because we never had that kind of relationship growing up. I wasn't about to force him to try it now.

Leo glanced up from his first aid responsibilities. "Tanner, man, what did you trip over, do you know?" He picked a chunk of glass out of the man's hand before opening an alcohol pad to clean the cut.

"I'm still trying to get the lay of the land since we rearranged the tables, and I got my foot tangled in one of the table legs. I'm okay, Leo. I'll go clean up the rest of that glass," Tanner announced as he tried to pull his hand away and stand, but Leo wouldn't let go of him.

"Do I need to put reflective tape on the floor? Will that help?" Leo suggested.

I suddenly felt like I'd blacked out and awakened in a different conversation. "What's going on?" I asked, looking between the two of them.

Leo gave me a look to shut up, but Tanner chuckled. "It's okay, Leo. He's been livin' out in the big world, and I'm guessin' you didn't tell him how I fucked up."

I felt my face flush and decided maybe it was best for me to leave the two of them alone. I turned to Leo. "Yeah, uh, get me the key. I'd like to wash up and maybe come back down and get a burger. I've been drivin' all day."

Leo offered a quick nod. "I'll get you the keys. Come back when you're ready to eat. Tanner, man, I think I better run you to the MedStop in Brownsville to make sure that cut doesn't need stitches."

I glanced around to see the bar was quite full, so I let out a sigh. "I'll take him. Looks like you have enough on your hands."

"Seriously, guys, I'm fine. It ain't deep enough to need stitches,"

Tanner objected.

"Come on, man, cut me a break. I'm responsible if you get lock jaw or some shit. When was the last time you had a tetanus shot?" Leo pressed.

"I got a shot before I got out, Leo. They pumped me so full of shit after I lost my eye, nothin' bad could survive inside-a me," Tanner joked, which really had me confused.

Leo laughed and stood, turning to me. "There's a MedStop in Brownsville on Boca Chica—I think that's the closest. Plug it into your phone, and it'll give you directions. You got a car?"

I nodded. "A rental. I backed into that damn pecan tree at the farm. Daddy was able to get the trunk to close, but it might not open again." I laughed as I remembered the sight of Daddy beating on the damn trunk, probably doing more damage to the car than the tree.

Not surprisingly, Leo barked out a loud laugh, which had heads turning. He reached into his pocket and pulled out his wallet, handing me a credit card. "Use this."

I wanted to say no, but I didn't want to make him feel as if I thought he wasn't successful. He had his own business, and apparently, it was doing quite well, so I took the card and put it into my pocket.

I turned to Tanner and offered a look that I hoped was friendly. "You ready?" I asked, so many questions circling through my mind. How had he fucked up? Where did he "get out" of? How did he lose his eye? What about his asshole little brother?

"Yeah, I'm ready, Kelso. Thanks for takin' me," Tanner responded, his voice quiet. He glanced up and looked at me, his face soft and a bit flushed.

I led the way out to the rental car and opened the door for him, which he surprisingly didn't complain about. What happened to the asshole I remembered from high school who strutted around like a peacock? What had happened to him that brought about such a change?

Read *Whiskey Dreams* today!

ABOUT THE AUTHOR

Sam E. Kraemer grew up in the rural Midwest before moving to the East Coast with a dashing young man who swept them off their feet, and the couple has now settled in the desert of Nevada. Sam writes M/M contemporary romance, subgenres: sweet low angst, age-gap, cowboys, mysteries, and military/mercenary. Sam is a firm believer in "Love is Love" regardless of how it presents itself and a staunch ally of the LGBTQIA+ community.

Sam has a loving, supportive family and feels blessed by the universe every day for all that has been given. Sam's old enough to know how to have fun, but too old to care what others think about their definition of a good time. In their heart and soul, Sam believes they've hit the cosmic jackpot!

Cheers!

If you enjoyed this book, I'd appreciate it if you'd leave a rating and/or a review at Amazon.com, BookBub, and/or Goodreads. If you have constructive criticism to help me evolve as a writer, please pass it along to me.

You can find me at: https://linktr.ee/SamE.Kraemer

I'd love to hear from you!